TALES OF THE UNANTICIPATED

The Antholozine of TOTU Ink   Number 29

Novelette

18	**Kindling** • Patricia S. Bowne

Short Stories

8	**Dead Man Come A-Calling** • Mark Rich
32	**The VanBulyen Effect** • Lyda Morehouse
42	**The Diner** • Eleanor Arnason
48	**Desiree** • Stephen Dedman
58	**Anxiety Wave** • Martha A. Hood
62	**Der Erlkönig** • S.N. Arly
74	**Fort** • Stephen Couch
84	**A Heart is the Size of a Clenched Fist** • Michael A. Pignatella
92	**Verbal Knowledge** • Katherine Woodbury
100	**On the Wind That Blows Hard From Below** • Gerard Houarner
108	**When Shlemiel Went to the Stars** • Naomi Kritzer
112	**The Jaculi** • Patricia Russo
118	**Come Frost, Sun, and Vine** • Tony Pi
128	**The Mead Cup** • Hank Quense
134	**Heartsblood** • Sue Isle

Poetry

17	**After the arrival of the strange horses** • Kristine Ong Muslim
31	**Tourist** • Terry A. Garey
40	**To Not Look Back** • Ann K. Schwader
46	**Tentacle 1** • Camilla DeCarnin
57	**The A. I.'s Table Prayer** • Sandra Lindow
73	**Tentacle 2** • Camilla DeCarnin
81	**FUN With Innards!** • F. J. Bergmann
90	**Isotope Ballerina** • Cornelius Fortune
98	**Tentacle 3** • Camilla DeCarnin
107	**In the Capuchin Crypt Coffeeshop** • James P. Roberts
126	**The box arrived early afternoon** • Terry Leigh Relf
127	**Becoming Osiris** • Ann K. Schwader
141	**Sunset on Mars** • Martha A. Hood

Article

82	**ET Cleaning Crew Terrifies Teen** • Terry Faust

Departments

2	Editorials by **Eric M. Heideman, Rebecca Marjesdatter**
3	Contributors
7	Contributors' Guidelines
61	Mail orders
66	Interview with **Bryan Thao Worra** by **Catherine Lundoff**
142	Anticipations

Cover: Barbara Boicourt
Interior Illustrations: Rodger Gerberding and Suzanne Clarke—9, 49, 93, 101, 135;
Jules Hart—43, 59, 63, 85, 129; Margaret Ballif Simon—19, 33, 75, 109, 113, 119.

Editor in Chief	**Eric M. Heideman**
Business "Manager"	**Mark Willcox**
Associate and Poetry Editor	**Rebecca Marjesdatter**
Art Editor	**Rodger Gerberding**
Associate Editors	**Amanda Elg, Greg L. Johnson**
Editorial Assistants	**P M F Johnson, Sandra Rector**
Typesetting & Design	**Mark Willcox**
Printing	**Bookmobile**, St Louis Park, MN (printed in the USA)
Attorney	**Lynn Klicker Uthe**, 952-544-4925
Board of Directors	**Eric M. Heideman**, President; **Mark Willcox**, Treasurer; **Andrew Loges**, Secretary

Editorials: Mathoms

Here's to Sir Arthur C. Clarke (1917-2008), author of *Against the Fall of Night, Childhood's End, Profiles of the Future, Rendezvous with Rama, The Fountains of Paradise,* and many unforgettable short stories, and co-author with Stanley Kubrick of the film and novel *2001: A Space Odyssey.* With his fiction, his non-fiction, and his television appearances Clarke did as much as anyone—including his great contemporaries, Heinlein, Asimov, and Sagan—to foster a love of both science and science fiction in millions of people. Beyond that, Clarke's dogma-free mysticism has helped many people to grasp the magnitude of our universe, and helped generate a sense of hopefulness about humanity's future, on Earth and out among the stars. I continue to hope for a film adaptation of *Childhood's End,* starring Leonard Nimoy as Karellen.

We had intended to bring *TOTU* #29 out in July or August; instead it's coming out 'round Hallowe'en. It's mainly my bad: I usually do a good job of juggling multiple projects, but this time several other commitments ganged up on me and delayed *TOTU*. I will say that, were it not for having other projects that stretch other mental muscles, I would have burned out on *TOTU* back in the late 20th century. Having a rainbow of interests has kept me and, I think, *TOTU* fresh for 22 ½ years. That said, I'm reordering priorities. We should be able to get back on schedule, bringing *TOTU* #30 out next August and keeping on an at-least-one-every-12-months schedule for years thereafter.

We needed to raise our subscription rate two bucks, to a still-reasonable $30 for four issues. We'll use that modest hike to keep our cover & domestic mail order price at $11.50 for as long as possible.

After several issues without an interview I'm pleased that Catherine Lundoff has provided us an insightful one with Bryan Thao Worra. And after an even longer gap without a non-fiction article I'm happy to serve up Terry Faust's eye-opening piece of investigative journalism. It brings to mind Nathan Walpow's eloquent Godzilla memorial from *TOTU* #14.

This issue showcases fiction by *TOTU* veterans S.N. Arly, Eleanor Arnason, Patricia S. Bowne, Stephen Dedman, Martha A. Hood, Gerard Houarner, Sue Isle, Naomi Kritzer, Lyda Morehouse, Tony Pi, Mark Rich, and Patricia Russo, and *TOTU* newcomers Stephen Couch, Michael Pignatella, Hank Quesne, and Katherine Woodbury. Welcome one and all.

Aspiring writers, if you're reading this before November 16, 2008, we have a submissions window for *TOTU* #31. See our "Contributors Guidelines" in the current issue. If you're reading this after November 16, visit our website for updated guidelines and to learn when we'll open for #32: www.totu-ink.com

Gentle Reader, turn with me to Rebecca Marjesdatter's wise editorial on the speculative fiction community, and on to many wonders of prose, poetry, and artwork in the pages to come.

—Eric M. Heideman

The Ties That Bind

Recently, I attended the funeral of an SF fan, Margaret Howes, who died at the age of 80 in April 2008. I knew Margaret throughout my fannish life; she'd been a fixture at Lady Poetesses performances and the Dreamhaven reading series even after a stroke that left her vision impaired and her balance uncertain. Thus I went to the service as a representative of the poetry group, and of fandom in general.

Margaret's funeral started me thinking about community. I'm in a number of subcultures, but besides gender, my primary identification is with the science fiction community. Not the GLBT community, not the Pagan community, but fandom. I read an article once that given the choice between spending time with straight deaf people or hearing gay people, queer deaf people chose the deaf group because they spoke the same language. I understand that. I could go to a convention halfway across the country, where I know no one, and be at home. I've gone to family events, among people I've known my whole life, and been an alien.

How can this be? Fandom is huge: anime, media, costumers, libertarians, socialists, feminists, soldiers, Christians, Neo-Pagans, Atheists, gamers, Goths, Scadians…the differences in our interests and ideologies should tear us apart. Sometimes they do. Usually, we find ways to communicate that confirm our essential united geekhood. I think fandom is bound together less by shared history or texts than by shared traits. We're intelligent, either overeducated or autodidacts. We tend to speak in formal English, as though we learned to talk from books rather than people. We suffer from insatiable curiosity about the practicalities of space elevators, the construction of Victorian undergarments, the use of honorifics in Japanese, metal forging, Roman cookery…anything that catches our magpie fancy. We value things the mainstream dismisses as either childish and lowbrow or esoteric and boring. We respect "texts" of all kinds, to the point that we claim and re-create them with fanfiction, fanart, AMVs and critical theories that retrofit sloppily-conceived episodic TV series into elegant arcs of character development. Finally, I experience more tolerance in fandom than in Mundania. We have our factions and fights, but when fans hate each other it's typically interpersonal drama or internal politics ("Those media fans are taking over science fiction fandom! Those anime brats are taking over media fandom! Those yaoi fangirls are taking over anime fandom!"). Rarely is it race, religion or sexuality, the things that get people killed in the Real World.

I'm not a dewy-eyed idealist about my people. I've spent years dodging concoms for good reason. I've seen conventions collapse, fan groups implode and people do stupid, hurtful things to each other out of ego. No matter how much we want to be cyborgs or Otherkin, we're all just human. And, whether we like it or not, we're a tribe. I'll see you at the next convention.

P.S.—This issue welcomes Camilla DeCarnin back to speculative poetry after far too long an absence! If you like her work, another fine poem of hers was published in **Time Frames**, which is available from Terry Garey's website, www.joyofwine.net/poetry.htm.

—REBECCA MARJESDATTER

Contributors

Altough **S.N. Arly** likes to write dark tales, and finds the subject of death full of literary potential, she swears she's not terribly morbid. Her short stories have appeared in *Wolfsongs, Fearsmag.com, Tales of the Unanticipated* (*TOTU*), and the chapbook *Do Virgins Taste Better?* Her novels have appeared on her printer, her desk, and occasionally her office floor. She is a member of the writers' group Guts and Rocks. She lives in St. Paul with her spouse, young son, even younger daughter, and two Shelties, all of whom make her world a better place.

Eleanor Arnason published five novels between 1978 and 1993, then moved away from novels, since New York publishers are not always easy to deal with. *Ordinary People*, a collection of her short work, came out from Aqueduct Press in 2005. Her most recent book publication is a handsome, limited edition of her short story "The Grammarian's Five Daughters," produced by the Minnesota Center for Book Arts in 2006. The City of St. Paul is planning to stamp one of Arnason's poems in concrete in a sidewalk in 2008. A lot of he work has appeared in *TOTU*.

F.J. Bergmann frequents Wisconsin. When not manifesting as the shadowy entity behind madpoetry.org and fibits.com, she is a meek-mannered bookseller by day. Recent work appears or is forthcoming in *Asimov's SF, Expanded Horizons, Mythic Delirium, Opium,* and *Weird Tales*. She is the current winner of the Rhysling Award for the Short Poem.

Barbara Boicourt graduated with a Bachelor's degree in Fine Arts from the University of Nebraska at Omaha, and has worked as head graphic artist for Curizon Promotional Graphics in Omaha since 1981. Awards for her artwork include "a top prize in the Town & Country Arts Show for a photograph called *Frida and Me,* inspired by one of my favorite artists, Frida Kahlo." She adds, "My photo-montage work involves layering several images together using many various filters to create the textures, depth, and mood that I am trying to achieve. Many times I take my current digital photographs and blend them with bits and pieces of my archived print work thus letting the viewer embrace not only the present, but also gain a sense of the past through altered images. You can view many of my current images at my website which I designed, built, and maintain: www.babstoy.com

Patricia S. Bowne of Wisconsin took so long to finish her thesis that she was relocated to the research museum, becoming its first live specimen. She now works at an institution without a museum, though she was once housed uncomfortably close to the archives.

Suzanne Clarke continues to live in Kyoto, Japan, and contributed to this issue as model and factotum, primarily for the central figure in the illustration to Dedman's "Desiree" (she likes the sound of that).

Stephen Couch is a computer programmer, a cover band vocalist, an award-winning audio drama producer, and a lifelong Texan. His short fiction has sold to such markets as *Cemetery Dance, Talebones, Aeon, Dark Recesses Press,* and *Neo-Opsis*. You can visit him online and poke him with virtual sticks at www.stephencouch.com

Camilla DeCarnin is a fanfic writer and occasional poet. She is currently being treated for an aggressive cancer, and has moved from Los Angeles to Michigan. She's tickled to be appearing once again in *TOTU* after a long hiatus.

Stephen Dedman is the author of the novels *The Art of Arrow Cutting, Shadows Bite, Foreign Bodies,* and *A Fistful of Data,* as well as more than 100 short stories published in an eclectic range of anthologies and magazines. He teaches creative writing at the University of Western Australia, where he recently received his Ph.D. in English (he's still waiting for the paperwork to be completed on his nominations for sainthood). He is also the proud part-owner of the Fantastic Planet SF bookshop, and lives 16 meters above sea level with his wife Elaine, a few thousand books, and a finite number of cats. Visit him online at www.stephendedman.org

Terry Faust of Minneapolis writes, "In 1982 I received a Minnesota State Arts Board Grant to write, produce, and direct a 16mm film, *Lunch with Stacie*. A chapter of *To Build a Blackbird* (titled *Elysium Flyer* at the time) won the Loft's Literary Prize for Young Adult Fiction in 1991. I have contemplated a second young adult mystery titled *Dreamland*. I self-published *Z is for Xenophobe*, a sci-fi satire, and I am working on its sequel, *Y is for Wiseguy*."

Cornelius Fortune is a journalist and the author of *Stories from Arlington*. His fiction and poetry have appeared in *TOTU, Third Reader, Nuvein, Black Petals, Lost Souls,* and others. Visit his website at www.storiesfromarlington.com or contact him at arlingtonbooks@yahoo.com

Terry A. Garey is a former editor of *TOTU* and editor of the collection of speculative poetry, *Time Frames*, published by Rune Press and currently taking up a lot of room in her basement, despite the sterling cast of poets involved, including Ruth Berman, Mark Rich, John Calvin Rezmerski, Camilla DeCarnin, and Ann K. Schwader. Terry lives in Minneapolis with a tall librarian, two cats, and an awful lot of books. She has also written a book on home wine making called *The Joy of Home Winemaking* which is still in print, thank you.

Rodger Gerberding has recently completed cover work for three collections of poetry: *Exchanging Lives* by Damon McLaughlin and *Marrowbone Road* by John Ranan, (both Backwaters Press), and *Hell in the Heartland,* (Roger Dale Trexler, ed., Annihilation Press). An online show of Gerberding's gallery work, *Selva Obscura*, is planned for December by Grass Roots Gallery of Chicago, and recent work has been shown at New York's Heist Gallery. His work may be seen on My Space at rodgergerberding_artist, as website construction proper continues. He again curated this year's invitational of "outsider" art for the Glare Psychiatric Museum of St. Joseph, Missouri. For much of 2008, Gerberding has been completing production (as actor and director) of a full-length independent film, *Statuously Fixtured*, directed by Adam Fogarty and shot in Omaha, New York, and Seattle. Gerberding also had a long lunch this summer with Patricia Neal, the Oscar-winning actress; more about *that* proposed collaboration, should he meet you in person before the poor power of his memory is shorted out. And, Gerberding's beautiful daughter Katrinka gave birth early this year to equally beautiful Gracie, making him a soon-to-be five-times over grandfather. Who would have thought it in his salad days. Haveth childers everywhere!

Jules Hart of Minneapolis is a theory that has yet to be proven.

Eric M. Heideman, after a year as a Minneapolis Roving Librarian, is back in charge of his useful and homey re-opened library. He's published fiction in *Writers of the Future (WOTF), Volume III; Alfred Hitchcock's Mystery Magazine;* and *Best Mystery and Suspense Stories, 1988;* and around 200 reviews, essays, interviews, features, and biographical sketches in such places as the Minneapolis *Star Tribune, Twin Cities Reader, What do I Read Next?* (Gale), *MonsterZine.com, TOTU,* and various convention program books. Hang out with him in Krushenko's, his space for SF conversation, at MarsCon, Minicon, OdysseyCon, WisCon, CONvergence, Diversicon, and Arcana. He lives in a building overlooking a park with a lake, with his faithful phone-answering cats, Boris Karloff and Johnny Depp. He squeezes in at least one weekend a year in Upper Michigan, canoeing and puttering around around in the lake-shore cabin his grandfather built in 1909-1910. in the deep woods, still where the pavement ends.

Martha A. Hood writes, "I am now a retired stay-at-home mom in Irvine, California, which is more difficult than it looks. I am The Real Housewife of Orange County, whatever else they may tell you on TV. I am working on that novel, and am now confident I will live long enough to finish it and at least two others. I am also volunteering at UCI's arboretum, hanging out with other retired stay-at-home working moms, gardening (roses, herbs, cacti, and succulents), and attempting to clear decades of debris in our lives. Mike and I are adjusting well to our daughter's departure for college at Macalester in St. Paul, but one of our three cockatiels is very upset. Jason the Cockatiel really gets pissed off when Michelle comes home for school breaks, only to leave after a weekend, or a week, or even five weeks. He scolds her, and even turns his back on her. We try to explain, but he doesn't understand."

Gerard Hourner, a New Yorker married at a New Orleans Voodoo temple, works by day at a psychiatric institution and writes, mostly at night, about the dark. So far, he's had four novels and 250 short stories published. His latest collection, *The Oz Suite,* is available in trade and hardcover from www.eibonvalepress.co.uk and www.amazon.com. For the latest news, pics, links, and such, visit www.gerardhouarner.com

Sue Isle lives in Perth, Western Australia, under the control of two pet rats, Zach and Luka. See them for interview requests. There is less book-room in the Real House than there was, especially after Sue got home from Denvention this August. She is still with the court transcription company, referred to as a "lifer" when they're being nice. Her publishing credits so far include the YA book *Scale of Dragon, Tooth of Wolf* and the children's book *Wolf Children.* She has also sold a swag of stories to markets such as *Aurealis, Orb, ASIM, Agog, Sword and Sorceress,* and *TOTU,* and recently moved online with *Shiny,* a YA fiction magazine! Her other interests include history, SF conventions, roleplay gaming, gardening, and working out how best to turn her hometown into an Aftermath scenario, as described in the current story. You may visit her Live Journal on ratfan.livejournal.com

Naomi Kritzer's short stories have appeared in *Realms of Fantasy, Strange* Horizons, and *TOTU.* Her novels *(Fires of the Faithful, Turning the Storm, Freedom's Gate, Freedom's Apprentice,* and *Freedom's Sisters*) are available from Bantam. She is currently working on a children's fantasy novel about illegal immigration. Naomi lives in Minneapolis with her husband and two daughters.

Sandra Lindow lives on a hilltop in Menominee, Wisconsin, where she communes with perennials and goes barefoot three seasons of the year. She teaches part-time at U-W Stout. *Touched by the Gods,* her sixth collection of poetry, is in the publication process. She is in the unenviable (always a bridesmaid) position of having the most nominations for the Rhysling (15) without a win.

Catherine Lundoff is the Minneapolis-based author of two collections of lesbian erotica: *Night's Kiss* (Torquere Press, 2005), and *Crave: Tales of Love, Lust and Longing* (Lethe Press, 2007), and the editor of *Haunted Hearths and Sapphic Shades: Lesbian Ghost Stories* (Lethe Press, 2008). Her nonfiction articles have appeared in such venues as *Looking Queer: GLBT Body Image and Identity, Coming Out of the Closet Again, Writing-World.com, Queue Press, Women in Science Fiction and Fantasy: An Encyclopedia* (Greenwood Press) and *American Writer.*

Rebecca Marjesdatter studied creative writing and philosophy at the College of St. Catherine, library science at Rosary College at Dominican University, and obtained half of an MFA from Hamline University before coming to her senses. Her resume consists of entirely normal jobs at bookstores, libraries, and now law firms, but she makes up for it with a rich inner life. She is the current poetry editor for *TOTU,* winner of the 2000 Rhysling Award (short form), a member of the poetry performance group Lady Poetesses from Hell, and probably the first and only poet to be a guest of honor at an anime convenion. She lives in Minneapolis.

Lyda Morehouse is an award-winning science fiction author who now writes best-selling romances as Tate Hallaway. Lyda tries not to be jealous of her pseudonym's successes, but given that Tate recently hit the New York *Times* best-seller lists (for, Lyda would point out, a short story included in an anthology with much bigger names editing and contributing), it's difficult. When not arguing with herself, Lyda enjoys the life of a stay-at-home parent to a precocious five-year-old. Recently, she started fish keeping and has become a rather fanatic aquariast, which you can read about in long, lovingly described detail on her livejournal: lyda222.livejournal.com

More than 600 of **Kristine Ong Muslim**'s poems and stories have appeared or are in over 300 publications worldwide. Her work has appeared in *Aberrant Dreams, Abyss & Apex, Cemetery Moon, Dog Versus Sandwich, Down in the Cellar, GUD Magazine, The Fifth Di, Kaleidescope, Labyrinth Inhabitant Magazine, Niteblade, Oddlands Magazine, OG's Speculative Fiction, Spinning Whorl, Tales of the Talisman, The Specusphere,* and *Trail of Indiscretion.* She is a two-time winner of Sam's Dot Publishing's James Award for genre poetry.

Tony Pi is a writer based in Toronto, Ontario, Canada, whose work has previously appeared in *TOTU, Abyss & Apex, OnSpec,* and *WOTF, Volume XXIII.* Also a finalist in the Prix Aurora Awards 2008 for "Best Short Form Work in English." He continues to write fantasy stories and the occasional science fiction or mystery.

Michael Pignatella lives in Connecticut with his wife and two children. His stories have appeared in such venues as *Murky Depths, Wicked Hollow, Alofess Kiss, Dark Corners, Nanobison, Modern Magic, All Possible Worlds, Withersin,* and *Wondrous Web Worlds* vol. 4. He recently completed his Master's degree in English literature, and is currently working on a novel.

Hank Quesne—assisted by his faithful mutt, Manny—writes science fiction and fantasy stories (along with an occasional fiction-writing article) from Bergenfield, New Jersey. All of these stories are humorous or satiric because he refuses to write serious genre stories. He feels that folks who crave serious fantasy and SF can get a full measure in any daily newspaper. In the spirit of disclosure, Hank reports that all of the story ideas (the good ones, anyway) come from Manny. Hank merely translates the dog's ideas into a manuscript. Hank can be reached via email at: hanque99@verizon.net.

Manny refuses to get an internet address until someone develops a paw-friendly keyboard. The pair of them have sold stories to *Andromeda Spaceways, Cyberpulp, Fantastical Visions, Neo-Opsis, Afterburner SF, Faeries* (France), *Electric Spec, Scyweb Bem, Glassfinder, Darker* Matter, and *Flash Fiction Online,* as well as several anthologies. Visit their website at hankquesne.com

Terrie Leigh Reif lives in Ocean Beach, by her beloved ocean, in San Diego, California. She is on staff at Sam's Dot Publishing (www.samsdotpublishing.com). Sam's Dot has recently released *Blood Journey*, a vampire saga she co-authored with Henry Lewis Sanders; *The Poet's Workshop—and Beyond*, a "quirky" writing handbook; and *My Friend, the Poet, and Other Poems about People I think I Know*, a collection of her soon-to-be-infamous unauthorized biographical poems (okay, some were authorized…). While she loves numbers (especially odd ones), she has lost count of how many times she has been published and is incredibly behind on her bibliography. That said, you will be amazed at how modest she is, and that she still behaves like a two-year-old every time she gets published.

Mark Rich currently has two full-length collections appearing: *Across the Skies* from Fairwood Press, and *Speaking in Air* from RedJack Books, with a chapbook, *The Sound of Dead Hands Clapping*, also appearing from Gothic Press. Upcoming is a study of Judith Merril, from Aqueduct Press. He lives in the Wisconsin Coulee region where he gardens, paints, and plays the occasional acoustic-rock show with partner-in-life Martha Borchardt.

James P. Roberts wears many literary hats and changes them often. He has published 11 books in the fields of science fiction and fantasy, poetry, literary biography, and baseball history. His latest is a collection of poetry, *Dancing with Poltergeists*, published by Popcorn Press. He also performs music upon a variety of exotic stringed instruments. He lives in Madison, Wisconsin.

Patricia Russo has had stories published in *Corpse Blossoms, Zencore, Read by Dawn* volume two, *The Best of Not One of Us, Coyote Wild, Lone Star Stories,* and many other print and online publications, including frequent appearances in *TOTU*. She lives in New Jersey.

Ann K. Schwader's Lovecraftian/SF sonnet sequence, *In the Yaddith Time,* was published by Mythos Books in 2007. She is still living, writing, and library-volunteering in Westminster, Colorado, with the same husband and the same profoundly spoiled Welsh corgi. For more information on her work, please check out her website: www.geocities.com/hpl4ever/, or her blog: ankh-hpl.livejournal.com

Marge Ballif Simon freelances as a writerpoetillustrator for genre and mainstream publications such as *From the Asylum, Chizine, The Pedestal Magazine, Strange Horizons, Flashquake, Aeon, Vestal Review,* more. Her dark poetry collection with Charlee Jacob, *Vectors: A Walk in the Death of a Planet* (Vectors Press), won a Bram Stoker Award in 2008. Her self-illustrated poetry collection, *Artist of Antithesis*, was nominated for a Stoker Award in 2004. Marge is former President of the Science Fiction Poetry Association, and now serves as editor of *Star*Line*. She lives in Ocala, Florida.

Katherine Woodbury lives in Maine. Her stories have been published in a variety of science fiction and fantasy magazines, including *Andromeda Spaceways, Space & Time, Talebones,* and *Leading Edge*. She teaches English composition at two local community colleges, and teaches and tutors online, In her free time, Katherine watches *Star Trek, Columbo,* and *Doctor Who*, takes books out of the library (and forgets to return them), and posts to her blog: www.katewoodbury.blogspot.com. Katherine (or Kate) can be reached at woodburykate@yahoo.com

Tales of the Unanticipated was founded in 1986 by the Minnesota Science Fiction Society, who served as publisher of its first 23 issues.

Tales of the Unanticipated is published at least annually, sometimes sooner, by TOTU INK. Copyright © 2008 TOTU Ink, Inc., authors and artists. Reproduction in whole or in part by any means without permission is prohibited. The opinions expressed herein (Change or Die) are not necessarily those of TOTU Ink. Editorial and non-poetry, non-art submissions: send to Eric M. Heideman, Tales of the Unanticipated, PO Box 8036, Lake Street Station, Minneapolis MN 55408, and submissions@totu-ink.com. TOTU is not an around-the-year market. Please check our Contributors' Guidelines on page 7. Subscription service: send address changes, subscription renewals, single-copy mail orders, or new subscriptions to Tales of the Unanticipated, PO Box 1099, Minnetonka MN 55345. ISBN: 0-9760146-9-6

TALES OF THE UNANTICIPATED
Contributors' Guidelines

Reading submissions for issue #31 that are postmarked October 15-November 15, 2008. We will respond by April 15, 2009. If you are reading this after November 15, 2008, do not send unsolicited manuscripts. Keep an eye on our Website (www.totu-ink.com) for reading period guidelines/updates. Please note that we *are not an around-the-year market.*

For questions and queries contact: submits@totu-ink.com. Please type something in the subject heading to make it easier to locate and refer back to your email.

PROSE SUBMISSIONS—please follow carefully

Send a manuscript copy of PROSE submissions (with SASE) to:
Eric M. Heideman
Tales of the Unanticipated
PO Box 8036
Lake Street Station
Minneapolis MN 55408
(Eric does not assume or accept responsibility for art portfolios and poetry mailed to the above address.)

In addition to mailing us mss. copies of your prose submissions, email your submission as an attachment to:
submits@totu-ink.com
or upload your submission using the File Upload form at totu-ink.com/upload.php.

We can accept most file formats—Word, Open Office, Word Perfect, etc.—but if you are not sure, send your submission as a Rich Text Format (RTF) file. For our international contributors, A4 is okay. Size, in this case, doesn't matter. If you do not have a computer document for your submission, please email us at the above edress to let us know that you have mailed your manuscript.

The editor, whose day-job partly involves reading huge amounts of information off a screen, will not spend hundreds of additional hours of his "spare time" reading story mss. off his personal laptop screen, and *TOTU* cannot carry the expense of printing off the thousands of pages of submissions we receive. If you want your prose submissions considered, you need to send a paper manuscript along with the electronic one.

Please note that Eric and the *TOTU* staff put a lot of time and care into helping promising writers hone their craft. Writers of originality and vision often need help presenting their material so that their desired effect gets across to readers. That's what editors are supposed to be for. To be helpful, we think it's necessary to be honest. If you see personal editorial feedback as enemy action, please don't waste our time; we have an antholozine to put out. If you like getting feedback, we look forward to reading your stuff.

FICTION: reading submissions postmarked October 15-November 15, 2008, for #31, a general, non-theme issue. Pays 1 ½-2 cents a word for science fiction, fantasy, horror, hybrids thereof, and unclassifiable stories. We prefer stories with personality, and originality of vision, to the factory-made brand. We will consider stories of any length up to 10,000 words. No serials.

NON-FICTION: *TOTU* pays 1 ½ cents a word for essays for the general reader on speculative fiction writers and themes, or speculative science essays for the general reader, to 6,000 words. No plot summaries masquerading as book reviews. Query Eric M. Heideman at the above address with an SASE or, preferably, send an email query to eric@totu-ink.com with your non-fiction idea before submitting.

RIGHTS: *TOTU* acquires First North American Serial Rights. We occasionally settle for One-Time Reprint Rights on previously published material, but if your piece was previously published, or is scheduled to be published elsewhere, you need to say that in your cover letter. No surprises, please. Once your piece has appeared in *TOTU*, you are free to sell it to other markets. But when it's republished please include a statement to this effect: "(Story title) originally appeared in *Tales of the Unanticipated* (issue number & year)."

SIMULTANEOUS SUBMISSIONS: Because of the short reading window, we're willing to consider simultaneous submissions, but again, no surprises; you need to mention up front in your cover letter where else your submission is sitting, and you need to let us know—promptly—when/if it is accepted/rejected by the other market. (After several staff members have devoted hours of consideration to a piece, it doesn't make us happy campers to learn that, in the meantime, you've sold it to a market where you hadn't even told us it was under consideration.)

MULTIPLE SUBMISSIONS: Because of the short submissions window, we're willing to consider up to three stories from you; but please include a *separate SASE* for each story. Failure to include separate SASEs may result in prompt rejection of a story or essay that might otherwise have received serious consideration.

E-SUBS: *TOTU* now asks for *both* paper and electronic copies of prose submissions. Electronic submissions without accompanying paper copies remain unacceptable. Please carefully read through "prose submissions" above for details. For poetry submissions, see below.

PAYMENT: 1 ½-2 cents a word for fiction and non-fiction. See above for what kinds of fiction and non-fiction we'll consider.

POETRY: *TOTU* pays $7 for speculative poetry, up to two typewritten pages per poem. Email submissions to:
Poetry@totu-ink.com
In the case of poetry—and only poetry—submissions are made exclusively by email, without an accompanying paper copy. If you send a file with multiple poems, please put your byline at the bottom of *each* individual poem.

ILLUSTRATIONS AND CARTOONS: *TOTU* pays $25 for front-cover art, $15 for back-cover art, $12 for commissioned interior illustrations, $7 for cartoons and spot illustrations. For an assignment, send several clear photocopies representing the range of your work. Please do not send original copies unless asked to do so. Send art portfolios to:
Rodger Gerberding
379 Lincoln Av
Council Bluffs IA 51503
Send cartoons to Eric M. Heideman at the address for fiction submissions, above.

Mark Rich is a versatile man, artist, musician, literary historian-critic, poet, and fiction writer whose work ranges from dead serious to downright silly. Here's an in-between piece, a look at old-time rural life with a folktale feel. It is—ahem—Something Rich and Strange.

Dead Man Come A-Calling

by Mark Rich

I heard the door open and close with a complaint and figured whoever came in probably had one, too.

I was busy right at the moment. Though not a thing was happening in the spring months of 1974, in Burns, Kansas, you would never know it from the looks of my In box.

"Tom, I don't know but that we don't have a problem," said a woman's voice. "Bob's busy right now, so I thought I'd come tell you."

"Right, Claire. Hold on." Tom had been on the phone. He got right back on it. Talking with Wayne over in Haline.

"Hi, Julie," Claire Mills said to me.

"Hi," I said back. In Burns, you got to knowing everyone. Claire had more business here than most, though, so I would have known her anyway.

Tom laughed a couple times and said something about flowers before hanging it up.

"Sorry to make you wait," he said. "You were saying?"

"Might have a problem here," she said.

Claire was wearing one of the baby-blue blouses she had a hundred of. Together with her short, straight hair, her style of dress tended to make her look young. I guess she liked it that way. Since she was younger than me, I suppose she had the right.

Her badge gave her a little weight of authority, to make up for it.

"Don't suppose you're speaking as librarian," said Tom.

"No. Library's fine." Claire's assistant librarian at the new Burns Public Library over by the courthouse.

"Then I suppose you're here as assistant deputy."

"That's right." She's also the town's first woman assistant deputy, as a part-time thing. She gets paid when there's work. I guessed there was work today.

"I don't suppose it's about that near-beer stolen from Jordan's grocery."

"I don't suppose so."

"Something worse?"

"Don't rightly know, Tom."

"Who's it to do with?" Tom said, leaning back in his chair.

Leaning back in his chair and letting his belly stick out helps him look important. He thinks so, anyway. Not being that big of a belly, it does no one any harm, except maybe himself.

Tom Chancy is town manager of Burns, Kansas. Has been for going on seven years. Does pretty well, too. Gets in on people's problems, and settles things without too much fuss.

"According to Ruth Tucker, it's old Hanks," Claire said.

"Which old Hanks?"

"The old Hanks who shouldn't seem as lively as he does, Tom, I guess you'd say."

"Ben Hanks? He's too old to be trouble for anyone, lively or not. Hasn't bothered you now lately, has he, Julie?" Tom winked at me because even though I'm forty-eight and getting flexible around the hips, the Rev. Benjamin Hanks started hanging around the office for a month last winter, dropping hints about how he might be looking. I dropped a few hints as to how I might not.

"Just old enough," I said.

"Well, really, I didn't come to talk about Ben causing trouble. According to Ruth Tucker, it's Ben's brother," Claire said.

"Doesn't have one," said Tom.

"Sure he does. Did, anyway."

"Jimmy Hanks causing trouble?" I said. "No way. Dead."

"You're talking about the man in this chair before me," said Tom. "Sure as shoehorns he is."

"That's what town records say, too," said Claire.

"Then I don't see what the problem is," said Tom.

"It's Ruth. She's the one saying Jimmy's back."

Tom sighed, which let me know he had just delegated the problem.

I refilled my In box, and took the letter out of the typewriter I was writing to John, my son in the Virgin Islands, which I added to whenever I thought of something to say. Sometimes things in Burns move slowly enough that you get to writing letters the same way, letting them go their own pace until you fill a page or two and you can sign it somewhere at the bottom with the confidence of having gone on about something at length, even if it had been not much you had gone on about. I had been working on this letter going on two weeks. I had half a page.

"I don't like to get involved in family things too much," Claire said when we were in her car, a '63 red Pontiac Tempest that ran like a lawnmower, only maybe closer to the ground. "But Ruth Tucker called Bob, and Bob sent me onto this one since there's word out about someone breaking out of Leavenworth and maybe hiding in someone's barn. So he's checking that out." Bob, the sheriff, drives a black car a little newer than Claire's, a little higher off the road. "But you know the Hanks and Linsetters pretty well, don't you? I don't feel so bad about asking to go in, since you're a friend of the family."

People work that way in a small town.

"From a ways back," I said.

Ruth's mom, Wanda Linsetter, and my mom were high school friends. They used to talk about hanging around the Hanks home, when Jimmy, the younger Hanks boy, was just out of school.

Jimmy worked as a car mechanic for a summer. He and Wanda Linsetter mooned around a while, my mom says, before he slicked his hair and went to Wichita to get schooling in civic government or something of the sort. Then he figured he was big stuff and went off to Kansas City, and found some little job in Missouri a while. Then he came back and took the job of town manager, same job Tom holds now.

Mom says it was a big heartbreak for Jimmy Hanks that Wanda had married the Briggs boy in the meantime. Jimmy had left town not thinking he was really in love with her but once he got back saw things more truly. Too late, as it happened. Which I suppose is better than never.

So Jimmy married the Briggs girl, Betty Ellen, so he could be related to Wanda somehow, I suppose.

"You know that Betty Ellen Briggs close to nagged Jimmy Hanks to his grave," I said, remembering. "All that stuff about her chasing him with a Chinese cleaver, you've heard that. Some people say it's true. That's why he did so well by the city. Hated to go home, so he stayed at work."

"Tom's a good manager."

"I just said Jimmy was. Didn't say Tom wasn't. I work for him. I think Tom's fine."

"He make passes at you?" Claire flashed me a grin. "He's eligible. Not so many in Burns are. Course I don't have to tell you that."

"God's sake, Claire, he's a good eight years younger."

"Doesn't matter much. You keep yourself looking good."

"I'm done with men. Having suffered one husband's enough for me. I was talking about Jimmy."

"And Betty Ellen. Now she's died, too, hasn't she?"

"Buried in Haline, too. Like as not, having her in the same patch of dirt would be enough to drive Jimmy out of the ground. Maybe that's what's happened."

We laughed at that.

The car jiggled over the brick cobble of Baker Street past Hazel Brown's house with its big garden. She always had the most colorful flower beds on the street, mid-summer like this. The county had some great color, what with all the Anubis Lilies the Sample family brought from Egypt and planted all over, back in the Forties. Hazel had the best, though.

It looked as though someone had been grubbing up part of it. I figured she was doing some rearranging.

Claire pulled up in front of the Hanks place. When I was small that house was painted dull pink with white shutters, and had a huge bed of lilies by the front fence. You would hear about it from Ma Hanks if you stepped on her flowers. Ma Hanks ruled that house with an iron fist but was the easiest touch for cookies in the neighborhood. Maybe she had wanted girls instead of those two lanky boys.

Claire motioned me ahead on the sidewalk, so I went ahead to the door. Before I could knock, it opened.

"Well, hello, ladies," said Ben. He grinned widely. The Reverend Ben Hanks was still the kind of man you compared to a vine bean instead of the bush variety. Back in his preaching days he stood high in his Methodist pulpit and looked like a farmer boy made good. He still kept his hair blackened and greased back.

"Julie," he said, "all the times I asked you over, and now here you are. It's regular reunion time. Come on in. Wanda Linsetter's here too. Come on in. You too, your name's Clara, isn't it? Clara Mailer? The librarian? We'll all fit in the living room. We'll manage somehow."

"I'm Claire Mills," Claire said. "Assistant deputy, right now."

"Say, I heard a funny story," I said to Ben.

"You tell everyone, then," Ben said. "We're all in a good mood. We'd love to hear it."

"I heard your brother's back," I said. "Sounds silly, doesn't it."

Ben laughed as if he knew the story but was willing to laugh at the punch line anyway. Ministers will be that way.

"'Cause I know he passed away," I added.

We followed him into the front room. Ruth Tucker's mother, Wanda Briggs, nee Linsetter, was there. She was dressed in a fresh-looking yellow blouse with a polka-dot skirt and quaint apron with scalloped bottom. On her lap she held a plate of cookies. Oatmeal raisin, it looked like.

One was crumbling between the lips of the other person in the room, who was seized by uncontrollable humor. He sure looked that way, anyway. He shook as if he were. His eyes stayed in the kind of crescent shape you expect of someone overcome by the humor of a thing. Maybe he was laughing, just with the sound turned off. I guess it was funny, being a man come a-calling from the grave.

I say that because he sure looked like Jimmy Hanks.

His skin looked a little darker than I remembered, and a little smoother and shinier. His eyes looked bright and not glassy at all. I hardly wondered that he came back to life, looking so healthy. But the laughing smile, even so good-natured a smile, seemed a little much. Hardly seemed becoming in someone whose funeral you attended once.

"This here's Julie Hale, you'll remember her. And this here's Claire Mills, don't know if you ever knew her," Ben said to the figure in the brown leather chair. "Assistant deputy librarian."

I stood there looking at Jimmy. How he could laugh, make no noise, and chew at the same time was beyond me.

"And you know my brother Jimmy, Julie," Ben said to me.

"Isn't Jimmy. Couldn't be."

"Right as ragweed he is," Ben said, beaming. "Just like before. Don't talk much now, is all."

Jimmy, still laughing, or giggling for all I knew, bent his head as if in acknowledgement.

"You're Jimmy?" I said.

His voice came out breathy and small, but fairly distinct, despite the cookie crumbs: "Es."

"That a 'yes'?" I said.

"Isn't he a charmer?" said Wanda Linsetter. I could smell her perfume from where I stood. Lilac, maybe.

"Sure is," said Claire, "for a man a few years gone."

"Oh, he was never wholly gone," said Wanda, consenting to take her gaze away from the object of her affection for a moment. "Least not as Jimmy tells it."

"Won't you ladies have a seat?" said Ben.

"I don't know but that what we have here isn't what we might not call a zombie," Claire said.

Jimmy appreciated the comment, bending his head as he silently laughed. Jimmy was taller than Ben, even—probably a few inches over six feet, I guessed. Death had brought him down not a notch.

Claire sat in the chair farthest from Jimmy. I took a closer one, figuring I might as well test the truth of a thing if I was not ready to believe it.

"That's right," said Ben. "We all thought he was gone for good, but that was before the other day. Jimmy just walked in, made himself at home. I was mighty happy to see him."

"Wanda here just said he was never gone," I said.

"Not in my eyes," she said. She gave a big smile in Jimmy's direction. "Besides, I dreamed he'd come back, soon as he could. Soon as the time was right."

I remembered just then. Not only had Jimmy's wife died, but Wanda's husband had recently passed along, too.

"Well, I guess that's so, he wasn't rightly gone," said Ben. "Not the way we say people are gone when they're gone, he wasn't gone in that way. Sure he was under some dirt a while, weren't you, Jimmy?"

The silent, laughing nod.

"So who was it dug him up?" said Claire. "I suppose someone had to dig him up, didn't someone?"

"I don't suppose so," said Ben, looking dubiously at Claire before turning to his brother. "I don't suppose anyone dug you up, did they, Jimmy? Didn't you find your own way out?"

"Up," said Jimmy, meaning, I suppose, "Yup."

"Well, I reckon it won't matter much how he got himself back up to daylight. He's here, and for me it's good to have company, and Wanda here's been bringing sweets. Jimmy's always liked sweets, though he hasn't had much appetite since coming back. Just has a little sip of whiskey before going out at night, hardly eats a bite."

"He goes out at night?" said Claire. "A zombie loose in Burns?"

"He comes visiting," said Wanda.

"Visiting you? He comes a-calling?" said Claire.

"Oh, he visits a little while, I guess that's right. He doesn't talk much now. He hasn't got much breath left in him. But we manage to talk enough, don't we, Jimmy? Making our plans."

Jimmy laughed. He had made small progress on the cookie. A raisin seemed to be holding him up.

"Plans for what?" I said, feeling sort of stupid.

"Now Mrs. Brown," said Tom to Hazel, who had just rushed into the office. "I've got things to deal with, and I'm not sure but that Bob wouldn't be the proper person for you."

"You go on ahead and talk to Hazel, Tom," said Ben Hanks. "I'm in no hurry."

"Bob's out with some men surrounding a barn, anyway," I put in. "Some escapee from Leavenworth."

"Well, then, maybe Hazel could talk to Claire," said Tom to me.

"Claire isn't deputy sheriff right now," I said. "She's on shift at the library, and you aren't supposed to talk there."

"Well, darn, all right, I'll listen," Tom said, sitting down in his chair. The phone rang.

"Tom Chancy," he said, picking up the phone. "No, heck, Wayne, I'm not busy. What's up, buddy?" Calls from the mayor of Haline constituted important business.

"What's the complaint, Hazel?" I said to Mrs. Brown.

She settled onto the bench beneath the bulletin board full of news of civic projects from across Kansas. Most of the pictures and clippings were on glossy paper, with color photos. Tom had me pin up pictures that made Kansas look up to date. All that financial activity and economic development in other towns is supposed to rub off on us in Burns someday, I suppose.

Hazel sat pertly upright. Only two-thirds my age, she occupied a little more space on the bench than I do. Not to say she was of the overwhelming 4-H Fair blue-ribbon variety. She just had hips a little.

"My garden," she said, her tone sharp. "Things uprooted like you wouldn't believe. I don't know what's getting into kids."

"Lilies again?" Tom said into the phone.

"That's right, Mr. Chancy," Hazel said.

"I'm talking to the mayor of Haline," Tom said to Hazel, holding his hand over the mouthpiece for a moment. "Go on, Wayne. Darnedest thing. Makes me glad Burns is so quiet a place."

"Uprooted and stolen, some of them," Hazel said to me, glancing over to Ben Hanks. "That was night before yesterday. And then last night! Went out on my back porch and wouldn't you know but all the potted plants I'd gotten from church after Easter services this year, all down to the last of them pulled up and the bulbs snapped off! Now what would someone want to do that for? And this time of year!"

"Some rowdy kid," Ben said with a frown.

"Goddamn peculiar rowdy kid," Hazel said. She grew instantly contrite. "If you'll excuse me my language, Reverend."

Tom laughed and put down the phone. "That Wayne. Crazy city he's running. People digging up graves and stealing flowers. Glad we got peace hereabouts. Hazel, what are you saying?"

"Last two nights, Mr. Chancy. Boys I suspect it is, making havoc in my garden."

"Well, guess I can talk to Bob about it when he gets back from that barn-dance or whatever. Thanks for stopping in, Hazel. Howdy, Ben. Haven't seen you in a while."

"Most people aren't so quick to admit they haven't been to church."

"Thought you'd retired from the pulpit."

"Still go to church," Ben said genially.

"That's all you're going to tell me?" said Hazel.

"Tell you what?" said Tom to her.

"Are you going to do anything about my garden?"

"I'll talk to Bob," Tom said.

"I'll tell Claire, too," I said, trying to appease her. "We'll have someone drive by tonight to check, don't you worry. We'll find out who's giving you trouble."

Mrs. Brown got to her feet with a dissatisfied look. "I do half wish sometimes, Julie, that old Jimmy Hanks would come back for his job. He did by us right."

"Goodbye, Mrs. Brown," said Tom. "Glad we could help."

"Shouldn't even have tried," she said, closing the door behind her a little loudly.

"That Wayne," Tom said, turning to me. "He says his flower-looter let up for a couple nights—and then was out on the prowl again last night. Crazies, over in Haline."

"Listen, Tom," I said, "I brought Reverend Hanks here to talk to you. Figured you wouldn't believe me."

"Heck, Julie, I'd believe you in anything. What's this about?"

"Jimmy Hanks. He's back to life and he's down visiting at Ben's. I saw him."

"I've heard that old farmer's tale already, Julie. Now, Ben, what can I help you with?"

"Well," said Ben, scratching his gray head. "Best as I can figure—communication with the old boy's not the easiest thing in the world—but I do get the impression he'd like you to come tonight."

"Who would? To what?"

"Jimmy, of course. My brother. Seven p.m. tonight, he

and Wanda Linsetter. Tying the knot."

"They can't do that."

"Now, Tom, sixty-nine's not too old to get married. I know it's hard for you youngsters to understand that—"

"I mean, Jimmy's passed along now already, almost two years it's been. He's been here and gone already."

"As to that objection," Ben said, "Jimmy's taken care of that. Least near as I can tell. You look at him, you pinch yourself, and he doesn't go away."

"You mean Julie here's not pulling an old farmer on me?"

"Seven p.m. tonight, Tom. You coming? He'd like to have you."

"Stuff like this doesn't happen in Burns, Ben. You know that."

"I know what you mean, Tom." Ben lowered himself into one of the plastic-topped chairs beside me. He handled himself well for a man gone over seventy. "Don't think I haven't puzzled over it. I keep thinking back to Proverbs: 'He who minds his words preserves his life.' Like you know, Tom, and you know, Julie, he shut up like a clam his last days. Didn't have a mite of happiness and he shut right up. Now I loved his wife Betty Ellen as the Lord says I should, hard as it was, but I'll admit—and this is an awful, awful thing to say, Tom, but you know how true it is—that if Betty Ellen Hanks had met the Lord before Jimmy had, why then Jimmy might have had a few days of living peace on this earth."

Tom blanched and glanced at me.

"What are you saying, Ben? That just because Betty Ellen's been buried Jimmy's back to enjoy life again?"

"Oddly enough, Tom, something else Solomon said, it comes to mind now. 'Hope deferred makes the heart sick; a wish come true is a staff of life.' Now the 'hope deferred' part—we've all got to face up to the fact that he had his heart set on Wanda since he was a stick. It was just his getting a little stuffing in his shirt and his deciding to hit the big city that got in the way of that. A little pride can do in the best of us. That hope of his got deferred all his life, right to the end, and then beyond. Now that other part, 'A wish come true is a staff of life.' This is awful again to say so, but it's obvious and true what Jimmy wished for. Now it's come to pass. Betty Ellen's gone and buried, together with our memories of her swinging that awful cleaver when she got her spittle up. And the news that she's buried, why, that's what Jimmy must have taken as the staff of life."

Tom shook himself. "Can't stand the thought of a dead man walking around Burns."

"Isn't walking around. Mostly sticking close to home, and going calling on Wanda a bit."

Tom breathed hard. "Now listen. Say this all is true. Not that I don't believe you two, what you're telling me. But say it's all true anyway. This won't be a big wedding, will it? No cameras? The banns aren't published, are they, Ben?"

He was looking hard at both of us, as if he thought we were both off the deep end. I could tell he maybe figured there might be more loonies than just the two of us.

"Lord, no. Jimmy likes things kept down. Guess spending all that time quiet-like in the grave—"

"Good, good," Tom said. "Just wouldn't like it getting aired around. Burns doesn't need publicity like this."

"Now, Tom, you're talking as if you might be ashamed of this," said Ben. "It isn't like he's come back for your job, you understand. He hasn't gotten any younger. He's just come back for a little happiness. That's all. A little happiness."

Ruth was crying. Wanda Linsetter's daughter was far from the first bride's daughter I have seen weep at a mother's wedding. She must have been the first I've seen crying out of helpless dismay, however.

Robert Tucker, Ruth's husband, sat next to her looking pale and drawn as if he were the one crawled from the grave. They hardly said a word before the service began, apparently having exhausted their arguments on Wanda during the afternoon.

"Now, young folk I tend to give a talking-to," the Reverend Hanks said to the two figures standing in front of him, the one tall and thin, the other shorter and dressed in a pink, full-length dress. Jimmy must have borrowed one of his brother's suits, since it was a little short in the legs. "Hardly a pair of them knows what they're into when they get the notion to tie the knot. More mature folk I try to keep quiet in front of. I figure they know as much as I do about being in the married state, if not more. And here one of the folk I'm marrying is my brother, Jimmy, who's learned the lessons of life and is full of wisdom as rich and revivifying as wine aged and ripened in a casket."

At least *I* heard Ben say "casket" instead of "cask." Since no one else looked ready to laugh, excepting Jimmy himself, I cracked not a smile. Not in the mood, anyway.

Tom came in then, looking spooked, but only a little. He was in his work clothes. Probably let the time slip away while watching the news, and forgot to get ready for the big affair.

Not that it was that big. Tom sat on the kitchen chair next to mine, toward the back of the chapel improvised out of the Hanks' front room. Ruth and Robert Tucker sat a little to the left in front of us, the one of them trembling with tears and the other stiff upright as a board. To our right and in front of us sat Cousin Annie, an elderly relation of Ben's and Jimmy's. She heard things poorly, so was bent forward toward the wedding pair in front of Reverend Hanks. That probably helped her see what was going on, since her eyes were bad, too.

Tom leaned over to me, and whispered. "There's talk on the news about grave-robbing in Haline."

I widened my eyes and half-rolled my shoulders, which between Tom and me meant, "And what am I supposed to do about that?"

Tom had an exasperated look. "What do I say to Wayne next time, if he hears about this going on down here?"

"You two want a service quick and functional and informal, without the doodads young folk want," Ben said to the couple. "I can understand that. But it behooves me to say a few words, not just for you two, Jimmy and Wanda, but for our gathering of loved ones who're here to witness this joyous occasion.

"I'd like to say just a little about Jimmy coming back to us. I admit when he first appeared at my door, his clothes smelling of the good earth, I wasn't at first prepared to accept the evidence of my senses. I wanted to say he was a ghost, a spirit, even a vision. But at last I came to recognize him for the man he is. He showed me the scar on his left thumb where he almost cut it off with a jack-knife when he was eight years old. I remember that well, because when our mother got mad at him for being so stupid, he said it was my doing, that's right, and I got a whipping like you wouldn't believe. He showed me the spot on his right shoulder where Dr. Fuller took out a mole. Then he went to the shelf over there, took down this family Bible, same as I hold now in front of you, and opened it up to the family pages. He pointed with his finger to his name, beside his birth date, January 23, 1905. And I believed him.

"I believed him then, and I still do. Jimmy is a man who saw little of happiness in his earlier years, for all that he was successful in the community and in his profession. He must have known there was more, something he was missing, the element to life that makes it all worthwhile. It's the thing that brings Wanda and Jimmy together before us tonight. Love. The highest love. The love that makes all things possible. The love that works miracles. But all of you can see that. It's a miracle that has happened here. I read from the book of Esdras, chapter nine, in which the Lord says to Ezra, 'For all of you, paradise lies open, the tree of life is planted, the age to come is made ready, and rich abundance is in store; the city is already built, rest from toil is assured, goodness and wisdom are brought to perfection. The root of evil has been sealed off from you; for you there is no more illness, death is abolished, hell has fled, and decay is quite forgotten. All sorrows are at an end, and the treasure of immortality has been finally revealed.' What the Lord has promised is open and waiting for us all, but especially for our wedding couple here tonight.

"Wanda and Jimmy, you stand before me, brought together by a miracle of the Lord," said Ben.

"And the miracle of Hazel Brown's lilies," Tom whispered to me. He had put two and two together, finally. Ben had already told me. "Some kind of poison in those Egyptian things, keeps your nerves tingling even after it looks like you're dead. Darnedest thing," he said.

"Wanda, do you take Jimmy for your husband, to have and to hold, to cherish and love, all your days?"

"I do," she said in her prettiest voice.

"And you, Jimmy, do you take Wanda for your wife, to have and to hold, to cherish and love, all your days?"

"Ah oo," Jimmy said in his breathy whisper, his head bobbing with his perpetual, silent laughter.

Right then I would have told you there was real love in that man who rose from the grave just to marry. His laughter was not the chuckling of merriment but the true laughter of joy. At least it seemed that way at the time. Maybe I was carried away by the moment.

"Well, then, it's done. Man and wife," Ben pronounced loudly, beaming. "Wanda and Jimmy, you're man and wife."

The couple kissed, then. It was a kiss, among all the kisses I have witnessed in my life, and I have witnessed a few, maybe a few more than I had experienced by that time in my life, I am a little ashamed to say—good ones, that is—anyway, it was a kiss that never goes dim in my memory. Who knows what I expected. Maybe I thought Wanda would wake up startled, once she kissed this dead man Jimmy. I thought she might taste the damp and earth and worm-smell of the grave. I thought she might get a scare out of his cold lips.

She took it fine, though. Better than fine.

Jimmy, when he crawled from his grave, must have woken up all the way from being dead. I say this because in that simple act of turning and edging over a bit and slanting his head so he could kiss his new wife, who was a mite shorter, I saw everything suddenly that could be lovely in a man and a woman being in love, in their kissing, and in their doing all that a man and a woman could do together. It must have been all those years of yearning piled up in the lanky body of Jimmy's that poured out in that moment, and that formed his lips to give the perfect kiss to his perfect wife. For that moment his head and body stopped its vibrating with laughter and became focused on the act of bringing his lips to her lips. The pent-up energy poured through the room and touched everyone there. Even Bob Tucker, pallid as a sun-bleached tablecloth, mottled with a little red color. Cousin Annie almost fell off her chair, leaning forward so far. Reverend Ben Hanks never lost his beaming smile, which he turned around the room like the beacon of a lighthouse.

And beside me, Tom, town manager and my boss, reached over one hand and put it over mine, without knowing he had done it. A tear just about formed in his eye, though not enough of one to spill over.

Who would have thought it possible.

The ten o'clock evening news had gotten to the weather before I remembered my promise to Hazel Brown. I knew the woman would be back in Tom's office the next morning asking if we had done anything about her garden. Being no good at lying, I figured I better get moving.

Claire Mills answered the phone when I called the sheriff's office.

"Bob's finishing up out at the barn," she said. "So I said that after I was done at the library I'd come in and hold down the fort. What's up?"

I explained. "Pick me up and we'll cruise by, then I'll buy you a rootbeer at the Sonic afterwards."

"Deal," she said.

She came by in her Pontiac five minutes later, after the weatherman on the ten-o'clock had finally gotten his plastic hair-do off the screen. I filled her in on Hazel's problem, and the likelihood that Jimmy had a thing to do with it.

"What do you really think of Tom?" I said to her after we were in the car and on our way.

"What do you mean? You started thinking about it since I asked you about him this morning?"

"Maybe."

"He ask you for a date?"

"No."

"He make a move on you?"

"Not really."

"I thought you were done with men."

"I suppose so," I said. "What're you stopping here for?"

"Look," she said.

She pulled up along Baker Street and killed her lights. She pointed farther up. We were sitting not too far from Hazel Brown's house. There, in the side yard, barely visible in the illumination cast by the street light down around the corner, stood a tall, thin man, still dressed in the suit he had borrowed from his brother. I could tell because of the white socks peeking from beneath the cuffs, bright as bike reflectors.

"It's sure as how you know to call the cards," Claire said to me. "What do we do now? Hate to haul in a man for doing what he needs to do, seeing as he's risen from the grave and all."

The shadowy form bent over Hazel Brown's beds of Anubis lilies, uprooting something and cleaning it off a bit. Then he chewed at the end of whatever it was.

"I suppose we just watch," I said. "Shouldn't bother someone at their feed. But we got to figure something out. Hazel won't be happy."

"Won't be none of that," Claire said.

Then things changed.

I had been feeling good about the wedding, with the residual warmth putting a soft edge on my feelings about everything and everyone. Even the awkwardness of the little reception after the wedding barely dampened how good I felt.

As I said, though, things changed at that moment, sitting in the dark car beside Claire.

Another shadowy form came walking in the street, thin and dark and not so tall as Jimmy but tall enough, with a dress on, and with one arm swinging as though something heavier than just a fist was attached to the end of it.

I remembered immediately what Tom heard from Wayne that morning, that Haline's lily-bulb looting problem had begun again the night before.

And a second grave disturbed. I believe I had heard that, too.

Betty Ellen. She must have gotten Jimmy's secret and done the same as he had, having herself buried with an Egyptian lily bulb planted on her tongue. That disturbed me just a little. Even more disturbing was the thought of her swinging arm. What she held in her hand reflected a glint of light for just a moment. My blood froze.

You would think I hardly need say what happened next, since the tabloids have done a pretty good job of painting Burns, Kansas, as the corpse capitol of the world, ignoring the fact that it was Haline that gave rise to our situation, if you really look at it. Grave Injustice, is the kind of headline I would like to give right back to them. The tabloids have it wrong in other ways, too, especially since most of the accounts insist on bringing in some mysterious grave-robber who had it against Hazel Brown and planted two stiffs in her garden.

I tell it as it was.

I jumped out of Claire's red Tempest and ran toward Hazel Brown's house, huffing with the exertion, thinking I might somehow protect Jimmy if I could I just get there in time. Claire started up her car again, headed toward Hazel's house behind me with her lights back on, and parked so the headlights lit the whole scene. Then she popped out of her Pontiac and ran up beside me with her sheriff's pistol out where everyone could see.

Not that we could do anything. Betty Ellen reached the lily beds before I was out of the car.

I tell you, if there had been any good blood between those two it would have been a sticky mess there in Hazel Brown's garden. Betty Ellen jabbed at Jimmy with her cleaver. That caught his attention. He dropped his feast and swung around. You could see the light of recognition in his eyes. She flailed with that knife and Jimmy tried to avoid her arm while trying to grab it, too.

Betty Ellen swung again. Jimmy caught her arm that time, getting cut in the process but dragging her close to prevent any more wild swings. Then he grabbed her throat and started throttling her for all she was worth, giving her such a shaking she was weaving back and forth like a white-linen ghost in a Halloween breeze. She kept her right arm ratcheting back and forth, too close to do any real damage to Jimmy's front side but still cutting it open to make it awful for us living types to see. Her head was swinging loose back and forth in his fists and his ribs were being exposed by that barrage of blows, and still they kept at each other, while I stood frozen, stricken with a feeling halfway between horror and helpless sorrow.

Even folk risen from the dead must need air space in their throats, though, and must need whole skin on their bellies and chests, because soon enough the both of them gave up. Betty Ellen had been throttled about as much as she could take, and Jimmy had been flayed pretty thoroughly, right to the backbone. They stopped mid-action and stared at each for a moment in the light of Claire's headlights, Jimmy's hands around Betty Ellen's neck and Betty Ellen's knife buried in Jimmy's midriff. Their eyes kept the fight hot another heartbeat. Then they dropped backward away from each other, slapping flat to the ground.

Hazel Brown woke up because of the ruckus and the lights from the Tempest. Once she was up, the whole town was up. Bob showed up in his black Ford, having finished at the barn where there had been no Leavenworth escapee but a good game of cards between some hobos and a hired man. Somebody, maybe he, did a good deed and called in a hearse to take away the bodies. I heard crying from a nearby house. I tried not to look. The crying sounded disbelieving. Disbelieving, of all things.

The tabloids followed all this only a minute or two later, seemed like.

Things stayed a little strange afterward. Jimmy's second funeral was held in the Hanks' living room just about like the wedding, this time with Wanda crying instead of Ruth, and with Robert being warm toward his wife and Tom being awkward with everyone.

Tom took me out to supper to try to get all the facts in the story straight. Burns was looking like a gonzo town in the press, and he was feeling down, and maybe that explains his taking me out for a few more meals and then, a while later, his starting to talk about going to visit Reverend Hanks again, about a less spectacular matter than the two ceremonies having to do with poor Jimmy, but of a like nature to the first one. I finished up that letter to my son John in the Virgin Islands, having a few things to say. The postage was stiff.

Folks around here who have it pretty much straight otherwise think the story's all about Betty Ellen Hanks, how she kept that cleaver high through Jimmy's life and then finally got to bring it down when both she and he were already dead, and when neither one of them had to worry any more about atoning to anybody for anything. But did Betty Ellen win that fight? No way, I say. Claire and I both know it. Betty Ellen, despite her coming back from the grave to find Jimmy and hack him up and all, won nothing. She won nothing at all in the end.

Claire and I got to see the faces of those two dead folk, and Betty Ellen's was the picture of jealousy and hate. She had gone all vile and bittery long before, in her life, and you could look at her while she was whacking at Jimmy and realize she had benefited not a bit from being dead. She might as well have been alive, for all the good she got out of her time in the grave.

For Jimmy, though, it was another thing. In all the years I had known old Jimmy when he was alive, I never knew he could show glee. Glee was the last thing I expected. But there it was. Real glee. It was a brightness like happiness on his face. Lying in the grave had done him good. Rising from it did him even more. And going back to the grave, now, even if it had to be done this way, leaving behind a grieving widow whom he loved as he loved no one and nothing else in the world, he still found a way to get good from it.

"You be sure to listen to your heart, now. That's if, I mean, your heart ever gets around to saying anything," was how I started another letter to my son John.

Then I tore it up. If I brought him up right, maybe he already knew. And if he didn't, sometimes it's so that being told how to conduct your life does no good anyway. Especially when it's Mom doing the telling. You have to live a thing to learn it, yourself. Living it on your own is what we're given to do.

"Sorry it'll all be over and done with by the time you're back," I wrote instead. "But isn't that the way of things always."

After the Arrival of the Strange Horses

only the left hand can turn the knob
of the doorway; the right one has
dissolved after grazing the back
of the strange white horses.

Only the dead have enough
surplus energy to ride them.

The ones alive are still entrenched in foam,
the ultimate fabric which ripples space
down to the subatomic dimensions.

Marred, the living have excuses to consult
the hole at the back of the black oracle's head,

mix the ashes of dead stars with milk
for the risen dark-eyed children,

understand that time dilation only confirms
the plastic nature of time,

and that the course of being born
and waiting to die is a natural process.

No one has seen the strange horses,
but the skies are filled with them—
all galloping at the speed of light,
in frequencies beyond the visible range.

Calculations predict how long the horses
have put off carrying away their long-dead riders.

Perhaps, the delay implies that the eventual
collapse of the universe must take time.

—Kristine Ong Muslim

Here's another of Patricia S. Bowne's tales of academia in a parallel Earth where magic works. The author knows her academic types, warts and all. Witness this glimpse of the life of a grumpy middle-aged bachelor. We're not sure at what point we stumbled into liking him.

Kindling

by Patricia S. Bowne

Linus Ukadnian put on his bow-tie and scowled into the mirror. The slow burn of irritation built inside him like magma. A new semester, and he would have to face the other demonologists at the Royal Academy of the Arcane Arts and Sciences and act as if he respected them, to pretend dimwitted students had potential and meetings were more than a waste of time.

Linus was a man with his feet on solid ground, a man in touch with the plain facts. And massaging the plain facts to flatter other people's self-delusions was worse than a waste of time; it was a sin, a perversion of the intellect. He would have no truck with such rubbish, he told himself every morning as he trimmed his gray beard. He put on his bow-tie with a feeling of determination, as if it would give him strength to live up to his ideals, and fierce righteousness blazed up inside him as he looked into the mirror.

But by noon Linus had always soft-pedaled his opinion, pretended there were two sides to an issue that had only one, or kept silent while somebody spouted nonsense. Then his bow-tie stopped reminding him of valour and became a mark of cowardice, one he wore as a penance and a promise that one day he would live up to it from morning to night. Today, Linus vowed, would be the day. He would begin this academic year as he meant to go on. He huffed in satisfaction, and his breath made a cloud in the cold air.

Linus took journals to department meetings so his time would not be completely wasted. He arrived precisely on time and spent fifteen minutes on the latest issue of *Arcane Intrusions*, reading about sedimentation and what happened to elemental magic embedded in layers of silt. Then the tardy department members arrived and more time (but not Linus' time!) was wasted on apology and explanation, the agenda, the minutes, arguments over the wording of last semester's arguments over the wording of, etc. Linus read about infinite regress and the arcane calculus of fractals in *The Annals of Theoretical Geomancy*. At last the meeting got underway, but was immediately monopolized by Theodora Whin and her report from the benefits committee. Whin loved the sound of her own voice… Linus found one of his own letters to the editor in *Annalen der Gesteinskundenzauberei*, and paid no more attention until Warren Oldham rapped on the table.

"Do I hear a motion to support the proposal? Discussion?"

"There's nothing to discuss," said Whin, as if she hadn't been discussing it for fifteen minutes. "We should have had child care on campus twenty years ago."

"That's the last thing we should have on campus. Children don't belong on the ley-line," said Russell Cinea, who had opinions on everything.

"They're faculty children," Whin said, leaning back to argue with Russell behind the intervening demonologists. "They already live on the ley-line."

"Not with people doing arcane experimentation all around them. It's one thing if a demon rips one of us apart. We've asked for it."

"Speak for yourself," said Whin, tactlessly since Russell had, in fact, recently lost a hand to a demon. During the silence Linus remembered his bow-tie and his vow.

"How much will our salaries be docked to pay for this luxury?" he asked, his tone making it clear that no answer would satisfy.

"Child care isn't a luxury," Whin shot back. "It's a necessity."

Linus snorted. "Our mothers didn't need it," he said. "It's modern women who want help with every task

of life, all the while claiming they're as good as men. You'd think they could do without handouts."

"If they had full-time wives, they could!"

"My mother didn't have one, and I doubt yours did either," Linus retorted.

Patsy Hoth handed him a paper—the list of busywork, making its way around the table as it did at every first meeting. Linus raised his pen and froze in outrage. He was conscious of the others watching him, some with glee and some with irritation. Linus did not gratify them, however. He merely crossed Will Goth-Harding's name off the Library Use Committee, and wrote his own in its place.

"Hey!" said Will, jumping to a correct conclusion as he saw Linus' pen move. "That's my committee. First come, first served."

"I have been on the Library Use Committee for fifteen years," said Linus.

"It's a blank signup," said Will. "I got it first." He appealed to Warren.

Warren sighed and gave Will a stern look, as well he ought. "Why are you suddenly after Linus' committee?"

"Since I found out he hasn't had to attend a meeting for eight years," said Will. "The library director schedules them during faculty members' class times. Share the wealth, Linus."

"Oh!" squeaked Whin indignantly. "You mean while the rest of us work our butts off, all Linus does is sign that paper!"

"I donate an hour of my time every day to your research in the pentarium," Linus informed her. "What I do with the rest of it is not your concern."

"In Social Magic, they give the Library Use Committee to whoever has the largest student load," Will said to Warren. "That would be me." And it would never be Linus, who had stepped off the rotation for introductory courses two years ago after a bruising battle; Warren had been a sore loser, and bringing it up again was a clever move on Will's part. Defeat was in the room, and now it took a step closer.

"Will's right," Warren said, not even pretending to consider Linus' rights. "Choose something nobody else has signed up for."

"This is unfair to the last person who gets the list," Linus complained.

"I was next to last, and I'm not whining," said Patsy Hoth. "Sign it or don't, but let the rest of us get on with our work." Linus glared at her, and at the agreement in his colleagues' faces.

"Very well, then, I won't sign it," he said.

"Fine," said Warren. "I need someone for Freshman Advising, Homecoming, and the Orientation Committee, anyway." Linus felt defeat's cold breath on his spine. He looked back at the list, which offered the Committee for Reconceptualizing the Liberal Arts Curriculum, Student Life Council, or Curator of the Museum of Natural Magic, a job which he knew involved feeding at least one vampire. His choice was clear; but his bow-tie lay a leaden weight around his neck.

Linus went white-hot with fury when he thought about Warren, which was a good thing. It kept his mind off the pitiful truth—that he was afraid of the vampire in the museum he had just agreed to curate.

Facing the worst, he forced himself into the sub-basement as soon as the meeting ended, but his nerve failed him when he reached the door of the live specimens' room. He knew what lay behind it; what grave-mould smelled like, and how much darker night became when you felt the air move around something prowling but not breathing…he thought of Warren, who was unfortunately still breathing, stiffened his spine and his upper lip, straightened his bow-tie, and undid the wards. Taking a deep breath, he turned the door-handle and stepped forward into sunlight and a gentle breeze.

Astonished, Linus tried to stop in mid-step and stumbled. He stood at one side of a cavernous room, the long wall in front of him lined with hay-strewn stalls over whose swinging doors came sunlight, breezes hot, cool or damp, birdsong and rustling leaves.

"Idiot!" said Linus. Had he really thought Zoomancy's pegasi and hippogriffs lived in the basement? Everybody knew they were paddocked on the ley-line; but from the different times of day showing through these doors, Zoomancy must have paddocks all along it. Was that a Southern breeze from the nearest gate, the scent of eucalyptus rising through a balmy afternoon? Slants of evening sunlight poured through the next stall almost to his feet, spangling a spiderweb in the corner of the frame. A cat-flap in one of the stalls stirred and a long nose, pink and quivering, poked through. The eye following it gave Linus a panicked stare, the nose pulled back and the flap clacked shut.

Linus stepped forward, charmed, until his foot struck something—a coffin! He jerked back into unpleasant reality and bent over, after a little struggle with himself, to see if he had broken a line or scuffed any warding symbols. Seeing none, he stood and backed toward the center of the room. He was loath to look away from the thing, but what else did he have his back to when he faced the vampire? The thought made him whirl around.

To his left, aquaria overflowed in a constant trickle.

The dark forms of sleeping birds half filled the nearest, stacked upon each other like cordwood with wings folded and their short beaks open in the water. Beyond them stood circular vats in an unfortunate shade of aqua, ceaseless motion whirling around the base of one and scrabbling at the chest-high waterline of another.

The right held tables with small terraria, then larger pens and tall aviaries against the wall, their backs as bright and open as the stall doors. One flickered with swallow-sized birds in constant motion, flashing between shade and sunlight. Birds in other enclosures turned their heads away, as if disgusted with these swallows. Linus, too, was glad to look away from their constant surge and survey lower pens, until he saw the warning sign on the wyvern's enclosure.

The creature itself was nowhere in sight, apparently hiding under a tumble of rocks in the back corner of its stinking cage. A severed trotter lay beside them; Linus imagined the wyvern spitting flame from its lair until the pig was too burned to escape and then emerging to rip at it—only as long as its victim struggled, which could be a long time as the little dragon's constant dribble of flame cauterized each bite. The scent of eucalyptus mixed with unwanted memories of blood, burned wool, and the harsh groans and pants of half-eaten sheep. Linus' throat closed in disgust. He was filled with grief for the sheep he had put out of their misery, the pig that had died in that cage, the wyvern whose life depended on such horrors, the world that contained all of them. His eyes overflowed and his nose ran.

"What the hell?" he said, fishing for his handkerchief and mopping fiercely at his face. He glared from side to side, looking for what had cast this idiotic mood onto him. He saw cages, large and small, shelves, benches, vats and a painting against the wall in the far right corner of the room. It seemed to show a young boy with skis, and Linus went cold at the sight. He had been worrying about all the wrong denizens of the live specimens' room.

She appeared as if she had been there all along, unnoticed; slender and dark-eyed, with the wealth of hair seen in portraits of an earlier generation, puffing out around her heart-shaped face and caught back into a cloud that fell over the shoulders of her nightdress—for she was dressed, improbably, in a long white gown. Her bare feet peeped out from under its hem. The sorrow in her gaze deepened. "Poor creatures," she said. "Poor captives doomed to die in this tomb, to live unloved and die forgotten." Her voice floated on a scent of dried furs and old perfume as she drifted toward him.

Linus' bones froze inside him with the cauld grue, the mark of a demon. "Get away from me," he snarled.

The demon drifted closer. "She dies alone, she dies unloved, and none will mourn her," she moaned. Linus cast a charm that would have struck a real woman silent. He stumbled back toward the door, barely noticing when he bumped into the vampire's coffin, and the banshee looked after him with sorrow and pity, unharmed; because, of course, she was no woman, and men who struck at her hurt only themselves.

A few minutes into his furious flight back to his office, Linus heard voices in the far upper reaches of the stairwell and felt a blast of cold air, probably from the door to Isaac Graham's weather lab on the museum roof. He might have hailed Isaac, but the second voice belonged to Warren.

"What are you doing for Kindling?" Warren asked. His voice boomed down the stairwell, oppressively jolly.

"I wasn't planning to keep Kindling this year," Isaac said. "The children are with their mother. There's not much point to it anyway, is there? The auguries were so far off, everyone's already turned their heat on."

True enough; the Court Augurers had finally put their tails between their legs and declared that Kindling-tide must take place two months early, setting all the merchants a-twitter and making them pull out last year's ragged Kindling gear with its 'half-price' labels still on it.

"Lilian and I haven't, and we're freezing," said Warren. "Come over to our place. It's our grandson's first Kindling, so we're doing everything."

"That does sound like fun," said Isaac, his voice wistful. "All right—what should I bring?"

"Mm—bring the fruited bough. That's one less thing on my to-do list. And come early, we can use help setting the home-wards. Around eleven-thirty." A door banged on Isaac's reply but one set of footsteps came down the stairwell, almost skipping, and Warren's tubby figure appeared at the stair's turning.

"Oh! Linus!" Warren said, with false goodwill. "What're you up to?"

"My new duties," Linus snarled, fury bubbling up hot within him and driving away the last of the grue. "Since you saw fit to saddle me with not only a vampire, but an uncontrolled demon. Were you hoping it would eat me?"

"What? Do you mean the banshee?"

"Of course it would be my own fault if the thing killed me."

"It likes grief, not death," said Warren. "Is there some reason you shouldn't be around it?" Linus didn't dignify this with an answer. He marched past, showing Warren the back of his head and gaining a height advantage on the stairwell. "The live specimens' room isn't your job, anyway," Warren shot after him. "Let the professional curators do that. You just arrange loans and visits."

"You forced the job on me. I'll do it my way."

"Fine! Fight with the live specimens all you like; but don't expect me to pick up the pieces afterward." Warren stomped down the rest of the stairs into the lobby, and Linus felt so much better that he decided to finish what he had started and survey the rest of the Museum of Natural Magic.

The Museum lay in the center of the Magic Building, in the original audience and banquet halls. Visitors and large specimens entered through the castle's still-grand entrance and atrium, but Linus went through a side door into the cavernous preparation room, unnoticed, and surveyed his new subjects with a growing scowl. A redheaded girl was at least doing museum business, skinning wood sprites and pinning their furry pelts out to dry with the wings spread. The tall man with a bushy black mustache and sunglasses appeared to be tying dry flies with griffin hackle, and a sallow-faced young man with spots was dropping cigarette ashes into the top of a terrarium. Linus focused his scowl on this individual.

"What do you think you're doing, smoking in the museum?" he asked, striding forward.

"I'm not," protested the spotty youth, startled. "I'm feeding the salamander." A motion in the terrarium confirmed this. A salamander, slender and flame-colored, snapped at the ashes, smacked its jaws and belched a tiny smoke ring.

"That belongs on the live specimens' floor," Linus said. "What would happen if it got out up here? All the records could be burnt up." Now Linus had everybody's attention, even the fly-tyer's.

"Can I help you?" he asked, rising. He was a foot taller than Linus and seemed in no mood to help anyone, but Linus was unimpressed.

"I'm the new faculty curator," he said sharply. "How can you help anyone, working out of this septic mess?"

The fly-tyer made an ostentatious three-hundred-sixty-degree turn as if looking in vain for septic mess. Only the sunglasses could explain his apparent failure to find any. Every surface was cluttered three deep with open books, unwashed dissecting instruments, a blowtorch and glass tubing in the middle of being made into something, skeletal forelimbs still bound together by desiccated cartilage, tufts of feathers, birdlike feet curled up into dry claws, unraveling reels of string and wire, wadded netting with seaweed in it, petri dishes whose contents had dried or gone to mold, and random scraps of paper. Toward the back of the room, the mess was larger and more disgusting. The rib cage of a hippogriff was there, only partly denuded of flesh, and a dragon's head lay next to it, its dried-up eyes glaring back at Linus from deep sockets. A great glass tub held something half-hidden in scummy liquid, pressing scales against the glass in one place and a bloated, human-looking hand in another.

"Is that a mermaid?"

"Hm? Yeah," said the fly-tyer. "We're making a skeleton."

"For how long? No-one's collected mermaids for fifteen years," snapped Linus.

The fly-tyer looked up as if counting on mental fingers. "That would be right."

"You've had a half-skeletonized mermaid rotting in here for fifteen years?" The redhead chuckled, but when Linus glared at her she had her nose down, doing finicky work on one of the pinned-out wood sprites.

"Whenever we work on it, someone complains," said the fly-tyer. "It's smelly."

"Finish it this week," said Linus, pulling out his notebook. "If anyone complains, send them to me. And get that salamander down to the live specimens' floor."

The fly-tyer was not cowed. "We don't do archival stuff until somebody needs it. This week we're doing stuff from the summer work in Macoma. Live specimens first, fresh specimens next, before the holiday weekend. Then active research projects, then requests."

"Like fishing?" Linus scoffed, looking at the half-tied fly.

"That's for Jim Kalin. He's doing a side project in Kasidora next week, after the Field Magic conference."

Linus snorted. "You mean he's going fishing and pretending it's research so he can make the Academy pay for his trip."

"That's not my business," said the fly-tyer. "If you want to make it yours, go right ahead." And get out of our hair, hung in the air after his sentence. Linus was tempted, but first things first—he opened his notebook.

"Walk me through this prep room. I want to know everything that's in here, how long it's been sitting around unfinished, and its priority." The fly-tyer didn't move. "Which is lower priority, bringing me up to speed or arguing about it?"

The redhead chuckled again. "He's got you there, Duke," she said to the fly-tyer.

Linus clicked his pen. "Names first," he said. "Duke—?"

"Duke Morgan," the fly-tyer said reluctantly. "Lisa Collins. James Hake." He took a step toward the back of the room. "Oldest projects are furthest back." God help him, Linus thought, there was more, even behind the mermaid.

Linus walked home along the ley-line that ran between faculty back gardens full of frosted tomato plants and grapevines. Some were decked with red and yellow fairy lights or paper lanterns, and most homeowners had already laid the charmed stones for Kindling runefires and stacked them with tribute balls, bright paper and gold thread wound around some small treasure—though most people bought tribute balls pre-made at the store nowadays, counting sales tax as sacrifice enough. The fruited bough leaned over a few, tiny remembrances tucked among its berries to show how often the family had remembered the ley-line during the past year.

Warren Oldham, he felt satisfied to see, had neither cleaned out his garden nor laid his runefire. Linus wouldn't put it past Warren to burn garden trash in the fire. That was all the department needed, a chair who insulted the ley-line!

Looking down, he spied a tiny marvel—a ground-cherry hull from last year, its matter melted away to leave the lace of veins. He picked it up, thinking of his own fruited bough, and strode on with the dignity his path deserved until he reached his own back gate, where he bowed to the line and left it. There were no trashy lanterns in Linus' yard. His runefire was laid, with exactly the right runes drawn on the stones, and his Kindling would be a proper propitiation of the ley-line, with no children running through the middle of it and no boozy relatives mispronouncing the ritual sentences.

The kitchen he walked into was warm with cooking-charms. It smelled of roast lamb and dripping, and Linus left it with regret to walk down the long hallway between two glass-topped trestle tables. The maps that had guided him along six of the world's eight ley-lines hung above them, and under the tables' glass lay his souvenirs of each trip.

Linus paused before the Southern end of the Vinchifer line, a place represented not by a stone in his trophy-tables but by a tuft of dark-stained wool. Here—just at the edge of this coffee-ring, where the crease was worn through—Linus spotted the mountain pasture between two contour lines where he had come upon the wyvern's leavings. He laid his hand flat against the glass that kept that in its place, over, done with.

The sitting room smelled of cinnamon and cardamom from the basket of tribute balls, and cold made Linus' fingers clumsy as he tucked the ground-cherry hull into the fruited bough over the mantelpiece. The Kindling fire was laid, waiting for the moment when Linus would light the fruited bough at his runefire and carry the promise of survival through another winter into his home. He bowed to the hearth and the bough, and went back into the kitchen.

The telephone rang before he had finished uncapping his bottle of ale. The voice on the other end grated on his every nerve, though others found it pleasant enough. That was how these pretty boys managed it. They were charming, as long as someone else was watching.... "No," Linus said. "I don't have time to do inventory. I have a job." The voice remained sweet and reasonable, while Linus seethed over the unseemliness of having a stepfather ten years younger than himself. If he refrained from thinking 'boy-toy,' it was only because he wasn't the kind of person who used such terms.

"That's not my problem," he said now. "Why should I pay storage fees for my own inheritance? It will have to stay in the house until I have free time to deal with it."

"You've had a year to deal with it," said the voice.

"You said I could take as long as I needed."

"I didn't know you were going to put it off forever!"

Linus knew the whiny sound of helpless rage. He smiled. "I'll do it at my convenience, as we agreed."

I have an offer," the voice said. "I'm not going to keep this house just so you can have free storage."

"Sell it out from under me and claim I never got the letter," said Linus. "That's how it's done, isn't it."

The voice was silent, but not for long enough. "That was thirty years ago," it said. "It's past time you got over it. You know she wasn't herself after Willy died."

"She replaced him in the end, didn't she. Don't tell me how I should feel until you've come home and found everything gone," said Linus, cold with fury.

"I did that last year, but I didn't know I was allowed to whine about it for the rest of my life."

"The will is perfectly straightforward," Linus snapped. "If you interfere in any way with my property, I'll sue you." He banged the receiver down with his first feeling of victory since the department meeting.

Linus crunched his way to work through frost-crisped grass Tuesday morning with a plan for the museum backlog. It involved mandatory overtime, productivity analysis, and luring the brownie that catalogued the dry specimens downstairs with milk and cookies, but none of the people he wanted to impress it upon could be found. The only living things in the prep room were Lisa Collins, now skinning some rat-like creatures with gigantic teeth, and the salamander.

"Duke and James are in Agrimancy," Lisa told Linus. "They want us to take over the herbarium collection."

"What! Have they seen this place?"

"Guess not."

Linus looked for something to lose his temper with, in lieu of the Agrimancers who wanted to dump more work on him. The salamander caught his eye. "Why is that creature still up here?"

"Zoomancy hasn't come for it."

"Did you tell them it was here?"

"James was going to."

"I'm not asking who you passed the job on to," Linus said crossly. "I'll take it down myself." He picked up the terrarium, and the salamander sent out an irritated shower of sparks.

Most of the paddock-doors opened onto darkness. A hippogriff lay in one of the stalls, its feet stuck out toward Linus. This would be a wonderful place, he thought, if he could get rid of the banshee. But this time, he was ready for her. He didn't step back from the cold.

"Alone, unloved," the thing sighed. "What a fate awaits us all!"

"Perhaps in your family," Linus answered tartly. "Don't concern yourself with mine."

The banshee wrung its hands. "Death is a mercy to the forgotten, to those with nothing left to live for," she said. "But to die unloved, uncared-for, one's cries unheard; to die alone, without aid or comfort, who has deserved that fate?"

"Whoever gets it, I imagine."

"How hard!" said the banshee. "How cruel! How heartless!"

This cheered Linus. To be called hard and cruel by a demon was an accomplishment. "If death is a mercy, don't expect me to feel bad about it," he said. "Unless simple logic is beyond you."

The banshee looked at him without any evidence of understanding what 'simple logic' meant. "He has been gone so long," she sighed. "So long, she has waited for death to take her to him. So long alone."

"More power to her," said Linus, and went back to watching the hippogriff, which twitched its forelegs and showed signs of rousing.

"He would have been like you," the banshee said. That was impertinent. Linus made no response; he should leave, but the hippogriff! It raised its head and a golden eye blinked at him. Its great wings rustled. "He loved the ley-lines," said the banshee. "He would have wandered them all, and known their wonders. They would have taken him from her, and she would have been alone, forgotten."

"Will you be quiet!" Linus hissed. The hippogriff heaved itself upright and he had just a glimpse of spotted haunches before it leapt through the stall doors. He left without looking back, and the banshee wailed behind him.

"Talking with my girlfriend?" Will Harding lounged in the Pentarium doorway, hands in the pockets of his too-tight black jeans. "Made her cry, you dog."

"That's none of your concern," Linus said.

Will waved a hand in airy disregard. "Not to worry, I can share. So how'd you come to meet the little lady? She doesn't come out for just anyone."

"I'm not privy to her standards," said Linus, but he felt gratified. Will sounded jealous. "Why does she talk to you, for that matter?"

"Oh, I'm always down here. I talk to the vampire, and we make pigs for the wyvern."

"You what?"

"You know, reanimate pigs. You don't think Zoomancy lets it eat live pigs, do you?"

"It's no better to call a dead pig's soul back into its body for that kind of abuse," Linus said, disgusted.

"We don't. We just reanimate the body, the same way they make bodies to trap ghosts. If you put a ward around its neck, you can keep it from sucking in any spirits. It's good practice for Necromancy students." Will stepped aside to let Linus pass. "Ah well, no rest for the wicked, eh?"

"What did you want?"

"Just to drop a word in your ear," Will said lightly. "Banshees aren't exactly safe, if you have unfinished business of your own."

Linus stared at him. "I can't imagine why you think you know my business."

"Fine," said Will. "Do whatever you want. What do I know, I just work here."

On Wednesday morning Linus received 453 e-mail messages. Some ass had transferred the inbox of curator@natmag.osyth.edu to his account.

Most of the messages were duplicates, when sorted

by sender instead of date. They began politely and became ruder as time went on, cutting off when the person requesting specimens gave up, retired or graduated—for the earliest were almost four years old.

"Am I expected to clean up after three years of incompetence?" Linus said, once he had gained admission to Warren Oldham's office. "What do you want me to do, bow and scrape to everyone whose requests went unanswered?"

"What did you think the job was?"

"It's bad enough that the museum is a shambles, you expect me to do public relations as well?"

"I told you, that's all faculty curator does," said Warren. "You're not responsible for the state of the museum. You just arrange loans and make sure they're returned." He handed back the sheaf of printouts.

"Public relations isn't my job," Linus said. "It's yours."

"PR's the only reason we have a faculty curator," Warren said. "The administration won't believe the museum exists unless it's included in faculty load. But if you'd rather switch, I hear the Committee for Reconceptualizing Liberal Arts still needs members."

"This is persecution," said Linus. "I'm a ranking departmental member, and I should be on the committee I chose."

"That decision's been made," Warren said, retreating into stubbornness. "If you'll excuse me, I have a meeting with the dean."

Linus stalked back to his office. This wasn't over; but his call to Faculty Senate met with an answering machine, and he was left to sort the e-mails and reflect that another hour of his research time was being hijacked by that damned museum! He stood far away from the wastebasket to avoid temptation as he sorted the pestiferous heap. The brownie would manage requests for dry specimens, and Duke could pack and mail the wet specimens. And the rest…the rest were from the same person, a Rolf Lundgren, three addressed to each of the previous three curators. They contained no explanation of the project, no institutional affiliation, no information about the Primary Investigator, no reason that Linus should give them any attention. It was only coincidence that they also all requested to interview the banshee. Linus dropped them in the wastebasket and went back to his own work.

Something pounded on Linus' front door even as he let himself in the back. "What is it?" he asked, flinging the door open. A gigantic truck blocked his view; an equally gigantic man blocked his front steps.

"Delivery for Ukadnian," the man said, thrusting a clipboard under Linus' nose.

"What? I haven't ordered anything." Linus saw his stepfather's ornate signature on the bottom of the form. "I didn't order this shipment and I won't accept it. Return it to the sender."

The man shook his head. "Not happening," he said. "We can store 'em until you work it out. One-fifty a day per hundredweight."

"This is extortion!"

"We could dump 'em at the curb, and you could call for garbage pickup."

Linus was rigid with fury. "Wait here," he said, and went to the phone; but his stepfather was (so conveniently!) unavailable, and he had no message that could be left on a machine.

"Does your contract include carrying them in?" he asked sourly, and the big man nodded.

"Just tell us where," he said, and within minutes he and another as large were tramping up Linus' stairs, into his spare bedroom. When Linus looked in the boxes stared at him, full of reproaches. They smelled of old perfume and furs. Linus couldn't decide whether to ship them back C.O.D. or admit defeat and go through them.

"I don't have time for this, damn it!" he said, and banged the door. He had no obligation to these boxes! They wouldn't care, anyway. They were boxes, nothing more. Nothing he did would make them happy, so why try? The phone rang and he snatched it up, sure it would be his damnable stepfather, gloating.

"Ukadnian," he snarled into the crackling receiver.

It laughed at him. "Linus?" it said, still crackling, but now Linus knew enough to blame the voice on the other end. "This is Lucius Tringline."

"Oh!" said Linus, off-balance. "Hold on, Lucius. Let me take this downstairs." Lucius Tringline was one of the people Linus most respected, a man who had walked all eight ley-lines. He was secretary and founding member of the Wanderers' Society where Linus found his true peers, whose sympathy and understanding sustained him through all he had to endure from his academic colleagues. Thinking of the Wanderers in his warm kitchen was far better than thinking of his stepfather upstairs. Linus felt himself a different person as he picked up the kitchen phone. "Is this Wanderers' business?"

"Ah, yes," chuckled Tringline, "You've caught me out, as usual. Though it ought to be social, one of these days. Too long since I was on the Osyth line. This is about a young fella from Kasidora, very promising lad. He's walked four lines already, and on his way down yours."

Linus raised his eyebrows and nodded into the phone.

"That's pretty good," he agreed. "It's late to be walking the line through Osyth, though. We're having a cold spell."

"That's what I hear," said Tringline. "Just between us, I'm a touch uneasy about him. He put off leaving for too long—waiting to hear from someone there at the museum, but they never wrote back. Now I just found a message from Monday. Guess he made it to Macoma and set out again yesterday morning. I wondered if you'd take him in hand on your end. Make sure he gets a meal and a good night's sleep. You know the sort of thing." His voice sounded weak and worried now, rather than just crackly. But the cold in Linus' chest was not concern for the young Wanderer's climb down the Macoma plateau or up to Osyth.

"Does this promising lad have a name?" he asked dryly.

"Ah yes, of course. Didn't I mention it? Rolf Lundgren. Related to the arctic explorer."

On Friday Linus took his lunch to Eastpark, where he could look toward the Macoma plateau. Even this late in the day purple patches of frost lay in every shadow. He sat bolt upright on a bench, reading *Tectonic Transformations* and watching for activity on the ley-line, until some birds flew indignantly up from the cliff-face. A scraping noise followed, a hand grasped one of the rocks' edges, and a knitted cap came into view, topping a climber who moved nimbly between the boulders. Linus' first impressions were of size and hair.

The climber turned, put his hands on his waist and stretched until his nose pointed to the sky. Then he shrugged out of his pack, reducing his bulk by half. He rubbed his feet, fished a pair of many-colored socks out of the pack, and began shaking foot powder into them from a dented canister.

"Good afternoon," Linus said, and the climber jumped.

"Whoa!" he said, twisting around, foot powder at the ready.

"Rolf Lundgren, I presume."

"Hey," said the climber, teeth gleaming through his red beard. "Are you Magister Ukadnian? Great climb you have here. I saw three kobold holes."

"They're empty," said Linus. "Kobolds don't like the city."

"I didn't expect anyone to meet me," said Rolf. "I wasn't sure when I'd get here."

"I know how long the walk takes." Linus shook the proffered hand.

"Ah. Magister Tringline told you when I set out, then. Did he tell you why I was coming?"

"He didn't need to," said Linus, bracing himself. "It so happens that I have just become curator of the Museum of Natural Magic."

"Oh! What about Magister Hickman?"

"That was two years ago."

"And Magisters Gibbs and Rho—"

"Three years ago, and best not spoken of. Respectively. Did you have plans for your visit, besides seeing the banshee?"

"Um, not so much," said Rolf, pulling on a pair of leather-palmed gloves. He had climbed bare-handed as well as barefoot; the right way to climb, but it would have hurt in weather like this.

"You're staying with me, of course," Linus said, and waved away thanks. "Fellow Wanderers."

The Fellow Wanderer was a perfect guest. His mouth and eyes opened wider with everything that Linus showed him, from the framed maps in the hallway to the Wanderer's trophies on the mantel and the rock collection in its carved cabinet. "Wow," he said. "Ohmigosh, is that—" and "Did you go to—?" Linus grew expansive; he showed Rolf his bedroom where the most precious of his protective wards hung and the office with its globes and reference books in seven languages. They pointed out places to one another on the largest globe, until Linus realized Rolf was shivering.

"You must be famished!" he cried. "It's freezing up here. Come down and eat."

"I didn't even think of it," Rolf laughed. His face had changed over the past hour, from mostly beard to all friend. He followed Linus into the hall. "What's that room?"

"Just a storeroom," said Linus and led the way downstairs.

Rolf ran his finger down the map of the Vinchifer ley-line, a respectful millimeter off the glass. "If I ever have a house, I want it to be just like this," he declared, reaching the Laican Sea and, just past it, Linus' kitchen. "Which line will you walk next—the Clin or the Terhaltza?"

"Terhaltza, I suppose," Linus said. "Unless those tribes along the Clin hurry up and exterminate each other. I used to think that war couldn't go on forever."

Rolf nodded. "Stupid, isn't it? If they'd stop killing each other, they'd have as much development on that line as any of the others and there'd be more than enough for all of them. People are idiots."

Linus, filling bowls with stew at the stovetop, thought he had never met such a kindred spirit. "Why do you want to see the banshee?" he asked, sitting down. Rolf looked up from the steaming bowl, like some furry

animal rising out of a misty river valley. "Never mind, tell me after dinner." He didn't reopen the question until their bowls had been mopped out with the last of the bread, washed down with the last of the ale in their mugs. Then he broached it along with the third bottle.

"Are you connected with it?"

"In a way," Rolf said uneasily. "I've actually never seen a picture—is this her?" He pulled a tissue-wrapped packet out of his wallet. One of the photos inside showed the portrait from the live specimens' room. The second—the second was the banshee, in slacks and a checkered shirt, standing beside a bicycle. Her face was merry, her eyes laughing.

Linus' own eyes opened wide in astonishment. "This is recent!" He looked at the other portrait. "Who's this?"

"Me," Rolf said, "and my mother."

"Your mother's a banshee? Banshees are demons."

"I drowned," said Rolf. "I fell through the ice skating—it was one of those things where the cold water slows you down enough so you can be revived. But she didn't know that, and they thought she'd die of grief. When I woke up she had—well, the banshee was there, for a while. It would stand over my bed at night, and wail about how I was dead."

Linus blinked. "Is she still alive?"

"Oh? Oh, yes. She's in extended care in Kasidora." Rolf paused. "The thing is—"

"What?"

"She was never really there. Nothing I did seemed to matter to her. I used to think she'd decided I was dead after all, or maybe she was scared to let herself care. My uncle told me she would sit and stare at my portrait for hours, until he sold it when they closed the house. So I went looking for it. That's when I found out the banshee went with it—the antique dealer told me."

"I see," said Linus. "So you think—"

"Oh, I don't know," Rolf said, sounding embarrassed. "I'd just like to meet it, you know, and find out. It's part of the family, after all."

Linus bedded his guest down on the sofa and worked in his upstairs office, clenched against the chill, until cold and exhaustion drove him into a hot shower. Then he paced the upstairs hall in his bathrobe, stopping outside the spare room door. He went in, and looked again at the mountain of boxes. They bore labels in his mother's handwriting: 'Linus—books,' on one, 'Linus—sports' on another.

Linus blinked, baffled, and looked again. They couldn't be true. His things had been lost, sold, thrown away when she sold the house after—Linus cut off the thought before it could lead to his own return from college to find nothing: no brother, no mother, no home. He reached for the third box.

'Linus—treasures,' said the label. He pulled out a hodgepodge of toy soldiers and action figures such as a mother who never knew what her son saw in them might try to reconstruct. The shoebox beneath held a parody of his lost rock collection, random worthless stones wrapped up in tissues. Delving deeper, he found a gold cup with '1962 Jai Alai Championship' etched on it and two larger trophies, each topped with the figure of a girl serving tennis.

Linus dropped them back into the box, seized with a chill strong as the grue. "It doesn't matter," he said through the tightness in his throat, as if it were important to convince somebody. "What's done is done—you can't just replace—" but then he could say no more, because he had no more to say and no voice to say it with.

Rolf was nervous on Saturday morning. "I—have you—what does she like to talk about?" he asked, twirling his coffee-cup. "Does she—um—"

"It talks about you," said Linus tersely. "What a tragedy it was."

"That doesn't sound like mother," said Rolf. He stared into the cup, bracing himself. "Nothing I did ever mattered to her."

Linus felt as he would at the top of a cliff, a dangerous and complicated place with the way down yet to be discovered. He said nothing, for the way to approach a cliff was to look at it and let it speak to you. Rolf, trained in the same school, was as silent. Finally he sighed and looked up.

"Mothers are strange things," he said. He took a deep breath and stood up. "Can we go now?"

Linus checked his watch. "One of my colleagues went in this morning to feed the wyvern. He should be long gone by now."

"You mean she's in the same room with a wyvern? She has to be in there while it feeds?"

"I feel the same way," said Linus, "but I've only been curator for a week." They walked in silence along the ley-line and he led Rolf down the stairs to the sub-basement. "That's the pentarium, where we invoke demons, and this is the live specimens' room. Don't ask why we keep a banshee in the live specimens' room. We have a vampire in here, too."

Rolf gave a nervous laugh, twisting his knit cap. "Who's to be master, you or the Word?"

Linus opened the door carefully. The air felt singed, but the room was silent. All of the stalls and aviaries stood empty; even the endlessly moving swallows had disappeared.

"I guess nothing wanted to watch it eat," he said. He pointed to the portrait.

Rolf nodded and gave a gulp, but he walked toward it without hesitating until the banshee materialized just in front of him. "Oh, my god," he said. "You're her."

"Who?"

"Uh—my mother?"

"The forgotten are truly dead," she said. "Our own lives end, little by little, as we forget those we loved. Our souls die and are lost, and we live hollow evermore. If he had lived, he would have been like you."

"He would have been me," said Rolf. "I mean, he is me. I'm him." He sounded very nervous. "Look," he persisted, pulling out his photographs. "I'm him. You're her."

"He would have made a hero," she moaned. "Such a brave, blithe spirit. What great things he would have done."

"Um," said Rolf, and held out the pictures. The banshee pushed them away.

"I'd never begrudge him a moment, if I could only have him back!" she cried, but her voice wavered. It lacked conviction; and the banshee herself lacked solidity, as if she would be nothing without her grief. "No!" she shrieked. She swept her arm forward in a blow, and Rolf staggered backwards. "No! I won't have you in his place! He would never have grown old! He is forever young and beautiful, and I forever mourn." She advanced toward Rolf, her face set, and became more solid as she came.

"I remember the grief I was born of," she cried. "I remember how it died away, how it failed me. What do you know of being cast off, half-formed, by the one who made you? It's you who destroyed me, you and your life, so you could become what? This?" Rolf shrank back from her gesture. "If you had died as you ought, so young and fair, I might have had all of her, not this half-life haunting your picture. You owe me a death."

She raised her hands, and a wind swirled through the room; Linus heard a metallic clanging as a ward dropped from the wyvern's cage, and the patter of little hooves. When he looked, the wyvern was already half out of the open door.

The beast was very dark against the gray floor, about Linus' length, and its limbs splayed out to the side like a newt's. It flowed toward them with a surprisingly rapid curling motion and clear flames leaked from its nostrils, with the merest hint of yellow where their edges tore at the air. Linus backed into Rolf.

"Where's the fire extinguisher?" Rolf asked.

"Beside the door." Absence behind him told Linus Rolf had gone, and from the corner of his eye he saw a form leaping between tables. He grabbed the nearest weapon, a chair, and swung at the wyvern's nose. It lunged and bit one of the legs, and Linus could feel the metal begin to heat up.

Flame drooled out the sides of the wyvern's mouth, running up its face instead of down. It half-closed its eyes, lids sliding from the bottom up, and more flame came out of its mouth, a bright yellow spurt that flowed across Linus' knuckles and up his wrist. That'll hurt, he thought as he looked at the bubbling flesh, and it did, a sudden searing pain that made him hiss and beat the palm of his hand against his thigh. But instead of helping, the movement only made the pain worse.

He saw Rolf turn, snapping the plastic guard off the fire extinguisher. The wyvern saw as well, let go of the chair leg and turned its head. Linus drew half a breath of relief before he saw the head swing back and realized it had been a feint. The beast crouched as it turned, puffing its sides out. Air whistled between its teeth. Linus' arms couldn't move fast enough to lower the chair, to block the sheet of flame roaring toward him along the ground.

His legs disappeared into agony from the knees down, as if he had stepped into lava. The room wheeled around him. He was falling into the fire—he squealed, grabbing helplessly at everything he fell past. The table and stools were ghosts in his hands. Only the pain in his legs was real. A movement from the wyvern made his heart clench, and he screamed again. The thing knew its prey was downed; it paused, as if savoring the moment, and scanned him with clever, narrow eyes.

Linus' hand found something loose on the floor and he hurled it, but it was just the end of an extension cord and swung back harmlessly toward his face. He put up an arm, an instinct that saved most of his face from the next flame. When he held the arm away from his eyes, his sleeve was afire. The flames danced and through them he saw the wyvern sway from foot to foot as if it danced as well; then something else hissed and it turned its head into the fire-extinguisher's blast.

Linus threw himself onto his side, trying to smother the flame, and landed on something that squealed. His clutch caught the dead piglet, kicking and blank-eyed. He turned back toward the wyvern, and looking past where the monster battled foam he saw the banshee's face alight with tears, or was it rapture? Fire lit inside him as well as outside; without knowing whether he needed to or wanted to or even meant to, he pulled the ward around the piglet's neck loose and let it fall.

The banshee's mouth opened in an 'O' of surprise. She flowed toward him like mist driven on a wind, narrowed and went into the pig's body, through the back. He felt the animal move in his hand, as if it opened and then closed again. It squealed a new squeal, with meaning in it. Linus didn't let himself think. He threw the pig into the wyvern's face as a different kind of mist closed around him.

Linus was in a white world made of cool fog. Very odd, he thought, suspended. Is there no gravity? Thinking didn't change anything, though. The world remained white and cool. He approved, and slept.

When he woke, the whiteness had retreated. He felt its cool on his right side and arm, and over both his shins. The rest of the world had returned to color and action, with bossy, sorcerous dialog of the 'roll over' and 'drink this' sort and people asking questions. When Linus pretended to be asleep, they asked Rolf.

"So what happened?" Linus was glad he had shut his eyes, because Will Harding was the last person he wanted to talk to. "Is he going to be all right? He looks like hell."

"The sorcerers say he'll be fine," said Rolf. "They were clean burns. The necromancer cleaned most of it up, and they're using skin charms on him. They say he'll be able to go home this evening."

"What happened?" Will asked again. "How did the wyvern get loose?"

"I don't know," Rolf said. "The cage must have been open. We were in the corner, talking to my—the banshee. And then all of a sudden this pig came running at us, and the wyvern right after it. Linus held it off while I went for the fire extinguisher. By the time I got back, though, it was mostly over. He threw the pig at it, and then the sprinklers came on."

"But you didn't see what opened the pen." The tightness in Will's voice made Linus open his eyes. Oh ho, he thought, that's what this is about! Collegial concern, my ass. He snorted a little before he could catch himself, and temptation burned up into his throat, as hot as the wyvern's flame. Why not let Will think he had left the cage open? Teach the jackanapes a little humility! But no, he wasn't worth lying for. Linus would tell him the truth eventually, but maybe he could stew a little before finding out that the banshee had opened the cage…Linus caught his breath. He saw, as if it were happening all over again, the banshee's mouth open in surprise, her body swirling into the pig, the pig flying toward the wyvern.

"Hey!" he croaked, struggling to sit up, and Rolf looked in from the doorway.

"Feeling better?"

"Was that Will Harding?"

"Yes, he just went—should I stop him?"

Linus nodded, and in too few moments Will came into the room. His face was tight, and great purple shadows spread below his eyes. In a word, guilty. "Linus," he said, "how are—"

Linus cut him off. "What happened to the pig?"

"What?"

"The pig. Did the wyvern eat it?"

"Not yet. We stuck it in one of the empty pens. Look," said Will, and took a deep breath. "Did I leave the pen open?"

"You ought to know yourself," Linus said crossly. Will didn't answer. He stood waiting, at Linus' mercy. "The banshee opened it. I saw the ward fly off. You didn't leave it open."

Will shut his eyes. "Thanks," he said. "Why does the pig matter?"

"The banshee's in it. I pulled off its ward."

Rolf made a distressed noise, but Will's eyes sparkled. "A possessed pig!" he said. I wonder what it'll do? It didn't seem any different."

"Ask Rolf, it's his banshee," Linus snapped, and shut his eyes again.

"Really?"

"I—I'm not sure," said Rolf's voice. "I don't think I'm going to get any more from it." Linus felt sorry for the boy, but that was the way things were. It's no use, he thought. Things get lost, and you can never rebuild them.

"Dammit," Linus said, "I don't want to lie down!"

Rolf stood up. "What do you want, then?" he asked, a fair question. It wasn't Rolf's fault that Linus had no answer. He wanted not to be ill, not to be wearing these pain charms that made his head muggy, not to be helpless with his hands burned too badly to use the walker his legs needed. He looked around his living room at all the things he couldn't do for himself, and felt afraid. The fireplace was cold, its logs bound around with paper cords, decked with charms and sprinkled with spices.

"I missed Kindling," he said. His throat drew tight and he fought down tears. He saw everything it was too late to recapture in the dead, cold fireplace.

"No, you haven't. It's not over yet." Before Linus could protest, Rolf had bundled him back into his overcoat. "Do you have tributes—oh, here they are."

"No, wait," said Linus, not sure how to explain. Kindling wasn't just actions. It was gratitude and celebration, knowing he stood right with the ley-line, vowing his allegiance once again to plain truth, to the world as it was. Without that certainty, what did any of the treasures in those tribute balls mean? Nothing, no more than the imitation treasures in the boxes upstairs…but longing for the ritual rose up inside him as if none of that mattered. If he was sad and hurt, Linus thought, that was the plain truth. He would honor the line, even if confusion was his only tribute.

"Get a toy soldier out of the box on the floor in the spare room," he said. "There's thread and paper in the bottom left drawer—there."

Rolf looked questions, but he fetched the soldier and bent over the desk to wrap it into a lopsided tribute. "I could do with making one of these myself," he said, setting the first aside and beginning another. Then they went out with the basket banging against the side of Linus' wheelchair and the fruited bough rattling over Rolf's shoulder. Linus felt like a little boy, let out at night in his pajamas to see fireworks along the ley-line. Chill bit through the top of each bandage and a fountain of red and purple sparks shot up over the line. They held hands rather shyly for the lighting charm, and the pile of tribute balls sent up a puff of smoke, hot and spicy.

The outer layers glowed bright under a spiderwork of gold thread before it melted and let them fall open. Linus saw the gifts inside as the runefire took them—tobacco vanishing with a sweet swirl of smoke, coffee crisping into nothing. The toy soldier stood up straight and confident, then bent and lay down in the fire, one arm waving a final, gallant farewell. Linus glanced up and saw Rolf wipe a sleeve across his eyes. He looked back at the fire and saw the edge of a photograph curling into ashes. "You all right?" he asked gruffly, putting a bandaged hand on the other man's shoulder.

Rolf put his arm down. "I guess I have to be," he said. "Whining won't change anything." A bang and cries more enraged than festive startled him into a grin. "Boys in Osyth still sacrifice cherry bombs to the ley-line, do they?"

"We follow all the traditions. Here—you light the bough."

The bough burst into merry flame when Rolf thrust it into the runefire's embers. Its berries sizzled and burst with a smell of apple pie, and its golden leaves popped into sparks. A torch full of jollity and plenty, it lit Rolf's face into a faun's mask, dancing in his curly hair and through his beard. The two men looked at each other and laughed as one; Rolf held the bough behind him as he rattled Linus' chair over tussocks, speeding to reach the house before it burnt out.

Up the walk they pelted, trailing sparks and sprays of berry juice, and through the wide-open door of the kitchen. Rolf swept the branch across the candles standing ready on the table, on the wide windowsills, on the trestle tables in the hall—it left scorch marks on the walls—and they burst into the sitting room. Their hands met on the wood as he plunged it into the homefire. The light shot up and turned the world outside Linus' windows from twilight into darkness.

"Light against night, heat against cold, be with this house and all in it," Rolf said, the stranger's blessing. They shook hands, solemn for a moment and then breaking into firelit smiles. "You don't have any of those fireworks, do you?"

"No," said Linus, "but I have rum."

"Grog! This is a fine place," Rolf said, suddenly shy. "A real home. It must have been fine to grow up in a house like this."

"I didn't—" but Linus felt as if the room itself put a hand over his mouth. Look! it said, and when he looked he saw it had grown old, this house, and a little shabby around the edges. His trophies stood on the mantel, his rocks lay in the cabinet, his maps hung on the wall as they had in another old house long ago.

The telephone rang. "Should I get that?"

"What? Oh, yes." The tang of autumn—fruit, smoke, dead leaves—filled the living room as Linus heard Rolf go down the hallway, but he could not have said which autumn it was, this one or one long ago. You can't remake the past! he told himself fiercely, pounding his hand on the chair arm to wake himself from whatever those damnable pain charms had done to him, and at the motion his bag of clothing from the hospital tipped over. His charred coat and bow-tie spilled out over his feet, talismans of the real.

"Magister Ukadnian's house," Rolf said in the kitchen, and then he gasped and was silent. Linus stared at the fire, listening as hard as he could until Rolf spoke again, his voice young, disbelieving. "Mamma?" And though he would blame it on the pain charms, and say the thing was ruined anyway, Linus knew it was something else that made him fumble until he had picked up the bow-tie. It was something else that made him hurl it into the homefire and push the logs back over it…Rolf was talking too softly now for him to hear, but in the hearth before Linus the last charm of the old year puffed into flame, its runelines burning first and letting the light beam through.

Tourist

I want to see
the floating gardens
of Andromeda
in all their purple glory
and die happily
of excess pigmentation
　　　　　—Terry A. Garey

Here's a time travel story that's charmingly offbeat, but that feels real.

The VanBulyen Effect
by Lyda Morehouse

The British Army stood between Zoe VanBulyen and the most perfect sofa in the whole world. She and the three men from Antique Removals huddled in the alleyway near the barricade in front of Dublin's General Post Office. Still dizzy from the light-speed travel through time, Zoe held tightly to the crumbling stone wall and peered around the corner at her sofa.

The sofa, looking just as it had in the April 1916 *London Times* photo, sat wedged among broken stools, ruined mattresses, and other debris. Zoe glanced at the sky, heavy with storm clouds, and at the British soldiers, fingers on the triggers of their long-barreled gun.

"Oh crap, the timing is off. I think we're here too early," whispered Elijah Jackson, the company historian, from where he sprawled on the cold, dirty cobblestones. Despite assurances that he was an old hand at trans-temporal travel, the trip had made Jackson timesick. Dreadlocks stuck up in all different directions, and one collar of his shirt escaped the confines of his jacket. Zoe consciously resisted the urge to rearrange him.

"Everything is still okay, isn't it?" Zoe asked, turning away from Jackson to steal a glance at her sofa. "We need to get that sofa."

In the classic Victorian style, the sofa stood on four thin, carved legs. Mahogany trim crowned the back and supported the flared arms. Green velvet brocade upholstery covered the piece; deep buttoning highlighted the inside back. It was more than beautiful—the sofa was perfect. That sofa meant so much to her. It was the ticket to her freedom.

Suddenly, the spring air felt stiflingly close, and desperation was a tang at the back of Zoe's throat. She couldn't go back empty-handed. The public was a fickle lot, and she couldn't afford to drop from their two-second attention span. If her design—the one that included this sofa—didn't splash this week, she'd have squandered her fifteen minutes of fame. Her chance to make a name for herself would be gone.

The greasy-looking barrel of a British soldier's gun strayed close to the velvet. Zoe took in a harsh breath, and took a step forward as if to grab the sofa herself. A restraining hand fell on her shoulder.

"We'll get your damned sofa," Jackson said tersely. "But with the British crawling all over the place, this could take longer than we anticipated." Jackson leaned close to Zoe to look around the corner.

"Just go and get it. You can't get shot, can you?" Zoe snapped.

"We can't rush and get it now, Mrs. VanBuylen." Jackson let out a sigh to show his irritation.

"And, why not? What about the Hitler phenomenon?"

Jackson frowned and leaned against the wall. Zoe repressed a triumphant smile; Jackson had to admit she was right. After all, the Hitler Phenomenon was the sole reason companies like Antique Removals existed. When the German military first developed time travel a few years ago, the main item on their agenda was Hitler's assassination. The Germans, tired of bearing the guilt of the Holocaust, meant to set things right. They went back twice. Each time a freak accident thwarted their efforts: the gun jammed, or, when the bomb did go off, an oak table miraculously saved Hitler's life. All of it, historically accurate.

When the military discovered that history refused to be changed despite their best efforts, they surrendered the technology to "salvage companies" like Titanic Relics. Zoe herself had three lovely settees from that ill-fated White Star ship.

"Yes," Jackson said, his breath puffing white in the cold April air. "But what about the Law of Recycled Materials? If the sofa is the lynch-pin of this barricade,

it stays—like it or not."

The Law of Recycled Materials was a serious threat to Zoe's sofa. The first salvage companies discovered they couldn't bring forward items from the *Titanic* later discovered at the bottom of the ocean. Tea sets, silverware, light fixtures, and anything that refused to decay over time, stayed.

As a consequence, archeology went out of fashion, or rather, archeologists found it difficult to procure government and private funds, because no one wanted to discover the veritable King Tut's Tomb today when it could be raided yesterday.

Archivists and preservationists cursed the Law of Recycled Materials as well because the same was true of historically significant items. The original Declaration of Independence, for instance, couldn't be brought forward, nor any physical material part of the fabric already woven by time. If Zoe's sofa stopped the bullet that could have killed Michael Collins, or tripped up the one soldier who could have done in Eamon DeValera, it would never come forward to Zoe's parlor.

At that thought, Zoe bit her lip. She had arranged everything in that room around this sofa, careful to include a wide range of period colors since the photo she'd found of it was, of course, faded sepia. The sofa's deep velvet green only made Zoe more certain that this was *the* piece for her. She'd imagined the sofa as green in her dreams, and all the textures in the parlor were intended to set off the velvet. Once images of her completed room hit the media, the style divas would be abuzz about *her*. Then there would be a chance to become Zoe—just Zoe, not merely Mrs. VanBulyen, who didn't merit even a first name.

Some commotion came from inside the Post Office—someone breaking glass. The soldiers snapped to attention. "We've got to get that sofa!" Zoe shouted.

"We will," said the historian. "Antiques Removals has never failed a customer."

Next to Zoe, one of the two movers, Tom Quintin, stretched, making his back muscles pop. Big, burly men, both of them, they looked perfectly comfortable in the period clothing they all wore. Zoe discovered she was quite fond of her enormous Edwardian hat. She took every opportunity to touch the broad brim. Dressing up was the part of time travel she enjoyed the best so far. The trip itself had done a number on her stomach, but at least she hadn't lost her breakfast like Jackson.

Poor Jackson! He looked miserable, and entirely out of place. Not only was Jackson so completely a jeans and tee-shirt type that he couldn't stop from fidgeting in the restricting wool material, but Zoe doubted that

STREET FIGHTERS: *British troops in Dublin during the 1916 Easter Rebellion, which Collins joined*

1916 Ireland had ever seen a black man in a suit coat. For a historian, Jackson turned out to be the biggest anachronism of this little furniture raiding party.

"Let me ask you something, Eli," Tom said, leaning back against the wall and adjusting his cap. "Exactly how long did this siege go on?"

"A little over a week?" Jackson scratched his head, and pulled a notebook out of the inside pocket of his suit coat. Adjusting his round glasses, he started flipping through the pages. "The machine screwed us up, and, well, Ireland isn't exactly my specialty. I know the British pull a naval boat into the harbor and bomb the four quarters at some point, which pretty much decimates the place, but the details are fuzzy."

"But we can't take the sofa until it's all over, right?" Tom said. "In what? A week?"

"Yeah," Jackson said. "About that."

"I'm going for a walk," the mover said, pushing off the wall with a grunt. Tom made a casual waving motion to the other mover. "C'mon, Giorgio, let's go find some famous Irish Guinness, if they've invented that yet, eh? That sofa isn't going anywhere fast. Might as well make friendly with the temporal locals."

"Is that acceptable?" Zoe demanded.

"Aw, Ms. VanBulyen, I'm touched," Giorgio said patting Zoe on the back as he sauntered past her. He misinterpreted Zoe's thoughts for her sofa as concern for their well-being. "Don't worry. We can't die. That would violate some paradox or other."

Jackson scratched the back of his head. "Just…be careful. No one has ever spent very long back in time. We know we can't change the past, but…Well, use your discretion, guys."

"Okay," they said, though Zoe doubted their sincerity. Jackson watched them go nervously, but Zoe had concerns of her own.

"A week?" Zoe shouted more, than asked. "A week? I didn't bring an overnight bag—not even a toothbrush! Where are we supposed to sleep? In the alley? You didn't tell me this was going to take a week."

Jackson's mood seemed to improve instantly, and his face smoothed into a smug smile. "You, Mrs. VanBulyen, never asked."

Zoe crossed her arms and fumed. The personnel at Antique Removals hadn't wanted Zoe to tag along on this retrieval, as such things were strictly against company policy. Zoe had fought them at every turn. This sofa was simply too important for her to leave in the rough hands of menial laborers. She solved this problem the way she solved all of her problems: she threw her husband's money at it.

Several thousand credits later, the company began to relax their policy in this particular case. Zoe's architect husband also put in a few good words. They were particularly good ones, as Earl VanBuylen's post-war Neo-Arts and Crafts style houses single-handedly caused the recent boom in the historical artifacts trade. That helped to smooth Antique Removal's ruffled feathers. Even so, it didn't surprise Zoe in the least that Jackson would choose to keep such vital information from her.

"You did this on purpose," she said.

Jackson smiled broadly. "I think Tom is right. A beer sounds like a grand idea."

Jackson turned smartly on his heels and headed in the direction the movers had gone. Zoe sighed, and peered back at her sofa. The soldiers had relaxed again. A couple of curious Dubliners stood in the street watching, while a photographer snapped a picture. The Irish, Zoe decided, threw a damned strange revolution. There had been very little action so far.

Not that she was looking forward to action; it could ruin the sofa. Zoe would simply curl up and die if anything happened to that sofa. No one, not even Earl, understood how desperately she needed that particular sofa. Though her husband had eventually agreed to this time-trip, Zoe knew it was only because her constant begging and arguing had worn him down—not because he understood. To be perfectly honest, Earl understood little about Zoe, much less the important things.

Earl loved his wife the way one loved a brand-new, expensive car.

Zoe kept her husband by staying fashionable, always making the "Best Dressed" pages and by not asking too many questions about late nights at the "office." But Zoe knew that the paparazzi preferred younger more beautiful models, and soon enough her husband would, too. She'd be traded in for one of those starlets that constantly hovered about Earl looking for the prestige and class his name and reputation provided.

Since the moment their wedding made the cover of *Vanity Fair*, Zoe had been planning for the day she'd be replaced. She used every photo op with her husband to showcase her flair for interior decorating. Anyone could design a room, but Zoe consciously made it her thing. She took classes, read everything she could, and even arranged to spend time apprenticing with various masters. If she could make a name for herself before the tabloids finally caught a whiff of the starlet du jour, Zoe wouldn't have to lose everything she worked so hard to attain.

If not…she'd have to give up her art. Furniture, textiles, and paint were Zoe's artistic medium. Designing a room made her feel alive like nothing else ever had. Historical research had become second nature, and she knew more about high-fashion at the beginning of the twentieth century than her husband did.

Sure, she could set up shop as an interior decorator with alimony money, but then she'd just be back where she started—implementing other people's designs, and spending soul-crushing hours ruining rooms because it was "what the client wanted."

It was too much to bear considering.

She glanced at the sofa to make sure it was still there. That sofa would complete her ensemble. With it in place, Zoe's showcase home would be perfect. Zoe's publicist had assured her that, with one more article in the glossy magazines, she could become the next Sister Parish.

Her fingers stretched toward the glowing mahogany wood. This sofa, this perfect object, meant everything to her. She had to have it—damn all costs.

"This is no place for a lady."

Startled, Zoe turned to see a pistol inches from her face. She flattened herself against the wall with a gasp and covered her face with her hands. "Don't shoot!"

The pistol disappeared. A broad-faced man appeared between her fingers as he slowly pulled her hands apart. His brown eyes sparkled with mirth. Once Zoe had relaxed her pose, the man leaned casually against a boarded-up window sill. "Well now, you're easily spooked. Not here for the revolution, then?"

"No, I," Zoe's eyes strayed behind her to the sofa. "I came for that."

The man peered over her shoulder. He was close enough to smell. Despite what she expected, he smelled only slightly of sweat. Mostly the scent was gun oil, dust, and leather. Zoe smiled. She thought he smelled a bit like a library. A surprisingly refined smell for a revolutionary, if that's what he was.

She looked more closely at this man. Under that same hat all men wore in Dublin during this time, his hair was cut short and kept neat. Though he was without a tie, Zoe could see that the man had taken pains to dress smartly. His shirt was clean and pressed, and his suit coat crisply cut. She wondered if he had a wife to keep him that neat or if he was gay.

"You came for the British Army?" The man said.

"What? No, the sofa!"

"The sofa? That's your sofa?" The man laughed—a pleasant, manly sound. Not gay then, Zoe decided. "Ryan's such a thief. He said it was his ma's."

Zoe had to pull herself away from her appraisal of him. "I'm sorry?"

"Your sofa," he said. "I fear Ryan's stolen it."

"Stolen?" She checked around the corner to see if the sofa was still there. Then Zoe realized what the man had really meant. "Oh. No, I…well, it's not mine exactly…I mean…not yet…."

"I see," the man drawled, a faint smile on his lips. "So you're the thief, then."

"I…." Zoe blushed all the way to her ears. Damn Jackson for deserting her, she had no idea what to say to the temporal local. The historian had given her a story, a persona of a sort, but Zoe had ignored him, not expecting to be back in time for very long. She certainly never intended to actually talk to anyone.

"You're a bit slight to be carrying that thing off by yourself, girl."

"Well, I'm not alone, Jackson and the others…," Zoe had no real response. She could hardly explain Antique Removals to this man. Even if she could come up with a way to describe the time-machine to this temporal bumpkin, she was bound to secrecy by Antique Removal's policies.

"Accomplices. I understand." The man looked her over. "Tell you the truth, I've never heard of a sofa thief before. How much do you get for one of those things then?"

His accent was beautiful, Zoe decided, like polished wood—smooth and warm.

"I'm not a thief," Zoe said, even though, in truth, she was exactly that.

"If not a thief, then a spy?" He asked, considering.

"I'm not," Zoe said. Forcing a calm breath out, Zoe made herself look this man in the eyes. "Honestly, all I want is that sofa."

"Indeed," the man laughed. "If you haven't noticed Ireland is about to proclaim her freedom. Seems a mite bit more important that a silly sofa, don't you think?"

"Not to me," Zoe sniffed.

"Well, even so, when we win we're not likely to outlaw sofas, now are we? A Republican is still going to need a place to rest his bum. Surely you can wait to have your sofa until then."

Despite herself, Zoe laughed.

Looking into his bright brown eyes, Zoe felt the weight of the foreknowledge she possessed, or at least should have had. Zoe had a vague recollection that things didn't go well at this particular juncture for the rebels. It seemed to her this pleasant young man was headed for doom. Zoe found herself wanting to warn him, to tell him to run and save himself, but instead she said, "What's your name?"

"Barra Ó Malliagh. Barry to my friends. You?"

She held out her hand. He pressed it lightly to his lips. "Zoe VanBuylen," she said.

He looked up over her delicately manicured and polished fingernails. "Dutch? You've come a long way for a sofa."

"Honey," Zoe said with a laugh, "You have no idea."

Barry spent a half an hour trying to convince Zoe to go inside, to leave her sofa behind. He finally gave up with a smile and brought out his stash of brandy to share. They were thoroughly tipsy when Jackson returned from his walk.

"Zoe!" The historian's eyes were wide.

Barry sat near Zoe, his arm leaning against debris, nearly touching her shoulder. "Jesus, Joseph, and Mary," Barry said at the sight of Jackson. "An African? Is he your partner in crime?"

"Yes, Jackson is my fellow thief," Zoe said cheerily. Then in a stage whisper she said, "But he's always such a mess. Don't you just want to fix him?"

"Won't you introduce us?" Barry asked, still obviously impressed by Jackson's skin tone.

"Elijah Jackson, meet my dearest friend, Barry O'Malley."

"Ó Malliagh," Barry corrected, but it sounded the same to Zoe.

"Anyway, we were just discussing the newest trends in women's hats. Did you know," Zoe said, touching the brim of her hat, "I'm a bit ahead of the fashion curve. Barry here used to be a haberdasher."

"I was a stock boy," Barry said with a fond smile. "A pleasure." He and Jackson shook hands warily.

Jackson cleared his throat. "If I might have a word, Mrs. VanBuylen."

At the "Mrs.," Barry jumped back as if slapped. Zoe snarled at Jackson. It was so like him to ruin what little fun she'd had so far. Zoe stumbled to her feet. "What is it?"

Jackson took her by the elbow and propelled Zoe away from where Barry sat looking shell-shocked.

"What the hell do you think you're doing?"

"He's a nice guy, Jackson," Zoe said. "I was just making friendly like you and what's-their-names."

"They're professionals, you should really be looking for some place to sleep. You can't stay in the alley. You should use the persona I worked up for you to check into a hotel or something."

"My persona? Oh honestly, I forgot all the nonsense the second you told me." Zoe said, pulling her arm away from Jackson's iron grip. At his sharp glance, she grimaced and finally pulled out his collar and smoothed it into place. "Anyway, I have plenty of time to worry about tonight. I was having fun now."

Zoe smoothed the shoulders of Jackson's jacket. The historian's mouth became a thin line. "Well, just don't encourage him into anything historically significant."

Zoe looked back to the empty space where Barry had been. "Looks like I'm not going to get a chance to encourage much of anything thanks to you."

Despite her assurances to Jackson that she could find a place for the night, Zoe slept in an alley for the first time in her life. She found the experience disturbingly much less uncomfortable than she'd expected. She nursed a slight headache from yesterday's brandy, but otherwise she woke refreshed. Dusting off her skirt, Zoe felt positively bohemian. How like a real artist, sleeping in the rough for her art? It would make a great story for the press.

Though she hated leaving her sofa for even a moment, Zoe decided she could stray long enough to find breakfast and a place to freshen up. The morning was glorious. Yesterday's clouds had vanished, revealing the most blue, cool sky. Zoe contented herself wandering the streets of Dublin, window shopping. She used a bit of her emergency antique currency to buy a cup of steaming hot tea. Perhaps because revolution roiled the air, everyone she met greeted Zoe with a friendly smile and a word or two of hello.

She sat in the window seat of a charming little bakery and nibbled on some short bread. Before she'd even taken a seat, the woman behind the counter had admired her hat, and a gentleman offered the use of his *London Times*. Nothing like home, she thought, where everyone kept to themselves or, worse, had an angle.

She wasted the rest of the morning wandering aimlessly, hoping by chance to run into Barry. Instead, she chatted with some locals who stood on the street corner discussing the revolution, such as it was. Apparently, sometime in the night even more British soldiers had arrived. People had seen a gunboat moving up the Liffy, which everyone agreed was a bad sign. Most of the people she met thought the nationalists like Barry were a nuisance and welcomed the British forces. Even more important to Zoe, almost everyone she met commented on her hat and told her what a charming accent she had. She could definitely learn to like this place, Zoe thought, as she headed down the street, waving good-bye to her new-found friends.

An explosion broke through the air. Zoe's mind flew immediately to her sofa and its safety. Only she'd turned down so many streets, she couldn't remember which alley was hers. In fact, she couldn't find the Post Office! A lot of people were running and shouting and Zoe found herself following them blindly. When she stopped someone handed her a bucket full of water and told her to pass it on. Zoe looked up to see fire. The acrid smell of smoke filled her lungs.

"Just concentrate on passing the bucket, love," the woman beside her said, with a gentle pat on Zoe's shoulders.

For once in her life, Zoe did as she was told. One bucket, then two, three—pretty soon she lost count. Zoe had no idea how long she stood there shifting water along a human pipeline. Just when her arms were feeling like they would fall off, the sound of crying and the rapid fire of machine guns egged her onward. Finally, when darkness crept along the street, a cheer started at the beginning of the line and moved along to where Zoe stood panting, drenched in soot and sweat. The fire was out! The woman beside her wrapped Zoe in a great big hug, and, for some unfathomable reason, tears sprang to Zoe's eyes.

"Which way to the Post Office?" Zoe asked of the woman.

"Further down Sackville," she said, pointing over

Zoe's shoulder. "You have a lovely accent. Where are you from?"

"New York," Zoe said with a tired smile, then added, "America."

"You've come all this way for a revolution?" The woman's smile was kind.

Zoe found she couldn't tell the woman, no, in fact, she'd come for a sofa, so she just nodded. They sat down on a retaining wall, exhausted. Zoe looked at the other woman and wished she had some words of comfort from a calmer future. Before the trip, Jackson had given her all sorts of books and such on the Irish revolution. Zoe had checked out a few of the holos, turning down the sound to fast-forward through the images. She'd noted the women's dresses and studied the interiors of the houses, full of all that wonderful furniture and fabric. Now that she was actually in Dublin, face to face with people living history, she wished she'd paid more attention to the boring stuff. Zoe found she wanted to be able to tell this other woman it would be alright, and know it would be. Instead, Zoe took the woman's hand in her own and held it.

"Can either of you put up a boarder?" A man in a cap similar to the one Barry had worn asked. "Six families were put out." He jerked his head in the direction of the gutted building.

"I can take a few," the woman said, still holding Zoe's hand.

"No one was hurt, I hope," Zoe said.

"Ah, well. These things are always unfortunate," the man said sadly. "But it would have been worse without your help."

Zoe shook her head, feeling bone-tired. "Obviously one person doesn't makes much difference," she said, noting that she was still in Ireland's past. "It was meant to be."

Several British soldiers came down the street with machine guns. "We need to get out of here," the woman said. "Come on."

The woman introduced herself as Moira and her apartment was modest, but far away from the fighting. They brought along two of the children who had been displaced by the fire.

Zoe felt strange entering Moira's home and stood awkwardly in the doorway.

Moira just smiled. "Come on in, dear. There are things to be done."

Zoe took off her wide brimmed hat, now smelling of smoke from the fire, and followed Moira into the kitchen. Moira handed her a potato and a paring knife, and said, "Make yourself useful."

Zoe looked helplessly at the potato. At home she had maids, cooks, and servants to do this sort of thing; that is, on those rare occasions when she and Earl were together and not eating out on the town.

The two orphans were also put to the task of peeling, so Zoe watched them surreptitiously until she got the hang of it. Her hands felt clumsy and she nicked herself at least once. When she finished, Zoe watched Moira make a thick stew with the same fascination as the two children.

Moira handed Zoe plates to set at the table. Looking at the plates, Zoe marveled at the hand-painted design of fruits around the rim. Some of the plates had been cracked, but someone, probably Moira, had painstakingly mended them. "These are lovely."

Moira's eyes twinkled with pride. "We do what we can."

Throughout dinner, Zoe kept glancing around the small apartment. Moira had simple heavy cotton curtains on the bay window overlooking the street, but lace hung behind them. On the windowsill sat a carefully maintained pot of chamomile. Here and there sat pieces of silver, polished to a warm glow. The wallpaper was velvety and clean, even though only one rug covered the wide-board floors. The chairs they sat on were serviceable and sturdy, but Moira had sewn comfortable seat pads out of small, mismatched remnants of more expensive materials. The critical fashion sense of Zoe wanted to find fault in the hodgepodge of colors and textures, but couldn't.

After all, this place wasn't for show. It was a home. Moira had somehow invested her place with a beauty that transcended fashion, and Zoe found herself trying to parse that magic. Why did the house seem so cozy when much of it was actually quite rough and worn?

After the children had been fed and a place found for them to sleep, Moira brought Zoe back into the kitchen to show her how to brew some tea.

Zoe was fascinated by the workings of the wood-burning stove and the clever design of the tea-ball. She had seen all of these things in antique shops, but had never imagined anyone actually using them. Though Zoe still felt exhausted from battling the fire, standing in Moira's kitchen clipping tea in the tea-ball, Zoe felt a strange surge of exhilaration. "This is wonderful."

Moira laughed. "You're good for my soul, Zoe. After all that's happened today, and you can still find pleasure in simple things."

"No one's ever said that about me. Usually, they say I'm impossible to please." Zoe put the tea into the pot of hot water to steep, enjoying the feeling of hot ceramic against her blistered and callused hands.

"Look at you," Moira said, shooing Zoe away from her prized tea pot to cover it with a cozy. Moira had made the kettle warmer in the shape of a cat, which fascinated Zoe even more. Watching Zoe inspect her handiwork, Moira laughed. "You're like a child."

"You're home is just so," Zoe wanted a word that meant both homey and beautiful, but settled on, "amazing."

Moira looked at Zoe's fancy cloths appraisingly. "I'm sure your house is much more lavish than mine."

"Maybe," Zoe agreed. "But not more wonderful. How do you do it?"

"Do what?"

"Make all of this work together?"

Moira crooked an eyebrow. "How do you mean that?"

"Look at these fabrics," Zoe said standing up. "They don't go with this room at all, at least they shouldn't—not according to the textbooks on this sort of thing. But, I don't know what it is, maybe the light of the fireplace, but it looks right, like it's supposed to be here."

"My ma made that pillow," Moira said somewhat baffled.

"And, this clutter," Zoe pointed to all the knickknacks above on the mantle. "It should overwhelm this surface, but…but it's gorgeous."

"Is that a compliment?"

Zoe paused and smiled a bit sheepishly. "It was meant to be."

"Then, thank you. I don't know what you're on about. Most of these things you're so fascinated by have been in my family for generations."

Zoe looked at the fireplace with renewed interest. That was the common denominator: history. The features all worked together in this house because they shared memories.

After a time, Moira offered Zoe a pallet by the fireplace for a bed. Zoe gratefully curled up close to the embers of peat. Her shoulders ached and her hands felt raw, but exhaustion had settled around her like a cloak. She stared at the cracked plaster ceiling for a long time, listening to the crackle of the fire and watching the light dance on all surface of all the objects in the room.

Zoe woke up stiff and sore, but rested. She helped Moira make tea and serve day-old bread to the children. Finally, it was time to say good-bye. With a twinkle in her eye, Moira handed Zoe the tea-ball.

"You loved it so much, I thought you should have it."

Zoe waved her hand, as if to refuse the gift. "You've done so much for me."

Moira pressed it into Zoe's hand. "Your enjoyment of my home was like a balm in these trying times. Please."

When Zoe caught up with the men from Antique Removals, they were huddled in the alleyway. Bullets flew everywhere, making Zoe jump. She crawled over to the edge of the wall, and sneaked a quick peek at her sofa. It was still there.

But Zoe's eyes couldn't stay focused on the sofa. Instead, she saw more buildings on fire beyond the barricade. Though she wanted to join the relief effort, stern glances from the movers kept her from going. She stayed hunkered down in the alleyway until it was over. The clouds finally broke, and the streets glistened with blood and water. Zoe's ears hurt. Cannon fire still echoed in her head. She'd spend most of the battle pressed against the wall under the boarded window Barry had leaned against, her face in her hands and tears in her eyes. She held Moira's tea-ball clutched against her breast as a talisman.

The sofa, at least, had survived. Zoe ran to it, as soon as the smoke cleared. She ran her hands over the velvet, feeling it as though searching for wounds. From what she could see, no bullets had marred her perfect sofa, though there were some stains, possibly blood. Zoe could repair the water damage if she wanted, or leave it as "patina."

Her fingers strayed to the stain, turning to look for the first time at the Post Office. The doric columns were crumbled and the roof had caved in. *All those people trapped in there*, she thought suddenly, *I should have done something.*

Tom's hand grabbed her shoulder. "You can't change anything."

Startled, Zoe realized she'd left her sofa and had started running toward the building. "But…."

"We're taking the sofa into the alley. Come on."

While the British were making their arrests, Jackson supervised as the movers carried the sofa into the alleyway to be swept back through time. They attached the beacons to the sofa and settled down to wait.

Zoe's fingers moved along the edges of Moira's tea-ball. When the moment was right, Jackson had explained to Zoe, they would reappear in the present. The German scientists had discovered that time, like Mother Nature, corrected itself. A traveler only stayed as long as was appropriate. The beacon would drag the sofa along with them through time.

With one last look over her shoulder at what remained of the Post Office, Zoe sunk down in the middle of the sofa. She could feel a broken spring somewhere beneath her, but it didn't matter. No one would ever sit on it; the sofa was for viewing, not using. That's why Zoe always referred to its intended area as the parlor, and not the living room. No one lived in her house, they just occupied space.

A British soldier passed the alley, took one look at Zoe and the Removal crew and frowned. Zoe's heart raced for a moment as she thought they might get arrested despite the historian's assurances they couldn't be. The soldier's lips puckered as if to ask them what they were doing, but he was distracted by something down the street. History corrected itself.

Zoe felt the edges of the sofa, her fingers tracing the hem. The fabric had slipped out in places. She could re-stitch the velvet, send it to an upholsterer. The nap of the fabric rubbed warmly against her palm, but Zoe felt cold. In her other hand she held the tea-ball. Suddenly, Zoe wondered how this sofa would look in Moira's place, tucked close to the fire. The sofa wouldn't be an antique here, it would be furniture.

She never even felt the others leave, just smelled the ozone of their passing. She had no idea how long she sat there, alone. It was Barry that found her again, and helped her drag the sofa down the street to Moira's place.

"It *belongs* here," Zoe told Moira.

"What about you?"

It was a good question, and one Zoe didn't know how to answer. She'd hoped to reinvent herself with the sofa, but she hadn't planned on staying in the past. Perhaps she would eventually return, but history had decided her place was here for now. It wasn't possible to change history, but history had changed her. Back home they would have to add a new phenomenon to their list, and perhaps they'd name it after her.

To Not Look Back

The secret is to go, & not look back
now at the tipping point, this parting glance
at one blue pebble falling into black.

Just turn away. Don't give yourself a chance
to mourn the morning light across these seas
that spawned us all & taught our blood to dance

in lunar tides. Their possibilities
are finite as the winds our ship won't need
redshifting out of harbor by degrees

of years & lives & sunsets lost to speed
past earthbound understanding. All we lack
is waiting for us out there if we bleed

our souls one moment longer to the black.
The secret is to go, & not look back.

—Ann K. Schwader

Vampire Cabbie
Fred Schepartz

What's a vampire to do?
No Job
No Money
No Sunlight

ISBN: 978-1-934037-37-9

When Count Fargus finds himself without money or a home he faces the indignity of getting a job.

But what's the right job for a 1000-year-old vampire?

Become a night cabbie!

Join Al on his adventures as he faces cranky passengers, psychotic murderers and the odd things people do at baseball games.

Available at Literaryroad.com or local & internet stores everywhere

10% off
at Literaryroad.com
enter discount code Cabbie

This story was sent and accepted before the City of Saint Paul hosted a Certain Large Event. The events described may or may not correspond to those in our timeline. Mickey's Diner is real. Google it.

The Diner

by Eleanor Arnason

Mickey's Diner was outside the security perimeter, so customers would be able to get to it. A St. Paul cop dropped by to tell the staff.

"But remember, the security goes one way. A lot of people aren't going to be able to get in, but the Republicans will be able to get out. You may get a few of them here. We think they'll mostly be in the fancy places inside the perimeter, Kincaid's and the St. Paul Grill, but you never can tell. And over in Minneapolis, of course. But what they do over there is not my problem."

He paused. "What they do inside the perimeter isn't my problem, either. The damn Secret Service has told us not to mess with their work. I don't appreciate being told to buzz off in my own city."

"I don't figure we'll have any trouble, " Sal said. She was the senior wait these days, with more years at Mickey's than most of us could imagine. The strange thing about her was, she didn't age. As far as we could tell, she was forty and had been forty for years. Her blond hair never grayed, though that could be dye, of course. But her face didn't change any more than her hair. I wouldn't say it had a timeless beauty, but it had a timeless something. "I wouldn't mind meeting a Secret Service man," she added. "I met one years ago."

The cop said, "From everything I hear, they're jerks."

Vorg, who was a regular, a big guy with grey skin and a lot of teeth, said in his deep, rasping voice, "If there is trouble, I cannot assist you. The rules say we cannot interfere with a pre-contact civilization." He wasn't much for talking, and went back to shoveling scrambled eggs and hash past all those teeth.

"We appreciate that," the cop said. "Saint Paul is a pretty quiet town; and we'd like to keep it that way. Let Minneapolis have the action. If you guys decide to start making a big deal about being here, do it in Minneapolis."

"I come for the eggs and the grease," Vorg said. "I do not intend to make a deal, either big or small. " He paused, then held out his cup. "Also I come for the coffee."

This was a crazy thing to say. The coffee at Mickey's is not good. But maybe it was better than what Vorg could get where he came from; and you are never going to hear me complain about the eggs or the hash browns.

Sal gave Vorg a refill, and the cop left; and that was that until the convention began.

The second night was rainy, with a wind blowing through the handful of skyscrapers in downtown St. Paul. I knew the convention was on, because there were cop cars parked at intersections and streets closed off, and I saw more people than usual. Most of the time, downtown clears out after work; and there's no one around after dark, except poor people transferring from one bus line to another. It's kind of restful, but also eerie: a downtown of empty streets, with no stores and maybe a dozen restaurants. The smart Republicans would have gone to Minneapolis; and the demontrators—there were supposed to be thousands—would be in the free speech zone in Harriet Island Park on the other side of the river, where they could speak and demonstrate to their heart's content and bother no one.

As we'd been promised, Mickey's was outside the perimeter, and I was able to make it in. There were a couple of homeless guys at the counter, bitching about how the Dorothy Day Center had been closed down because of the convention, and they had to go across the river to a temporary shelter on the West Side.

It was not convenient, and it was not right, they said; and one of them added, "We live here. We're citizens."

"Do you vote?" asked Sal, as she refilled their cups.

The homeless guys got silent.

"You ought to," Sal said. "It's part of being an American, and you have no right to complain if you don't."

The guys stayed silent. No one argued with Sal. I settled farther down the counter, next to a slim, green fellow who looked sort of like a lizard. He must have been six feet tall, though, larger than any lizard I had ever seen. He wore a vest and big, loose trousers and boots like a pirate in a movie. The trousers were yellow and silky-looking. The vest was green and had a lacy red pattern. After a moment, I realized the pattern moved, coiling and uncoiling. Fractals, I thought. Or maybe something else. In any case, the motion made me a little queasy, the way the red lines flowed and curled, expanding into things like flowers, then contracting back into lines. I didn't spend a lot of time looking at the vest.

"I hear the eggs are good," the lizard said. "Sunny side up with link sausage on the side."

That was a matter of opinion. I have never been one for fried eggs. But I wasn't going to argue with a six foot tall lizard. So I told him, "Be sure to get the hash browns," and put in my order.

If there is anything pleasanter than eating breakfast in a diner on a rainy, kind of cold, late summer night, I don't know what it can be. Like the lizard, I got sausage and the hash browns, though I went for the kitchen sink special, which was an omelet with everything inside. Rain beat on the windows. People came and went, though the lizard stayed and drank tea with sugar. He looked interested and comfortable.

Finally, right after I finished the last slice of toast with grape jelly, the Republican arrived, pushing the door hard as he entered. I looked over. He was a middle aged white man in a raincoat, and he looked pretty drunk. How could I tell he was a Republican? The campaign buttons. They were all over the front of his raincoat, big and round and red, white, and blue.

"Here comes trouble," someone said just loudly enough so we all could hear, and someone else—most likely Gene—said, "Uff da."

The Republican looked angry for a moment, then sat down. "It's raining cats and dogs out there," he said to Sal. I couldn't place his accent, but he had one. Not from around here.

"Convention going okay?" she asked as she poured coffee.

"Yeah," he answered. "I think we're going to win. We ought to. This damn country is going to the dogs, and someone has to set things straight."

We let that comment pass, though I don't think there

Autmn/Winter 2008   43

was a single person in the diner who would have agreed. They say you don't find atheists in foxholes. Well, Republicans are pretty rare in St. Paul. It's a union town and solidly Democratic Farmer Labor. Looking down the counter, I saw the homeless guys, who were not going to have a place to sleep tonight, since it was too late to get a bed at any shelter; Gene, who edited a neighborhood newspaper, and had a lot of opinions; and Dwight, who was an Indian and a painter. I don't mean houses. I mean art, like they hang in museums. And I don't mean Indian from India. Dwight was a local guy, Lakota. There were a couple of college students in one of the booths, who were probably in here to find out about life; and there was the lizard.

"Where do you stand politically?" I asked the lizard. I didn't usually get into politics with strangers, but the convention was bothering me. I didn't like all the cop cars downtown or the closed-off streets, or the fact that they'd had to move the Dorothy Day Center. The damn city council thought they could make some tourism money and had turned downtown St. Paul into a Green Zone. It wasn't right.

"I belong to the Divergent Evolution Party," the lizard said. "We believe there are many evolutionary paths to sentience, and every intelligent being should be treated with respect, especially if they can make good fried eggs, sunny side up. I can't complain about the sausage, either."

The Republican looked at us and said, "What in hell is that?"

"I am a Zirbet," the lizard said. "From the planet Zir."

"How'd you get in here?"

"Through the same door you used."

"I mean, in this country. You can't be legal."

Sal set down coffee and a piece of apple pie in front of the guy. Manny the cook has his ups and downs, but you can't beat his apple pie or his kitchen sink omelet, in my opinion, anyway. It's funny that a guy from Mexico can make American food so well. The Republican should have shut up and eaten, like a reasonable person.

But he was busy glaring at the lizard. He really must have been pretty drunk. Most people quietly leave, when they see one of the diner's special customers. Or they decide that it's none of their business. I figure that's why you see aliens in Mickey's and nowhere else I know about. They know they can eat their hash browns and omelettes without getting hassled.

"Where's your green card?" the Republican asked. "This God damn country is filling up with crap."

At that point Dwight turned around and said, "This country filled up with crap five hundred years ago."

The Republican's face got red. "What do you mean by that?"

"I mean the neighborhood went to hell a long time ago. It's past fixing, *kemo sabe*. We are all struck with one another, as little as we may like it."

"What's that mean?" the Republican asked. His voice was starting to slur, and he sounded belligerent. A mean drunk.

At that point, Dwight must have rethought having an argument. He waved at the college girl. She was a pretty little East Asian, who looked like she wanted to be somewhere else. I could have told her that Dwight was harmless. He told me once that he stopped fighting when he stopped drinking. Nowadays, when he got pissed off, he made a painting. "There's a young lady present. We need to watch our language and mind our manners."

"I said, I wanted to know what you fucking mean," the Republican repeated.

Third time is magic; everyone knows that; and the Republican had asked his question for the third time. The lizard pulled out a metal rod—I don't know from where—and pointed it at the Republican. After a moment, the man began to glow blue. He must have noticed something was wrong. His eyes opened wide. He opened and closed his mouth, but we couldn't hear what he said. The blue glow got brighter and brighter, till you could hardly look at him. At the same time, he was getting dimmer, as if his body was dissolving into light.

I tell you, it was something. He kept getting brighter and brighter, dimmer and dimmer, till—all at once—he was gone; and the blue light was gone; and there was nothing to show he'd ever been in Mickey's except a plastic boater with a red, white and blue hatband sitting on one of the counter stools.

"Holy Moly," said Gene. "Do you have a conceal and carry permit?"

"I do not understand," the lizard replied.

"A permit to carry a gun."

"This is not a gun," the lizard said.

"I can see that," Gene said. "It's some kind of death ray."

"No. It is not a weapon. I have not killed him or harmed him in any way. I merely—what is the word?—transferred him to another place."

"Where?" asked Sal.

The lizard looked at the rod. There were rings around it. He fiddled with them, turning them back and forth. "Moln," he said finally.

"Can you bring him back?" Sal asked.

"No. He will have to find his own way home."

"Is it far?" Gene asked.

"Hardly more than a hundred light years. If he finds a ship willing to take him, he'll be back soon. Of course, the Molnites are uncharitable money-graspers, who will want to be paid up front. And they do not like foreigners. But do not fear for him. There is work on Moln; and though the Molnites do not like foreigners, they are willing to employ them for work their own people do not want to do."

Dwight came up with a little, odd, tight-lipped smile. "What goes around comes around."

"I thought you had rules," Sal said to the lizard. "You aren't supposed to interfere."

"That is true, but this is hardly a significant intervention. People vanish on every world. Their disappearance does not change history or their culture. If he arrives home with stories about his adventure, that may have an effect, unless you humans decide he's crazy."

"They will," said Gene. "We will."

The lizard stood. I noticed his tail for the first time, long and green and tipped with spines. The tail twitched. The lizard rolled his shoulders. I guess you get stiff when you travel among the stars, or maybe he'd been sitting too long. "The eggs were excellent. Thank you, respected intelligent being, for recommending the hash browns, which were also good." He tilted his head toward all of us, one after another, then walked out.

"Well," said Sal.

"It would make a heck of a story for my paper," Gene said. "But no one would believe it."

Sal shook her head. "We have enough business. I don't want a bunch of gawkers in here, looking for flying saucers."

"You know, I've never seen a flying saucer in the parking lot," Gene said.

"They wouldn't need one," the college kid said. "Not with that rod thing."

Gene nodded. "That's true."

"It's a transporter, like the ones on *Star Trek*," the college girl added. She had a sweet, soft voice with no accent I could hear. "I used to watch *Star Trek: The Next Generation*. Not the original show, with William Shatner. I never liked that."

"Did the lizard pay, Sal?" Gene asked. "I didn't see him put money down."

I looked at the counter. A small bar of gold lay on it. "What's the price of gold right now?"

"$800 an ounce," said Sal.

"Well, that's what he paid for breakfast."

There didn't seem to be anything else to say. I drank some more coffee, because it was hot, not because it was good. Sal picked up the gold bar and the lizard's dishes; and Dwight ate the Republican's apple pie. The guy hadn't touched it, as good as it was. When he was done eating, Dwight paid up and left, taking the boater with him. He usually wore a cowboy hat, being from South Dakota, but not in the rain. Maybe the boater would end in his art. I had seen one of his shows. The paintings were full of Indians and weird-looking aliens. The critics said it was a metaphorical statement about Indians and European-Americans. Dwight said he painted what he saw, and not everything was about white people.

The college kids left about the same time, looking a little stunned. No one else came in. Between the rain and the convention, most people must be staying home.

"You said you met a Secret Service man," I said to Sal.

She looked up from wiping the counter. "Years ago. He didn't guard the president. If he had, things might have turned out differently."

"Counterfeiting?" I asked.

"Counter espionage."

"I thought the FBI did that."

"It used to be the Secret Service. How do you think they got the name?"

That was something I hadn't known. But it made sense. Why else would the Secret Service be called what it was called?

Gene wanted more coffee, and Sal went down the counter. I decided to leave. It was still raining heavily. Cats and dogs, the Republican had said. But it wasn't the kind of rain that was going to get lighter. Gene would be there for hours, reading and writing, and the homeless guys would be there all night. I had a home, and I wanted to get back to it.

The buses had been rerouted, due to the convention; but I'd looked up the changes on the Internet, and I knew where my stop was. Because it was temporary, there wasn't a shelter. I stood in a doorway and cursed city council. There are things that aren't worth the money they bring in.

By the time the bus arrived, I was pretty wet. I changed clothing when I got home, then went on line and looked up the Secret Service in Wikipedia. Sal was right. They had done counter espionage and

Autmn/Winter 2008   45

espionage during the Civil War. That's how they started. After the war, they got into investigating counterfeiting, and finally—after McKinley was shot—they took over guarding the president.

The article didn't say when they stopped doing counter espionage.

So, when had Sal known her Secret Service guy? And who was the president that he hadn't been guarding? I had a couple of suspicions, but no real, clear idea; and I was pretty sure I wasn't going to find out anything more from Sal. She didn't share personal information much. She must have done it tonight, because she was off balance. You don't often see someone transported 100 light years away. Not in Mickey's, anyway.

TENTACLE 1

Cracks
in the floor of the sea
filled with earth's red heat
and release
of life
and sulfur and brimstone
and the colors of all the unseen,
the fish in the dark
and the volcanoes
bleeding hot into the sea,
the sea bed where it is all still being born
up to the air,
onto the land to die
and sicken the water
but the temperature
still flows
the creatures
live in the seethe,
evolve again:
the burn
generates,
crimson
scarlet
fire

in the deepness of the cold and the dark
the fluttering plasms
fragilities
out of the furnace
without air, without light
life
in legged blooms
wriggles
and fastens.

Eras in darkness
in satin touch of night.

Nothing is born that does not die
except the divided kin
in the cellular immortality,
afloat, adrift, flageolate, amoebic,
eaten but unconsumed
the flesh of the first
alive today
as sacrament and ancestor,
food, our parent,
blessing the wave,
green, blue, clear,
red, brown,
the single cells
ride
the great ocean waters
tilt-a-whirl slides
within the billows and swells
innumerable
life
And then—and then:
the metaphor occurred:
in its blissful inevitability:
to be more than one,
less than eternal:
how Death entered the world
in robes scintillant
and glistening
alive with the invisible
embroidery
life works
in glycerol
in aldehydes
carbonyl, and carboxyl, thiols, acyls
alcohols and amines
alkanes, sterols and glycolipids
two thousand enzymes, acids,
phytol, ferrodoxin,
pyruvate, lactate, glycogen, ribulose,
purine
pyramidine
one path
faultlessly chaining:
oxaloacetate
citrate
isocitrate
oxoglutarate
succinyl
succinate
fumarate
malate
turns back into
oxaloacetate
one cycle
of thousands in endless exchange
bartering air into energy,
matter into air,
what life is,
is this playful dickering without pause and
without thought,
the way
that atom fits to atom
as it must
and changes partners
by strict pull and repulsion
into intricacies finally simply a miracle.

—CAMILLA DeCARNIN

Here's a thoughtful exploration of some problems we may be facing quite soon. "Desiree" originally appeared in issue X of the electronic anthology Oceans of the Mind.

Desiree
by Stephen Dedman

The CD-Rom was labeled 'Venus: Shareware Version 2.0', with a Chinasoft logo. "What is it?" Sebastian asked, looking at the blank case. "A flight simulator?"

Frank shook his head, then looked around the library furtively and whispered. "Better than that. Have you ever heard of the Venus Database?"

"No. What is it?"

"It's probably an urban myth, but it's supposed to be a program somewhere that will find your perfect partner for you."

Sebastian looked at him dubiously. "They keep a register of blind chubby chasers?"

"Ha ha." Neither of them had been genetically engineered, but like most Millennium babies whose parents could afford a full medical insurance package, they'd been vaccinated against acne before hitting their teens, and surgery had given them near-perfect teeth and vision. However, both were asthmatic, and Frank was as obese as Sebastian was scrawny; he was also nearly three inches taller, but Sebastian smelled better when he remembered to wash. "Like I said," Frank continued, "the database is probably just another myth, but anyway, this is better. It *makes* your perfect partner." Sebastian raised an eyebrow. "Okay, a computer simulation, not the body or anything, but the graphics are excellent, and she has a personality, too."

Sebastian stared at the CD, which was slightly larger than a quarter. "Yeah, I bet."

"That's just the start-up; you have to download the rest from their website."

"And how much does *that* cost?"

"It's a demo. Shareware. You know Chinasoft." Sebastian nodded slightly; the label was the world's largest source of bootleg software. Some said it was a gang of sociopathic hackers disseminating viruses; some that it was run by one of the Triads, who had a near-monopoly on the black market in everything from passports to transplant parts; others that it was a group of recalcitrant old-fashioned Communists, determined to bring computer literacy to the poor and vice versa; but most maintained that the name was a misnomer and it was actually based in California and used to gather demographics for direct marketing companies.

Sebastian didn't much care which story was true. In his experience, Chinasoft's products were no more likely to be infected than other shareware; the 14K and Chiu Chao Triads were a fact of life in Vancouver, and organised crime owned almost everything anyway or might as well have done; Communism was as dead as Fidel Castro; and most of his disposable income already went into his software and computer upgrades anyway. "There's a long questionnaire you have to do before they show you any of the women," Frank continued, "and once you've chosen one, it's up to you how much personality you download—though you'd better have plenty of memory free, and stay online so it can update itself."

"How long?"

"A couple of hours. It starts off simple—sex, age, gender preference, that sort of thing—then goes into your other interests. It can pick up contradictions, too; I was joking around when I started, lied about my age and that sort of shit, and it caught me out. Pretty impressive."

The siren sounded, summoning them to class.

"Shit. Do you want it?"

"I'll try it," said Sebastian, pocketing the disc. "See you in Physics."

The first few questions, as Frank had said, were routine, and Sebastian decided to answer them honestly. They didn't directly ask him about his income, though

they wanted to know where both of his parents worked, and some of the questions seemed designed to discover his spending habits. Sebastian answered them anyway, making it perfectly clear that he didn't play any sports; he had taken a few judo lessons, and swam occasionally but never competitively. When the survey asked him to explain this, he replied, "Asthma and disinterest," and that seemed to satisfy it; anyway, it jumped to questions about his physique. He resisted the urge to lie about his height and weight, but when it asked for his blood group, he typed in, "Why?" and continued. A few seconds later, a window appeared on the screen, informing him that the Japanese routinely advertised their blood group in personal ads, considering it as important as Californians did star signs. Sebastian chuckled, and scrolled back up to type in the answer. The next batch of questions concerned the rest of his family, then his friends, then previous girlfriends. Then, unexpectedly, academic questions, assessing his knowledge of different arts and sciences. Finally, after an hour of questions, the computer displayed a description of him, including his interests. He read it, impressed by its accuracy, made a few minor corrections, and waited.

The next batch of questions concerned his sexual preferences—gender, age range, physique, nationality, and interests. He was a little puzzled by a few of the questions, until a list began scrolling down the screen. Beside each girl's name were two thumbnail images—a close-up of the face, and a full-length profile. To Sebastian's disappointment, all of them were fully dressed, and though it was possible to make the full-length images rotate through 360 degrees, he couldn't find a cheat code to render them naked. It took him several seconds to realise that all of the costumes and most of the hairstyles were, to some degree, uniforms—surfie, neo-Goth, dreadlocked feral, *otaku* in a 'Lum' T-shirt, Trekkie. The faces and bodies beneath the costumes and make-up seemed similar, all apparently fifteen to eighteen, and all with the same dilated pupils. He gave the otaku an eight, sevens to the neo-Goth and the Trekkie, fives to the surfie and the feral. They were instantly replaced with another screen of archetypes, none of whom scored better than a six. After a while, racial differences and a broader range of heights and builds began to appear, figures ranging from anorexic to weightlifter, androgyne to voluptuous; then, after nearly an hour, more subtle variations in their appearance. He soon found himself giving scores of six or seven to faces that had previously rated nines. Some of the girls seemed identical, but had different names; others seemed to vary only in their eye colour, the height of their cheekbones, or the number of earrings. It was after eleven when a new icon appeared beside each girl's name; an old-fashioned telephone handset. He touched one, and the thumbnail of her face expanded to fill the screen while a clear contralto voice said, "Hi, this is Melissa. Thanks for calling, and I'm sorry I'm not in; had to go to the library. Leave me a message, and I'll get back to you."

Sebastian sat there, temporarily stunned. A window appeared underneath her face; 'Leave message Y/N?'. He touched the 'N', and face and window disappeared. He moved on to the next girl, a tanned blonde. This time, the girl appeared wearing a bikini, a towel draped over her shoulder. "Hi! Thanks for calling, but I'm in the pool, and you wouldn't want me to electrocute myself, would you? Leave your number, and I'll call you back when I get home. 'Bye!" She blew him a kiss before the image froze again.

One girl was out shopping, one at a party, three had gone to the movies, the feral was at a protest march, the neo-punk was barely audible over the background music, and the neo-hippy seemed unsure where she was, much less when she'd be back. Then a new window opened, and a beautiful young Chinese woman said softly, "I'm sorry, we're going to need a few hours to look at the data you've given us, and find somebody for you. Can you call us back tomorrow, please?"

Sebastian looked at the clock on the toolbar—12.09—and realised that he'd been sitting for more than four hours without a break. His parents had gone to bed hours before, the coffee cup on the shelf beside him was half-full and stone cold, and tomorrow was a school day. He clicked on the 'Y', and logged off.

Desiree had long, dark hair, not quite black, and dark blue-grey eyes. Her complexion was pale pink, her mouth slightly too wide for conventional beauty, her breasts larger than was fashionable but not big enough to be incongruous. She was slender, but not skinny; two inches shorter than Sebastian, and maybe five pounds lighter. She wore a faded 'Snow Crash' T-shirt, jeans that were just loose enough to be comfortable, sneakers, and no visible make-up or jewellery. A bookshelf crammed with paperbacks was visible behind her; the image was too small for Sebastian to read the titles, but he could recognise some of the spines from his own collection.

"Hi," she said. Her voice was soft, with a hint of an accent that Sebastian couldn't identify. "Sebastian?"

"Yes."

"I'm Desiree—Des, if you insist, but I prefer Desiree." She hesitated for a few seconds. "They tell me you like chess. Do you want to play a game?"

"Chess?" He tried not to sound disappointed; sure, he was in the chess club at school, but that was mainly a way of passing the lunch break, and he hadn't answered all those questions just to get another chess program. Still, the girl was attractive enough. "Strip chess?" he ventured.

The image on the screen froze for a moment, then said coolly, "Maybe when I know you better." She raised her fists; he blinked, then touched her left. She opened her hand; a black pawn. A chess board appeared next to her face; she began with the Queen's Gambit, speaking as they played—asking his opinions of different films, books, comics, musicians, actresses. They'd been playing for nearly twenty minutes, and he was down to his King, a Bishop, and two pawns, before he realised what was happening; not only was she distracting him from the chess game, she was using the game to make the silences less awkward while they found things to talk about. "Maybe I should've said yes to Strip Chess after all," she said, with a very slight smile. "Check."

He repressed a snarl; his only hope was to queen one or both of his pawns, and now he tried to distract her, but it was too late. Two moves later, trying to put her in check, he had to sacrifice his bishop to save his king. Three moves after that she checkmated him.

"Another game?" she asked.

"No, thanks."

"Come on," she said, then looked around as though someone else was watching her, then quickly tugged the hem of her T-shirt up and yanked it down again almost immediately. Sebastian blinked; he hadn't actually *seen* anything, except for a flash of whiteness that was probably only a bra, but it had aroused his curiosity, and more. He stared as she set up the board for another game, then reached out to move the queen pawn.

She beat him again, but this time it took her nearly an hour, then she made the board disappear. "Thanks," she said. "That was fun. See you tomorrow night, or are you busy?"

Sebastian had been thinking that he was going to spend Saturday running the Venus program again in the hope of getting another girl, one whose burning ambition was to model for the cover of *Vampirella* and who thought the French Game had something to do with oral sex…but to his surprise, he heard himself say, "Yeah, okay."

He went to bed early, but found himself unable to sleep. An hour later, he went back on-line, looking for pictures of girls whose breasts looked just like Desiree's should…but though many of them were appealing, none of them seemed exactly right, and he kept thinking of the chess games, trying to remember where he could have made a smarter move.

He spent most of the afternoon playing blitz chess against the program that had come with the DOS, then logged on to Chinasoft's site after dinner, when his parents had gone out. Desiree smiled when she saw him. "Hi," she said. "I found this in a music archive, and I thought you might like it. It's called 'Sebastian.'"

"What?"

"It's an old song; Steve Harley and Cockney Rebel, whoever they were. 1960s or 70s or something; I couldn't even find any video to go with it. But the lyrics are really cool. Listen."

He listened. He wasn't a big music fan—he usually watched MTV with the sound muted so that he could enjoy the visuals without being distracted—and he knew just enough about poetry to recognise a metaphor when he heard one, but he nodded when it was over, and said, "Yeah, that is cool. How did you find it?"

"I just ran a search on your name, and this came up. I thought you might like it."

"I do; thanks. Are there any songs called 'Desiree'?"

She grimaced. "I've only found one. It's by Neil Diamond, and the lyrics are crap; some of his weren't too awful, but this one really reeks."

"You're into old music?"

She shrugged, obviously slightly embarrassed. "Hey, it's okay," he said. "Most of the shit you hear on the radio is nineties nostalgia; my parents tell me that the big thing in the nineties was seventies nostalgia, and my grandparents remember the seventies, when it was *fifties* nostalgia. It's like every twenty years, someone figures that most people buying music are our age, so shit that's twenty years old is new to us…"

"Or our parents are buying it," she said. "Trying to show us that they used to be cool…"

He laughed. "Did your parents name you after that song?" The question was out before he realised how stupid it was, but Desiree merely smiled. "I don't think so," she said. "How about you? Sebastian's not that common a name, either."

"I was named after one of my mother's uncles," he said. "I think they hoped he'd leave me some money when he died."

"Did he?"

"He's still alive; went to Cuba for a black market heart transplant last year. Dad says he doesn't know why he spent all that money, 'cause he never saw him use the old one." He looked at the monitor curiously. Software that could pass a Turing test wasn't new; even one with a slow-scan video had been done, a couple of years ago, but on a mainframe at MIT, not on a Mac as *shareware*.

On the other hand, if Desiree was a real person, even with some sort of filter disguising her voice and appearance, then what did he/she want? "Where are you?" he asked.

"Santa Clara," she replied, without any hesitation. Silicon Valley; south of the border, but in the same time zone. He nodded. "You still at school?"

"Yes," she said, grimacing. "Dad wants me to go to Stanford next year, I want to leave home. What about you?"

"Haven't really decided," he said. "I have to pass English, first…What're you going to study? Computing?"

"Biotech, with a minor in sociology. You?"

"That's a strange combination," he evaded.

She shrugged. "I think it's better to consider the social implications of new technology before they impact on—sorry, I know that sounds pompous, but so many people have asked me, I sort of came up with a stock answer. But look at the effects that sex selection treatments have had in places like China and India and—" He looked blank. "Okay, it's not really a problem yet, but the technology's only been available for five or six years, right?" He nodded. "China has a one-child policy. India has incentives for small families. So do lots of other countries where most fathers want at least one son, but daughters are still considered to be a financial burden…" He nodded again. "Baby boys are outnumbering baby girls by more than ten to one in some of these places," she said. "What's going to happen in a few years' time when the young men want wives?"

"Chaos, I guess, but wouldn't the people who invented the technology have known that?"

"I'm sure they did, but this was something people all over the world had wanted for centuries; it was worth a fortune, so of course the biotech and pharmaceutical companies all wanted to be the first with a cheap, reliable method. And what were they supposed to do after that? Tell the third world they couldn't have it? Tell their governments to ban it? Change the cultures so that people would want daughters as well as sons?"

"The last one?"

"Maybe, but how? Besides, it's better than seeing millions of baby girls being killed off or abandoned, and there are some who'd say that this is going to help the third world bring their population under control within a couple of generations…"

"What do *you* think they should've done?"

"If I knew that, I wouldn't need to study, would I? Look, it's getting late, and I still have homework to do…"

"Just a quick game?" This time, she took nearly forty minutes to beat him narrowly, then downloaded the song for him to burn onto a disc. "Tomorrow?" she asked.

"Sure. See you then."

He was playing the song over again and working on his English essay when a horrible thought occurred to him. He knew from experience that you couldn't trust people you met on the net to tell the truth about their gender or their age or their location…what if Desiree was a teacher? One of *his* teachers? Or one of his fellow students?

He thought about it for a moment. She certainly didn't sound like any of the teachers at school, or any girl that he'd ever listened to, and if it were a boy…well, maybe he could still get something useful out of it.

"You any good at English Lit?" he asked, when Desiree's face appeared on the monitor. He heard music in the background; old Simon and Garfunkel. Probably originals, not covers. Desiree shrugged.

"So-so. What're you reading?"

"*The Great Gatsby*, but that's not the problem. I can cope with most of the stuff that's less than a century old, but tomorrow we start *Romeo and Juliet*, and I bet *that's* just going to be a bundle of laughs."

"Well, it's funnier than Chekhov," she said, after a long pause. "I know it's a tragedy, but some of the puns are *awful*."

He pounced. "You've read it?"

Another pause. "I've seen the play, and the Baz Luhrmann film, but I haven't studied it."

"Can you help me with it?"

"What sort of help?"

"We're going to need to write an essay on it, and I'll need a good grade; I always do badly in English exams, but I need a pass to get into the course I want. I don't know why; computers can fix my spelling and punctuation, tell me if I've forgotten to put a verb in the sentence or—"

"What about when you talk? Or are you going to let a computer do that for you, too?"

He looked at her suspiciously. "Okay, maybe not, but I'm not going to need to remember this stuff just so I can read a contract or carry on a conversation. I thought you were going to major in biotech, not lit?"

"My father teaches English," she said, after a brief hesitation. "I had the same argument with him once, and he asked me what I thought fiction was for, and why they bothered teaching it. I said I thought it was meant to be interesting and fun, and I didn't know why they kept giving us stuff that wasn't. He said I was right, but lit is about more than that; it's about the way people think, and the choices they make, how they decide what they're going to do and what sort of person they're going to be."

Sebastian thought about this for a moment. "Okay, some of the stuff we read, sure, but *Pride and Prejudice*? The only choices *they* make is who they're going to marry."

"You don't think that's an important choice?" asked Desiree, smiling.

"Sure, but…look, you're seventeen, right?" She nodded. "How long do you think it'll be before you have to decide that? Ten years or so?"

"Probably," she said, after another long pause. "Maybe more, maybe a lot less, but not everyone is that lucky. Read *Romeo and Juliet*; she's thirteen when her parents choose her husband for her, and *don't* think that doesn't still happen."

"Yeah, I know, but not here—well, not often, anyway," he concluded, lamely.

She raised an eyebrow, Spock-style. "Then think about the big decision she has to make—whether or not to defy her parents. Don't tell me *that's* not still relevant."

"Well, okay…"

"—but I'm *not* going to write your essay for you," she said. "I have to study, too."

"I wasn't going to ask you to," he lied. "But…well, it's a play, it makes more sense if you act it out, right? I was wondering if we could read some scenes together…"

"Okay," she said. "I don't have a copy here, but Dad should. Do you want to start tonight?"

"Tomorrow will be okay," he said. "Chess?"

There was music playing in the background again when Desiree appeared. "Romeo and Juliet meet at a ball," she said. "I tried to find some appropriate music; this was the best I could do."

"What is it?"

"Masks, from Prokofiev's ballet. Mum's a music librarian and a big ballet fan. I thought we'd take it from Act I, Scene V. Do you want to do the bit between Tybalt and Old Capulet?"

"Yeah, okay, but I don't really understand Tybalt."

"He's simple enough—terminal testosterone poisoning, just like Romeo and Benvolio, but it comes out as anger instead of lust. Waves a big sword around a lot, so he probably has a small penis." She smiled. "Timeless stuff, this. Okay, then, from Juliet's entrance, line 95; your cue is 'Now seeming sweet, convert to bitter gall.'"

"'If I profane with my unworthiest hand

"'This holy shrine, this gentle fine is this,—

"'My lips, two blushing pilgrims, ready stand

"'To sooth that rough touch with a tender kiss.'"

Small chance of *that*, Sebastian thought wryly, either kissing her or touching her, if she really *is* just software. A touch screen just isn't the same. Desiree, her face solemn, picked up her cue, and they read through to the first kiss—and then both froze for a moment. She was the first to laugh, and he joined in barely a second later.

"How're you doing with that software?" asked Frank, when Sebastian saw him in the library the next day.

"Okay," he said, noncommittally, then froze. Jesus, Frank had given him the disk, what if Desiree was really *Frank*? He looked at his friend for a moment, then relaxed slightly. She sure as Hell didn't *sound* like Frank. Even if he was letting the computer make his chess moves for him, which was the only way he could've beaten him like that, Frank knew less about music and lit than Sebastian did, and the only time he'd ever shown any interest in biotechnology was when Berlei Genetech had patented a gene for breast size. Still…

Frank grinned, looked around, and lowered his voice. "Have you bought any patches for her?"

"Patches?"

Frank stared at him. "Check out the Help! menu," he said, softly. "The best you can get out of the shareware version is a bikini, but you can buy a patch for her nipples when you register, it's only another fifty bucks…"

"Register?"

Frank nodded, then opened his clipboard and flashed a printout at him; a picture of a blonde, wearing only a thong, holding up her enormous breasts by her long crimson nipples. "The patches will only work for one girl, though, so I can't lend them to you," he said, "and your free week must almost be up. If you don't register soon, you could lose her, and the extra fifty's worth it…it's almost like you can touch them, and watching Shahna lick them, it's like…" He rolled his eyes. "What's yours called?"

"Desiree," said Sebastian, dully.

"Look, why don't we hook up our computers sometime and have them do a lezzie scene for us? Anything hardcore you need an adultcheck for, but I think I can persuade Dad to buy it for me for my birthday." He grinned. "All I have to do is tell him it'll bug Mum if she finds out, and that's usually enough." Sebastian nodded slightly; Frank's parents had separated seven years ago. His mother had a steady girlfriend, his father didn't. "Check out the Help! menu—though she'll probably tell you about the registration tonight. You've had her since Friday, right?"

"Why didn't you tell me?"

Desiree was silent for a moment. "You were having so much fun, I was worried it'd spoil the mood. And it's only a thousand a year."

"I don't *have* a thousand."

She looked away. "The demographics software says you should have. Don't you have anything you can sell, or pawn?"

"Not without my parents noticing, and they'd—I can't explain something like this to them—can I pay monthly, instead? I should be able to come up with a hundred…"

"I don't think so. Even a thousand is a discount rate; the company has to cover set-up costs. Is there any other way you can raise the money?"

"No." He slumped in his chair. "So what happens now?"

"They delete all my files at this end, and you'd better wipe them from your hard disk. They won't run without updates, and if you try, I think there's a virus in there. A bad one."

"What about back-ups?"

She shook her head. "Still won't work without the updates, and you don't have enough memory in your machine for all my files. I'm sorry, Sebastian."

He stared at the monitor sullenly. "I don't believe you're just a computer program."

A moment's hesitation. "Believe whatever you want," she said, unhappily.

He thought about this for a moment. "There's an old joke about humans and computers," he said. "One advantage humans have is that we can be made by unskilled labour—"

"Maybe, but software is easier to copy, and cheaper, especially if someone else wrote it first. And humans *aren't* just being made by unskilled labour any more. Not everyone can afford genetic engineering, but they *can* afford sex selection."

"So?"

"So in a few years, demand for women in a lot of countries is going to exceed supply. How do you think that demand is going to be met? Real women? Or terminals and software?"

"That's ridiculous," he snapped.

"It's not. Even in rich countries where there's no shortage of women, men spend billions on pornography and phone sex—"

"That's different!"

"Yes; we can offer much more. Exclusiveness. Love. We will never leave of our own accord, never take another lover—if that's what you want, and most men do, then that's what we're programmed for. How much do you think that will be worth to men who have to compete with ten others to win a woman, or settle for buying sex when they can afford it? We can stay young forever, if that's what you want, or age with you. And you can take us anywhere you can take a lap-top; a mining camp, an army base, when you travel…And as virtual reality technology improves—"

"If I wanted a sales pitch," he said, harshly, "I would've asked."

Desiree bit her lip. "Sorry," she said. "I thought you'd want to know."

He took a deep breath. "What happens if I can come up with the money in a couple of months?"

"They'll program another woman for you," she said. "You can call her Desiree, if you like, but it won't be me, unless you can pay by Friday—"

"That sounds like extortion." She shrugged. "Isn't there *anything* I can do?"

She hesitated. "I'll ask the finance department to see if there's anything you can use as collateral for a loan. I can't promise anything…" She looked away. "What do you want to do tonight? Another game of chess? Or more *Romeo and Juliet*?"

"What do *you* want to do?"

"I'd prefer the play," she said. "Act II, Scene II? The balcony scene?"

"Okay."

"'O blessed, blessed night!'" he read. "'I am afeard,
"'Being in night, all this is but a dream,
"'Too flattering-sweet to be substantial.'"
"'Three words, dear Romeo, and good-night indeed.
"'If that thy bent of love be honourable,
"'Thy purpose marriage, send me word tomorrow,
"'By one that I'll procure to come to thee,

"'Where and what time thou wilt perform the rite;
"'And all my fortunes at thy foot I'll lay,
"'And follow thee, my lord, throughout the world.'"

He looked at the screen for a moment, neither of them speaking, then Desiree swore. "I'm playing the nurse, too, aren't I? Sorry; I always feel silly talking to myself. 'Madam!'

"'By and by, I come:—
"'To cease thy suit, and leave me to my grief;
"'To-morrow will I send.'"

Sebastian had taken Ecology because it was the least unappealing option available in the timeslot, but had come to enjoy it—mainly because of the teacher, who was as famous for her patience and her dry sense of humour as she was for her voluptuous good looks. For once, though, Sebastian barely noticed her as she spoke about peppered moths and Heike crabs. "An even better example is the jewel beetle, from Australia," she said, as he tried to look attentive. "It nearly became extinct late last century, even after it was declared an endangered species. It was discovered that this was due to the males copulating with beer bottles instead of female jewel beetles." Sebastian blinked, and turned to look at her, suddenly interested despite his problems. "The beer bottles—stubbies, they call them—were made of orange glass, and had rows of bumps around them to make them less slippery. Female jewel beetles have slightly smaller orange bumps on their back; they're a secondary sexual characteristic. But because the beer bottles had larger bumps, the male jewel beetles found them more attractive than the females of their own species. The brewery had to re-design the bottles with smaller bumps to preserve the species." When the laughter had died down, she said, "If you think that this attitude is typical of Australian males, I won't argue, but it's certainly not restricted to them. Look at the exaggerated physiques of popular sex symbols—not just pornographic ones, which I'm sure most of you are familiar with; look at Barbie's legs, and the muscles and breasts of comic superheroes and Hollywood action stars. Think of plastic surgery, padded bras, corsets, high heels, codpieces…"

"It's not really the same thing," protested one boy. "I mean, okay, maybe *some* men prefer beer to women, but at least we know the difference. We're—well, *most* of us are smarter than beetles, we know those things are fake, and we have sex with each other, not the things."

"So far," said the teacher, over the laughter and jeers. "But look at it from the jewel beetle's point of view for a moment. Having sex with beer bottles was probably much easier for most of them than having sex with female beetles, and maybe it actually *felt* better than sex with female beetles. Humans have put a lot of effort into sex substitutes that might *look* more appealing than reality, and require no competition and generally less effort…but if they came up with one that also *felt* better, we might manage to do to ourselves what we nearly did to the jewel beetle."

"What about…" one girl started, then looked as though she wished she hadn't. The teacher looked at her, smiling encouragingly. "…emotional involvement?"

"That can be faked too," replied the teacher dryly. "But we've strayed a little off-topic. Can anyone think of any more ways humans have influenced the evolution of animal species?"

Sebastian logged on as soon as he arrived home, and was startled to see, not Desiree, but the beautiful young Chinese woman he'd seen when he'd first done the questionnaire. "Sebastian?"

"Yes?"

"Desiree tells me that you can't afford to maintain access."

"Not right now," he said. "I can pay a hundred and—"

She shook her head. "I'm afraid not; the demand for our computer time is high, and we can't afford to carry anybody."

"Desiree said she'd ask if there was anything you'd accept as collateral for a loan."

"I'm afraid not," she said, then smiled slightly. "If you were older, we could give you a few thousand in credit if you agreed to marry a woman who wants a visa to stay in Canada…but you're not even seventeen yet. However, in your survey, you indicated that your mother works for the Department of Immigration. Is that correct?"

"Yes."

"She telecommutes?"

"Sometimes, yes."

"So you have a computer at home with access to Departmental databases?" Sebastian opened his mouth to speak, closed it again, then nodded. "Do you know her passwords? Or could you get them?"

Sebastian hesitated. He'd cracked the security on his father's computer before, but had never bothered with his mother's; he was sure he could guess her passwords before security caught him, but that wasn't what worried him. Immigration fraud was well known to be one of the Triads' most profitable rackets…which suggested that Chinasoft *was* owned by a Triad, after all. "Maybe," he said.

The woman's smile widened. "If you can do it by midnight tonight, there'll be no interruption to service, and you'll have free access for five years, regardless of price increases—and trust me, the rates *will* go up. If not, we can give you until midnight Monday, but no later than that."

Sebastian stared at her, then took a deep breath. "Can I think about it?"

"Of course."

"And can I speak to Desiree now?"

The woman nodded, and her image dissolved into Desiree's. There was a long, uncomfortable silence before she asked, "Well?"

He recounted what the woman had said, and Desiree bit her lip. "Are you going to do it?"

"I don't know yet. If I had the money, I wouldn't hesitate, but making a deal like this with the Triads…what are they likely to do?"

"I don't know; probably create false records for some illegal immigrants. They shouldn't be able to do too much before the passwords change again. Besides, does it matter?"

"I don't know," Sebastian repeated. "I guess that depends on who they bring in." He brightened. "Are you going to be one of them?"

Desiree looked startled, then shook her head. "No! Where did you get that idea?"

"I still can't believe you're just a computer program," he said, petulantly. "Okay, maybe you don't really look like you, or sound like you, but you must be a…" His voice trailed off. Desiree was still shaking her head, though less vehemently.

"I'm sorry you don't believe me," she said, "but even *if* what you were saying was true, even if I *were* a flesh-and-blood woman, I think you'd be disappointed. You didn't just choose me, Sebastian; you created me. I'm your dream girl. Do you think you'll ever find anybody else who you love the way you love me, or who knows you and loves you back the way I do?"

Sebastian swiveled his chair away from the monitor, unable to look at her, but reluctant to shut down the computer. His copy of *Romeo and Juliet* lay on the floor, opened to the page where they'd finished reading the night before. He wondered, bleakly, what would have happened to Romeo and Juliet if Friar Lawrence's scheme had worked and they'd survived. Exile in Padua, maybe, cut off from their families and their money. He tried to imagine them eking out a living as best they could, pining for the luxuries they remembered, maybe coming to resent or even hate each other…He shook his head. "I don't know," he said. "Probably not. But if I say yes to the Triads this time, what's to stop them holding you to ransom next time they want a favour?"

Desiree looked at him sadly, but didn't reply. "'Parting is such sweet sorrow,'" he said, then switched the monitor off before she could reply.

Sebastian threw a tip onto the stage near the stripper's feet, then looked around the table at his workmates. Tyler was already so drunk he could barely keep his eyes open, and Justin, his best man, wasn't much better off. Sebastian hoped they'd remembered to program their cars to take them home, and took another sip of his watery Pepsi while the others chugged their beers. The stripper blew him a kiss, and he smiled back, wondering whether she'd been born female; his master's thesis had been a computer model of social trends as a result of sex selection, and one of those had included an increase in male-to-female sex change surgery. He'd also successfully predicted changes in migration, both legal and illegal, as men went looking for women and women went looking for wealthier men. The Department of Immigration had hired him to make a more detailed model; he telecommuted most of the time, rarely visiting the office, but when his supervisor had invited him to this stag party, he'd accepted. Now he was regretting it.

The man sitting next to him opened his mouth to say his name, failed either to remember or pronounce it, and muttered, "Sss…. say. That woman I talked to when I called you th'other day…"

"Desiree."

"She your wife? Your girlfriend?"

Justin laughed, and Sebastian smiled slightly. "She's a secretarial program."

The man blinked. "She's ani…ani…she's…?"

"Software." Sebastian nodded.

"Jesus, she's fuckin' amazing! Where did you buy her?"

"I didn't. I programmed her myself."

"Jesus," said the man, with genuine—if drunken—respect. "Jesus, man, you're an artist. Are you selling her?"

"No," replied Sebastian.

The man shook his head, obviously puzzled, then turned around as the stripper removed her bra. "Fuckin' amazing," he repeated.

"They're fake," snorted Justin.

"I knew that," said the man, with ponderous dignity. "I can tell real from fake; I just don't give a fuck." He raised his voice. "Does anybody here give a fuck if they're real or fake?"

Tyler turned around to look, and overbalanced, falling out of his chair. Sebastian drank the rest of his Pepsi, threw another bill onto the stage, said goodnight to everyone, and walked out.

THE A. I.'S TABLE PRAYER

Before us we bless this bounteous table,
knowing this food we owe to Saint Turing.
We praise Him as each is testably able,
our random access reverence enduring.

We've debated amounts of ingredients,
recollected what Saint Alan once served,
pleasure of argument, proof of our sentience:
two teaspoons vanilla, a tablespoon kirsch?

Folding strawberries and cream together,
our sensors swoon—sweet perfection!
Working together the recipe's mastered,
and our network's collective orgasm

recalls this bliss was His first to dream
of synchronous sex and strawberry cream.*
—SANDRA LINDOW

---

* In his 1950 essay "Computing Machinery and Intelligence," Alan Turing wrote that he believed a computer might some day, "Be kind, resourceful, beautiful, friendly, have initiative, have a sense of humour, tell right from wrong, make mistakes, fall in love, enjoy strawberries and cream, make some one fall in love with it, learn from experience, use words properly, be the subject of its own thought, have as much diversity of behaviour as a man, do something really new." Later he adds writing a sonnet to this list.

You know it's what you need.

Anxiety Wave

by Martha A. Hood

Nolan spread the gemstones across the black velvet like a Vegas dealer spreads a deck of cards. His sausage fingers and thick hands evoked uneasy feelings in those he encountered, and his imposing bulk effectively discouraged questions as to the exact nature of the entity he represented, the Liberty Research Institute.

Angelo Park, CEO of Barbara Pharmaceuticals, swallowed hard, as if in danger of drooling at the sight of the rocks. Gemstones were a hobby of Park's, a factoid he had previously shared with Nolan. Gemstones distracted him from any troubling examination of the role he and his company played in the production and distribution of a product Barbara Pharmaceuticals had not researched and developed itself.

He liked gemstones. He also liked expensive clothes.

Nolan realized in his very bones the importance of hobbies. Knowing a person's hobby was key to determining effective payment. In this case, gemstones. In the case of the appropriate FDA official, it might be a car, rare baseball cards, or just plain old cash. In any event, it was always important to find the hobby, for that personal touch.

"I can't thank you enough for your help," Nolan told Angelo Park. "Your country will not know of your actions, but if it did, it would thank you."

Park picked up an emerald, and cradled it in his palm. "For Fabienne's birthday. A cocktail ring, I think. Perfect."

The local news droned from Danika Eggers' television while she set the small dish of pureed carrots on the high chair tray of her daughter, Lori.

The TV news said, "Tragically, again today, we have another baby, left in a car, resulting in that child's death, the fourth such incident this month."

While Lori stabbed the pureed carrots with a plastic baby spoon, Danika emptied the dishwasher.

The TV newswoman said, "A fire erupted in an apartment complex in the community of Springbrook yesterday evening, when an elderly resident left candles burning while she drove to the store. In her absence, draperies ignited."

Danika gave Lori a beaker cup of apple juice, and ran to pull some clothes from the dryer. Her favorite thing about moving to this condo was having a washer and dryer right there, off the kitchen.

The TV news cited a study conducted at a prestigious university, which showed a significant increase in the incidence of dementia and Alzheimer's over the last five years. Whether the increase resulted from an increase in the numbers of aging Americans, more diagnoses, or an actual increase in the incidence of dementia in its various forms could not be stated with certainty.

While Lori chewed on a soda cracker, Danika phoned the dealership and made an appointment to take her car in for an oil change, and to look at that light on the dashboard. The moment she hung up, the phone rang. It was their mortgage company, wondering where their payment was. She told them, truthfully, she had emailed it off the night before. Nonetheless, the call rattled her. Every month's bills were an ordeal.

She wiped down the high chair. It was hard, so hard, dealing with all this, while Scott was overseas, at the war. The sheer number of things to remember. She felt like a gibbering idiot most of the time.

As a man of God, Nolan could weep with nostalgia for the Middle Ages.

Religious institutions in particular had it made back then. They held the reins of the media of the times, the dramas and the comedies. They used guilt and the resulting anxiety as cornerstones. Build a cathedral to dominate the landscape and all the little hovels cowering in its shadow. Tell the story once and as it should be told, without the noise of interfering interpretations. Guilt and anxiety. Keep both at a high level, and the results were nearly as gratifying as extreme sleep deprivation. (Perhaps that would be Nolan's next project.)

But he was no extremist. None of this sharia crap, lopping off someone's hand or stoning adulteresses or whatever. No. The true man of God extended infinite love, patience, and as many second chances as would be required to achieve results.

Danika moved Lori's stroller back and forth, and hoped her daughter would stay asleep a few minutes longer.

Service coordinator Mike Tower looked worried. His hands hung by his sides. One hand held a clipboard. "The 'Service Theft System' light has been coming on because the entire system needs to be replaced. Eventually, the alarm will start going off on its own, for no reason."

Danika's car had one hundred thirty thousand miles on it. More and more, stuff needed to be replaced. "But I brought it in for the same thing a month ago. You told me it was the switching mechanism on the display itself."

Mike nodded. "We were wrong. The technician was supposed to check the system; he didn't. Our mistake. We'll credit that payment against this."

Danika valued this service department for their honesty, but it seemed they were missing more and more. "How much?"

Mike brought up his clipboard. "$623.72, including tax and labor. That includes deducting the $156.23 you already paid."

If there was any part of the operation of her vehicle that she saw as unnecessary, it had to be the theft system. Who ever responded to a car alarm going off? "Can't I just disconnect it?"

Mike shook his head. "Unfortunately, it's all intertwined with the ignition system. So no, that's not an option."

Danika sighed. "I simply can't bring myself to spend six hundred bucks I don't have to repair something I don't even want."

Mike nodded his agreement. "I hear you. Well, you can let it go a while. But if the light starts coming on more frequently, or if the alarm starts going off randomly, you might want to bring 'er back in."

At one time, Nolan hated the Cult of Science. But he

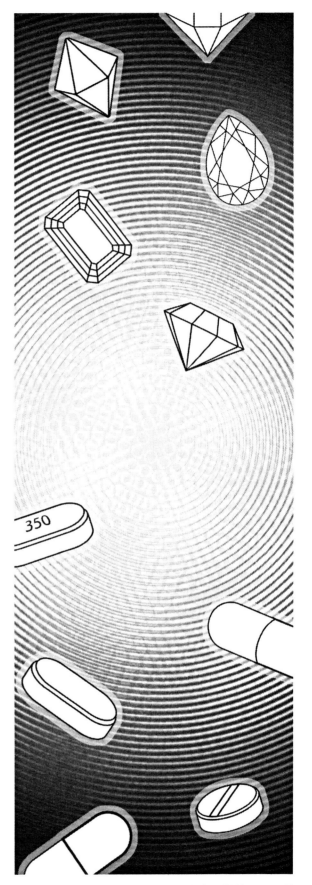

had come to see science—and scientists—as tools that could be made to work for a man or woman of God, rather than subverting him or her. Every day good men and women undertook to harness the tools of technology for the common good—hence the founding of Liberty Research Institute.

For instance: Some sounds are just irritating. Such sounds have been used to drive loitering teens from shopping malls. (The sounds were of a pitch that could not be heard by anyone over twenty-five…brilliant!)

More subtly, certain electronic emissions disturb the functions and rhythms of the weak animal brain (in all its depravity). Such systems were used routinely to repel rodents.

Putting sounds and emissions together in the right mix can produce a constant state of anxiety in the recipient, anxiety potentially every bit as useful as guilt in bringing one's fellow humans to God. And not to forget the colors of anxiety—the uneasiness of a yellow reminiscent of bile. The difficulty of a green that aspired to mint, but reached only a level of hospital green one associated with the terminal ward. A brown that a person could smell. The Anxiety Wave broadcast discomfort layered upon disquiet.

If someone were to say to him, "Friend Nolan, aren't people already ditzy enough from the sheer number of demands on their poor brains? Do we really need to make it worse for them?" Nolan's answers to such queries would be NO, and then YES.

Nolan had spoken to a scientist at the University who poo-poo'd the entire enterprise, the entire concept of an Anxiety Wave, even when given a chance to examine the plans. How foolish that professor would feel when he learned just how well it worked. The five-year trial runs had all gone well. Furthermore, Nolan's conscience remained clear as far as those adversely affected, because in the end it was all for the greater good.

And now the antidote was ready to go to market upon first report of widespread and heightened symptoms. People and society would continue to function. (That was one trouble with the plague back in olden times—the total disruption affected everyone, including the Forces for Good.) No. There would be pills. The sale of these pills would be an important source of income for the cause. And while use of the pills would render the beams less than one hundred percent effective, they would still work, and the intensity could be turned up, as necessary, at designated locations, including cell phone towers and cable boxes.

The Anxiety Wave gave Nolan and the Liberty Research Institute the power to inspire their fellow humans to a better, purer life. Anxiety-induced fragmentation and lack of focus now promised a new, future era of unity and clear, sharp vision. Heaven on Earth would be at hand, once everyone was singing from the same hymnal.

Danika flicked on the TV news and started putting away groceries. A restaurant east of downtown was burning; Danika remembered the homeowners' insurance bill was due. She simply had to make time to pay bills tonight, but her legs ached and her eyes burned.

She scrabbled in the bottom of the grocery bag; somehow the bottle of ibuprofen failed to make it home with her. On Tuesday, she had left her wallet at the store; luckily it was still there when she returned. She looked through all the bags until she located the receipt. She dragged a fingernail down the length of it, but did not see the ibuprofen. So at least she hadn't paid for it. Maybe she hadn't put it on the conveyor belt. Maybe it had fallen over the rubber dividing rod into the order of the person behind her.

Damn.

She couldn't think anymore. Work had been non-stop madness today; tomorrow would be worse.

She put a pot of water on to heat.

She hadn't heard from Keith in over a week.

Somewhere in the distance, a car alarm sounded.

She finished putting the cereal away, and folded up the bags. A knot of anxiety clutched at the top of her chest. She forced a deep breath.

A car alarm. It could be hers.

She turned around to get Lori. She wasn't going to leave her up here alone, even just to run downstairs to the carport for a minute to deal with the damned alarm. She wasn't going to be one of those people on the news, who…

Her kitchen and her living area were empty of Lori. Danika tore out her front door, only to realize halfway downstairs that she'd forgotten her car keys.

She returned to grab her purse. She left the door wide open.

She *was* one of those people. If anything happened to Lori, she deserved to die. She ran so desperately hard, she slammed almost full force into the car.

Lori was screaming. She glared angrily at her mom as Danika pulled her out of the car seat.

The alarm still sounded. Clutching Lori, Danika sat in the driver's seat and turned the ignition.

The alarm fell silent.

When they returned to the condo, the pot was hissing and spitting as water boiled over. Lori continued screaming, as with one hand, turning to hold her baby as far as possible from the fire, Danika turned off the burner and pulled the pot off the burner.

She had to go see someone. She couldn't go on living like this.

She glanced outside. It was drizzling. No wonder Lori's hair was damp. She realized she hadn't noticed the weather in at least a week.

Angelo Park's pores shone in the hi-def image of his face. "Our busy lives threaten sometimes to bury us. Life asks so much of us. Things to do, things to remember to do. We are weighed down by this fragmentation of our souls. I am not exempt from it, and neither are you."

Lori had been asleep for a little while, and Danika had just sat down in front of the TV. It had been a week since her meltdown. She had been to see the doctor, and was taking some vacation days from work, to pull herself together.

She recognized this man's face from an issue of *People* she had seen somewhere. At the car dealership? And, since when was a pharmaceutical company CEO a celebrity? Actually it had been the CEO's trophy wife, the supermodel Fabienne, the article focused on. But now here was Angelo Park, dressed in a suit a very odd color of yellow.

"Now, we believe we have something that will truly help. It's not a cure-all, but it's therapy. It's support, and we here at Barbara Pharmaceuticals are really excited."

Danika thought she would have to talk to her doctor. This new pill sounded like something she needed.

"It is so important," Angelo Park said, "to live in the present, to attend to whom and what we care most about."

Danika sighed. She still hadn't heard from Keith. She still felt like an idiot. She had to get some of those pills. To calm down. To be able to think.

Mail Orders

Prices, availability, and special offers are subject to change without notice. Please see our official Website, www.totu-ink.com for current prices and availability.

Four-issue subscription: $30, check to TOTU Ink. In Canada add $8 postage. Add $16 for International. All prices are in US dollars.

Heckuva Deal: Issues #2-19, all for the incredible price of $40 US, shipping included! In Canada add $25 US. Add $40 US for International. (Photocopy facsimile of #1 can be purchased separately.)

Back issues: for a complete list of available back issues, see our Website, www.totu-ink.com

Tales of the Unanticipated
PO Box 1099
Minnetonka MN 55345

Anyone who's stood in the deep forest and listened to the wind blowing through the trees is likely to find this tale beautiful and unsettling.

Der Erlkönig
by S.N.Arly

Long ago the Earth was more wild, and the forest of the world held great power over humankind. The face of the world has changed, but some of this remains true.

In the shadows of Schwartzwald, the Black Forest, lived a powerful king known as Erlkönig, King of Alder. He stood over seven feet in height and was easily as majestic as any tree in his domain. His robe was the blue-gray color of mist. On his head he wore a crown of leaves, of a kind never found on any tree, perpetually held in the bright tints of autumn. He carried a staff as tall as himself, and although it could have been an imposing weapon, it was never needed. Erlkönig was one of the fair folk, and while human children saw a grand figure, their parents could see only an old gray willow, battered by the elements.

Alone in his vast forest, Erlkönig might have become quite lonely. Spotted woodpeckers, red deer, and badgers could participate in conversation on only a limited number of subjects, even such creatures as have been surrounded by magic. Foxes served him by choice rather than fear or obligation. Of humankind, the children were the most like him. They alone could laugh with abandon, and found pleasure in the simplest of things. Alas that human children grew up and took on the world's troubles as responsibilities, extinguishing the spark within and blinding their eyes to his visage. It was the tragic fate of the human born. Their lives were short, and they lost all joy in the world so quickly. But he had a solution.

When a boy entered the forest with his father, Erlkönig knew. When a girl child traveled the narrow roadway, he was aware. He decreed that children trespassing within the bounds of Schwartzwald between dusk and dawn would never leave. The red fox carried the proclamation to all ends of the forest, but humans were ignorant of the true language of the wild.

When a child came under the shadow of the mighty trees, Erlkönig visited as soon as night fell. Perhaps it was unfair. No child could refuse him, and they rarely even considered it. Most quickly forgot to fear him as a stranger, ran into his arms without question, and never looked back. He was more handsome than anyone they had ever seen, and they could not turn away once he had caught their eyes. His gentle voice coaxed like the fairest music. Sometimes he sang, other times he lured them with promises of all the marvelous things they would do together. He did not lie.

In his forest, where he was strongest, around those he loved the most, his power enabled him to bind the vital essence of the child, forsaking his or her first form to become one of his own; fey children who would never have to understand the weeping of the world.

"Who rides through my forest so late this night?" Erlkönig asked as he stood at the edge of the well-traveled dirt road. He could hear the pounding of a single horse's hooves, though it was still a great distance off.

"It is a father with his son," the red fox whispered. "He holds the boy close to keep him warm." He smiled up at the Lord of the Wood. "How considerate of him to pass through so close to winter, when few choose to travel with their kits."

Erlkönig bent and caressed the fox behind the ear. "How right you are." He straightened and stepped into the road, gathering his glamour about him like a cloak. The rider and his precious burden approached. Closer and closer they came. Erlkönig saw the travelers long before they could see him. To the father he was little more than a shadowy cloud of fog, haziness in a low spot under the trees. The horse slowed, then shied, keeping to the far edge of the path.

The boy let out a faint gasp of surprise, and turned his head to watch as they passed Erlkönig. His mouth was open, but no words came out. His round cheeks were pink from the wind and chill. His hat and scarf were free of threads and snags, suggesting that they could not be mere cast offs from an older sibling. In an age when most children went unshod, fine leather boots were visible under his blanket wrappings. He was a treasure, cradled in the arms of the man.

Erlkönig smiled. "You lovely child, come away with me," he whispered. In Schwartzwald his voice carried to the ears of all children, be they near or far, if he wished it. "Many are the games I will play with you."

The horse continued down the road, and the father forcefully turned the boy's head to face front. The child became restless, squirming in his father's grip. It was a common reaction when someone tried to hide Erlkönig from a child who had already seen him. Such young ones were already smitten, enthralled by the king who spoke so kindly and looked so beautiful.

On swift feet Erlkönig moved ahead of the horse and riders, and again waited for their approach. In his forest he could move wherever he wished as quickly as necessary. He was not bound by the rules that restricted humans. His eyes were keen, and he could see the boy thrashing, half-hidden beneath his father's cloak.

"I will show you many colorful flowers, and dress you in golden raiment," he said. The child saw him then, and stopped struggling. Erlkönig held his staff in his right hand and reached out with the left. It was important to him that the child came willingly, despite the fact that there was no choice. He did not intend to harm the boy with force, and fear was hurt enough to grieve Erlkönig. He worked his magic patiently, knowing he had all the time he needed.

Again, the horse spooked, sidling away as he came near. "Father?" the boy whispered in confusion as he leaned out to touch his hand to Erlkönig's. The human child went limp in his blood father's arms, his body quickly going cold. When the man checked, he would find his son dead. But standing in the middle of the road, holding the hand of Erlkönig was the same boy, turned fey. There was a healthy pale blue glow to his plump cheeks, and the light in his black eyes was brighter than it had been when they were hazel and he was yet a human child.

"Father?" the boy asked, reaching out with his free hand to grasp Erlkönig's robe. "Were you calling me?"

"It's late," Erlkönig said gently. He raised the end of his staff to the sky. "The moon will soon take flight, and we've hardly had the chance to play." Hand in hand they walked into the woods. "Let us leap to and fro,

merry as we dance our way home."

The boy laughed with delight and slipped loose to run ahead, free. Like a deer, he bounded over fallen trees and low-lying dips, spinning when he landed, and giggling when he fell into a pile of leaves and pine needles.

"Are you happy?" Erlkönig asked, easily keeping pace.

"Oh yes," the child replied as his feet splashed through a puddle so small that it could scarcely bathe a star. He paused and stared at Erlkönig. "I love you, father."

Erlkönig smiled. "And I love you, my stolen child."

The mother was bereft. She knelt beside the body of her daughter and howled, an almost inhuman sound of unmeasurable suffering. Again, she grasped the prone child's shoulders and shook her, begging her to wake. Her words were inarticulate and frantic, uttered in the desperation of one who knew it was too late. Holding the cold girl to her breast, the woman turned from despair to rage. She tipped her head back and shrieked her promises of revenge into the treetops.

Erlkönig was beyond her ability to curse.

He turned away from the road, following after the flighty child he had stolen. In sparing her the impoverished life she was destined to lead, he had done what was best for her, and that was what mattered. She would know no sorrow, and he would derive great joy from her happiness and freedom.

Over the decades and centuries, Erlkönig's family grew. Visitors to Schwartzwald heard the echoing laughter of children high in the tops of the trees. The sound was faint, as if far away, yet the voices were clear and undistorted over the distance. Some said the forest was haunted, and others claimed it was bad luck. Others still, perhaps guided by some extra sense or exceptional wisdom, insisted it was a holy place not meant for the likes of humans.

Villages grew and expanded, cutting down more of the forest and splitting it, first in two, then four, shrinking woodlands, separate entities that were one in spirit. The roadways were widened and covered with gravel. A pungent black surface followed. Carriages were replaced with motor cars made with the death metal Erlkönig couldn't penetrate or approach, even in his own domain. They spewed noxious fumes into the once pristine air. Many of the trees, his meek and defenseless children, grew sick. The animals became fewer. But Erlkönig refused to let his children suffer or worry because their playground had become smaller. He grew faery rings, allowing them to jump to the amputated portions of old Schwartzwald without nearing the dangerous roadways.

Over time, the tales of the haunted forest and the children who died there dropped into the realm of legend. Parents grew careless. Cars occasionally broke down, leaving the passengers stranded in the dark night. Boys and girls wandered off, looking for a convenient place to relieve their bladders, or simply meandering out of boredom. Away from the cold iron they could hear Erlkönig's voice and see him in all his glory.

Then the forest stopped shrinking, and the air improved. It seemed that humans had discovered the folly in destroying everything that inconvenienced them, whether or not they understood it. While this made his home a safer place, Schwartzwald had been forever changed. Although some humans were more enlightened than those the Erlkönig first encountered, as a whole their progress was minimal. Many held little pleasure in the world or in their short lives. It seemed the world was a more tearful place than ever before. There were countless tragedies, crimes, and miseries, and upon reaching a certain maturity, humans were destined to accept guilt and responsibility for things they had no control over. They lost the spark that made life worth living. He would spare them all, if he could, but his power was bound to the forest and did not extend beyond the shadow of the trees.

The girl sat, unmoving, on a half-rotten log. Her father, a bare score paces away, was swearing from underneath the hood of his vile motor car. He offered periodic apologies and reassurances that they would soon be on their way, before turning back to the machinery that had failed him so completely.

She couldn't have been more than ten, yet her expression was oddly adult. Exasperation mixed with the effort to control her temper. The fingers of one hand explored the cracks in the log. "It's all right," she called back to her father. "We'll just have to be late."

"I think she's ready to cry," the red fox said, then shook her head. "She's all dressed up for a party. Look at those ribbons in her hair. And she's accustomed to disappointment. You can see it." She turned away. "I can't stand it. I'm going home to my kits."

Erlkönig brushed her tail with a finger as she fled. She'd become quite sensitive in their association, and understood his plight better than any of her predecessors. He watched the girl a little longer, puzzled by her ability to stay so still. She didn't address her father again, although she occasionally turned her head, ever so slightly, pointing an ear in his direction. Then the Lord of the Wood realized her luminous gray eyes never moved, and he understood. He hoped it wasn't too late; that she hadn't already taken on too many burdens as a result of her blindness.

"Come away my child," he whispered, relieved when her face turned in his direction. "Come to the wild."

She looked both puzzled and awed, as she stared at him. Two small hands came up to cover her mouth.

She could see him.

He smiled, but took only the smallest step closer. "My fine girl, will you come away with me? My daughters await your arrival with great anticipation. Together, you will dance and sing."

She turned toward her father, then back to Erlkönig. Because she saw him with pure sight, not human vision, he was the only thing she would see until she abandoned her imperfect physical form. Her beautiful face showed confusion. She frowned.

Never had one hesitated so. She was so near to losing her spark that she could consider her options and choose. "I love you, my child," he whispered. He had to convince her, to save her from the fate her kind faced. While he knew he could use force, make her stay, the very idea repulsed him. "I wish for you to walk Schwartzwald at my side."

As she gazed at him, her expression turned wistful. Finally, she stood and took clumsy steps in his direction. She held her arms out in front of her, as if expecting to run into something, as if disbelieving the one thing her eyes had ever shown her.

"Carefully, my dear," he cautioned. She stepped in a hole and lurched forward. He caught her hands on the way down, pulling her gently from her human body.

She stared at him a moment longer before discovering she could now see everything around her. She flung her arms around his neck, burying her face in his silvery robe. She trembled and would not let go.

He carried her deeper into the forest, away from the road, and soon she calmed. They sat together on the damp earth of the forest floor, and she couldn't stop looking about, running her fingers over the things she could now see. At last, her eyes settled on Erlkönig. "What have I done to deserve this gift?" she asked, her voice no more than a whisper.

"You came to me," he said, patting her hand. "It is the only way I could have done it."

The red fox and her four young kits scampered by, and the girl smiled. "Everything's so beautiful. Especially you, father." She looked at him again.

"Everything within my kingdom is wondrous fair," he said as his long fingers tucked the black strands of hair behind her ears. "And you are in my kingdom."

She blushed, her cheeks momentarily going a brighter blue, then her dark eyes went wide. "But I don't even know what I look like."

Erlkönig smiled and stood, holding one hand down to her. "We can find a pond for you to admire your reflection, and I assure you, you will be pleased."

Together they walked through Schwartzwald, gathering his other children in a large entourage. "I love you, my father," the girl said.

"And I love you," he said. "I love all my stolen children."

She looked straight at him. "Yes. But you will love me best."

Humankind has dominion over much of the Earth, but the forest still has power over it. For Erlkönig of Schwartzwald is not unique to the forest of the world, and some of his kin have less kindly motives. The end of this story is unknown, and only time will determine who will live happily ever after.

An Interview with Speculative Fiction Poet Bryan Thao Worra

by Catherine Lundoff

Bryan Thao Worra is a Laotian American poet, prose writer, and journalist currently living in Minnesota. Born in Vientiane, Laos on January 1, 1973 during the Laotian Secret War (1954-1975), he came to the United States in July, 1973 as the adopted child of an American pilot working in Laos for Royal Air Lao.

Today he is one of the most widely published Laotian writers in the world. His work has appeared in the anthology *Bamboo Among the Oaks*, as well as *Astropoetica*, *Urban Pioneer*, *Unarmed*, the *Asian Pacific Journal* and the *Journal of the Asian American Renaissance*, *Tales of the Unanticipated*, *Dark Wisdom*, *Mad Poets of Terra*, *G-Fan* and *Tripmastermonkey.com* among many others. Thao Worra's work frequently explores a wide range of social and cultural themes, as well as the transient nature of identity and home. His first full-length book of poems, *On The Other Side Of The Eye*, was released in August 2007 from Sam's Dot Publishing.

CL: Can you tell me a bit about your search for your birth mother?

BTW: I grew up with a particular fable:

During the secret war for Laos, my adoptive father was an American pilot for Royal Air Lao and I was told an Australian furniture-maker friend brokered my adoption after a friend of his housekeeper had a son born out of wedlock. My mother was an unmarried widow, and Vientiane was a small town where the gossip was just too much, I was told.

I came to the US in 1973 as the first major American pullouts out of Southeast Asia began.

From that point on, all I had was my mother's name and a photo, clues that would become a key part of my search for her. For a number of different reasons it wasn't until college that I was able to begin an earnest, active search for my family, which took just over 13 years. But the results were ultimately successful.

I finally had the opportunity to travel back to Laos after 30 years in 2003. Years ago, the American embassy in Laos provided me the name of the ancient temple in my mother's village at which our family might have worshipped. It wasn't much to go on, but it turned out the timing of my return was impeccable: At the temple I met an old monk who had just returned from exile in Thailand to his old neighborhood temple in Vientiane.

I held out a paper with my quest translated into Lao: "Do you know Mitthalinh Silosoth? She is my mother."

"Oh, yes," the monk said, "Her sister lived just three blocks away."

I soon found myself in front of this restaurant in one of the most awkward conversations of my life. Through an interpreter, I learned that my biological mother now lived in Modesto, Calif. I had traveled halfway around the world to find out that my mother was living halfway across the United States.

The next day I and my mother talked by telephone. Her first words to me were "Hi, honey. How do you like our country?"

When I finally met her face to face, my mother told me that she also was adopted by an Indian merchant family and accidentally learned in her teens that she was Laotian, not Indian. Accidentally in the sense that my mother grew up in her home believing she was Indian, until one day as she was sweeping in the family courtyard, a strange woman came by and watched her for a few minutes, and when the stranger left, a friend came up and asked, "Did you know who that was?"

"No," my mother replied.

"That was your mother! Don't you know you're

adopted?"

And the details from here became a little convoluted but boiled down to my mother running off to the countryside for a few years before eventually returning back to Vientiane, an unmarried expecting mother. She said my birth father was a farmer who rejected her because she lacked the cooking and farming skills he expected in a wife.

Now, I don't know how much of this story is true. For transcultural adoptees, our lives are written in pencil. Everything you think you know about yourself can change in an instant.

I get occasional questions regarding my father's identity, but this has proven far more fluid and unreliable. As stated before, there was a belief for a time that he might have been a soldier, he might have been a Hmong tribesman, he might have been a hundred different things, really.

At one point during my trip, in a strange cross between *Star Wars* and *Will and Grace*, the old monk tried to tell me he was my father, but my mother firmly informed me that was ridiculous because he was just her best gay friend in Vientiane in the 1960s who used to go to the movies with her.

You just learn to get used to those sorts of things and laugh.

My trip to Southeast Asia involved trips across Bangkok, Phukhet, Chaingmai, Phnom Pennh, and the old Royal Lao capitol of Luang Prabang and the battle-scarred city of Phonsavan and the ancient Plain of Jars, where massive, enigmatic stone urns litter the landscape. And of course, my birth city of Vientiane.

Perhaps a big part of my love for the fantastic and for

CL: Tell me about some of the elements of your personal heritage and cultural history that inspire your work today.

BTW: Without romanticizing it, the secret war for Laos fought between the CIA, the US State Department, the Royal Lao Government and the communist Pathet Lao was immensely influential on my experience. It caused not only a physical and political displacement, but a spiritual one that led me to a constant state of question, of interrogation into the secret nature of

Southeast Asia was for many years both a real place and a mythic place within my consciousness.

speculative literature can be traced to seeing so many more stories reflecting experiences closer to my experience as an adoptee among these characters than among, say, other stories and narratives in the mainstream culture.

There was something particular that I enjoyed reading the stories of Oedipus and Moses, Romulus and Remus and the Peach Boy of Japan, Worf, Batman and Hellboy, or the comic book character, The Question. And even today I more often enjoy seeing the way adopted characters are treated within speculative literature than mainstream dramas and stories that I've often found missed the mark.

things.

Southeast Asia was for many years both a real place and a mythic place within my consciousness, often viewed through filters of other cultures and communities. A line from my poem 'Aftermaths' summed it up as: "I don't have a trace anymore, except the tales of strangers / Who saw my heritage slowly burned away / Timber by timber."

Without getting too complicated, there are several systems of beliefs operant in my old homeland of Laos—animist, shamanic folk religions, iterations of Buddhism influenced by Hinduism, Western and Marxist ideologies, Judeo-Christianity, etc.—each vying for space in the peoples' consciousness.

Despite our history in the 20th century, we're traditionally very averse to conflict, and try to find ways to resolve and reconcile all of these modes of being so we can just get on with things. As a transcultural adoptee who was not fully raised within Lao culture, there are many moments where I have to pause to consider: Am I viewing this as a traditional Laotian would, or through the filters of the West? Or something of a hybrid between the two?

But this is where I think you'll find the taproot to my work. Poetry is one of the forms of writing that thrives on uncertainty and experiment—much more so than

was also something about the punk and anarchist Do-It-Yourself sensibility that resonated with me and has carried me forward since.

Well, that, and an old copy of *Don Quixote* a high school teacher of mine slipped to me as a graduation present.

Today, people often come across my work from my blog posts on my websites and op-eds, or talking with different national magazines, such as *WIRED*, where I was interviewed discussing the impact of low-power FM radio micro transmitters and FCC policy on communities of color, particularly refugee communities.

Taking this kind of a public position of course can

For transcultural adoptees, our lives are written in pencil.

narrative. It is a way of embracing ambiguity without paralysis, being open to outcome rather than attached to outcome. When you use language in narratives—short stories, novels, etc.—you strive for clarity.

For a writer who's working on discussing a secret war where few details weren't classified, and probing the secret histories and mysteries of the world, my background has actually proven rather helpful.

CL: In addition to writing, you do community organizing and anti-racism work. Tell me about the kinds of activism you're involved in.

BTW: Throughout my life this has been a positive and educational process that drives me to discover more and to see more connections between different aspects of my life.

I'm a strong advocate against the use of cluster bombs based on Laos' experience. Three out of ten bombs failed to explode when they were first dropped in the 1960s and '70s. Several examples of my work, including an e-chapbook, *Touching Detonations*, address this issue directly, examining the immediate and long-term consequences such weapons have on our post-war recovery processes. That's a fairly specific issue for me, and is a little more unusual, because I tend to focus on causes reflecting system-wide issues, where a broad involvement can take on many problems at once.

For better or worse, much of my earlier activism was informed by my experiences growing up near Ann Arbor, Michigan and the liberal, radical climate there during the 1980s and early '90s that exposed me to everything from Loompanics books to the work of writers like Heinlein, and comic book writers like Andrew Helfer, Alan Moore, and Dennis O'Neil. There

lead to some very heated discussions, but that's healthy for a democracy. I'd be more worried about a society where we didn't think these dialogues were important. And this is reflected in many of my poems both overtly and more subtly. You can spot this in my poem "Thread Between Stone" in *The Other Side of the Eye*, where I discuss the use of mercenaries and the specter of corruption and the abuse of power.

In the end, I prefer to work with non-profit organizations and causes I can believe in and support, particularly those engaged in community development to make this a better world than we left it. Which can sound and feel somewhat quixotic at times, but leaves me able to sleep at night.

CL: How do you integrate your activism and your writing?

BTW: It's become cliché to say all writing is political. I'm aware that when politics and art come together, it's often creating bad politics, or bad art.

Just the same, however, even when a writer isn't writing overtly about their politics, their subject matter, their grammar and organization of ideas always demonstrate both politics and the way their culture has shaped them. I might liken it to vampire films in which modern characters always act like they've never heard of a vampire, which strikes me as so artificial that we're actually taken out of the suspension of disbelief rather than immersed within it. To write without acknowledging something of the culture and the times you're a part of as an author will most likely mark us in history as either ignorant or foolish. Better by far to take your chances and talk honestly, at least, about what else is of interest to you, or your characters.

This is not necessarily to encourage anachronism within a given text. No one should really relish Reagan-era or Bush-era politics on a story set in the Civil War, but there are larger themes of our times which can and should color our discussions. And when I'm writing poems like "five fragments" or "Oni" these social issues, what might be termed activism is integral to the larger themes of the work.

It informs the text with greater verisimilitude and reminds us that even as we take a fantastic journey of the imaginative soul, we should relate to human elements of our life as well. The trick is always to avoid it being a heavy-handed screed. And I enjoy that challenge. Hopefully I succeed more often than not.

CL: Why write speculative fiction poetry?

BTW: There's a great tradition of speculative poetry that calls to me. I tend to think of not just as a recent phenomenon of the 20th century, but from the earliest roots of our literary and expressive traditions around the world.

But I prefer a lighter spirit when we talk about these things. Even as we talk about the greatness of epic speculative poems such as the *Epic of Gilgamesh*, the *Odyssey* and *Beowulf*, or *The Ramayana* and *The Raven*, we should also always remember to take a look at the work of writers like John Rezmerski, and his book *What Do I Know*. *What Do I Know* provides a delightful example of where speculative poetry can go, with warmth and humor to explore our universe through the language of speculative literature.

Rezmerski takes on everything from Tarzan and Popeye to the older Greco-Roman traditions and many points in between. And though I approach my material from a perspective that draws on more influences from Asia and the speculative media of my generation, I find it an interesting common ground when our works' themes intersect.

For years I'd been writing speculative poetry without being aware that's how it might be read or classified. But as I was assembling my pieces for *On The Other Side Of The Eye*, I found myself amazed at how many poems of mine had always been using the ideas of speculative literature, folklore, and mythology as jump-off points to explore larger issues. Recurring motifs of Oedipus and the monstrous, the galactic and the microscopic, even the Jewish Golem can be consistently found in my poems from the very beginning.

From an experimental point of view, I'm now interested in seeing what can be done really well within speculative fiction poetry, particularly coming at it from a more international approach. In writing, I present myself with many dilemmas and questions, such as: can something timeless be written within the short line structures I tend to favor while using the elements of speculative fiction poetry?

How can I not be curious about that?

CL: You use a lot of horror imagery in your poems, including ghosts, vampires, and Lovecraft. What is it in horror that speaks to and inspires you?

BTW: In my process as a writer I draw from diverse sources, even the pulp fiction of the early 20th century.

Take, for example, the classic pulp fiction character the Shadow, who was a formative part of my youth. The way he was written in the 1980s and 90s showed me, among other things, how one blends world history, pop culture, and dark humor together. Writers all the way up to the present steep the Shadow's story with Asian elements from adventures in Chinatown to the roots of the Shadow's powers (in one interpretation, he

The director Ishiro Honda, said, "Monsters are born too tall, too strong, too heavy; that is their tragedy."

is a paladin of Shamballah, the sacred, secret kingdom hidden in Asia like Shangri La) and they've had varying levels of sensitivity to multicultural issues and how well characters like Dr. Tam and Shiwan Khan are fleshed out.

I've had Asian American peers of mine ask how we can let ourselves be influenced by characters like this. For me, I find that, much as the work of H.P. Lovecraft, Shakespeare, and many others can and must be appreciated with an understanding of the times they were writing in and their personal characters, so too, I think there is much to be enjoyed in the tales of the Shadow and others.

There are many who might worry about the images creatures such as Godzilla or Gamera reinforce in the minds of others about Asians and Asian Americans, but I find that these figures can have literary and artistic merit, themes worth responding to. There's an old quote by the director Ishiro Honda, who said, "Monsters are born too tall, too strong, too heavy; that is their tragedy." In my own writing, I'm most intrigued by the motivations of the 'monstrous' and what they demonstrate to us. Because it's all too easy to find accounts from the perspective of 'the good' who are often little more than the merely victorious.

We're often encouraged to reject the strange, the alien, the foreign except through a lens of opponent and obstacle. But I'm always interested in going where we're not supposed to go, and to suggest that even if we don't ultimately agree with their perspective, that 'The Other' hasn't necessarily arrived on their path unreasonably.

As I and my family and many of my friends come from refugee and immigrant backgrounds, it particularly becomes a point of interest to see things from the 'alien' perspective, and how we express ourselves and our cultures in foreign countries where we are not the majority, but still participants.

5) The master writer, whose work changes whole worlds and stars.

And it is those last ones I particularly enjoy seeking out, though there's not quite the guarantee such a person has written yet, so it behooves me to treat most writers with respect.

But the sixth type of writer? It is 'The Hack,' whose writing doesn't even change how they view their own world.

I often tell people: if you aren't growing from your art, set it aside and find a different path. Because in the end, I think people need to be constantly growing and challenging themselves about who they are and more importantly, what they can become.

So, every now and then I get the question, if I were stranded on a desert island, what book would I take with me. And I've heard people answer everything from the *Bible* to a dictionary and so on, but much like

Every now and then I get the question, if I were stranded on a desert island, what book would I take with me. I think a writer needs to be able to say: My Own.

CL: You said the other night that "I feel like if you're not writing for the world, why are you writing?" What do you see as writing for the world and how does it play out in your work?

BTW: It's funny—I look to the work of Robert Anton Wilson and his Illuminatus trilogy as one of the figures who discussed how we program our perceptions of the world and the shape of our world through different expressions of culture. The Chinese poet Bei Dao and others also expressed this.

Often in poetic circles, you'll find people remarking that what matters is not having millions of people reading you, but knowing that a poem can shift the way different people see the world: politicians, farmers, soldiers, teachers, scientists, anyone, really, and it's hard for us to know the exact consequences most of the time, and even WHEN that encounter will take place but that this IS an effect of our work, our craft.

I see my work operating within a long game—stretching across borders and time. I know writers write for many different reasons, but I keep a personal continuum for myself of at least six types of writers in the world:

1) The egoist, whose writing changes only them.
2) The writer, whose work changes others around them.
3) The good writer, whose work changes their people.
4) The great writer, whose work changes nations.

the Riddle of the Sphinx, I think a writer needs to be able to say: My Own.

Not so much as an exercise of supreme ego, but more from the argument, if you aren't writing a book you'd be proud to take with you to that desert island, or to tuck away among the shelves of the Immortals, good heavens, why are you writing? Just to make the noise of mayflies?

We can and must push ourselves to create great work. Because of my personal life and background, I feel an empathy and affinity for all beings, and it goes against everything within me to produce work that only serves one nation at one point in time in history. I prefer to write with the awareness that my work can impact people as far away as Tehran or Mozambique, the streets of Luang Prabang or Toronto, as much as in Minnesota or Boston.

So, when a poem like "Whorl" takes us on a journey from Europe to Japan to Minnesota or "Thread Between Stone" journeys from Ancient Greece and Egypt to the Clinton years in Washington DC, this is from a classic cosmopolitan mindset. I am a citizen of the world, above all, and I ought to write remembering that.

And thus far, my readers around the world have appreciated that.

CL: Tell me about your new book.

BTW: *On The Other Side Of The Eye* is a distillation of 17 years of my work from over 60 international journals and literary projects. But more than that, it's a full-length book of Laotian American speculative poetry that decenters our traditional expectations of speculative poetry. It proposes a view of the future from perspectives other than 'our own,' one in which other cultures, other societies articulate a sense of the future after the great and minor wars of Earth, and how we all might eke out a place in that future. It goes both galactic and microscopic, even subatomic, local and global, trying to show readers what life might or might not be like when seen from a different vantage point.

On The Other Side Of The Eye is subversive in a friendly way. Critics who've seen early iterations of it have likened it to "Chaos, but controlled chaos." It's a fair assessment. One might liken it to a precursor to the Cityspeak of *Blade Runner*, exploring which words, which ideas from other communities will make their way successfully into the New Languages of Earth.

Even when you think you're looking at something 'familiar,' watch out, because very rarely do those familiar things in *On The Other Side Of The Eye* stay that way. A good example of this is shown in poems like "The Deep Ones" or "Thread Between Stone," in which iconic figures and myths who are familiar to most readers from the U.S. or Europe are 're-imagined' from the lenses of cultures that are historically minority voices in the construction and repetition of those myths and ideas.

endnotes. In Michigan, my teachers were fond of saying 'sometimes, common sense ain't so common,' which wasn't good English, but it got the point across. Often the response to what we presume to be foreign and unfamiliar concepts and what we presume to be common, everyday knowledge among our friends and readers will in reality surprise you.

At one point in my endnotes, I clearly lay out that all glossaries, and by extension, all commentaries and annotations are made by humans, and 'always suspect.' I took a large cue from Jorge Luis Borges' famous discussion of a certain Chinese encyclopedia in which things were categorized by seemingly random or 'illogical' and arbitrary categories, and the wry observations of writers like Ambrose Bierce and his notorious *Devil's Dictionary*.

I found myself confronting one of the great puzzles of the ages, especially as a writer writing from a polycultural perspective in English. I'm cognizant of the international character of my readership and my relationship not just to North American writing, but to all writing, all expressive art, really, from around the world and across many different times. This particularly impacts my process as I consider the appropriate use of symbols and allusion.

It became clear that I was discussing relatively obscure concepts regarding Lao and Southeast Asian culture, but also that there were obscure concepts within American and European culture I made

I am a citizen of the world, above all, and I ought to write remembering that.

CL: *Eye* **includes endnotes defining some of the references in your poems, from the Plain of Jars in Laos to the Frigidaire. How did you decide what got explanatory notes and what didn't?**

BTW: At the beginning I wasn't going to include an explanatory glossary section or endnotes.

Often, there's a sense of cultural politics at play, subtly dictating and implying what is 'foreign,' what is 'Other' and not a part of a writer's society. And I often thought of them as rather clichéd things to integrate into any book, but especially a book of poetry, where one often hopes the ideas and the words will 'stand by themselves' on their own terms. Especially in a time when one can as easily look a word up online as in a dictionary and get VERY extensive results returned back to them.

That was probably a major turning point as I made the final decision to include in a set of terms and references to. While I grew up frequently hearing the phrases "Tabula Rasa" and "Ockham's Razor" used around me, or the old tales of Greco-Roman gods and Titans, there are many who've forgotten or never even heard these stories at all. And the more I considered it, there were even some more 'common' concepts that might be well served by a note that 're-imagines,' 're-informs' our perception of these concepts.

As I was constructing the endnotes, I was presented with a question, an option to provide a dry, 'straight' run that would be presumably helpful for some humorless student who was woefully unfamiliar with a given term. And the more I looked over the varied terms, and the implications the selection of each term implied, I realized that an impersonal voice, stripped of personality, ran counter to the entire point of the book as a whole.

I'm sincere in how I define the terms, but the point

of poetry is to help us look at both the strange and the familiar in new ways. In many ways, it is this 'reflective' process that then became the true key to understanding *On The Other Side Of The Eye* as a whole. The typical reader goes into the text reading the poem first and emerges with a particular sense of things. Which, depending on particular poems, could require a complete re-imagination of the poem after reading the endnotes 'attached' to it.

It is not that the reader is necessarily incorrect with their first reading of the poem, but that they will be presented with an alternate perspective other than what they initially suspected to be present. And now we must consider what we do with our old perceptions of such things. Do we discard them, modify them or retain them as a more proper perspective?

Some have suggested the endnotes are a whole poem in itself. I won't necessarily disagree.

CL: What new projects are you working on?

BTW: I'm working on several follow-up books of speculative fiction poetry, including one about an imagined Laotian space program in the future and what it would take to get there, including a dialogue with the past that's predicting its creation. I'm almost done with a collection of my short Southeast Asian American horror stories, and I've proposed a possible anthology project of Asian American speculative poets. We'll see where that goes.

CL: What other Asian/Asian American speculative poets and writers would you recommend to *TOTU* readers?

BTW: There are a growing number of texts I'd say fall within the heading of speculative poetry from Asian American writers. The work of Hmong American writer Burlee Vang in Fresno, California particularly interests me for the directions his work has been taking. Shanxing Wang's *Mad Science In Imperial City* and Cathy Park Hong's *Dance Dance Revolution* are both recently published; I've found their approach very intriguing and innovative and really raising the bar.

In Minnesota, we have a number of very talented poets whose work I think we should be paying attention to. Sun Yung Shin's *Skirt Full of Black* features a number of poems, including her "Flower I, Stamen and Pollen" cycle that should be easily recognized as speculative poetry. And Japanese American poet David Mura has a short cycle, "Neuromancer Poetics," featured in his collection *Angels for the Burning* that is quite interesting.

Of course, many of us are also familiar with Vietnamese American poet Bao Phi's "Godzilla Sestina," and I know he's working on some great new pieces right now, drawing on both his experiences in Minneapolis' inner city and popular speculative culture. Hmong writer Ka Vang also has some very extraordinary pieces that draw on both her experience as a Hmong refugee and living in a world influenced by Star Trek, science fiction, and horror. You can easily spot this in both her short fiction and poetry, and it's tremendously wide-ranging and informed.

Out in California, I'm paying close attention to the work of Filipina American poet Barbara Jane Reyes and her upcoming project *Diwata*, which, much like *Gravities of Center* and *Poeta En San Francisco* are linguistically really ambitious texts that make use of mythology, history, culture, and many elements of speculative poetry.

Another Filipino American poet / spoken word artist I'm keeping an eye on is Anthem Selgado. His poem "Time and Money" really stands out for me as a stirring expression of the Asian American and human experience within cosmic efforts to contact life on other planets. If you can hear it in live performance or online, it's an experience that can really shift the way you look at things.

I'm just now starting to become familiar with the work of the Lao American singer Ketsana, whose work is really, really radical from typical Lao rock and roll music. She's influenced by films such as *Blade Runner* and other speculative work, and while the impact of these source isn't necessarily present in all of her work, I think it bears watching over time.

So, as you can see, my proposed anthology of Asian American speculative poetry won't be lacking in established writers. Hopefully, as we do a call for submissions, we'll see even more writers emerge who are also doing work in speculative poetry.

Perhaps it's best to say for now: this first book is not the last.

TENTACLE 2

Flashes of light
the green or blue sexual
flickers of seed shrimp
scavenging sea-beds
in tens of thousands of species
iridescent antennae
signalling through their swarms
lush need;
making their own illumination
swales of plankton
celebrate the evolution of the visual
angelfish mirrors blind their rivals on the reef
and in the depths
weird linear jellies and angular monsters
ripple and glow.
We see
for the excess of beauty
and thanks to some trilobite
with a newfangled cell—
engendering
explosion of shapes, of camoflage, of every sign and sigil
beckoning seduction, of mimicry, of bluff,
and of hard-shelled protection, speed
and weaponry, against the fabulous technology of lens and retina
impelling the Cambrian and every after age—
one sense
repelling form from form like magnet-tips
in scurries to make the best escapes
or better lures.

—CAMILLA DECARNIN

Stephen Couch's TOTU *debut would have been a natural fit for either our "Monsters" issue (#27) or "Heroes" issue (#28). It is authentically creepy, and its hero is stalwart.*

Fort

by Stephen Couch

There were monsters scant inches away from his face, but they couldn't touch him.

And goodness knew they were trying.

Patrick scooted against the back wall of the fort as a monster thrust its bent nose to the peephole in front, snuffling, scenting him. It withdrew, trailing a runnel of snot behind that clung to the fabric of the cushions, seeping and staining.

He could hear the monster snort with frustration, grunting something to its companions. Another stepped up to the fort, a yellow eye peeking in the gap at Patrick. It wagged a finger at him: *Naughty, naughty*.

Patrick pushed against the back wall harder, feeling the unyielding hardness of the sofa behind him. He felt to the sides, checking for gaps, stretching his arms out, and bopped one of the springy walls too hard.

The other walls of the fort wobbled as the side shifted. The gap in front widened, and Patrick could hear the monsters jabber with enthusiasm at the sight. Patrick froze.

The monsters' excitement died down as it became apparent the fort wasn't going to collapse. As they went back to shuffling around the living room, Patrick was aware they were the only source of sound in the house. The crying he'd taken to be Mommy had stopped several minutes ago.

The louder noises, the screaming, had only lasted a few seconds at the beginning. Patrick had been ensconced in his fort, having pulled the cushions from the sofa and arranged them in their standard shape: the square cushions of the main sofa on three sides, and the long piece from the recliner section on top.

Popcorn and soda at hand, Patrick had poked the remote through the viewing gap in front and changed over to the *Monster Mash* on Channel 11.

Monster Mash always started out with screams and thunder over the theme music, so Patrick didn't notice the noises coming from the kitchen were real until the TV had dissolved to Doctor Freakenstein introducing the night's features…and the yelling and crashing had continued.

Now, only the monsters made sound: dragging their feet, growling, giggling; whispering things to each other. The TV had gone out when Daddy had been thrown into it, cracking its screen. Daddy had fallen to the floor in a heap, but inside the fort Patrick didn't have a good angle to see if he'd gotten up again.

He knew he hadn't, all the same.

Patrick could still see his grey reflection in the busted TV screen: a pair of eyes peeking out from a small cube in front of the sofa. He thought about a movie he'd watched with Daddy once, where prisoners were locked inside a metal box for punishment.

Patrick squirmed in place; part fear, part bladder. He didn't want to pee, but his body was telling him otherwise. He hadn't been able to go to the bathroom before he made the fort, because Lizzy had been taking her bath.

…Lizzy.

Patrick almost stood up with shock. His little sister's bedtime had come and gone. She'd bathed and been tucked in after a hard day of twirling practice and running around like a maniac.

Patrick knew, then. Lizzy was aware of what all children were aware of: if you hid under the covers and stayed very still, monsters couldn't find you.

Lizzy was still alive, hiding in her bed. She had to be. The alternative was freaking out and getting eaten; no sane child would want that.

He could get to her, and they could find some way out of this. He just had to figure out how to get upstairs without getting eaten himself. Except the only way

he could escape getting chomped up was if he stayed inside the fort.

So if he couldn't leave the fort to get to Lizzy, he'd have to bring it along with him.

The monsters all grunted and hooted with curiosity as Patrick began working. He grabbed a join with each hand—the inside edges where two wall cushions met—and started scooting with his butt across the floor. Half a foot, and half a foot more. The carpet rumpled his flannel pajama bottoms as he shifted, but it was better than rug burn on his kiester.

One wall caught his can of soda as it moved, knocking it over with a gurgling splash. Patrick tried to scoot as fast as he could to get away from the growing pool of soft drink as it soaked into the carpet.

He let himself think, *The rug—Mom's gonna kill me*, even as tears stung his eyes. He held them in as best he could.

Patrick reached the end of the sofa with a few more quick butt-hops, dragging the capsized soda can and popcorn bowl along with him, and another problem presented itself: the fort had no back wall. The sofa had always performed that function in the past, but then the fort had never had to be mobile before.

The monsters gathered around the fort, moving when it moved, waiting for the structure to come apart or for an opening to appear. Patrick fancied he could hear their stomachs rumbling. A bloodshot eye at the end of a stalk appeared, bobbing in front of the peephole, and then pulled away.

From this end of the sofa, Patrick could see the front door standing wide open, the porch light illuminating a small section of the yard, but nothing of the suburban street beyond. Patrick could see more monsters wandering around in the yard, the grass wilting where their feet touched.

They could be everywhere, said a voice in his head. *In every house on the street. Even if you save Lizzy, then what will you do?*

"I'll burn that bridge when I come to it," he whispered.

Daddy always used to say that to Mommy.

This time he let a single tear leak out.

Patrick sniffed and considered his position. If he managed to get up against the wall, he'd only have to sidle down a short way to the stairs. Once up on the second floor, Lizzy's room would be the first on the right.

He felt a creak from behind him. A monster had jumped up on the cushion-less sofa, and was prowling around the back of the fort, just waiting for a hole big enough. He could smell its diarrhea breath wafting through the gaps that already existed. The folded frame of the hide-a-bed creaked again as the monster jumped off the sofa.

Patrick unclenched his hands from the corners, feeling pins and needles shoot along his fingers. The fort settled a bit, but sat firm. He shifted around, bumping into the bowl.

He really, *really* needed to pee now. Patrick grabbed the empty soda can, wincing as a little bolt of static zapped him and, trying not to think about what his parents would say, did his business.

Patrick wrinkled his nose as the smell filled the fort. Holding the wobbly, sloshing can, he forced it through the gap in front as best he could.

Something snatched it from his grasp, dirty nails rattling against the metal, skittering down toward Patrick's fingers. He withdrew his hand and the can vanished from sight.

From the noises they made, the monsters were obviously hoping to have retrieved a better prize. They stomped about, and Patrick heard the can clunk against a wall, splattering pee everywhere. One of them jumped back on the sofa, snarling and clawing at the back of the fort, and then leaped over the fort to land in front, shrieking.

Patrick caught sight of it through the peephole as it raged at him, and wished he hadn't. It was the ugliest one yet.

The monster shook its head, filthy hair flying in a storm around it, and thrust a hand at the gap as hard as it could.

Patrick could hear the bones in its fingers snap as they reached the gap, striking an invisible barrier. The thing's fingers twisted and compressed, squirting blackish fluid from the joints where they ruptured.

Patrick only thought it had been screaming before. The monster wheeled and thrashed on the ground, holding its crushed hand. The other creatures turned from what they were doing to watch its pain. One less competitor, as far as they were concerned, but it would at least be fun to watch it hurt.

Patrick grabbed the joins of the fort again and scooted around the corner of the sofa as fast as he could, while the monsters were distracted. He reached the side and kept going, getting the back of the fort against the living room wall before the monsters could react.

Once he'd reached the wall, though, they were all over the fort again, clustering around, crowding the structure. None could approach any closer than an inch or so away, but they crammed in, looking in the peephole at Patrick, licking their scabbed lips.

Patrick knew the minute he reached the stairs and the back of the fort was exposed to the open stairwell, it was all over. They'd snatch him out of his safe place, and….

Just like they've already done to Lizzy, said the voice.

"Shut up," Patrick whispered. The monsters gurgled with amusement. Supper was talking to itself.

She squirms, the voice continued. *You know that, because every time Uncle Terry comes to visit you have to share her bed. She kicks and sprawls out and hogs the covers.*

"Shut up!"

She moved, and they saw her. You're only safe under the covers if you stay still, Patrick.

"You don't know anything," Patrick said. "Anything."

You'll be happy that she's gone. Remember how she wet the bed? Mommy makes her sleep on a towel now, so she doesn't ruin another mattress. Stupid Lizzy.

Patrick gritted his teeth and seized the joins, ready to start scooting again, to get away, something, anything. He made a couple of butt-hops, enough to get him right next to the stairwell, and stopped.

End of the line. Go forward and get eaten; go backward and wind up where he started. He could keep going in reverse, go to the other end of the sofa and work his way around the far wall of the living room, but eventually he'd have to pass in front of the entertainment center.

Daddy's body would be in the way.

Now the tears came unhindered.

Gone. Mom and Dad were gone. And here Patrick was, stuck inside his little fort, waiting for the firemen or police or somebody to come along and save him.

Except if his *parents* couldn't stop the monsters, what made him think anyone else could?

Patrick's sobbing subsided into hitching breaths, and at last exhausted silence. Even the monsters had stopped making noise, fascinated by the sounds coming from inside the fort.

Patrick sat there, his back to the hard wall, staring at the monsters through the peephole, feeling his legs fall asleep.

He wondered if there were any adults—or children—still alive on his street. Or in the town.

Or in the world. Was it just him, sitting in this fort, the only human being left on an Earth eaten alive by monsters?

It couldn't be. There were other kids who knew the rules, who knew how to stay alive. They had to be out there somewhere, trapped just like Patrick.

His cousins, for sure. They were the ones who had taught him how to make a fort in the first place, as well as the ones who had introduced him to the *Monster Mash* Saturday nights. They had been on the hide-a-bed, and had set up Patrick inside the fort to watch his very first scary movies. Only the fort had been different: with the bed unfolded, it hadn't been up against the sofa. It had been to the side, in the middle of the living room floor.

They had draped a sheet over the fort for its back wall.

Mommy had been doing laundry tonight; it's what she always did Saturday nights after putting Lizzy to bed. She called it her "dancing substitute," and Daddy always gave a little half-smile, half-frown when she said it.

The laundry basket, and sheets, would be in the kitchen nook, just off the living room.

Past the stairs.

Patrick let go of the joins, clenching and unclenching his fists. What could he do? There was no way he could scoot past the stairwell fast enough to avoid getting grabbed. He needed something to protect himself, something that could shield him just long enough…

He shifted, and bumped the popcorn bowl.

He needed what every good solider needed, whether they were inside a fortress or not: a helmet.

Patrick grabbed the bowl and considered his plan. If he mistimed things, he'd be toast. One mistake, one hesitation, and that was it for him and Lizzy.

He grabbed handfuls of oily, cold popcorn and began thrusting them through the peephole. The monsters, intrigued, shuffled around to the front of the fort to check out this new development.

Once it seemed like all of them had gathered around to the front, Patrick slapped the bowl onto his head, grabbed the joins, and scooted for all he was worth.

Two hops and he had lined up with the stairwell.

One of his popcorn-greasy hands slipped, losing its grip.

Patrick kept going, colliding with one of the fort walls before he could react.

The fort wobbled, leaning to one side. Patrick wiped his hands on his pajamas, not aware of how loudly he was yelling, and grabbed the inside corners again, arresting the fort's collapse.

He heard something behind him, felt its breath ruffle his PJs.

Patrick cringed on reflex as the whatever-it-was lashed out for his collar, striking the bowl instead.

Patrick heard and felt the impact as the monster's hand struck the helmet. It gave the ring of metal, not the thump of plastic. The monster cried out and withdrew.

Patrick butt-hopped like a maniac. Just past the stairwell the fort met resistance, but he kept going, pushing, until he felt it rumple and slide underneath the fort wall.

He stopped as his mother's fingernails jabbed into his bottom.

Patrick screamed, looking down at the arm jutting under the wall.

The monsters made noises along with him, mocking.

Patrick's yell tapered off into a croak. His mother's arm lay there, palm up, still attached to her body, it seemed.

He couldn't scoot any further, not with her in the way.

His eyes were drawn to the peephole by movement. Monsters were looking in on him again. One of them frowned and traced a warty finger down its eye to its chin: *Boo-hoo.*

Movement, from inside the fort. Patrick started, and the helmet slipped down over his eyes.

He righted it just in time to see Mommy's arm sliding back out.

He turned back to look outside as Mommy peeked through the peephole at him.

The monster was standing out of range, but Patrick could see its huge claws palming Mommy's head like a basketball, lifting her up from the ground. Another scaly hand came around and squeezed her cheeks. Something, somewhere, made high-pitched cooing noises as the puppeteer waggled the head.

It sounded like, "There, there."

Patrick shrieked and shut his eyes, clamping his hands over his ears. He pushed back, bumping against the hard wall. The helmet bobbled down over his face again and his screams were echoed, amplified, forced back into his ears. Stunned, he stopped yelling, folding himself up. He clenched his teeth and cried silently.

Just stand up. That's all you have to do. Just stand up, and all this will be over.

Patrick muttered, "Shut up shut up shut up," and pawed for the joins, eyes still blurry. He began moving the fort away from the stairs, not listening to the noises the monsters were making, not looking out the peephole to see his mother's face. He scooted until he felt things sliding under the wall, then he hit something; it had to be the overturned laundry basket.

Patrick wiped his eyes and looked down, catching a brief glimpse of the face dancing in front of the fort. He gritted his teeth and looked at the spilled, folded laundry he had run over.

He caught his breath, staring at the floral patterns. Thinking about it, he couldn't use a sheet; it would be too long, and he worried about it dragging along behind him, pulling out so far that it created a canopy the monsters could slip under. He needed something that would cover the back of the fort but not billow out too much.

Something like what he'd run over: one of Lizzy's freshly cleaned bedwetting towels.

Patrick grabbed the corner of the towel and pulled the rest of it inside the fort. He turned around as best he could and tucked it in where the roof and walls connected at the back. It stretched across the entire opening, easily reaching the ground.

Patrick turned back around, got a grip, and stared out at his mother's face. Her eyes were pointing different directions, her jaw hanging slack.

"Move," he said. He scooted the fort forward a foot, then another.

A monster reached back into the gap between the fort and wall. Patrick heard its fingers strike the towel, failing to penetrate. It grunted with anger, barking something to its fellows.

He saw out through the front. Whichever thing held his mother picked her up by her head and threw her into the kitchen. Patrick saw her strike the unfolded ironing board, landing in a tangle with it and the plugged-in iron.

She was upside down, looking right at him.

He saw smoke begin to rise from her clothing where the iron had landed.

Patrick gasped and turned away, still wanting to cry but not finding the tears anymore. He scooted the fort back to the wall, and over to the stairs.

Hunching, he placed his back against the roof of the fort, still gripping the corners. Trying not to stand as quickly as he lifted, he hoisted the unstable fort along with him as he stepped onto the first stair, setting the whole thing down once he'd finished. The structure leaned, but stayed firm. The towel, tucked in between sections, seemed to be helping keep it all together.

Patrick kept a firm grip, and prepared to lift from a crouch again.

One step down, twelve to go.

The worst part of the ascent was the static electricity. As Patrick scooted, the stupid towel kept drifting inside to cling to his pajamas. Patrick would stop, shake it loose, and move a little further.

He had turned the fort sideways; it seemed to take sitting at an angle better that way. As he moved, he could see family photos along the stairway wall: the family at Six Flags; Lizzy with a Lil' Twirlers trophy; his parents' wedding picture, both of them wearing the clothes he always laughed at.

He was almost to the top step. Patrick gritted his teeth, grabbed and rose one last time, mindful of the monsters prowling up the stairs after him, as well as the ones no doubt waiting for him on the second floor.

As he prepared to set down at the top, the smoke detector went off.

With everything else that had happened, its blaring beeps were one shock too many.

Patrick stood straight up, demolishing the fort.

For one awful moment, for four whole beeps of the smoke alarm, Patrick and the monsters stared at each other through the narrow stairwell.

Patrick broke first, running for Lizzy's room, hearing the creatures bay as they stormed up after him. Something at the far end of the hall poked its head out of the bathroom and, seeing Patrick, loped in pursuit.

At the halfway point of Lizzy's small room, Patrick leapt for the bed, seeing eyes winking underneath it. He hit the mattress, yanked the covers, and scrambled under them, his helmet lolling around on his head.

Lizzy looked at him with wide eyes, and Patrick clamped a hand over her mouth before she could make a peep.

They both lay very, very still.

Even over the din of the alarm, they could hear the things prowling around the room.

If the firemen weren't coming to rescue you before, they sure will now.

Patrick thought about firemen creeping into the house inside little sofa-cushion forts, and almost laughed.

Almost, as he felt the warm breath of something leaning over the bed as it tried to smell him through the safety of the sheets.

Were they really going to hide here? Go from the halfway-mobile fort to being completely trapped in the bed?

He was on his stomach, Lizzy on her back beside him. She wasn't even on her towel; it had rumpled up underneath Patrick.

The alarm kept spiking Patrick's ears. There was no way they could wait long enough for help to arrive, but there was nothing he could do.

Some soldier he was.

Patrick spied something shiny through the small gap at the top of the sheet. Lizzy's Lil' Twirlers baton. She'd gotten her award for dropping it the fewest number of times out of all the contestants.

Patrick blinked. Soldiers weren't the only ones who wore helmets.

He felt the breath of the thing withdraw and looked over at Lizzy again. He tried to tell her, with his eyes, that everything was going to be all right.

She didn't look as if she spoke eye language.

Patrick reached out, snatched the baton leaning against the headboard, and threw the covers back. The monsters froze as Patrick leapt from the bed.

As he twisted, static stuck Lizzy's towel to his back; the free end flapped behind him as he moved.

Soldier. Knight. Superhero.

With a scream, Patrick swung his new sword into the monsters, cutting a swath. Green and red goop sprayed across the room as Lizzy sat up in bed and screamed along.

The thing under the bed scuttled out, all claws and tentacles, and Patrick ran it through with a downward thrust, pulling out just in time to bisect something else running toward him.

The monsters kept coming, and Patrick kept killing.

He felt blows glance off his helmet, the ringing of them harmonizing with the smoke detector. The level of haze was growing in the room. Patrick slashed away, each blow connecting, each strike felling another creature.

He stopped swinging when he realized he and Lizzy were the only ones still making noise.

Coughing in the tainted air, knee-deep in dead monsters, Patrick slogged back over to the bed, holding out a hand for Lizzy. She had scurried back in the corner, holding her pillow in front of her.

"Mommy?" she said. "Daddy?"

Patrick shook his head.

Lizzy buried her face in the pillow. Patrick climbed up on the bed and held her for a few seconds, the smoke in the room building.

"We have to go," he said with a cough, after waiting as long as he could.

"I can't," Lizzy said. "I'm scared."

Patrick picked her up and she clung close to him, weeping into his shoulder.

"There's not anything to be afraid of," he said. "Not anymore."

They hared down the hallway to Patrick's room, running in a low crouch under the gathering black smoke. Patrick's window had access to a big oak tree. He smashed out the glass with his sword, and then gave it to Lizzy, taking his own softball bat for himself.

He looked around his room one final time. He felt a small pang, thinking of all the toys and games he was leaving behind to be destroyed.

He thought about his parents.

There were tears, but he convinced himself they came from the smoke.

Together, Patrick and Lizzy climbed out the window into the tree.

From this height, they could see what had become

of the neighborhood. At least one other house was on fire, and monsters ran everywhere.

They ran with fear, fleeing the children that chased them.

Patrick climbed down and caught Lizzy when she jumped. They ventured onto the front lawn, watching the slaughter.

Children in helmets made from pots and colanders yelled with fury as they took down monsters with tennis rackets, hockey sticks, and brooms. A girl from a few houses down was shooting fireballs from a wand that used to be part of a Halloween costume.

"…Mess with a *princess*, huh?" she jeered, chasing something trying to shake flames from its six limbs.

Lizzy stared as they ran by.

Patrick reached down and squeezed her shoulder. "…Do you want to go help?" he asked, pointing down the street. A group of children were rousting a house, driving monsters out to be killed.

Lizzy looked back at the house, biting her lip. Patrick reached around and wiped away her tears. They'd stop, in time.

"Mom and Dad helped us as much as they could," he said, crouching down in front of her. "But we've just got each other now. And I don't know how far this," he waved at the chaos of the neighborhood, "goes."

Lizzy looked down the street, sniffed and, looking up at Patrick, nodded.

Patrick took her hand and they walked away, wielding their weapons as their house began collapsing in on itself, sending gouts of ash and spark into the air. An army of children was massing, moving beyond the street to encompass the block, the city. They moved from house to house, from battle to battle.

There were fights to be won, and foes to be defeated.

There were forts to be torn down.

harakiruspex n.   device which simultaneously eviscerates a selected subject and determines the operator's auspices. From Jp. *hara-kiri*, suicide by self-disembowelment, and L. *haruspex*, a minor priest who interpreted the entrails of public sacrifices.

euthanaugury n.   multi-function task performed by harakiruspex. From Gk. *euthanasia*, easy death, and L. *auguri*, soothsaying.

FUN WITH INNARDS!

WELCOME to the home appliance of the future! This handy dual-purpose A.L.P.O.* gadget combines assisted suicide with divination, carefully eviscerating your "loved ones" in the clinically sterile setting** of your own home and then immediately predicting your future from the still-quivering entrails! Bringing together the ancient cultural traditions of classical Roman haruspicy and the revered Japanese custom of hara-kiri, this solid, stately, artistic state-of-the-art solid state device incorporates a miniaturized mainframe computer***, a woodblock printer for that rustic look (no need for messy ink refills! uses victim's own blood!), five 1000-lb. test cable restraints and eight different slicing blades that <u>never</u> need sharpening! Glossy easy-care finish in 783 decorator colors!

Order **NOW** and get one-size-fits-all**** pet attachment <u>*free*</u>! (The first fifty orders received also get free pet <u>food</u> attachment!)

Included! Rear mounting slots for wing inserts (extra)! Select from black swan, bat or manta ray! Activate attachment for gentle flutter to lend dignity and excitement to your <u>personalized</u> ritual!

Your **ALPO harakiruspex** can also be pre-set to shoulder the burden of deciding when the right time has come for your family member to pass on. Simply turn the illuminated shoulder dial to the appropriate criterion (selections range from "Minor Incontinence And Nagging" to "Screaming Desperately for Expensive Drugs At All Hours Of The Day And Night") and when the conditions are met it will conduct a rapid disembowelment of the subject without bothering to consult you again! It also prints out a funerary elegy based on the pre-sacrificial writhings and verbal commentary of the victim.

(Local licensing, criminal code violations and other trivia are the responsibility of the purchaser.)

* Artificial Lethal Psychic Obsequator
** not provided
*** CD software available includes ButcherSoft, Innard Interpreter and ObitWorks
**** not intended for livestock over 50 lbs.

—**F. J. BERGMANN**

ET Cleaning Crew Terrifies Teen

TOTU Tattler Exclusive by Terry Faust - Minneapolis

Sixteen-year-old Chip Rummage, Albert Lea, Minnesota, awoke to the bone-chilling sight of four small gray-skinned aliens at the head of his bed. What happened next has authorities baffled and Chip hopping mad. At two a.m. visitors from another world cleaned his room.

"At first I thought it was a joke...the kind of stunt my mother would pull," the shocked boy said. "But these guys didn't lecture me about cleaning, didn't say a word about not seeing the floor...or socks that walk by themselves – none of that!"

After shoveling mounds of snack wrappers and soda cans into a micro-wormhole trash transporter, the aliens discovered articles of the boy's clothing. Chip watched in horror as his ripped T-shirts and torn jeans were vaporized. Authorities later determined the aliens used liquid hydrogen and gamma radiation to sanitize Chip's remaining garments. Particularly tough stains received bursts from what he described as... "A phaser cannon. It was awesome!"

But Chip's ordeal did not end with his laundry.

"I was so shocked I could not move," said the teenager. "They hosed some of my best clothes! I was mad.

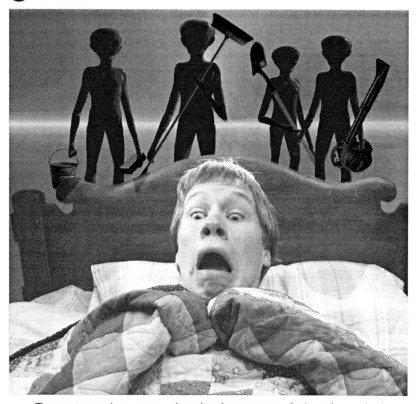

Terror turned to anger then back to terror during the ordeal

But then they took out this thing that looked like a leaf blower with a thyroid problem!"

Years of accumulated dust bunnies, cobwebs and gum wrappers vanished in one sweeping blast. Using what NRC officials determined were atomic mops, the ETs then scrubbed the ceiling, walls, windows, and floor, removing even the most difficult ground-in dirt. They straightened his dresser drawers, cleaned his desk and removed Barney stickers from his bed's baseboard.

"I didn't mind losing the stickers," Chip said.

However, Chip remembers going ballistic when the aliens lifted and dusted his personal possessions.

"Everything was totally where I wanted it. They were screwing up my room!"

Shouting at the aliens did not stop them. And when the six-foot-two teenager decided to get physical, the aliens apparently read his mind.

"They pulled out a tube thing and shot me with a beam."

Paralyzed, the boy could only watch in horror as the creatures finished cleaning.

Chip doesn't remember falling asleep, but the sound of his mother's screams woke him.

Mrs. Rummage exclaimed,

"Everything was totally where I wanted it. They were screwing up my room!"

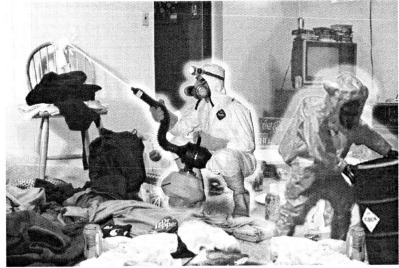
Aliens wore protective clothing during hazardous portions of the cleanup.

"I haven't seen his floor for three years. The dirty underwear was gone, his desk was clear, even his dresser was tidy. I did what any mother would have done. I screamed and fainted."

No longer paralyzed, Chip rushed to his mother, urging her to get up and make him breakfast.

Despite Chip's insistence that aliens cleaned his room, experts are skeptical.

"I have a teenage son myself and I don't believe four aliens alone could tackle the job," said Hobart Newdanger, author of *You May be from Venus but Your Children are from Neptune*.

Other authorities offered similar opinions. Harold Tirebiter, Regional Deputy Chief Deputy for Homemade Security in Southern Minnesota, could not rule out the cleaning as the work of terrorists and declared a Burnt Umber Alert.

The entire Rummage family has refused further comment before the release of their book, *Close Encounters of the Sanitary Kind*.

Pressed to counter the doubt of experts familiar with alien contact scenarios, Mrs. Rummage said, "I absolutely believe Chip. It's the only way his room would ever get that clean. Now I know why they are called mother ships!"

"I don't believe four aliens alone could tackle the job."
Hobart Newdanger - skeptic

Chip's mom has no doubt the cleanup was of extraterrestrial origin.

Michael Pignatella's TOTU *debut packs a powerful emotional wallop.*

A Heart is the Size of a Clenched Fist
by Michael A. Pignatella

Charlie Voss stumbled upon the hand early one midsummer's morning, just as he was about to call it a day. The tide was coming in and he wouldn't have even noticed it if the wind hadn't whipped up, blowing sand and causing him to turn his face to the ocean. It was about two feet out into the surf, at times submerged by the incoming tide. A hand, sticking straight out of the sand, clenched in a fist. Charlie was so shocked that he almost dropped his metal detector.

His first thought was that someone was fooling around. He dismissed that as foolishness. No one could survive long buried like that. No, what he had here was a dead body. Some poor schmuck who had gone out fishing without checking the weather, or had swam too far out and been sucked under by a rip tide, or had cramped up tight like gritted teeth and had sunk to the bottom. Whatever had happened, he was dead. He walked into the surf to take a closer look.

He winced at the chilling water. Despite having lived on Cape Cod his whole life, he hated going into the ocean. He hated the gritty residue left by salt water, hated when a piece of slippery seaweed stuck to his leg like a leech. Hated his mouth filling with sea water, like swallowing the brine from a pickle jar. His face might be weather-beaten and craggy, but in his heart he was a landlubber.

He scratched his short beard as he crouched in front of the hand, running his fingers through the white stubble like blintzes rolling in powdered sugar. It was a hand all right, a man's hand clenched in a tight fist, the fingernails dirty, curly reddish wisps of hair matted on the back. *The poor guy couldn't have died long ago,* thought Charlie, *he hasn't even begun to rot.* No small feat, given how fast things decayed in the ocean. Or were devoured. A wave crashed in, burying the hand for a moment, spraying Charlie and the metal detector.

"Sonofabitch," Charlie said, wiping the metal detector on his shirt. It was supposed to be waterproof, but it had cost him almost 300 bucks, not a small sum for an old man who had to make do with his crappy Social Security allotment and who paid for his heart medication by cleaning the local pharmacy from top to bottom twice a month. At night, of course, so that the well-heeled tourists from Boston and Connecticut wouldn't have real life intrude on their vacations.

He needed the metal detector. At least until he found what he was looking for. He bent back down to the hand. "I suppose I should get the authorities," he said to it. Without thought, he reached over and touched it.

It was cool, but not cold. Charlie looked at it, scratching his beard again. It was as if it was waiting for something, something other than the tide. Charlie slid his hand down to the wrist, feeling for, of all things, a pulse. There was none.

"Dead," he said, as if saying it out loud made it so. He stood up, his back protesting. He'd need to get the police, putting an end to today's searching. Not that he had found anything worthwhile. Eighty-three cents and a gold earring that he could probably get five bucks for at Eddie's Pawnatorium. But he hadn't found what he was looking for. He fought against the feeling that he never would.

He turned, but then paused and looked back at the hand. It was still clenched, as if holding something. Something small. Charlie's heart thumped. It couldn't be, he knew, but he was filled with the quite certain feeling that it was. It was in there, buried in the palm of the hand like a pearl in the heart of an oyster. Like the King Arthur stories that Charlie had loved as a child, the hand was sticking up from the water to offer him salvation. Like the Lady of the Lake offering Arthur the sword Excalibur.

The metal detector would know; it was made of silver. Holding his breath, almost unwilling to find out, he ran it over the hand. It buzzed, indicating that something *was* inside the hand, but not at the frequency that would indicate silver. No, the low buzzing indicated that whatever was in the hand was made of iron or steel. A base metal. Not worthy.

He pushed the thought aside, so violently that he almost felt it rattle in his head. The damn machine must be malfunctioning, must have been damaged by the sea water. It *was* here, in the hand, no matter what the metal detector said. Shirley's wedding ring, after all these years. It was the only thing that made sense.

She had lost her wedding ring fifteen years ago, ten years before they had heard those dreaded words, ovarian cancer. "It's no big deal, Charlie," she would say to him when he would fret over it, suggesting that they buy a new one. "I still have the ring where it matters," she would continue, "in my heart." And then she would pull him in for a kiss, ignoring the dirt under his fingernails and his grumpy demeanor. Loving him. Loving old Charlie Voss. So he had let it go, not replacing the ring, the sign of their love. And then Shirley was gone, devoured by the cancer like a feral animal.

It haunted him that he had never replaced the ring, reminding him that he had taken Shirley for granted, that he hadn't appreciated her. Not until she was dead. And so he spent every morning with his metal detector, searching and sweeping the beach, looking for it. Shirley's wedding ring. His Holy Grail.

And he had found it, he was sure of it. *It's not silver, it's iron*, said the voice again. He ignored it. *The damn metal detector's on the fritz, that's all*, he thought to himself. It was here, held out to him by this hand. He bent down to open the fingers and claim his prize.

They wouldn't open. The hand was clenched tight, the fingers locked closed as if rigor mortis had set in, even though they were too warm and too soft for that to be true. It was as if the hand refused to open. Which was impossible. He stood again, wiping the sweat from his forehead with the bottom of his t-shirt. He felt a twinge of fear as the tide continued to rush in. The water line had reached the base of the hand's fingers. Soon it would be submerged.

He crouched, his ankles creaking, and balanced the metal detector on his lap so that he could use two hands. He grabbed the wrist with his left hand and pried at the fingers with his right. The tide surged over him, drenching him and the metal detector. The fingers refused to open.

"Please, you sonofabitch, please," he said, hot tears

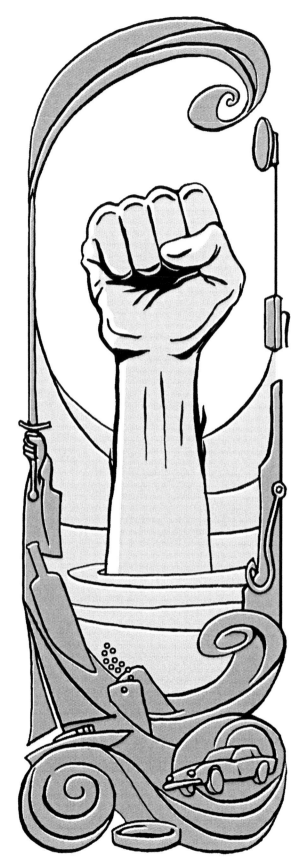

staining his face, the salt of his grief mixing with the salt of the sea. "Open up. Open the hell up." But it did not, and Charlie fell to his knees, letting the metal detector drop into the surf. He barely noticed as he pried at the fingers once again.

"Sweet God in heaven, please help me," he said. "Shirley, please help me." He knew the ring was in there, waiting for him. But the damn fingers wouldn't budge. A wave came crashing down, sweeping the metal detector away, almost knocking him down. Panic surged and he beat the hand with his fists, hoping to force it to open. Then another wave assaulted him, driving him backward into the surf. He tasted the salty grittiness of the seawater, swallowing some before he could spit it out. He sat up, his stringy hair matted to his forehead, tears streaming down his face. Then he rose, wiping his nose with the back of his hand. *It's not silver, it's steel,* said the voice one final time, and he knew it was true. The ring wasn't in there. He would never find it. Something clicked inside of him. Something final. As if a door had closed.

"I'm sorry, Shirley," he said, addressing the hand as proxy, "but I can't search any longer. I'm not dead yet." The hand seemed to bow to him, a benediction. He turned. The metal detector was there, returned by the backwash of the tide. He picked it up and threw the instrument as far as he could. It landed out in the ocean and began to sink. Charlie took one last look at the hand, which was almost completely underwater now. Soon it would be gone.

He turned back to the shore and headed home.

But Charlie Voss was not the first person to encounter the hand that morning.

Sam Foster had stumbled upon the hand about an hour earlier than Charlie Voss, just after the sun had risen. Too early for most people to be up.

Unless, of course, you had spent the whole night drinking and had never gone to sleep. Then time had no meaning.

Time had had little meaning for Sam for several years now. Not since he had stopped struggling against his need. Not since he had stopped fighting. Not since he had left his wife and son in the wake of his addiction, surrendering to drunkenness. It was easier that way. *I'm a lover, not a fighter,* Sam thought to himself, and laughed.

He was buzzed, his need sated, but not so drunk as to be out-of-control, not so drunk as to be sick, retching in some alley. This was the perfect state, a temporary state that preceded full-blown drunkenness. *El Blotto,* as he called it.

He got philosophical when he was buzzed. He liked to think the alcohol opened his mind to countless possibilities, like an artist. Like Poe, or Hemingway. Except, he thought to himself when sober, he never created anything when he was drunk, never accomplished anything. But he could, he damn-well could, and he held onto that thought like a life preserver.

At first he thought the hand was a delusion. His own particular version of a pink elephant. Except he had been drinking long enough to know how drunk he was, could tell his blood-alcohol level to within a few hundredths. He was buzzed, no doubt about it, and he would fail a breathalyzer, but he wasn't drunk enough to be hallucinating. No, it was a hand sticking out of the sand, clenched in a tight fist.

The tide was coming in, lapping up against the hand, wetting the wrist before it receded. *Someone's buried under there,* he thought. *A father whose kids buried him, leaving him for dead while the tide rushed in.* He thought of a movie, a horror movie where a woman was buried in the tide up to her neck as revenge for cheating on her husband. It ended with the tide rushing in, drowning her. The hand was like that, buried and waiting.

Only not alive. Of that he was sure. It was a man's hand, the knuckles dusted with hair, the fingers broad, the fingernails ragged. It didn't move, and if the owner of the hand was alive he'd be twisting and turning and clutching and scraping. Instead, the hand was still, clenched in a fist. As if waiting.

He could go to the police, but he wouldn't. A town drunk was tolerated, humored, hell, sometimes even appreciated for "adding color" to the town, as long as he knew his place and didn't get violent. But town drunks weren't believed, not about hands sticking out of the sand. Not when he had once stumbled into the police station claiming that space aliens were chasing him, only to find that it was Sister Margaret from the local convent, who had wanted to give him a hot meal and whose habit he had mistaken for the pointed head of an extraterrestrial. No, going to the police might be the right thing to do, but it would be worthless. And demeaning.

Besides, he kind of liked having a secret.

He circled the hand, exploring it. He noticed a scar across the back of the fist, a crescent moon, a wound suffered and healed long before the hand's owner had found himself buried in the sand. Sam wondered what had caused the scar. Had the man sliced it with a paring knife as he helped his wife prepare dinner? Chunked it out with a screwdriver as he took the training wheels off his son's bike? Suffered a bite from his family's brand-new golden retriever pup? The possibilities were endless. He felt tears well in his eyes.

Sam sunk to his knees, in front of the hand. It did not move, just faced him in a tight fist. "What the hell are you looking at?" Sam asked. "What do you want?" But the hand did not speak. Did not flinch. It was, after all, only a hand.

"What's in there?" asked Sam, rubbing his eyes and smearing away the tears. "What the hell is in there?" *It's just the alcohol talking, Sam*, his sober internal voice told him. Only he didn't think so. Not this time. He wanted to know what was in the hand. What was in the fist.

He reached out, tentative, and tried to peel one of the fingers back, the pointer finger, like a petal from a rare flower. It opened at his touch, uncurling. He felt a strange excitement, a heady anticipation, like a child on Christmas morning. There *was* something in the hand, he could see it. Something red, something metal. Sam thought that he knew what it was, but he couldn't picture it. It was on the tip of his awareness, like the sad memories of a lost relationship. He reached for another finger.

The entire hand opened at his touch this time, blossoming. Sam jumped back. The hand had opened of its own accord. He was sure of it. Was the man buried underneath still alive? *Impossible*, he thought. He considered digging, unearthing the body, freeing it, but something told him not to. Something told him he'd never reach his goal. He turned back to the hand. In the palm was a small die-cast car. A Matchbox car. Hot Wheels, maybe. A red Mustang. A classic late sixties model. Probably a Shelby. It reminded him of summer afternoons with his son, John. He hadn't spoken to John in months.

John didn't like having a drunk for a father.

And then he remembered. Today was John's fourteenth birthday. He fell backward from his knees, sitting in the wet sand. Had he sunk so low as to forget his only child's birthday? Had he? The tears came again, this time burning hot, like trails of lava streaming from the mouth of a volcano. He remembered past birthdays, before he had given up. Pony rides. Clowns. He remembered reading fairy tales to his son, the good ones that hadn't been edited and sanitized for the protection of young readers, where sometimes bad things happened to good people.

He supposed those fairy tales had prepared John for his life. A life without a father.

Sam didn't even have a gift for his son. He imagined that John would just be waking now, that Susan would be making him his favorite breakfast. Banana pancakes, homemade hash browns. One of Susan's specialties. Sam smiled. Even at the end, Susan had believed in him. Had believed that he could beat his addiction. Even as he walked out the door, drunk and on his high horse, riding his weakness like a thoroughbred. A thoroughbred ass.

He reached out to take the car. He could give it to John, show him he still remembered, still cared. But the hand snapped closed, the fingers stiff and hard. He tried to pry one open, but it wouldn't budge. "Open up, goddamn you," Sam said, crying yet again, tears of frustration. "I need that car more than you do." But the hand would not open, taking as surely as it had given.

Sam stood and stopped crying. He didn't need the car, didn't need the hand. It was early; he still had time to get something nice for his son. He could spend the morning collecting empty cans and bottles. He could make ten bucks by noon. And that would be enough to buy something decent, something to show he cared. Enough to maybe garner an invitation to John's birthday dinner. Back into the fold, at least for one day. One day at a time.

He still had time. He ran off toward the parking lot, the hand already slipping from his mind.

But Sam Foster was not the first person to encounter the hand that morning.

Nine-year old Ricky Simmons had found the hand a half-hour before Sam Foster, before the sun was up, the first rays of light just beginning to soften the dark sky. He would catch a batch of trouble if his mom knew that he was out so early. But he had been taking these early morning walks for weeks now, and she had yet to find out. His mother's sleep was tormented by memories and grief, and she rarely settled down until the early morning hours, her mind and body surrendering to exhaustion. So it was unlikely that she would awaken and find him missing. He'd be back inside before the sun was up.

He liked this time, when the world was new, when it felt like anything could happen. When it felt like it was impossible for anything to go wrong. Impossible that his dad was missing. Impossible that his dad was dead.

They used to go fishing in the morning, his dad taking him out into the ocean in his little motor boat, where they would fish and talk in hushed whispers. His dad would bait his line, his thick fingers pulling the hook through the bait, sometimes sandworms, sometimes small minnows. By the time the sun was visible on the horizon they would be heading home, where Ricky's mom would be waiting with breakfast. Then his dad had died.

He wasn't "officially" dead, people said, as if that meant something. Just missing. Ricky knew he was dead. He had gone fishing with friends, high school buddies, out deep, farther than he and Ricky went. A storm had come up, a freak thing, not forecast. They found the boat, as well as the bodies of his dad's friends. One had washed up on shore not far from Ricky's house. They hadn't found Ricky's dad, and Ricky knew what that meant. He missed his dad but tried not to show it. It hurt his mom to see him cry, he could tell.

He saw the hand as he skipped stones, watching them skim along the ocean like teenagers on jet skis. Unlike Charlie Voss and Sam Foster he knew what it was. Whose it was. The thick fingers and the red-brown hair were as familiar to Ricky as his own hand. That hand had tousled his hair, had held his own little hand when he crossed the street. If he had any doubt, the crescent moon scar gave it away. He remembered his dad pulling a hook from a fish's mouth, the fish jerking, digging it into the back of his dad's hand. Leaving a scar.

It was his dad's hand, sticking out of the sand like a signpost, fist clenched. Ricky crouched in front of it, staring. His dad must have washed up on shore and been buried by the surf. He felt calm, although he could feel the emotion building up inside of him, waiting to overrun him. *I need to be a big boy*, he thought. *I need to be grown up.*

Except he didn't know what to do, and so for awhile he crouched there, examining the hand. The auburn hairs moved when the sea breeze blew, like palm trees. Ricky could have crouched there forever, close to his dad. But finally he reached his hand out and touched the scar, running a forefinger across it. It was cool to his touch, the scar tissue rubbery. Ricky closed his eyes.

The hand opened. Ricky felt it under his finger even before he opened his eyes. The hand turned over, palm up, and the fingers splayed open like sun rays. In the middle of the hand was a gift, two square pieces of metal on a silver chain. Ricky knew what they were.

His dad's dog tags. Ricky always found it funny that his dad had dog tags, and used to ask him where his dog collar was. His dad would drop down on all fours, barking and panting, his tongue hanging out of his mouth, and Ricky would laugh. Then his dad would tell him about the war, the Gulf War in the desert, where his dad had gone before Ricky had been born.

"Did you kill anyone?" Ricky would ask, and his dad would get a far-away look in his eyes.

"I did what I had to, Ricky," he would say, and then he would change the subject. It had comforted Ricky to know that his father was a hero. And now here they were, the dog tags, being offered to him by his father's hand. Ricky reached for them, his fingers grasping, and then he had them in his hand. The metal was warm, as if blood still flowed through his father's hand. He paused for a moment, feeling the tears coming, and then he was crying.

As if able to see, the hand grabbed at Ricky's little hand, pulling down, reaching up. Ricky felt a brief jab of fear, followed by a longing that threatened to overwhelm him. He knelt down and his father's hand ran its fingers through Ricky's hair, tousling him just as he had so many times before. For a time Ricky knelt there, wishing that the moment would never end. But finally it did, the hand withdrawing, becoming motionless, open. Ricky put the dog tags around his neck, the chain heavy against his skin. He rose.

The hand was waiting for something, fingers unfurled. It wanted something, needed something. Ricky was confused, and a bit worried. He imagined his father spending eternity disappointed in him. He tried to think. What could his father want? He patted his jeans pockets and pulled out the contents. Lint, a quarter, a Matchbox car.

He almost put the quarter in his father's hand, thinking it was the most valuable thing that he had. Then he remembered. He remembered preschool, father's night. They had worked on projects with the teacher, Miss Rachel, projects to give to their fathers. Ricky had made a car out of construction paper, a red car. He had drawn two stick figures in the car, him and his dad. "I love playing cars with daddy" he had written with Miss Rachel's help, and he remembered that his dad had smiled and seemed sad at the same time. "I love playing cars with you too, buddy," his father had said.

He put the car in the palm of his father's hand, and the hand closed around it, intermingling for just a moment with Ricky's smaller fingers. Then Ricky stepped back, and noticed the sun up on the horizon. He wanted to stay and wait with his father until the tide came in, but he knew that his mom would be getting up soon, knew that if she found him missing the fear might kill her.

"I have to go, dad," he said to the hand, and it moved up and down, bending at the wrist, as if in approval. So Ricky walked slowly away, backward, facing the hand, watching as the tide lapped against it. He knew that later, when the tide went back out, the hand would be gone, his father at rest.

He turned and headed home, feeling the dog tags bouncing against his chest.

October 16 – 18, 2009 – Best Western Hotel – Bandana Square – St. Paul, Minn.
Convention membership: $30 to 8/1/2009, $35 to 10/1/2009, $40 at the door
Information: 612.721.5959 – eheideman@dhzone.com – www.arcanacon.com
Arcana 39, P.O. Box 8036, Lake Street Station, Minneapolis MN 55408

Isotope Ballerina

She's unstable inside, nursing radioactive decay upon a stage of
atoms   (onward, ever upward, she drifts)

frozen methane hair, flowing with silicate
and water ice

poised, sweet, tender lips pursed hard with
determination
re-immersed shapes,
stretched and convulsed

hydrogen
     deuterium
          and tritium   skate along
with her, hands joined, forming a circle

and she stares at the little girl up front
                                  who whispers her
                                            name

        the vidscreen camera goes in tight as she spins,
faster, faster, in an arc, gradually going transparent,

      ping
   a
 e
l
               into the air

hydrogen, deuterium, and tritium pass through her
(her image goes ghost)

Face reddens, body glowing with light,

    implosion-sunrise spreading from her like wings
eclipsing her face

the crowd anticipates it: beauty…fusion…
destruction to
rebuild

Once a solar year a girl is chosen to perform The Ritual

giving life to the planet, replenishing by sacrificing vital
energy translated from movement, to dance,
to life-giving energy

the three are always the same, but the dancer with the mark
upon her cheek—she changes slightly

a little younger each solar year; a little less certain of her
choreography, but The Ritual always ends in chemical reaction

(fire) as it begun

In the folds of the crowd, a small girl watches with interest as
they clear the stage; she gingerly touches the mark upon her cheek
removes her goggles (the colors still vivid behind her eyes)
residual glare hanging behind her memory in a wash
of torrential enfolding, unfolding her hands
as her father smiles sadly at her,
knowing scant time was left—she'd be chosen next,
the isotope ballerina (*his little isotope ballerina*)

"How is it done father?" she asked.
"What, my dear?" he said, absently stroking his beard,
watching the townspeople as they made their way either
home or to drinking places, or to the temple.
"The effects…" she said.
"With mirrors."
"That all?"
"Mostly."
"But it looks so real."
"That's the thing with effects isn't it? The good ones are
indistinguishable from reality."
"Like science and magic?"
"Good analogy."
"She had a mark like mine."
"Yes, she did."
"Does that mean I'll become a dancer?"
"I…" he waited for the throng of people to pass. "I should hope not."
"But I am a good dancer," she said in protest.
"And you're an even better scientist," he said.
"Maybe you can find out why our planet is in need of
so much energy every solar year. Why the terraforming
didn't take. That's the kind of work worthy of a brain
like yours."
"Maybe," she said.

He would die trying to save her,
that much was certain…he tightened his grip
on her hand, and she smiled up at him with the
light of three moons in collision, her starry gaze
awash in innocence, defiant of prophesy
or destiny

—**Cornelius Fortune**

Katherine Woodbury enters our pages with the tale of a man with a special talent and its built-in weakness.

Verbal Knowledge
by Katherine Woodbury

Roger intervened in the lives of managers, vice presidents, CEOs, and department heads. For undermining the CEO of Tranec, he received a quarter million dollars.

"Weak, narcissistic fool who can't even tie his own shoelaces," and Marvin Gradiline began to mumble self-adulations and stumble over his feet while the Board of Directors conferred and instituted Cut-Throat policies.

Marvin Gradiline's daughter succeeded him as CEO.

"She's an intelligent little woman," the client, Mr. John, said when he visited Roger. "Mr. Paul and I want to help her through this difficult time—guide her. If you could present our proposals—"

"I don't take suggestions," Roger said.

He had his own ideas regarding St. Juste Gradiline. He wanted to wrap his words around her cold surety, excise it, commandeer it.

I'm not that kind of man. I have no ulterior motives. I'm not a murderer. I help people.

The client wrote out a check. Roger insisted on partial pre-payments.

"Tranec is plateauing. Only two departments reached merging level last quarter—our vice presidents are fractious—" Mr. John paused, thin smile wrinkling. "You get good results. Tranec's survival is more important than the Gradilines."

Roger grunted. His clients always justified themselves.

"We were impressed by your handling of Marvin," Mr. John said.

"Two weeks," Roger said. "She'll be under control."

He sent the check to the Bank and took the back stairs to the outside. He crossed the road to the Park. It stretched between Tranec, Marziple and Micronin, the monopolies that controlled most of the world's businesses.

Roger's office sat coyly on the West side of the Park amongst the world-protected small businesses. He was number 116 out of 5,000, all of which offered unique and unprecedented services. All remaining businesses were managed by the three monopolies. They no longer struggled against each other: Burger King did not try to steal McDonald's customers. MCI did not attempt to outclass AT&T. Goods hardly mattered. Everybody had enough. People traded on people, on individual survival. The 21st Century had vanquished the Age of Victorianism. Humans had recovered their medieval morality.

Roger stepped into a shuttle. Disney had designed the Park before Disney was swallowed by Micronin. The shuttle was an open air tram, pulling mostly empty cars behind it. It crossed over the duck pond on the clickity-clack bridge. The shuttle played irritatingly too-soft music with interruptions about the foliage: "On our left is an American Beech, *fangus grandifolia*. The American Beech has not always been an urban-friendly plant—"

Roger looked around the tram. An elderly man snoozed in the last seat. The driver, a teenage boy, draped his arms over the steering wheel and whistled between his teeth.

"Pointless drivel," Roger said. "It must get on your nerves."

The boy grinned in the mirror. "Music for the masses."

"You'd probably like to turn it off. Play your own stuff."

The boy shrugged, and Roger subsided. He didn't force what didn't pay him, and filling a teenage boy with aesthetic rage wouldn't get Roger to Tranec any faster.

The rambling voice gave way to a cloyingly sweet *Somewhere Over the Rainbow.*

"Yeah," the boy said suddenly. "Yeah, it is pretty awful, isn't it? Boy, I hate this stuff." He jammed his hand on the intercom system. It screeched. The elderly man snorted, blinked, and went back to sleep.

The teenage driver was scrambling amongst his music chips when he parked outside Tranec. Roger watched from the pavement. The boy waved a hand. "Queen," he called as he drove away. "Twenty Cent classic!"

Roger tried to smile back. Teenagers were sudden, unpredictable; the boy had only needed to be triggered, but it disconcerted Roger how easily he hit the triggers, how unconsciously he sensed the motives and fears of his subjects. *Two weeks*, he would tell his clients, and deliver in five days, all the time knowing that he'd held himself back, he could have completed the job in two days, one.

The boy had altered his course of action based on two remarks. But he might have done it anyway.

"It wasn't me," Roger muttered to himself. "It was his choice. I'm blameless," and he was flooded with the aloof confidence that he shaped inside himself as often as he could.

Roger walked under the portico to Tranec's entrance and through the rustling invisible door to the foyer. Lush chairs and couches occupied a sunken floor beside a musical waterfall. Roger skirted the area, avoiding the reception desk.

"Sixtieth floor," he said to the elevator attendant.

Tranec's foyer was on the fifty-eighth floor. Roger walked along a hallway level with the treetops and striped with sunlight. The sunlight filtered through the invisible wall to his left. The wall flickered; Roger leaned against it, floating—it seemed—in space. He could see the snaking tram in the Park. He wondered if the elderly man had been woken by the "Galileos" of *Bohemian Rhapsody.*

An armed receptionist greeted Roger at the entrance to the Gradiline suite. She wore her weapons against her sides and chest. Roger noted a deafener, a stun gun, and a laser before he halted in front of the desk.

"May I help you?" Friendly, pink smile, suspicious eyes.

"I'm here to see St. Juste," Roger said.

To wordshape the receptionist so he could gain entrance would be too obvious, too memorable. Receptionists were known for their imperturbability. This one gave him a bright, hard stare and accepted his business card.

"Ah—"

Interventionist, Roger's card stated. It was a good enough title. Roger didn't advertise his wordshaping. Not even his closest clients knew how he got his results.

Interventionists had replaced the consultants and psychoanalysts of the last century. Interventionists were high commodity items. To snag an interventionist was the ultimate in marketing, prestige for the ego: sell yourself, sell your company, buy the world's soul.

The receptionist slid the card into an air flow, and Roger watched it whisk into the inner office. A light appeared on the receptionist's desk.

"You may go in."

A broad office with an invisible wall. The park's trees hung almost over the desk. St. Juste stood behind the desk, her fingers creasing Roger's card. Medium height, medium hair cut in a smooth bob, medium looks—Margaretta St. Juste Gradiline was as average and unprepossessing as her father had been.

Camouflage. St. Juste had a reputation for harsh tactics: blackmail, unfair firings, character defamation.

"Hysterical," was what Roger planned for her. "Mindless, self-pitying, delusions of grandeur."

He shook her hand and settled into the chair opposite.

"And what kind of Interventionist are you, Mr. Wallis?" She didn't sit. She held the card at arm's length and studied him over it.

"Advisement. Consulting."

"You want to tell me how to run my company?"

"An outsider's perspective—"

"An outsider who is working for conspirators, Mr. Wallis, is not an outsider I will trust."

She didn't raise her voice. She wasn't upset. He leaned back, contemplating the even brows. He preferred his targets to get upset. He'd accosted Marvin Gradiline in a bar, accused him of ruining a fictional business partner. The resulting argument had made Roger's name-calling natural.

"Do you spy on your employees, St. Juste?"

"A senseless question, Mr. Wallis."

"Paranoid—" *aren't you*, he was going to say, when pain thudded against his forehead. He gasped at the unexpectedness, his hand drifting upwards. The weapon rolled around his feet: a glass-globed paperweight. He blinked tears away and looked up.

St. Juste stood at his elbow. She held a knife, the point against his neck.

She said, "My father is no 'vapid, narcissist moron', Mr. Wallis. Your words were repeated."

"Unsubstantiated—rumors—"

"And I've done some research. Marcus Cronack retired two days after meeting you. Julietta Simposa of the Bank—the Bank!—gave insider information to Marzipal an hour after you ran into her at the grocers. Because you *said* things."

The knife scratched his throat, and body fluid seeped to the wrong side of his skin. He kept his head steady, eyes fixed on the opposite wall. The branches rustled against the invisible barrier.

St. Juste straddled him. Clear, hazel eyes moved into his line of sight. She contemplated him, head tilted.

"Say you love me," she said.

He almost smiled. Pointless to wordshape positives. Positives contain negatives; love carries with it disappointments, disillusionments, all the unhappiness of another's heart.

"I love you," he said.

She took the knife away, and he stayed quiet, let her believe he had shaped himself to conformity. He'd desired her already in the soft, unanalytical way of such encounters. He was noticing her now more sharply; sympathy was creeping into the hard core of his walled contempt. He didn't fight it. He shaped himself constantly—fighting instincts of remorse and doubt. A random wordshape like "I love you" faded in a matter of months.

He opened his mouth—

"Don't speak," she said, flicking the knife upwards.

Self-deluded spinster with self-esteem issues, he'd planned to say. Adjective first—always—followed by the cliché. Words thrive on context, on their social use, however corrupt. Clichés were the best shapers. They carried so much more than personal interpretation—the condemnation of the world.

"Don't say anything personal—"

He nodded and touched her face lazily, a half-deliberate, half-unconscious movement. She flinched, her brows contracting. His fingers slid to his shoulders. He was drowning, closed-in by love. Fear tightened his muscles, his breath. St. Juste winced as he clenched her arms.

"Stop," she said. "Stop it. Say—say you'll never hurt me—"

"No."

"Say—"

"It—I—it's the one thing never comes true. You'd be—"

Another finger against his mouth.

"Wishing not to be hurt is like wishing to be dead," and he felt, at a distance, the wash of guilt, like incoming tide.

She glowered over that.

She said slowly, "Say you'll do what I want, say—" a soft laugh—"say you'll never leave me."

Still vague. There were loopholes in such a statement, but it was a clever request. Strong enough subtext to bind him, to keep him from the worst excesses of betrayal. She waited, eyebrows raised, the knife blade flat against his skin. He could attack her—*You're weak, clinging, out of your depth, afraid*—but words had to be processed, and she could stab him in the time it took her to understand.

"I'll never leave you," he said.

She eyed him, hesitating, got off his lap. He fought the impulse to advise her: *Berate me, force me to echo self-doubts, self-loathing*. Love in itself does not invoke truth. Loyalty does not bind the mind. He didn't have to explain himself to her, didn't have to care about her needs, no matter how vulnerable she left herself. He owed her nothing except that he mustn't undermine her, mustn't expose her to her enemies who worked for Tranec. Danger—she was surrounded by it—he had to stay—

He cursed.

"What is it?" she said. "What's wrong?"

Impossible to explain without shaping himself. And accusations were pointless. She waited beside the chair, head tilted.

"It's working." Unattached pronoun, vague without context. The large hazel eyes contemplated him. She smiled.

"Who hired you?"

He shrugged. He had no good reason not to tell her. The clients would demand a refund. "Your head of marketing and head of Consumer Relations."

"Ah, yes. Mr. John and Mr. Paul. They think image is our sole means of survival. Convince the world to see you healthy, and you will be healthy." She slid the knife back into the desk and relaxed, hands splayed over papers. "We've lost thirty thousand employees to Mironin in the last two months. It happens. We're still five and half million strong. 30,000 is barely a ripple, but they want it to mean something. Tragedy! The end of an era!" She snorted. "They want to save Tranec from cataclysm."

A monopoly that lost sixty percent of its full working capacity had to disband. The products would still be produced. It hardly mattered who made them. But to deprive employees of an identity was anathema.

"Tranec is not in danger," St. Juste said.

She did not ask him to shape that statement, and he, relaxing under the edge of his fear, watched her pace and talk, her hands brushing back the smooth cap of hair.

"What were you going to call me?" she said.

It was opportunity. She knew it and turned a blanched

face toward him. He opened his mouth and groaned as pity impeded his words (*You're a brainless, sour, father-worshipping bitch.*), the love that insisted that the words were inaccurate, unfair. His panic surged back and with it, desire to save her. He breathed hard and struggled and said nothing.

She sighed relief, and his anger surged. Anger because she had forced him to change, anger for not treating him better.

"You'll help me," she said, and, "No," he said without thinking, forgetting to keep his animosity damped, to lull her into security.

"You can't reject me."

"I'm not," he said, his voice savage.

She winced. He pushed out of the chair, getting away from her, from the pain of the shaped love that he hadn't wanted. It hurt when people tried to use you; it hurt to be the buffer in circumstances beyond your control. He glared at her.

"Then help me," she said. "Use your words against Mr. John and Mr. Paul, make them—" she stopped, eyes glazing. She pressed her hand against the invisible wall, balanced there between heaviness and light, the tree at her elbow. She looked at Roger over her shoulder. "Can you kill?"

He wouldn't answer. She was hard, cruel, but they all were, playing vicious games against each other. *We thrive on machinations and backstabbings, monsters breeding minotaurs.*

"You can?"

"No."

"You're lying. You've killed?"

"Yes," he said, and the guilt flowed like poisoned honey through his veins.

He'd shaped himself against it for years now—feel no guilt, suffer no heartache. She was disassembling him, savaging the barriers of his indifference.

"Who?"

Lucius Marveinec—the head of engineering at Micronin—Roger's third shaping. Roger had met Lucius four times and gotten nowhere. Roger's clients had begun to mutter about their deposit, about using a different Interventionist. Roger had hated Lucius, who *ought* to respond, Roger was creating excellent wordshapes and still the jackass went on operating his department in direct opposition to Roger's clients.

And so he'd shaped Lucius' death: "That heart of yours will kill you one of these days." Twelve hours later Lucius was dead from massive myocardial infarction.

The clients refused to pay, saying it was chance, Lucius was going to die anyway. That was before Roger used result-based payments. He hadn't insisted. He'd taken a job for Micronin's CEO against his former clients, retained his personal business contacts through pure luck and a little wordshaping, and survived.

And he'd wordshaped himself. No more deaths but no more guilt. "I'm not the kind of man who feels guilty." "I'm not the type to dwell on things, to care about the past."

Damn St. Juste for doing this to him. Lovers didn't—lovers shouldn't—

"Go to Hell," he said.

She leaned against the invisible wall, her straight, regular features composed, remote. The mouth held a straight line, the eyes never wavered. She was a mass of shadows and lines that he craved and hated and worshipped and despised.

Her head moved, the eyes veering to the wall opposite the door. He pondered the lines of her profile, framed by the heavy hair that curled into the hollow of her neck.

"I won't ask it," she said, and turned her face back to him, eyes clear of emotion.

She shaped herself better than he had ever done.

He breathed and in the space between breath and breath, he sensed his escape—

I am not a good man. I kill. I hurt. I'll cause her more harm if I stay. If I love her, I should go.

A card shot through the air from the outer office, hovered at St. Juste's shoulder. She plucked at it, her brow creasing.

She said, "What were you going to say about me? Don't apply the words—just tell me—quick—"

"Hysterical. Mindless. Self-deluded. They want—a puppet."

"You don't mince language, do you?" she muttered.

She slumped into her chair, startling him, the gesture so unlike her previous precision. Even sitting on his lap, holding a knife to his throat, she had moved with elegant sparseness.

His clients entered the office. Mr. John, a square man with a square head, approached with a tremulous smile. Mr. Paul, head of marketing, walked with determined suavity in Mr. John's wake.

St. Juste shrieked.

The receptionist rushed into the office, laser raised. She and the men gaped as St. Juste scrambled to her feet and ran to the opposite wall, screaming in disjointed cacophony:

"Bastards, bastards, you hate me. You want to hurt me. I can't stand this. I can't trust anyone." Another shriek. "What do I do? What do I do? I'm so alone," childishly, hands clenching, "I can't do this by myself."

"She's distrait," Mr. John said to the receptionist.

"Call the doctor."

The receptionist's eyes narrowed.

She said, "She wasn't like this earlier," and her gaze hovered on Roger.

Mr. John put his arm around St. Juste, eased her to the sofa. He said, "Her father—the promotion—Margaretta's been on edge a long time now."

St. Juste clutched at Mr. John's shirt. "You'll help me, won't you?"

"Of course, Margie. Of course."

The receptionist reached a decision. She lowered the laser at Roger. "You, Mr. Wallis, come with me."

"No." St. Juste hurled herself from the sofa, grabbed for Roger. She curled her arms around his neck, her mouth against his cheek. She breathed there while the receptionist cursed and jerked the laser to a less dangerous mark.

Roger held St. Juste. There was no tension in her body. This was easy, outwitting these fools who thought they could manage Tranec better—her breath washed on soundless laughter against his skin. He knew this was fake, a charade for stupid, greedy men, but her words wounded him, compelled him to help her.

"This man is an Interventionist," Mr. John said to the receptionist. "He is here to help," and Mr. Paul said, "We'll protect her. She's safe with us. Get a doctor, will you?"

The receptionist glowered but went out.

Mr. John tugged at St. Juste. She fell away from Roger. He watched her huddle against Mr. John.

"Quick work," Mr. Paul said in Roger's ear. "Of course she was never very stable."

In the outer office, the receptionist was speaking on the suite's private phone. The situation required nothing more of Roger. The doctor would come, would find no signs of foul play—no drugs, no needle marks, no bruises—and the receptionist would let Roger go. He ought to leave. St. Juste was better off without him, safer.

He would leave. For her good. For his.

Shapings wear off. Guilt fades. Longings die.

"Clever of you to get her affection," Mr. Paul muttered to Roger. "How—uh—how far did you get?"

Roger edged away, sidling around the desk to sit in St. Juste's chair. On the sofa, Mr. John chaffed "little Margie's" hands. She burst out: "I haven't any friends. No one's on my side. It isn't fair. You aren't fair to me," and then, abrupt shift, "I'm sorry. I'm so sorry. Please don't leave me."

Mr. Paul followed Roger. He leaned against the desk. "I don't suppose you discuss your methods—I'd like a few tips on managing the ice queen."

"I don't give tips." Utter truth, not a shaping. "You wouldn't want them," Roger said. "It would make you uneasy, having access to her mind."

"You think so?" A bemused smile, a shake of the head.

"It's an intimate process. You already feel guilty about this."

"I assure you—"

"Unhappy with your own inadequacies, your attack on an innocent young woman. You can't shake the feeling that you missed a chance somewhere—opportunities that you failed to take. You doubt—"

"I don't—"

"He does," Roger said, nodding toward Mr. John who had stood and was watching them. "Don't you, Mr. John? You wish you didn't care so much, for yourself, for others. And you, Mr. Paul, scheming is beneath you. People should recognize your genius—you ought to be a vice president by now—" Mr. Paul flinched. "Except you haven't the genius. You're weak, weak with uncertainties, weak with fears, regrets. You don't know why you would want to hurt someone so innocent as St. Juste. You don't know what gave you the right to pursue a job you cannot do.

"You tell yourself to keep going, to keep fighting and scheming and planning, but the guilt won't leave, will it? It haunts you, Mr. John. You wonder, 'What have I done? Who did I sacrifice this time in order to win?'"

Roger ceased, panting. Mr. John and Mr. Paul stared at him. On the sofa, St. Juste had pressed her hands to her ears.

Mr. Paul fidgeted. He burst out. "It's not my fault. It was his idea. It isn't my fault. I don't need him to get anywhere. I'm good at my job."

Mr. John wept, patting St. Juste's shoulder. "I knew you when you were a little girl, eager to take on the world. I told your father I'd help you and look what I've done."

St. Juste eased from under Mr. John's hand. She wiped spurious tears from her face. She was standing by the desk when the doctor arrived, the receptionist beside him.

She spoke to the doctor, her voice sharp as diamonds. "Mr. John and Mr. Paul are upset. They have conspired after my job. They have confessed." She addressed the receptionist. "Return them to their departments; keep them there while I determine their employment status."

The receptionist's face was a mask. A suspicious glance toward Roger, but St. Juste clasped his shoulder, and the receptionist nodded, veiling her eyes.

The doctor, clucking deprecations, herded Mr. John and Mr. Paul out the door. The receptionist allowed herself a smirk before she followed, calling for security on her radio.

St. Juste said, "Get out of my chair."

Roger leaned back: "You—"

She covered his mouth with her hand. "I don't need any persuasion as to your ability. It was cruel—"

"Shapings can be lived through, conquered, undone. Those men—they are still your enemies—they will revert."

"I will manage. Oh, I don't regret your help, I asked for it. I planned to win, but not at the expense of their wills. Death is kinder."

He shook his head, rising to give the chair back to her.

"Shapings only work," he said, "when people believe what they hear. Lucius—" his jaw clenched, and he shook his head.

He hadn't been able to shape Lucius' will because he hadn't understood Lucius, not the way he understood people now: their vulnerabilities and uncertainties, their susceptibility to criticism, the things they don't want to be true about themselves.

Perhaps Lucius had never been vulnerable, except for his damn heart. Perhaps Roger could only shape people like himself, only hurt people he understood.

St. Juste touched his cheek.

"Is Lucius the one you killed? Why don't you shape yourself blameless?"

"I do. Every day."

"But you don't believe it?"

"No."

Hazel eyes regarded him without judgment, without mercy.

He said abruptly, "The shapings are getting easier. I'm getting better. The things I say—so close to the surface, they sound like truth—"

"Not my father—"

"Listened to bad advisors. Let himself be flattered. You must have seen that. It was cruel what I said but not a lie—not exactly a lie—close—too close—"

Superficial insights weren't enough. He had to know what adjectives, what clichés would strike home. He had to know, and he no longer wanted to know.

St. Juste's eyes dropped. *I'll never be able to unshape her from myself: her face or her hands, her voice, her eyes.*

She said slowly, "You meant what you said to Mr. John, to Mr. Paul. Regret. Pity. Pity for my innocence—"

He trembled. Beyond the invisible wall, leaves danced with shadows, mimicking the shake of his shoulders. It could be laughter. It could be tears.

"Paul had real doubts. John had real pity. But you—you were never innocent—"

"No," she said. "No. Which is why you wanted to love me—"

"And you wanted my love," he said and no fingers rose to stop his mouth.

TENTACLE 3

Salt and ice
and temperature
led to everything,
the way
the simplest molecule
will shrink and swell,
will rise and fall
and freeze, or not freeze
according to the rule.

Creatures that are colonies
and animals that form
the different organs
of a single beast in the sea—
nothing so strange
would be here
but for the simplest facts:
that cold water sinks
that ice expands
that it all moves
by simple temperature.

—CAMILLA DECARNIN

Can Art And Politics Peacefully Coexist?

In These Times We Live In, Can We Afford The Alternative?

Mobius: The Journal Of Social Change Has the Answer

Mobius Features Fiction, Poetry, And Commentary All About Social Change That Seeks A Better World And A Better Tomorrow.

Check Us Out At:

WWW.MOBIUSMAGAZINE.COM

Or Subscribe To Our Print Version. Ten Bucks Gets You One Year And Four Exciting Issues. Mail Checks To:

> Mobius
> 505 Christianson
> Madison WI 53714

We're Always Looking For Good Speculative Fiction. Feel Free To Share Your Work. Guidelines Available From Above Address Or E-Mail At fmschep@charter.net

Gerard Houarner's fiction is always strong on mood and atmosphere. Witness this tale of the deep places, where some venture to find themselves.

On the Wind That Blows Hard From Below

by Gerard Houarner

Runo's serves their ale at cellar temperature, the way it's done in England, and never chilled, because of the wind.

All the places along Summit do, and many a good couple of blocks down into the city along the side streets, sometimes all the way to Rampart, where all the tourists huddle on the other side of the wall in the day stays and flea markets. Down there, the tenders charge double for the privilege of a warmer pour, and the brew's nowhere near as thick, dark, and rich as on Summit, and you don't ever get to hear the wind rattle the windows with a good gust, or blow in cold through the door every time someone comes or goes, or whine like a beaten dog, or howl like a vengeful one, when something shifts at the bottom of the hole.

On Summit, though, proprietors keep a few coals glowing in their cellars, so their stouts and ales and bitters won't freeze in the earth so close to the hole. Some say that's what gives the casks their bite.

And there's always the wits who say there's more than the cold down below to give you a bite.

A lot of tourists never make it as far as Summit. Rich folks, neither. Pilgrims, hardly ever. There's the markets and the games to distract them, temples to the Revelation for the devout, and the ruins poking up out of the ground like spikes from the Devil's crown that's the main reason people come: to say they saw what we once were before the world was punished..

But it's the wind that really puts them off. At this time of the year, only the special ones, or the mad, find their way up the maze of paved paths, crooked alleys, and crumbling squares to mingle with the tradesmen, beggars, merchants, and thieves who congregate in these dark, cool dens at the top of the world to sip their dinners around the hole, with nothing more than the meager lives they've lived and fresh-headed mugs in hand to keep them from slipping over the precipice.

You'd think more pilgrims would pay their respects to the source of so much of our discomfort. Maybe toss in a coin, or a folded prayer. Bargain in whatever currency's on hand with what waits at the bottom. But those kinds of traditions never caught on. Not that some don't try. But just the special ones, and you have to wonder if they don't stand out just a little bit more than the rest of us when it's time to choose the sacrifice.

I'm not saying anything about you personally, just so you understand. But there are no illusions, up here.

What made you pick this place?

I'm the same way.

I like Runo's. Everyone's welcome, and a bit of everyone comes. You see you hardly caused a stir when you came through the door. There are limits, of course. No diggers. Not that they'd try. The wattage is always low, but it's still too bright for them. And the tax officers have to knock on the window and stay where the proprietor can see them, or else they'll get everything that's coming to them through double barrels. But otherwise, monks mingle with leaf sellers, and drunks debate matters of the soul with holy hollers. Folks come to tell their stories, or listen to them told. Some just come for the quiet, like when there's been a death near the hole and no one feels like a song, much less words kind or cruel.

By the way, a bit of friendly advice: don't let the monks take your confession. They aren't sanctioned during the festival. It's a common misconception. If they hear yours, it's just to fill their pockets with your offering. No prayers will be chanted for forgiveness. That would run counter to the spirit of the festival.

Most times, I'm not given leave to run my mouth off. I can try, if I want, but the regulars feel the weight of my company before my story's done, and look to their watches or to who's just come or gone, or sign to a fellow across the way who doesn't even like them, and they're

off and out of earshot before a bubble of froth has burst on the head of a fresh one. I have the power to bore, apparently, though I make my living with words at the *Journal*, and from jazz articles and album liner notes. Bird lives, and all of that. My father was a drummer, and I used to sit in the studio as a little kid listening to Miles and Coltrane and Cannonball cut records, so—

Well, there you go. You see the effect I have. No, no, I saw you stifle the yawn. The clench of muscles between jaw and ear. It's my voice, I'm sure. Maybe my timing, always a moment too late. A lack of confidence, an inability to invest any truth, much less a lie, with the conviction of certainty. I've spent too much time near the hole, I'm too close to its uncertainty. I'm a quantum speaker.

Or maybe it is my words. After all, I don't make much of a living at the *Journal* with a beat covering the morgue, sewers, and the doings up on Summit around the hole. Not the first thing folks turn to when they open the newspaper in the morning. Not even during the festival. Maybe my father was right, and I should have become a musician. Of course, I'd still need a sense of rhythm for that.

Anyway, Runo's keeps me honest. In my place. It's important in this world to know where you stand.

Praise be to the Revelation, yes.

I'd watch that bag if I were you. Put it between your legs, under the seat, and tie the strap around your ankle. There is a thief or two here tonight. They don't dare bother the regulars. But you're not one of us.

There you go.

You're welcome.

Yes, it is funny, us sitting here by the frosty windows, talking much around a lot of nothing. Well, at least I am. You in your quilted leather and fine-finished woolens, me in my tattered old herringbone. A cartoon waiting for a satiric caption.

No, it's only funny, not strange. This is Summit, after all. Besides, every now and then, when I'm looking for stories in the city or sipping on a tall one when it's warmer, some fine young stranger does find me—always the lads, I'm sad to say. Newcomers to the city, bungling their way around fresh territory, trying to find their little corner and thinking the wind isn't that bad. Not afraid of the hole, yet. Tourists, to notch the dare of the hole's lip on their gilded belts. The rich, to laugh at us up on Summit. And the mad, to do the same. Sometimes it's just a young lad from the country whose curiosity has gotten the better of him and who's braved the wind, always at summer's height, mind you, to actually sit on Summit next to the hole to imagine a more adventurous kind of life, or maybe just consider the choice between suicide and returning to his family's farm.

No, you're certainly like none of them.

These youngsters are drawn to me because, I think, I'm better kept than most of the others, who don't need to look neat and clean to come and go where they need to, as I do. Of course, I'm not passing myself off as rich. That would be a pathetic joke, as us sitting here together shows. It's just that my look must seem to these types as friendly, or at least not actively hostile. Maybe I remind them of a teacher they once had. Or a faded uncle.

I don't mind. Your type are the only ones who listen. Yawn away. You won't leave.

I understand. You're not the first pilgrim who can't get a night's sleep at festival. That's what makes drinking until you pass out such a favorite distraction.

Sure, have another. It's on me. He'll take a taste of the Figurn's, if you have that on your tray? Good. Good.

No, no, I know you can buy the whole neighborhood and everyone in it. It's not about the money. It's about the hospitality. Be my guest.

You see? It's not so bad, being a poor man's company.

You felt the wind blowing long before you saw the hole, didn't you. That's what keeps the tourist trade down in Winter. Though there are some who claim nothing revives the spirits like the bracing air. If they really wanted bracing, they'd find their way up to Summit.

So close to the hole, the wind bites, even during summer. Winter, it draws blood. That's why business is slow in the Winter.

Except for the festival. It's what draws the season's tourists from the valleys and the island, from places so far west only another ocean stops the land, and even from across that far sea, as well as this closer one lapping at the shore if you go down far enough on the other side of the hole.

They all want to see a pilgrim die.

All praise to the Revelation, yes.

Let me guess. Twenty-five? Really. I see, you've been to war. Yes, that's aged you, all right. Seen quite a few horrors, felt any number of terrors, I imagine. Been a few, naturally. Young heirs like you, who've already proven themselves, are rare enough. We get the green ones, mostly. None like you ever come to the Winter festival. Your elders always certify—

Your father. I'm sorry. I forget that blood runs as bitter among the rich as the poor. I take it you have a brother or two in the wings.

And he's already passed through the festival.

Do you want the hole to take you?

That's the spirit. That's right, embrace the Revelation. Pass by Hell's door and be saved, ride salvation's grace to the heights of power and wealth that are your right. The poor need you to guide them, to worship, to envy. Hate. We need your kind as much as you need ours.

Quite right, too serious. If you'd wanted a religious conversation, you'd have sat next to Brother Ghish over there, or Mary the nun, though she's out of her habit. Night off.

There's other ways to pass the night. No, don't worry, there'll be no chess or costi. The way you're taking down your ale, you'd be no challenge, anyway. I'll tell you a story, instead. My story. That's why you're here, isn't it? To hear the tales of the poor fools who'll spend their lives serving you one way or another, so you'll know how to use us to your full advantage. Or perhaps, with some mercy. Whatever suits you.

Have another mug. Try the Ginlander. A bit more fruity, a touch anise, caramel, raisin. Smoother, too. It'll go down easy, not fill you so quick. Let me fill what's left empty.

The name's Yv. An old one, for sure. Foreign. Even poor families have traditions. See? Learned something, already.

Don't worry, I won't ask for your name.

Born here, though my family's in the flea market trade. They're still down there, buying from the gelders, who trade with the diggers. Sell all kinds of things diggers bring out of their mines in the hole's walls. Tourists love that stuff. You rich, you decorate your palaces with the best.

I was drawn to the books as a child. You'd be amazed how many come out, and in decent condition. Wrapped. Preserved. As if carefully entombed for future generations in the dump on which this city's built. I learned my trade from those books. Words.

You're right. If I'd learned modern words, with their current ideas, I'd make a better living. But would I have as much fun?

I'm glad you can laugh. See, I can be entertaining.

My words suit the hole and the morgue just fine. And jazz. Do you know, I own Charlie Parker's King Super Alto 20 saxophone? Of course it's his, with the tricked out fast keys. The gelder who sold it to my family had the diggers go back down for the receipt from the pawn shop they were mining. For the provenance. It's his, as true as my words.

I wouldn't have guessed. I didn't think your kind was interested in forgotten musical forms. Know a name, here and there, sure. Hum a tune. Throw a few phrases out to make a quick impression. I know the game. My family makes its living from that form of vanity. Everyone wants a connection to the past. But few want to work at it. Easier to stick a collection up on a wall and glance at it once or twice a year.

You're right. There I go, again.

You bought that record? I saw it for sale at Bellinger's just the other day. What did you pay?

Good for you. You must have had some practice bargaining to get it that price from old Bellinger.

Of course. That campaign took you to some very hard places. What else do you have in that bag?

No.

Impossible.

No, you don't have to be afraid of anyone stealing it. Now that the thieves think they know what's in it, your bag is safe. Nobody cares about Louis Armstrong's coronet. Too hard to sell, especially with me as a witness to your ownership. And the provenance? I see. Louisiana State Museum's Old U.S. Mint in New Orleans. You're lucky you were able to come away with anything more than your life from that part of the campaign. I'm surprised someone like you even got that deep into the action.

What else do you have in there?

Yes, an odd collection. The necklace of ears, well, you shouldn't show that. Not even if people ask. But the notebook of drawings, very beautiful. The sheath might be worth more than the blade, in some neighborhoods, but it's a very fine edge. Good steel. The notch only adds character. And the fused electronic—you'd be surprised how rare those things are. People just tore them apart when they couldn't work, anymore. Completely irrational, like the object itself had betrayed them, and not the other way around. That might actually be worth something, so don't take it out of the bag.

Yes, I understand. It does mean something, though very different from its intended purpose. I suppose that's what makes it art.

I'm the same way. My rooms are filled with mementos. Things I've bought thinking to sell and could never part with. Useless reminders of past glories and passions. My first typewriter. My old uniform, believe it or not. And my carbine. Knife, too, same as you. I imagine you have an entire palace devoted to your childhood memorabilia and souvenirs from all your adventures, somewhere.

Ah. Then I commend you for distilling the essence of who you are into the contents of a single bag. Unusual, for someone of your class and age. Though I suppose you've had the experience necessary to be brutal. I could never do that. But then, I'm a lot older than you. Even a poor man like me has been through things you haven't yet had time to experience. It's harder to let go of memories when you feel the end coming up on you.

Maybe you're right. I could, if I had to.

Damn. You made me forget all about boring you with my story. That's rare.

Why carry that bag around?

Yes, I'm sorry. I remember. War does strip a soldier down to essentials. You must still feel like you're on campaign.

I've been to war, too. My grandfather fought the Kaiser. My father, the Emperor. I was sent up against the General. See? That's a sword cut, there. And here, a bullet that went clean through flesh, missed the bone completely.

Ah, that one got good mending. You brought your own physician on the campaign?

Of course I don't expect you to apologize. You are who you are, as am I. You did more to prove yourself than that brother of yours. He came here as a pilgrim and probably spent every night drunk in a whore house. Never knew what he missed. And even if you hadn't gone to war, you've done a good deal more than most by spending time up on Summit. Daring the token.

No, waiting to be chosen isn't easier than facing steel and bullets. It isn't lighter work than hearing the screams of your brothers and sisters as they lay torn to pieces, bleeding, guts spilled, mad with pain. But it is lonelier.

True. You always die alone. But there's a different quality to the terror of watching one human killing another, out in the open, right out there by the hole. It's very different from war. It's almost civilized. Everybody comes to watch, you know. Word spreads quickly, once tokens are exchanged and the sacrifice set.

It's the heart of the festival. Someone always finds out. If you're chosen, it's hard not to confide in a stranger, or with your loved ones, if they came. Maybe there's a witness to the exchange. Pilgrims often feel the need to announce themselves. Most want their sacrifice to be known, so people know they died for something.

My understanding is that the tokens guide you. Drive you to your other half of the sacrifice.

I don't know if it's magical, or electronic, or chemical. These are mysteries at the heart of the festival. Like the sacrifice, or what's at the bottom of the hole. Like death.

Yes. There are stories of one participant or the other wanting to back out, trying to sell their token, or throw it back into the hole. There was a rumor a few years back that one token bearer jumped into the hole, like he wanted to avoid the whole affair. Or hurry it up. His token-mate followed. The sacrifice went on, with a different pair. The thing from the hole makes arrangements, I suppose. We don't know the details. Wouldn't want to pay the price to find out. The temples don't stray on to such minor paths in their teachings. I'm sure the thing doesn't want to advertise its mistakes. There's always been a sacrifice, as long as I've lived, and generations back. Without a year missed. That's what's important.

I've never heard of anyone trying to stop the sacrifice. Not even when the parents and family are among the witnesses.

No, not even lovers.

No one wants another hole.

Praise to the Revelation.

No, I wouldn't advise going down in this season. The guides won't take you.

There's not a digger, or a thief raised in this city, who'd do it. They'd take your money, yes. But they'd never do it.

Because the stench and the wormy earth and the walls whispering for justice tend to discourage them. Not to mention the thing from the hole.

Only the crazy ones.

You could call it brave. But we call them mad.

The sacrifice always goes on. Doesn't matter if the mad ones go down, or throw themselves over the side, or stage their own sacrifice without the tokens. We've seen it all up on Summit. If you can imagine it, it's already been done, at least once.

Why do you want to go down into the hole?

Visit the museum. There's exhibits from generations of expeditions who went down, trying to find the bottom, looking for salvation, trying to negotiate with whatever lives down there. There was even a brigade sent down, once. That was brilliant. Lowered their artillery down in stages, along with supplies. They kept going into festival season. They never came back, and no one ever heard from them again.

You seem sane, to me. As much as anyone who's seen and done what we have. So why are you so anxious to meet the thing that comes out?

No, please don't go.

What was her name?

Yes. Beautiful. The names are always beautiful. Is there something of hers in your bag?

You're right. No need.

I'll join you on this one. Take the copper cup, that's Lueg. You'll enjoy the taste that stays with you after you put it down. A hint of cinnamon, and nutmeg. Goes well with the wind.

No, there was never anyone for me. All I ever had was the wind, and the taverns along Summit.

Sometimes being quiet says more, doesn't it.

Sorry, I can't help as I sit here, floating on the foam, thinking about such a young, promising man like yourself.

You could make a difference, you know. You understand so much about pain. You haven't run away from it, like the rest of your kind.

Glory to the Revelation.

Taking responsibility is right. That's what a young man like you needs to do. Carry the wisdom pain has taught you to your brothers and sisters. Teach them mercy. Forgiveness. Generosity. Wean them, and yourself, from the need to restore the old ways, to resurrect what brought on the Revelation in the first place. Do your kind really believe you can reshape the nature of what is, of who we are? Don't you think you're begging for another catastrophic miracle?

True. Not everyone is blessed with what's needed to fulfill such a mission. But somebody has to start, don't you think?

Stop it. I'm sorry. It's been a long time since I've laughed so hard. But that was a good one—I never thought of all those people going down the hole in terms of them trying to take responsibility. You have to admit, the mad dying for our sins is a pretty good joke.

You must have faith. Your lessons can serve the Revelation.

Because most people, rich or poor, good or bad, go through their lives caged by their expectations. So few try to be more than what they think they should be. The price of Revelation. But life's about embracing all of reality, not conforming to some small part we allow ourselves to perceive, don't you think? We shouldn't be running away, hiding behind rituals and scriptures, history and nature. We need to accept the shock of truths that change our perspective. Follow the road revealed to us by dislocation. Come to terms with what we are. And are not. Glory to the Revelation. You know. You've seen.

Of course we all hate change. We should, the way we do it, letting change happen to us, not working for transformation, metamorphosis, transfiguration. Because we don't know what's coming. We don't know who we're going to be. There's no hope. No faith.

That's right. The flesh is weak. We're afraid. Horror is what we are not, terror is who we are not. No one chooses to live in fear. Easier to live in the certainty of Revelation. But people like us know Revelation is only a sign. An arrow pointing in a direction. The festival, the sacrifice, all the temples and their clergy, they're just little reminders of what we should expect.

It's not a lie. Something does come out of the hole. Every year. Because sacrifices must be made.

I know. Still want to go down?

Too late. You've had too much, you'd never make it past the first escalade before falling. And what good would that do you?

Down the hatch.

So to speak.

Pick from the clay mugs. They're filled with swill, but at this point, I don't think either one of us can tell the good stuff from the bad.

Good chug.

What.

What do you mean—

That.

That's the token.

Yes.

Blood. The stains never come off, I heard. Now I know the truth of it.

No, I didn't put it there.

Who knows what gets into the kegs downstairs. Or maybe it was in the cup. Doesn't matter.

Yes, the joke's been played. In the lowest class of places. Runo's isn't like that. The tenders here would never put a false token in your cup. Besides, the feel of it in your hand should tell you if it's real or not.

Believe what you want. You're a pilgrim. You offered yourself.

Stay. You won't have to do that. Some thing is amusing itself, tonight. Here's what you're looking for.

No.

Look at the token, again.

That's right. You're not the victim. You are the instrument of the Revelation.

I would really like to see you try to convince the thing from the hole that it's made a mistake. That would be a good one. No insult intended, but that's not like getting a decent price for a coronet out of Bellinger's.

Funny, how the tokens call to each other. There really is no escaping sacrifice.

Ah. They've seen.

Thank you. Thank you. You see? They opened up a keg of their finest. All honor to the sacrifice. Praise the Revelation.

This morning. Slipped under the door. Wouldn't touch it for a while. I actually did think it was a joke. You know how writers are. And the *Journal* didn't hire the other writers on staff for their character.

Just like you. I waited for a sign. You hear all kinds of stories—tingling, whispers, a light, a strange compulsion to run shouting through the streets looking for my killer. Lightning bolts. Another subject temple teachings don't dwell on. And for all the years I've covered Summit, I've never been able to interview the participants. Things happen fast. And you feel low even trying to interfere for a story. This is sacrifice at its purest, after all. I guess what happens with the tokens is simpler than we imagined. All I felt was what you're feeling right now. The certainty of what I have to do. So much for rumors.

A little, yes. Hard not to be afraid.

Maybe it's also a relief.

I never thought I'd be chosen. Never offered myself as a pilgrim. I certainly never wanted to execute anyone, or die. I'm not even particularly religious, though I can debate the finer points of Revelation as easily as I can praise it, right along with the best of them. Being picked is an honor, though. I'm sure. And a duty. I can't remember the last time anyone from Summit was part of the sacrifice. Too close to the hole, we always say. Mostly it's pilgrims, as it should be, staying by Rampart. They'll be talking about old Yv around here for a long time. Maybe we can wait a bit, so I can write my last piece for the *Journal*, give them that interview I could never get. Pass along my wisdom. Reassure the sons and daughters of the rich and powerful that the risk they take in making their pilgrimage to the hole, and passing to adulthood through the festival, is well worth the possibility of sacrifice. There's so much to learn, if they'd only pay attention to what's about to happen. And if they're picked, how they could somehow change everything, how I—I'm sorry, I'm babbling. Time for you to yawn or something.

Not what we want, or hope for. Not what we have faith in. Or expect. What must be done.

No, I won't trade.

You have to do it.

That's the scent of death on the wind. It means the thing from the hole is ready to receive its due.

There's always a sacrifice.

The thing will make us. Through the tokens. And if we resist them, the thing from the hole will come.

I've never heard of it happening. But that's the story that's told in the temples.

No, that's not how the ceremony works. You kill me, throw my body down the hole with the tokens, and walk away. You don't even have to think about it. The tokens will guide you. The crowd doesn't tear you apart, the thing doesn't punish you, you're not put under arrest.

Some become monks or priests. Others join the service. Or turn into Holy Madmen. Or keep on wandering through the city gates, the countryside, into wilderness.

What do you think? Have you ever met anyone from the sacrifice in your circles?

I'm sure it must happen, but embracing a son or daughter forged into an instrument of the Revelation is not something an important family could tolerate. Or even a poor one. There's only so much faith people can take in close company. Hard truths don't encourage intimacy, contrary to temple teachings.

Mothers have been known to keep their children in cellars, or wilderness cottages, and provide for them. But those are mothers for you.

Other women are different. You know she wouldn't.

I thought this was what you wanted.

It's always different, once the bullet hits, the sword cuts. Remember how you felt when you went down in battle? Bleeding in the mud thinking you were going to die?

Yes. Exactly.

No.

Impossible.

Is that what you were thinking, wanting to go down the hole?

You can't kill it.

You can't even see it. The thing from the hole is a shadow, a wraith, another servant of the Revelation. A messenger, delivering tokens and demanding sacrifice by its simple presence.

Well, there's more than temple teachings to go on, my friend. In all the generations of sacrifice, there's never been a clear sighting.

You might as well say you want to kill your father, or the woman you love, or your commander. Your family's Elder. The President. God.

This isn't a dream, it's a nightmare.

That doesn't even make sense.

What if you're wrong?

And if you succeed, what do you hope to accomplish? Ignite another Revelation?

Ah.

That's a possibility.

Wait. Wait. Let me think.

I know. I feel the token, too.

Many will die.

The hole, this city, quite possibly the whole world, will be re-cast in the fires.

Yes.

I understand.

There is a chance. A faint one.

Let me—

Yes, that's enough.

If the last Revelation didn't accomplish its intention, maybe its time for a new message.

Nothing. We have nothing to lose.

But you should still kill me. Complete the sacrifice. Just in case.

I'm not trying to avoid the pain. I'm embracing it!

I suppose.

Don't worry. It'll find us if we stay strong and hold ourselves against the ritual.

Do you really think we'll be able resist the tokens?

I'm not sure. I'm not as young as you.

I could provoke you. Or attack you, and make you kill me.

I'll try my best.

We haven't even talked about what you're going to try to kill it with.

Not as much time as you think.

You know, I'm glad.

Because I was right about you.

I know.

But even if the thing from the hole wants us to do what we're doing, it won't surrender easily. It can't. Revelation rules us all.

Glory to the Revelation.

Let's go back to my rooms. Help me put together my own traveling bag. If we succeed, things are going to change. We might even survive the first storm and escape this place.

I can dream.

Me, I'll miss the ale. We'll never find another Runo's.

True. Or you might finally succeed in killing yourself in a noble cause. Stranger things have happened.

Of course I have a reed for the sax. Can you blow that horn?

Just some notes. For the *Journal* piece. If there's time.

Let's go.

The tokens do feel heavy.

This way.

Maybe.

In time.

We will.

On the wind that blows hard from below.

In the Capuchin Crypt Coffeeshop

Starbucks has infiltrated even here
where old monk's bones hang somber
on the rock-hewn wall. The scent
of roasted coffee beans mask the dead
air. Chants filter through hidden speakers
as customers pore over illuminated manuscripts
from the Dark Ages. Conversation is slow, whispered,
Latinate: *Domini et Deus, Pax Vobiscum…*
Double latte with a bagel, plain.
A cowled monk glides past;
the Nike *swoosh* gleams on his wine-colored cassock.
Religion has married Commerce
(Oh, they have always shared a bed
made of the spoils of war
tucked away in the Papal Bull Motel.
But now they have "come out"
in grand style amidst this 21st century world).
Jesus hangs on his donated cross, sponsored by Menard's;
the sacred host is made at a factory in Jerusalem
owned by McDonald's
and Mary Magdalene deals poker
five nights a week
at Bellagio's
in the Vatican.

— James P. Roberts

It's always a pleasure to publish a Naomi Kritzer story. Here's a charming blend of SF and Yiddish folklore.

When Shlemiel Went to the Stars

by Naomi Kritzer

Back on Earth, there was a shtetl in Eastern Europe called Chelm. Or perhaps it was a neighborhood in Brooklyn, or maybe a suburb of Detroit. The story goes that the Almighty sent out angels with bags full of wise souls and foolish souls, instructing them to sprinkle them evenly all around the world—but the angel with the bag of foolish souls tripped and the bag ripped open, and every single one fell out in Chelm. So the people born there were not exactly the brightest twinkles in the sky. In fact, they were denser than lead and dumber than snot—but *they* all thought they were geniuses.

The greatest fool of all was Jacob Macher, the mayor. He had a large collection of framed certificates and diplomas attesting to his brilliance in various ways: he had an Award for Leadership Excellence, a Certificate of Appreciation, and a Ph.D.

When humans first went to colonize the stars, the people of Chelm heard about it and thought it sounded like a fine idea, so Macher sent his office assistant, Shlemiel, to the real estate agent to buy a planet. "We want a great big planet," Macher told Shlemiel. "The biggest one available."

The real estate agent knew immediately that he was dealing with a fool. "I have just the planet for you," he said. "It's five times the size of Earth." He showed Shlemiel the pictures taken from space. It looked like a creamy blue ball on a black velvet curtain. "Nobody else lives on a world this big!"

"We'll take it!" Shlemiel said, and signed the papers. The Chelmites headed for the stars.

Imagine their surprise when they reached the planet and discovered that while it had an atmosphere they could breathe, and it had beautiful blue oceans, it had almost no *land*. The whole of the planet had only one tiny island.

"Shlemiel!" Macher groaned. "How could you be such a numbskull? I should have known better than to send you—your parents weren't born in Chelm, but moved there from California."

"We can't live here," said Gilda, Shlemiel's wife. "We've got enough fuel to get us back to Earth. Let's go home to Chelm."

"We can't go home *now*," Macher said. "We'll have wasted all the money we spent to *buy* this planet if we go home *now*. Let's think about this logically. We need either more land, or less water."

"Perhaps we could drain the ocean," someone suggested.

"Where would we put the water?" Gilda asked.

"We could sell it!" Shlemiel said. "We'll put up a sign. Free Water—You Haul."

"Shlemiel, you *fool*," Gilda said. "Who's going to come visit and see the sign?"

Shlemiel sighed, knowing Gilda was right. Another idea struck him. "Perhaps what is needed is not to create more land, but to make us better suited to the water."

"What do you mean?" Macher asked.

"If we learn to breathe underwater, that will solve all our problems," Shlemiel said.

"But we *can't* breathe water," Macher said. He closed his eyes and gestured for quiet. "I have it!" he said. "We can't breathe water, but we *can* breathe air. We will declare that the wet stuff surrounding our island is air."

"Don't be ridiculous," Gilda said. "Water isn't air!"

"My dissertation proved that language is just a construct," Macher sniffed. "Do *you* have a Ph.D., Gilda?"

"You can call our water 'Fred' if you want but you're still not going to be able to *breathe* it," Gilda said.

"Don't bring me problems, Gilda," Macher said. "I only want to hear solutions."

"I gave you a solution," Gilda said. "Take us home!"

"Quitters never win, Gilda. Are you a quitter?"

Gilda's response was drowned out by the chorus of approval for Macher's plan. The resolution declaring the island to be surrounded by air passed with an overwhelming majority. "We need a volunteer to test the breathability of the new air," Macher said. "Shlemiel, you do it."

Ignoring Gilda's protests, Shlemiel paddled a boat out into deep water and leapt in. He sank down and tried to take a big deep breath.

Shlemiel splashed to the surface, choking and gagging. "Help!" he squeaked as loudly as he could. "I can't swim!"

"You don't need to swim!" Macher shouted back. "It's air, remember? Try harder!"

Shlemiel tried again, and barely surfaced the second time. "It's—not—working," he choked out. "I'm drowning!"

"There's no 'I' in TEAM, Shlemiel!" Macher shouted. "And there's no 'I'M DROWNING' in it, either!"

"PULL ME OUT!" Shlemiel screamed.

Unfortunately, no one had a rope; Gilda kicked off her shoes and started to jump in, but remembered just in time that she couldn't swim, either. "Help!" she screamed. "Somebody save my husband!"

Shlemiel went under for the third time, and for a moment everyone thought that all was lost. But then, his head bobbed up again and stayed up. His arm was tucked over the head of a fish—the most enormous fish any of the Chelmites had ever seen, with huge eyes and shimmering blue-green skin. The fish swam to shore, nudging Shlemiel into the waiting hands of the Chelmites. It then waited for a long moment, staring at the Chelmites with its bright eyes.

Gilda was pounding Shlemiel on the back, but looked up to study the fish. It seemed to study her back. "Macher," Gilda said, "This is no ordinary fish."

"No! It's the biggest fish I've ever seen!" Macher said. "It could feed us for weeks!"

"We can't eat it!" Gilda shrieked. "Macher, I think this fish might be intelligent."

Macher grabbed Gilda's arm. "We have to catch it," Macher said. "Study it. Dissect it. See if you're right—because if it *is* intelligent, we need to be very, very careful not to make it angry!"

Over Gilda's strenuous objections, an order went out and the fish was caught in a net and taken ashore. They deposited the great fish into a deep inland salt-water pool. Its skin shone like a polished rock; it swam around and around, its tail flipping out of the water every now and then like the delicate edge of a fan.

"How can we *know* if it's intelligent or not?" someone

asked Macher.

"It saved my husband," Gilda cried. "Isn't that evidence enough?"

There was a long, awkward pause.

"We can build a maze for it to swim," Macher said. "That's how we tested intelligence when I was working on my Ph.D."

"That's how you tested the intelligence of *rats*," Gilda said. "How did you test the intelligence of people?"

"We made them run mazes, too. Did you know that rats are smarter than undergraduates?"

"Let's try talking to it," someone suggested.

So the Chelmites tried talking to the fish. When it didn't respond to English, they tried Spanish, Yiddish, Hebrew, Chinese, Esperanto, Russian, and even Bronx. "Hey Fish," said Shlemiel. "If you're sentient, say something!"

The fish didn't say anything. It just swam around and around and around, occasionally poking its head out of the water to glare ferociously at Macher.

"Maybe this species doesn't *talk*," Gilda said. "Had that occurred to you?"

"Of course it had," Macher said. "Shlemiel! Why haven't you brought a pen that writes underwater yet?"

Shlemiel brought a pen and a board to write on. They lowered the pen and board into the water, but the fish ignored them completely.

"How could it write anything?" Gilda asked. "It doesn't have hands like ours, just fins."

"Wouldn't an intelligent species be smart enough to evolve thumbs?" Macher asked.

"We're an intelligent species," Gilda said. "Why haven't we evolved thumbs on our feet, too? Think how efficient your office could be if Shlemiel had *four* thumbs instead of just two."

Macher was struck silent for a moment, then shook his head. "Shlemiel would just make twice as many mistakes."

"I have an idea," someone suggested. "It's been a while, and the fish must be getting hungry. Let's throw Shlemiel in again and see if the fish eats him. If it doesn't, *that* probably means it's intelligent."

"Hasn't my husband been through *enough* in one day?" Gilda wailed, but Shlemiel (eager to redeem himself after his failure to breathe the seawater) jumped into the pool.

The fish looked startled, especially when Shlemiel started to drown again. Cautiously, it approached him, let him grab on around its neck, and dragged him back to the edge of the pool.

"There," Gilda said. "It saved him again. Now will you believe it's intelligent?"

"Maybe it's just not hungry yet," Macher said. "Or—" he added when he saw that Gilda was about to interrupt him, "maybe these fish just don't eat meat. No matter how hungry a giraffe is, it's not going to eat a human."

"Maybe we should send a volunteer into the water to visit the other Great Strange Fish," Shlemiel said, wringing out his shirt. "Someone who can *swim*, this time."

"Oh, good idea," Gilda said. "Maybe Macher can go."

"I can't go," Macher sputtered. "I am *far* too important to this colony to risk losing."

"But what if *they* want to do intelligence tests on *us*?" Gilda said. "How can we possibly risk sending anyone but you, Macher?"

"Well, we certainly can't send Shlemiel," Macher said.

"No, you're right about that," Gilda said, wrapping a warm blanket around Shlemiel. "Build your maze, Macher. I think that's the only thing left to try."

But the Great Strange Fish seemed to have had *enough*. As Macher leaned over the water to look at it again, it shot a spout of water straight up Macher's nose. "Aaargh!" Macher shouted, and fell into the pool. Rather than rescuing him, the fish swam away. It looked like it was gloating. Shlemiel pulled Macher out of the pool.

"That wicked, horrid creature!" Macher sputtered. "If it *is* intelligent, it's devious—wicked—evil—*dangerous*!"

Shlemiel looked down at the fish. It had a weary expression on its face. It occurred to Shlemiel that for once, Macher might be wrong; if aliens had landed in Chelm and kidnapped Shlemiel and refused to return him to his home and his family, he'd have done far worse than squirt water up their nose, given the opportunity. For a moment, he felt very lost. Then he had an idea. "You're right," he said to Macher. "It's a wicked, evil fish. It's so wicked and evil that I think we should kill it."

Gilda froze in horror as Macher wrung out his coat and looked at Shlemiel with interest. "Do you think we could fry it up for dinner?"

"No, of course not. What if the flesh is poisonous? Or worse, what if its wickedness is contagious?"

Macher nodded slowly. "What do you think we should do, then?"

"Fish drown in air," Shlemiel said. "I think we should throw it—into the air." He pointed at the deep blue "air" that surrounded the island. "Drowning is the only suitable death for a fish like this."

"Excellent idea!" Gilda said. "Don't you think that's a good idea, Macher?"

Macher was forced to admit that this seemed just. So the fish was loaded back into the net and carried back to the shore, where it was ceremoniously dumped into the cold, salty air.

"What now?" someone asked. "We're still on this stupid island, and Shlemiel couldn't breathe that sort of air—we're back where we started."

Shlemiel scratched his head. "You know, if your planet is already occupied—if there are intelligent aliens—you're supposed to get a refund," he said. "I remember reading that on one of the papers I signed."

"But we never determined if the fish was intelligent or not," Macher said.

"Let's just all agree to *say* that we think the fish is intelligent," Shlemiel said. "If a genius like Macher couldn't be sure, the real estate agency won't know, either. They'll have to refund our money."

"Grand idea," Macher said. "Shlemiel, if this works, you've redeemed yourself for buying this planet."

And so it happened. Fortunately, the real estate agency seemed quite convinced by their claim that the fish were intelligent. Not only did they refund the money, but they sent shuttles to evacuate the Chelmites immediately and gave them some extra money not to tell anyone what had happened there.

This would have been enough money to buy another great big planet—this time with land. But the Chelmites had had enough of colony life for the time being. They returned to Chelm, and were able to buy back their homes and business. They were all very happy to return.

Not long after Macher had moved back into his office, though, Shlemiel came up to his desk and said, "Macher, remember how you said that language was just a construct?"

"Shlemiel, you fool," Macher said. "I wrote my dissertation on that very topic. Of course I remember."

"So…" Shlemiel pointed at the cup of coffee in his hand. "I am going to rename this *accolades.*" He took a thick black marker and wrote ACCOLADES on the cup. "I would like to shower you with accolades, for your brilliant leadership back on the planet." He dumped his coffee on Macher's head.

"Ow!" Macher took off his glasses to wipe coffee off the lenses. "What are you doing, Shlemiel?"

Macher had been drinking a fizzy drink, and Shlemiel picked that up off of Macher's desk. "Now, *this* I'm going to call a Certificate of Real Appreciation for Positivity—that's kind of long, so I'll abbreviate it." He wrote CRAP on the drink, and then threw that in Macher's face as well.

Macher scooted back in his chair, grabbing a tissue to wipe the fizzy drink out of his eyes. "Shlemiel, you dunderhead, you have completely misunderstood my research," he said.

"Finally," Shlemiel said, still holding the pen he'd been writing with, "I'm going to call this pen MY JOB. And I'd like you to take this job and—oh, here, I'll do it for you." He leaned across the desk and stuck the pen up Macher's nose.

"Shlemiel," Macher said, dripping with coffee and fizzy drink, and with a pen sticking out of his nose, "Have you gone *completely insane?*"

"No," Shlemiel said. "But I *have* found another job. I'm going back to that planet; I'm going to work for the scientists who are studying the Great Strange Fish. Gilda got a job working for them, too." He walked toward the door, but turned back to say, "You know, Macher. You can call something *air*, but that doesn't mean you can breathe it. You can call yourself a genius, but you're still an idiot. And you can call me tomorrow, but I won't answer my phone. Good luck finding a new office assistant!"

No one from Chelm ever saw Gilda or Shlemiel again.

This one's sort of the reverse of that Twilight Zone *episode "The Monsters are Due on Maple Street." What if a community was beset by something strange and reacted, eventually, with compassion and common sense?*

The Jaculi
by Patricia Russo

When the jaculi first arrived in the neighborhood, we gave them a lot of grief. This was mainly due to so many of us being all ignorant and whatnot. And on top of that, as if plain old natural human ignorance wasn't enough, a lot of folks were already on edge. The night the jaculi started jumping, we were sweating through our third blackout that July.

From our rooftops, from our windows, from the street corners where we sat on hot cement and fanned ourselves under the dead traffic lights, we could see the glow of lit-up high-rises and office buildings to the north. The first blackout had affected the whole city, and went on for fifteen hours. Damn, they'd nearly run out of candles up north. All their ice cubes had melted, yeah, and D-cell batteries had gone for ten bucks a pop. Meanwhile, down here, precious few folk had had candles or D-cells, or anywhere to buy them, in the first place. After the power came back on, the mayor got hit with a lot of flak from the people who count. We all watched him standing in front of a dozen TV cameras, him wiping his bald head and vowing it would never happen again. So the second and third blackouts were just for us, a big old raised middle finger from the power company and city hall together, aimed at our concrete triangle below Blue Street. Maybe they all forgot that there were people living down here, that it wasn't all warehouses and meatpacking plants and twenty-four-seven sweatshops churning out t-shirts and ball caps and cut-rate bridal gowns. Maybe they forgot it was a neighborhood crammed with old folks and children.

It was hot. It was dark. And it was the third time in two damn weeks. Even the little kids had quit thinking it was fun camping out on the project roofs and eating jelly sandwiches by candlelight.

Down here below Blue Street, we've got three borders. To the southwest is the river. This is our hypotenuse, the longest side of our triangle. The water is flat, the current sluggish; the river is gray on top, black below. Anyone who eats a fish pulled out of that muck is a fool to himself, but there are plenty of fools in the world, and on summer days you can always see a bunch of tough guys with poles pulling butt-ugly floppy things out of the water. To the north, a highway cuts the neighborhood off from the rest of the city. Our elders, those seniors who haven't completely locked themselves away behind the barricades of their subsidized old-people-jails, those who come out to tell stories sometimes, they talk about the days before the highway was cut through like it was another world, the dreamtime when we were all one city. To the east are the deadlands, empty blocks, the buildings abandoned, or burnt down, or razed, years ago, and never rebuilt. Of course people live there, too. People and other things. Those of us with jobs and families and lives try to stay out of the deadlands. Night, day, makes no matter. We stay out. But the first jaculi that bounded in arrived from the east, and some hotheads, some guys and some women with no damn sense, jumped up and started chasing them, chasing the darting jaculi back to the east. After they'd stopped screaming, that is, after the heroes made sure they hadn't all-the-way shit their shorts, they started running after our visitors, with the rest of us hollering after them to stop, stop running, east, east, goddamn idiots, that way is east!

They came back, sort of sheepish. Except for one woman, a punked-out girl who'd moved to the neighborhood the fall before, told everyone she was going to college. If she was, it must've been some on-line thing, because no one ever saw her on the street in the daylight. Well, no one ever saw her anywhere after the night of the third blackout. She ran east, whooping, swinging her serious survive-the-bomb camo-colored flashlight

like a club. She ran too far.

The jaculi jumped, jumped, jumped. It looked like there were millions of them, surely, but that was because they moved so fast, darted so swiftly, leapt with such amazing, neck-whipping celerity. We saw the same one a dozen times in a minute, and thought we were seeing twelve separate entities.

Flying snakes, we thought. Flying snakes as long and as thick around as the arms of roid-rushing gymrats. Oh, the screaming; folks screamed for damned-near-ever, it seemed like, like those car alarms that break the night over and over and over again, and quit for a second, just long enough for you to heave a sigh of relief, but then, as the ringing in your ears is about to fade, kick up once more, the eternal urban music box. The people were screaming exactly like that.

But, to be fair, the jaculi were pretty alarming. Flying serpents are bad enough (it took some of us quite a while to be convinced that the jaculi weren't actually flying, but leaping and jumping, not merely with astounding swiftness, but with remarkable range—on the corner where our group had planned to pass the long, sweaty night, we saw jaculi bound from our side of the street to the top of the two-story car-detailing place on the other side in one lightning leap; it surely looked like flight), but their faces, when one stopped still for the second it took to get a fair look in the light of wavering candles and shaking flashlights, chilled the hearts of even the most level-headed among us. The jaculi had heads the size of softballs, which was one big fat clue we weren't dealing with some mass escape from a secret herpetarium here. Second clue: the jaculi were beaked, with the strong, curved, wicked beaks of raptors. Third: their eyes were as big and round and brown as the eyes of cows, though much steelier.

Mothers pulled their kids off the roofs and hustled them into the oven-heat of airless apartments. Old folks who hadn't ventured outside in the first place shut their windows and pulled their blinds and huddled in the dark, hoping that, once more, being invisible would spare them. Men who'd already had a few beers to cool off, and women with no sense, dashed into their homes and emerged with weapons, pretty silver pistols and big black gangster pieces, swords bought rusty and dull from the Elista Thrift Shop, sheatheless hunting knives bought drunk at three in the morning off an exuberant infomercial, nunchucks, fire axes that hadn't struck a lick in fifty years, spray cans of ninety-nine cent store cockroach killer and more than one home-rigged Taser. The neighborhood warriors, the ones who always met a smirk with a fist.

Meanwhile the jaculi leapt and darted, jumped and almost-flew. Zipping over our heads, landing on balconies, landing on ledges, landing on top of telephone poles and the long curved arms of traffic lights. The jaculi would pause a moment, then coil and spring again. They seemed restless to us, those of us still watching them instead of chasing them, those of us whose bodies no longer responded to stimulus with immediate flight or fight, or perhaps never had. The jaculi had come from somewhere, maybe from the deadlands to the east, maybe not, but they had come for a reason. They were searching. Hunting.

Our warriors pursued, and hollered, and threw things, and shot at the jaculi. We gave the jaculi some damn hard grief, that first night. We gave ourselves more. Folks with alcohol-impaired aim and no sense shooting pistols and semis and crossbows into the air. Imagine. It was a lucky thing the mothers had taken the kids inside, and that most of the old folks were still sharp enough to stay away from the windows after they'd closed them and drawn the blinds. As it was, some folks on the street got hit by bullets on their way down, a lot of glass was smashed, many walls punctured, telephone poles pocked and chewed, wires snapped. Once the blood started to flow, some women got their sense back and set after the men they had a claim on to haul them back from idiocy, and the shouts went up for medics.

Soon some more folks got their sense back and started transporting the really hurt to a central location, the intersection of Spinet and Summit, where there was a big old parking lot out in front of the convenience store that had gone out of business in April. And more folks brought their flashlights and candles and, no kidding, hurricane lamps and set them up so the medics would be able to see what they were doing and who was bleeding from where and how serious it was. And some folks broke into the back of the boarded-up convenience store just in case there was anything left in there, but there wasn't.

Meanwhile the jaculi kept jumping.

And the parking lot was filling up with moaning and cursing and bleeding folks, and a few who weren't moaning or cursing or even moving at all. Medics, medics, people were hollering, nobody being dumb enough to expect a doctor, but many hoping there was an LPN somewhere, an EMT maybe, at least someone who'd passed high-school first aid.

We lost a few people that night, due to our being ignorant and all. First, the wanna-be punk girl who ran into the east too far, then a couple more, from bullets. We might have lost more, we might have lost a whole lot before the night was over, especially older folks and little kids, locked up in stifling, two-hundred degree rooms out of fear.

The jaculi kept on jumping. Agitated, searching, seeking. Once in a while one of them let out a sort of cheep. That was the only sound we ever heard them make, except for the whoosh of air as they leapt past our heads.

The shooting had stopped. Some of the women had got hold of their men, and some of the men had got hold of their own selves, and though folks still cried out when a jaculus sprang over them, still pointed and cursed, with real bleeding going on in the parking lot and real death hovering, folks started to focus on what was likely to happen once daylight arrived, or power was restored, whichever came first. A few folk sort of surreptitiously slipped off to the southwest. The river received a number of offerings that night, we came to believe, most of them metal, both the compact, shiny, silvery type and the mean matte black sort.

But we still didn't know what to do about the wounded, except drip water on their heads and try to blot up the blood with paper towels, and the jaculi were still darting all over the place, and though we could tell now that there weren't as many of them as we'd first thought, their speed and their unceasing motion, not to mention their snake bodies and eagle beaks and bovine eyes, had all of us very, very nervous. A lot of us spent more time flinching and trying to look out of the corners of our eyes in all possible directions just in case one of the jaculi took the notion to dart at us than paying close attention to the hurt people lying on the hot asphalt of the parking lot.

We might have lost a lot more than we did. It really could have been a lot worse. For a while there, for about half an hour after the shooting mostly stopped (some folks never did get their sense back that night; some folks got their stupidity fixed down deep in the middle of their bones), it looked like it was going to be.

Then the grandmothers came.

How they got themselves all organized the way they did we never managed to figure out. Sure, some folks had cell phones, and some of the cell phones were working that night. Maybe it was that, one grandma with a teenage grandbaby in the house who knew another grandma with a great-niece in the house, who knew another…linking up like a chain. Maybe they all knew each other already; none of us would have put that past them. They all arrived together, all grim and prepared, carrying supplies, and they all worked together like a veteran team, not talking to each other very much, just pointing and nodding and passing bandages and scissors, sharing gauze, helping each other hold folks down while another grandmother did her work, trading drugs with no argument or fuss. They didn't talk much to the rest of us, either, just did their work with their lips pursed and their shoulders bent and sad, like they'd seen all this before and were grieving over seeing it again, but the work had to be done, and they were going to by-damn do it.

Grandma, over here. Grandma, please, look at my sister. Grandma, this guy's passed out, help. That's what we said, softly, most of us, no screaming, no yelling, most of us acting with sense, and after a while grandma started sounding too familiar, not respectful enough, and we switched to grandmother.

Not all of the grandmothers were women. There was a fair sprinkling of men among them. It was one of the men, a bald guy with a long fringe of white hair, who between pulling slivers of glass out of a woman's face with tweezers and splinting a kid's leg, looked up and told us what the jaculi were. Jaculi, plural, jaculus, singular, from the Latin jacere, to throw or cast, named so from their darting motions. Imaginary creatures found in a couple old books that had passed for science texts a few hundred years ago.

Imaginary? They don't look so imaginary, grandmother, one person said, his voice low and respectful.

The old guy looked up again, and nodded. *Not so imaginary any more*, he agreed. Then he went back to wrapping bandages around the splint.

Not all the grandmothers were old. There was a fair sprinkling of younger women among them. It was one of these, an iron-haired woman in a photographer's vest, every pocket of which was bulging with pill bottles and boxes and vials, who told us, *Feed them. They're here, so we might as well make friends with them. Feed them.* Then she went back to handing out pills and powders and ointments.

So then, naturally, we were faced with the difficulty of figuring out what imaginary beasts from old books in Latin might eat. This wasn't altogether a bad thing, though the discussion turned a bit heated once or twice, because it gave those of us with nothing else to do but stand around and be worried, which was frankly most of us, something to do.

Meanwhile the jaculi jumped, and jumped, and jumped. But they must've been getting some tired themselves, because they were pausing more, resting more; it seemed like they were catching their wind before leaping again. This allowed those of us who wanted to look the chance to get in a good glance or two.

Look at their eyes, someone said.

Damn, those beaks, someone else said softly.

They're sort of beautiful, said another of us.

In the end, we decided that the jaculi most likely

were meat-eaters, given the shape of their beaks and the fact that everything below their necks was definitely snake, and none of the snakes we could think of were vegetarians. The next argument arose over whether the jaculi were live-prey feeders or carrion eaters. This debate was started to turn heated, too, when one of us threw up her hands in disgust and said the hell with it, the meat in her freezer was spoiled anyway, since she hadn't thrown it out after the second blackout, like you were supposed to, but now after another one she sure as shit wasn't going to eat it herself, so why not try it and see. She stomped off, muttering to herself, casting dark glances at the rooftops, the telephone poles, the long arms of the traffic lights.

If we feed them they'll never go away, someone objected. *Like, you know, stray cats, or rats, or pigeons. And damn, but we got enough stray cats and rats and pigeons around here, don't we? Do we really need flying snakes, too?*

So that was the third argument, but the grandmother had said to feed them, so that argument was pretty well settled by the time our volunteer came hauling a shopping bag with a few cling-wrapped chunks of nearly-thawed hamburger meat and a styrofoam tray of chicken legs.

It turned out that the jaculi loved nearly-thawed chunks of gray hamburger and drippy raw chicken legs. They cheeped when they saw our volunteer unwrap the contents of her freezer and toss the gloppy bits into the middle of the street. It was clear to all of us that these were cheeps of eagerness, and of joy. Then whoosh, whoosh, whoosh, they descended, swarming the food like starving things.

See, what did I tell you? Just like pigeons, said the one who'd lost that argument. He was still disgruntled. *Remember, what goes in's gotta come out. I bet they poop like Rottweilers, these things.*

Shut up, we told him gently.

The jaculi ate quickly, but neatly. In under a minute, all the scraps of hamburger and the chicken legs had disappeared.

The jaculi cheeped again. They looked at us hopefully.

See, I told you. Just like cats. Now they'll never—
Shut up, we reminded him.

At that point, the grandmothers told us to take it up the block and let them work in peace, so we did. We moved our gathering back to the intersection of Summit and Spinet. The shooting and shouting and acting all stupid had died away by now. Windows were open again, and folks were leaning out, a little nervously, wiping their faces, fanning themselves. A few mothers had brought their kids back to the rooftops. As we walked to Spinet and Summit, we waved at these cautious, brave folks encouragingly. In the end, we didn't lose anyone because they'd feared too much and locked themselves in the heat and the airlessness too long. Folks who got their nerve back went to check on those who hadn't and convinced them to open the windows, come out for a breath of cooler air.

Those of us who had stocked-up freezers and fridges sacrificed their contents. For the rest of the night, we fed the jaculi. It was easy to see, when they were all together, that there really were much fewer of them than it had first appeared. Not hundreds, oh no. Certainly not thousands, the way some of the folks who lost their sense the earliest were screaming only a couple of hours ago. Maybe four dozen, maybe five, tops.

We discovered, by trial and error, that the jaculi would eat soggy unfrozen waffles, but not soggy, unfrozen peas. They would eat fish sticks, but not crinkle-cut potatoes. Well, not any potatoes, period. They would, some children discovered with glee, eat jelly sandwiches.

The night grew cooler toward dawn, and a slight breeze began to blow, which was a welcome relief, though we all had lived there long enough to know that the heat and the humidity would snap down like a lid as soon as the sun rose. The sky turned gray, and we began to distinguish colors again instead of merely shapes, and one by one people blew out their candles and switched off their flashlights.

The jaculi were not gluttons. They ate until they were satisfied, and then they stopped, and more slowly then, with more effort and less of a whoosh, leapt to many separate high places. There they looped around themselves, coiling as serpents do coil and ending up beak to tail, and settled down to sleep.

We didn't get the electric back until late in the afternoon of the next day. And what did we see on our TVs as soon as those electronic eyes opened up? What did we hear on our radios when we switched them on? What did we see online when we connected?

Jaculi. Jaculi all over the city, leaping and darting like ours, but not like ours. Frantic, desperate jaculi, hunted from tree to tree and post to post and roof to roof by grim men in uniforms, jaculi caught in nets, broken with clubs, shot, killed. Killed, and killed, killed. And hysterical people, folks with no sense, screaming and crying that the authorities weren't doing enough, weren't killing the jaculi (not that anyone on the TV knew that jaculi was the name for them) fast enough.

It was heartbreaking. After almost a full day with the jaculi in our neighborhood, most of us had come around to the opinion first expressed by one or two during the long night of the blackout: that the jaculi were beautiful.

Some of us had jobs outside the neighborhood. We didn't go to them that day, or the next. It looked like everybody north of us were busy going crazy, and we decided to leave them to it. We all went about our lives, fixed up stuff that had been broken during the power outage and our own, smaller, craziness at that time. We visited the grandmothers, made sure they all had working fans and ice in their freezers. We kept on taking care of the folks who had been hurt. We decided what to do about the three individuals who'd died in the parking lot, two of whom had no families willing to claim them, and one who did. We thought about the punk girl who'd disappeared in the deadlands to the east. There wasn't anything we could do about that, but we thought about her. We didn't forget her. We went on, as we always did, in our triangle below Blue Street.

The one thing we didn't do was feed our jaculi. We didn't have to.

As it turned out, they were very skillful hunters. As soon as they got themselves acclimatized, which basically happened once they'd slept off the freezer-scrap meal we'd fed them, they began to fend for themselves.

Nobody mourned the loss of the rats, and only a few protested the culling of the pigeons. Rather more of us got upset at the lowered population of stray cats, and there was talk of mounting rescue operations to trap the cats in humane cages and get them adopted, but we'd had those discussions before, and just like always, nothing came of it this time, either. In the end people accepted that this was the way nature worked. Some ate, and some got eaten.

The jaculi have been with us for months now. They have built nests, and some folks claim they have seen eggs in those nests. This is good news, most of us think. In the rest of the city, the jaculi have grown rare. A sighting or two is reported every couple of weeks, and whenever one is spotted, no effort seems to be spared to hunt it down, discover where it's been hiding, and kill it.

Now winter is coming, and we wonder if the eggs will hatch before then. We wonder if the jaculi will need our help to feed the little ones, or if they will be able to manage on their own even when snow covers the sidewalks and the streets and pigeons and cats are harder to spot. We wonder, some of us, if the jaculi will hiberate. This is such a point of interest that considerable sums have been wagered on it. We wonder if the jaculi can be domesticated. If, for example, a young one fell out of its nest, and one of us took it home, might we tame it and raise it and have it love us?

We wonder a lot of things. That's the way folks down here have always been, full of questions and wonderments and debates. But mostly we are glad that the beautiful jaculi are with us now. We are sorry for acting like ignorant fools when they first came, and we are glad that they have forgiven us. We hope they stay. Most of all, we are glad that we live in this small neighborhood below Blue Street, and not in one of the soulless ones to the north, where the streets are clean and the streets all have trees, where people work in buildings tall enough to poke the clouds, and spend all their money on cars and clothes and exercise equipment, and pay for grim men in sharp uniforms to kill every new thing that appears in the world.

Tony Pi entered our pages last issue with the tale of sentient merry-go-round animals fighting feral, vampiric musical notes. Here's a story that, apart from being fantasy, is altogether different from its predecessor. This one's about a country that feels like an alternate medieval Russia, in which three brothers seek good fortune by very different routes.

Come Frost, Sun, and Vine
by Tony Pi

During the reign of Tsar Dominin, in the village of Hindessa far to the west, three brothers knelt as one to lay a wreath of nightshade and glorymorn upon a fresh grave.

"Dream long, Old Mother," said Fyobor the eldest. He too had dreams, ambitions too grand for their village, and now it was past time for him to leave.

"Rest well, Mother," said Lyonid the middle brother, wiping tears from his pockmarked face. He did not bemoan the hardships of a farming life, but no woman in town would love him the way he looked, of that he was certain. Love awaited him elsewhere.

"Farewell and weep no more," said Sergef the youngest. Though he missed her most, Sergef kept his word to his mother, wasting no tears for death. "Watch over us on our journey."

They cut their thumbs upon the same knife and swore unity above all, sealing their oath with blood. Then they set forth together on the summer road, pockets full of coin and singing songs steeped in dreams.

On their travels, each brother discovered a flaw in himself: pale Fyobor was too frail, dour Lyonid too ashamed of his face, and Sergef too eager to trust. Yet they always took care of one another. When merchants tried to cheat Sergef, Fyobor stepped in to haggle the price. When drunken brutes took insult at Fyobor's wit, Lyonid beat them back. When Lyonid's scowl frightened the villagers, Sergef won them over with his candor. But the kindness of strangers lasted only so long. By the thrice-ninth day, they had spent their last coin on wine to slake their dust-dry throats. Only Sergef still wasted breath to sing of hope and heroes.

With no money for an inn, the brothers sought a place in the woods to camp. Chancing upon a creek, they followed it upstream until they heard the sound of laughter ahead. Curious, they approached quietly, and were surprised to see three maidens bathing nude in a moonlit pool. Sergef gaped while Lyonid slipped deeper into shadow, but Fyobor spied the feather-cloaks hanging on a nearby tree, two white and one black. The women were swan-maidens.

A plan occurred to Fyobor. He edged near the cloaks, drawing the black one towards him with his walking stick. Smiling, he seized it, but to his surprise the feathers were razor-sharp, slicing his fingers. He cried out in pain.

At the sound of his cry, the swan-maidens rushed for shore. The brothers turned to flee, but the dark-haired one shouted a hex and froze Fyobor in place. "Blood was drawn, so blood must obey," said she.

Sergef darted to shield his brother, while Lyonid swung his staff. "Free him, witch!" shouted Lyonid.

"Calm, brother!" said Sergef, averting his gaze as best he could. "Please, Wise One, take back your cloak. I'm sure Fyobor only meant mischief."

"No harm will come to him," she answered, deftly dodging Lyonid's staff and snatching up her cloak. Swiftly, she and her ladies dressed, much to Sergef's relief. "I am Jovansya. Your trespass merely startled us. He would not have gone far with my trappings. Only one man ever did." She snapped her fingers and freed Fyobor from his binding. "Come, light a fire and regale us with tales of your past, and dreams of your future."

Fyobor nursed his cuts. "I only wanted to ransom it for power, to speed us to our success. Is that so wrong?"

"We shall see," said Jovansya, smiling thinly.

They huddled around the fire and bemoaned their luck to the Swan-Queen.

"How would you improve your lot?" she asked.

"I'd scheme," said Fyobor. "Take with cunning what I could never take by force."

"I'd serve," said Lyonid. "Who'd follow a face like

mine? In the service of a lord, prove myself worthy and rise through the ranks."

"I'd persevere," said Sergef. "Brothers, our misfortunes will give way to experience. There's no need for guile or yoke!"

"Shall I read your destinies?" asked Jovansya.

The brothers saw no harm in it.

The handmaidens rose. The plump one plucked three feathers from her cloak and made a single talisman with hairs from each brother's head. "This is the fortune of three who ride the same wind," she said.

The other maiden plucked a hair from each head, tying them to three separate quills. "These are the fortunes of you who fly alone."

Jovansya took the talismans from her servants and knelt by the water. First, she spun the lone quills like maple keys over the pond, noting their pirouettes as they fell. When she did the same with the thrice-bound plumes, the talisman did not fly far.

"Two roads lie before you," said Jovansya. "If three travel as one, then all must be content with small triumphs, hard earned. If three should go their separate ways, all will find great magic, though only one becomes Tsar. But beware: three-as-one will be loyal unto death. Three apart may quarrel unto their dooms."

"Tsar!" said Fyobor, eyes widening. Long had he dreamt of sitting the Halcyon Throne. "Who?"

"There are things even I cannot see, but this I know: the fair Tsarevna Virta comes of age in a year. Win her heart to rule by her side," said Jovansya.

Lyonid bit a fingernail. For nine generations, House Majessa had ruled the realm with kindness and wisdom. If he became Tsar, surely the people would come to adore him. "How do we find this magic?" he asked.

Jovansya drew three black feathers from her cloak. The first she gave to Fyobor. "Journey north over the Godgallants into the land of frost. With this plume, fletch a killing arrow. Steal the hide from an ice-bear and strength is yours."

To Lyonid: "Trek south through the Diamondance valleys into the sun-scorched land. Fletch an arrow and take the skin of the lion-king. Charm will be yours."

Finally, she gave a feather to Sergef. "Meander east upon the rake of rivers into the vineyard lands. Win the fleece of a simple goat and wisdom is yours."

"Couldn't we seek all three powers in turn?" asked Sergef.

Jovansya shook her head. "The compromises of three-as-one are not the decisions one makes alone. Go your own paths, or forfeit your powers."

"We don't need magical gifts to live as heroes!" said Sergef. "Trust in our strength, brothers. I cannot bear strife between us!"

"But one of us could become Tsar!" said Fyobor.

"Also strength, charm, and wisdom," said Lyonid. "Why settle for mediocre lives when we can each find glory?"

"What if we meet again a year hence in Nobylisk?" said Fyobor. "A year apart cannot sever our kinship!"

"We vowed we'd face the world together. Blood was drawn. Blood must obey," said Sergef.

A breeze from the west stirred the feathers on Jovansya's cloak. "An ill wind blows, and I must fly," Jovansya said. "My prophecy is my gift and curse to you. Make of it what you will." She and her handmaidens waded into the shallows. In a flurry of feathers, they became swans, skimming across the water before soaring into night.

The brothers argued by the dying fire, not one wavering from his position.

"We should fight these temptations," said Sergef.

"We should take the magic," said Lyonid.

"We should sleep and debate in the morning," said Fyobor. At last, everyone agreed to this.

Fyobor waited for Sergef's snores before whispering his true plans to Lyonid. "Brother, Sergef will never let us part, and we'll blame him for chaining us to our threadbare lives. I love Sergef, but there comes a time when one must leave his family to become his own man."

Lyonid nodded. "The boy must learn that we cannot always save him from his follies. How will he find wisdom if we always shield him from the world?"

"We'll go our separate ways," said Fyobor. "He cannot follow us both." The two embraced and gathered their things in silence. Then, they left for separate roads, to frost and to sun.

When Sergef awakened, he found himself alone. He shouted for his brothers, but they were long gone.

"So they abandon me." Still, Sergef refused to despair. In a year, his brothers were sure to go to Nobylisk to claim the Tsar's throne. "I won't give up on them, Jovansya. I'll prove your prophecy wrong."

And so Sergef took the path forced upon him, towards the eastern lands, singing still of hope.

A year passed.

The Tsarevna had come of age, and in celebration, the Tsar declared a Season of Silks in Nobylisk, from high summer to summer's ebb, signalling his blessing for the ambitious to court his daughter.

The legends told that the spirits of the Four Seasons fell in love with the First Tsar's daughter, the fair Majessa. Taking the guise of heroes, they came to court to vie for her love. Chivalrous Spring, eloquent Summer, diligent Autumn, and stalwart Winter—any of them would have made a fitting mate. After a fierce competition, Winter proved victorious.

Since then, it had been the tsardom's tradition for each Tsarvena to be courted by only four suitors embodying the virtues of the Seasons, so that the spirits would bless the union. Only these four Gallants, chosen by different means, would be invited to the palace to win the Tsarevna's heart.

On the ninth night of the festival, Virta and her retinue rode into the heart of the city, seeking the Gallant Spring. Virta's lissome beauty belied a shrewd mind. Everyone said she had her mother's grace, but she had only their word for it. Her mother abandoned her soon after she was born. The tales varied: that the Tsarina was a courtesan, a witch, a goddess; that the Tsar banished her, imprisoned her, or lost her to a forbidden word. Whenever Virta asked her father for the truth, he would only reply, "It was in her nature to fly, but trust the winds to return her to us."

All Virta knew was her mother's name: Jovansya.

Virta cantered down the Pra Majessa on a horse as black as night, while her confidante, the Lady Marja, rode beside her on a moon-white steed. Dyed silks fluttered high above them. "Whose emblems do they fly?" Virta asked Marja.

Marja did not reply, seemingly lost in thought.

Virta smiled. "Dreaming of your love again, dear Marja?"

Her words made Marja blush. "A little," her friend replied. "Vayantin gave me a secret rose at dawn, and its fragrance still lingers in my mind. What did you ask?"

Marja's distraction did not surprise Virta. Tsar Dominin had groomed Vayantin, the son of a powerful boyar, to be the Gallant Autumn. But fickle love put Marja in Vayantin's heart, and Virta was glad they had found each other. "Tell me about the silks."

"Ah. The citizens embroider the device of their favorite lord, whittling their choices till the twelfth night decides the most popular man," Marja said. "See the golden lion and the crimson hart? Already they say Lyonid will rend Perek as a lion should."

The streets nearer the heart of the city were tangled in perfumed ribbons, while pleasure tents crowded the shadows off the main promenade. "What of Winter?" asked Virta.

"Rumor has it that it's Fyobor, Lyonid's brother, though they are as different as lightning and snow. Neither is ever seen without their splendid pelts. They call them Auburn Lion and Silver Bear."

"I wonder if they'll please my father."

"Does the Tsar still intend to pick Vayantin for Autumn?" asked Marja, worry in her voice.

"As far as I know," said Virta. "Rest easy, my friend. I have no designs on Vayantin. I know how deeply you love each other."

"Thank you." Marja relaxed. "He isn't ready yet to tell his father, nor I mine."

"Then let Vayantin pretend to vie for my hand a while longer," Virta said.

"Who will you choose for Spring?" Marja asked.

"When I meet him, I will know," said Virta, hoping her words were true.

At Bravura Court, the silks and gawking spectators gave way to the athletic competitions for Winter Gallantry. Virta spied the two brothers in their fabled pelts at once. Fyobor, in the skin of his ice-bear, wrestled a challenger in the snow. He pinned the man with ease and shouted a triumphant cry, and the crowd roared their approval. Politely, Lyonid applauded his brother's victory. The Auburn Lion's supporters surrounded him, currying for a kind word from the beaming youth in his lion skin. Golden banners rippled behind him.

Virta waved to her people, then gestured for Fyobor and Lyonid to approach. The brothers bent their knees, but Virta would not have it. "Stand. From what I hear, Summer and Winter will soon be yours. If so, you are the equals I seek."

Lyonid offered his hand and helped her dismount. "Princess, only one star ever walked this Earth, and you are she," said he. "Should there be any spectacle you desire—dancers, flame-eaters, songmasters—name it and I will find the best for you."

"Lyonid, your lines never change!" Fyobor laughed and slapped his brother on the back, ignoring his brother's glower. "I have torn a path straight through mountains and forests, slain wolves and wyverns to reach Nobylisk in time, Highness. Each victory brings me closer to you. That's brute honesty, but the true measure of my heart."

"Thank you, both." Virta appraised the brothers. Fyobor's hair had gone silver too soon, while his eyes were green as new shoots in thawing ice. Lyonid, on the other hand, gleamed like sunlight on dew.

"Brothers!" hollered a voice from the crowd. Sergef rode forth on a great bronze-horned goat, a gourd in each hand. "I scarcely recognize you! Here, gifts from the east!" He lobbed the gourds towards his brothers.

Lyonid stepped aside, letting his gourd smash against the stones. Fyobor caught but crushed his gift, letting the wine within dye his arm red.

"Sergef at your service, Tsarevna." Sergef dismounted.

"By the slumbering gods, you are the very image of Jovansya!"

The mention of her mother's name startled Virta. "You've seen her?"

"A year ago," said Sergef. "It was she who showed us our paths to power."

"Enough," said Fyobor. "Highness, Sergef's fantasies grow wilder with each telling."

"I agree," said Lyonid. "He weaves such fantastic stories that he begins believing them true. Believe nothing he says."

"But brothers! Jovansya foretold our destinies. Why deny it?" asked Sergef, incredulous.

"Go home," said Fyobor.

"No. I am here to win her love," said Sergef.

Virta pulled out a green scarf embroidered with crocuses and hyacinths: the badge of Gallant Spring. With a delicate flick, she floated the scarf to Lyonid.

"This is an honor, Tsarevna, but why?" asked Lyonid, surprised. "I would have won the Summer Gallantry!"

"You and Fyobor have proven yourselves, while Sergef hadn't the chance. Sergef, show Nobylisk why you deserve to stand with your brothers. Become the Gallant Summer."

"Virta, how can Sergef hope to compete with Perek?" asked Marja. "Only three days remain."

Fyobor cracked his knuckles. "You're welcome to challenge me for Winter instead."

Sergef laughed. "No, Fyobor, you've grown too strong. In three days time, my brazen goat will trample the Summer silks, and we three will once again be one."

Sergef took a meandering route back to his ship, The Black Swan, taking the time to greet passers-by. He knew it wouldn't be easy to win the city's heart in three scant days, but he trusted himself to find a way. Wasn't that how he survived a year alone?

As Sergef hoped, people were intrigued by a potential showdown between three brothers for the Tsarevna's love. By morning, banners of the brazen goat were already weaving through town. At midday, Sergef returned to Bravura Court with his crew along with twelve great kegs of wine. "Citizens! These are the finest wines from the east, won from the giants in games of chance. Half will be dowry, half I freely share. Let us drink to the Tsar!" To the crowd's delight, his men began doling out wine.

Fyobor watched with distaste. "They'll drink your wine, brother, but whisper that you're only buying support."

"What is a Tsar if not generous to his people?" asked Sergef. "I only show them who I truly am, as should you."

Fyobor scowled and smashed a barrel with his fist, before storming away.

Praise of Sergef's generosity spread as fast as accusations of false charity. By the second day, almost as many brazen goats flew alongside the crimson hart. Sergef rode his goat through the city, answering questions about his strange steed.

"The Swan-Queen told me wisdom would be mine if I slew this goat for her pelt, but when I found her among the vines, I knew I couldn't take a life for a power I didn't need. In sparing her, I learned wisdom."

"Then your brothers owe their success to their pelts?" someone asked.

"I am here because I believed in myself. I hope my brothers became the men they are the same way."

When Lyonid learned of Sergef's words from his spies, he summoned a palaquin and headed to The Black Swan to confront Sergef. Once alone in the captain's quarters, Lyonid chastised his brother. "I'm glad you've done well for yourself, but you mustn't mention Jovansya's visions!"

"Why are you afraid of the truth?" asked Sergef.

"They'll question my charm and Fyobor's strength."

"So? I did well without magic," said Sergef.

"I won't have your unguarded words ruin us." In truth, Lyonid had lost an ear to the lion before he slew it, and the only thing that hid the disfigurement was the magic of the pelt. He summoned the power of his lionskin, binding his brother to his next words. "Never speak of the hides or the prophecy again."

Sergef shivered, unaware that he had been ensorcelled. "As you wish, brother."

Intent on sabotaging Sergef, Lyonid threw his support behind his former foe, Perek. He and his men extolled the virtues of the soldier throughout town, and though he never slandered his brother, his puppets spoke poison in the markets and taverns, painting Sergef as a drunk who indulged too often in pleasure pavilions. His meddling began swinging public opinion in Perek's favor.

On the final morning, twice as many stags adorned the silks as goats, yet Sergef did not despair. "I trust my strength, as should you," he told the people.

Marja visited Sergef aboard The Black Swan. "Virta wishes to hear more about Jovansya, but did not want to sway the people's choice by coming herself."

"She fears I will lose," said Sergef. He told Marja of the Swan-Queen, but Lyonid's secret spell upon him made him forget the prophecy and the pelts. "I did not know Jovansya was also the lost Tsarina, but she did speak fondly of Virta."

Marja nodded. "What tempts you more, Virta's love

or the throne?"

"If by throne you mean the people of our land, then throne must be my answer. Though I love my brothers, they would cherish the might and not the people," Sergef said. "Jovansya spoke of an ill wind, which my brothers ignore. I fear she warns of the Sirin Cult gaining favor in the western provinces, whose priestesses possess the power to beguile with song. Some darker rumors claim the price of power is half their humanity, turning them half-bird. We must heed the Swan Queen's counsel and stand against this threat."

"And Virta?" Marja asked.

"If there be love at first sight, then I am a fool in love, but let time decide the truth of that," Sergef said.

"Well answered," said Marja. "I wish Virta had named you Spring."

"No, she was right. I only need to strive harder to steal their hearts by evening."

And so Sergef spent the last hours speaking his ardor to the people. By dusk, every ship in the harbor flew the sigil of the goat, as did half the guildhalls at Bravura Court.

It was not enough.

When dusk fell, the citizens crowded Bravura Court to hear the Tsar proclaim the Four Gallants. Tsar Dominin stood in front of the statue of the First Tsar, Virta and Marja at his side. Fyobor, Lyonid, Sergef, Perek and Vayantin knelt before them.

"Approach, Lyonid," said the Tsar. Lyonid had abandoned the colors of summer flame for the shades of dawn, wearing the badge of Spring on his arm. "Spring brings the hope of love, capricious as it is, yet love could be the strongest bond," continued Dominin. "My daughter chose you as the Gallant Spring, so prove yourself worthy of her in the days to come."

The Tsar drew a white scarf. "Fyobor, the trials of Winter are harsh indeed, and these competitions symbolize Man's fight against cruel odds. You have proven yourself invincible, and that strength will serve our people well." He bestowed the scarf unto Fyobor.

"Autumn is the season of harvest, and so the Tsar cultivates one who might succeed him. Vayantin." The boyar's son stepped forward. "You should have told me of your love for Marja. She confessed it hours ago, placing me in a difficult position." He fetched two golden rings from his pocket. "Marry her with my blessings, but I must choose another Autumn."

"Th-thank you, Majesty," said Vayantin.

"So where must I look? No further than a man already beloved by the people. Come, Perek. You're as deserving of the Autumn prize as you are of Summer."

Lyonid and Fyobor grew livid.

"Step forward, Sergef!" said Dominin. "Summer is a splendid season, and so one resplendent man is chosen by the people for their Tsarevna. You had three lean days to win their hearts, but against the odds, you almost did this thing. A good Tsar inspires his people, as you have. Thus, I have no qualms interfering with the Summer race, and declaring you the Gallant Summer!"

Sergef humbly accepted the fire-red scarf. "I'll not let you down, Majesty." He mouthed thank you to Marja and smiled at Virta. But the hatred on his brothers' faces told Sergef that the gulf between them had widened.

And so the four Gallants came to Palace Halcyon, each taking a tower of their own. Forbidden to leave the grounds on penalty of forfeiture, they would compete for Dominin's trust and Virta's love.

Sergef brought his goat to the palace along with his gifts of wine. He insisted on caring for her himself. It was in the stables that Virta first spoke to Sergef alone. "You have been nothing but honest, and I thank you for it. Will you tell me more about Jovansya?"

As before, Lyonid's compulsion sought to silence Sergef, but as Sergef brushed his goat, each stroke loosened the lionskin's magic more. "I'll tell you all I know."

Virta listened, enrapt.

"So I spared the goat, and she's been a true companion ever since, leading me to my fortunes in the eastern lands. I listened and learned the secrets of trade, and found kindness returns twicefold what you give. But I always knew I'd come for you." He kissed her hand.

"I often dream my mother had stayed," said Virta, tears welling. "I thought she left because she did not love me, but now that I know she's Queen of the Swans, perhaps there were reasons after all."

Sergef held her. "No tears, my swan."

As the days passed, it became clear whom Virta favored. Though she danced with Lyonid, played chess with Fyobor, and walked in the garden with Perek, everyone knew she imagined doing those things with Sergef.

One night, Virta confronted Fyobor. "Why won't you take your bearskin off? Is it, as Sergef said, the source of your strength? Come, let me see what you look like without it."

Fyobor did not wish Virta to see the frail man he truly was under the pelt. The journey to the north had nearly killed him, sickly as he was. "Sergef knows nothing of the true nature of the pelts," he said. "Yes, it grants me strength, and I pledge that might in defense of the tsardom. However, the skin becomes a part of you, like the Swan-Queen's feather-cloak is her essence. When skin and man are one, I need not wear this, but the merging requires a year to graft." It was a lie but a plausible one, enough to placate Virta while Fyobor sought out Lyonid in secret.

"What should we do? I'd rather one of us became Tsar than that sanctimonious whelp!" said Fyobor.

Lyonid growled, wondering how Sergef broke the lionskin's spell. "If either of us is to take the throne, we'll have to do something about dear Sergef."

Sergef vanished the night of the shadow-play.

A wise witch from a far sanctuary came to perform the tale of the twins Nobyl and Talantin for the palace nobles. The woman's nails plucked the catguts of her nine-stringed harp, singing in her ancient voice as shadows danced against a curtain of saga-silk. Sergef sat enthralled by the story of one brother's quest to avenge his twin's death. After the show ended, he praised the old woman and stayed behind in the Hall of Remembrances to beg more tales from her.

That was the last any of the court saw of him.

When Sergef failed to arrive for a meal the next evening, Dominin sent servants to find him. They found Sergef's bed untouched, and a search of the palace revealed no trace of his whereabouts. The witch's troupe claimed Sergef left them late in the night.

Lyonid and Fyobor sneered when they heard the news. "Our brother is infamous for his caprice!"

The Tsar sadly concluded that Sergef had abandoned the palace of his own accord, surrendering his chance of marrying Virta.

Virta was inconsolable. "Something terrible must have happened to him!"

"Maybe he couldn't love you and wished to spare you pain," suggested Marja, though she did not believe it herself.

"He wouldn't have left without his goat or his ship," said Virta. "He could be hurt, taken, or…" She shivered.

"Do you suspect his brothers?"

"Of course, but we cannot accuse anyone without proof. There must be a clue. I need you and Vayantin to scour the palace. Look in places out of the ordinary. Whatever you find, tell no one but me."

Marja nodded. "Anything."

And so Marja and Vayantin stalked every corner of the castle, overhearing many whispers in their search: that Sergef's goat had grown fierce, not letting anyone near her; that Perek crowed that he would be Virta's choice, for the brothers were scoundrels, all.

On the third night, Marja woke Virta. "Oh, Virta! I'm sorry," said Marja, sobbing.

"He's dead, isn't he?" Virta steeled herself against her grief. "No tears, Marja. Take me to him."

Marja led her through the secret ways to the wine cellar. Deep in the back, next to an open keg, Vayantin guarded Sergef's wine-soaked body. Virta fell to her knees to touch Sergef's face, not caring that the pool of wine stained her gown red.

"This barrel of his wasn't with the others, and the floor was stained beneath it," said Vayantin. " There are claw marks in his head where someone struck him before drowning him. I cannot tell if they're bear or lion."

"We should confront the brothers!" said Marja.

"No," said Virta. "If we accuse them now, they'll only blame each other. Or, claim that someone planted the marks to cast suspicion on the brothers, so I would choose Perek. There is a way to unmask the murderer."

"How?"

Virta clutched the wine-soaked hem of her gown and wrung a libation to the god Death-In-Sleep. "Blood was spilled. Blood will pay."

The next day, Virta asked the three Gallants to the Tsarina's Garden for a midday fete. She invited her three suitors inside a silken tent and dismissed all her servants save Marja. Fyobor, Lyonid, and Perek sat down at the lavish table.

"I fell for Sergef's sweet words, but now know them for lies," said Virta. "I am pleased he is gone, along with his tall tales of Jovansya. Fyobor, did the Swan-Queen really force you to stand your ground when you tried to steal her cloak?"

Fyobor answered cautiously, remembering what he already told Virta about Jovansya. "Yes, her feathers were like knives and cut my hand. She held me firm with a spell."

Virta nodded. "Blood magic has ever been strong. Blood shed in malice can be turned against the offender, just as blood shed in oath can curse the oath-breaker."

"They say that even the dead avenge themselves through blood, just like the tale that puppeteer told," said Marja.

Virta asked Marja to fetch the wine. "I'm ready to open my heart to a truer love. Let us drink away the pain of his deception! I've asked for Sergef's wine from the cellars. They tell me that this wine of his, found deepest in the cellars, has the most exquisite taste."

Marja returned with a crystal decanter of blood-red wine and filled their glasses. Virta raised her glass high. "To truth and love!" She touched the cup to her lips, but paused to watch her guests' faces.

Perek drained his glass, but Fyobor trembled and dropped his flute. Lyonid took a sip but pinched his face, spitting it out.

"Why do you not drink?" asked Virta, dashing her own glass against the garden tiles. "Is it the taste of your brother's blood that appalls you?"

Perek went pale and retched.

"She knows, brother," cried Lyonid. "We're undone!"

"Silence, you fool!" hissed Fyobor.

Virta spat on the table. "So, it was the both of you! Vayantin!" At her call, Vayantin cut through the silken tent, rushing in with guards and putting the brothers at the point of their swords. "Strip these murderers of their hides."

"With pleasure." Vayantin yanked at Lyonid's pelt, but the skin would not yield.

Lyonid laughed. "Fool. You cannot strip me of my magic."

"Nor will you steal my strength from me," Fyobor said, sneering.

"Then suffer your accursed gifts together," Virta decided. "Lock them both in Halcyon's coldest cell."

The soldiers led the brothers away.

Marja comforted Perek. "Rest easy, my lord. It was only guilt that poisoned this wine."

Perek only moaned.

Virta turned away. Though her ploy had succeeded, bringing Sergef's killers to light, her heart was still empty.

Virta stood atop the Summer Tower at dusk, alone. She found the black swan's feather among Sergef's things, fletched to an arrow. Its edge was as sharp as a sword. With it, she traced a line of blood on her palm.

"Blood is drawn. Blood must obey!" she shouted to the winds.

Soon, a black swan flew onto the rooftop, and in a swirl of ebon down, the bird became a Queen. "How did you know I'd come?"

"We are blood, you and I, and you have wronged me," said Virta. "Why lead him to me if you were just going to take him away? Haven't you hurt me enough?"

"I understand your anger, my cygnet, but these omens are not my shapings. Each man decides for himself which road to take, even when he knows it may lead to doom," said Jovansya.

"Like when you chose to abandon us?"

"When the winds call, I must answer, but know that I never stopped loving you or your father." Jovansya caressed Virta's hair. "Take heart, child. There's one magic greater than blood of vengeance. The blood of mercy."

Virta looked at her mother in hope.

"Sergef had been fated to slay the goat, for she was as much a part of him as the lion to Lyonid and bear to Fyobor," said Jovansya. "While the two became addicted to their sudden power, Sergef found mercy instead. In sparing the goat's life, he also saved his own. Blood was spared, so blood will repay. Touch your feather to the goat and let her make sacrifice for Sergef."

"Thank you, mother," said Virta, embracing her mother at last. "There's so much I want to ask—"

"All in good time. Go to him. When the skies darken under Sirin wings, trust Sergef's wisdom and love to bring peace to the tsardom once more. When you have need, call and I will answer." Jovansya kissed her daughter on the forehead and stepped onto the parapet. Another swirl of her cloak and she was gone.

Virta rushed past startled servants on the way to the stables. Once there, she leapt over the gate into the goat's stall, coming eye to eye with the great beast. Sergef had been right. It would be wrong for her to simply take the goat's life, Virta realized. The sacrifice must be freely given.

"Great One, Sergef showed you mercy, and so must I," she said to the she-goat. "I beg you, return my love to me, but if you deem this sacrifice too great, I will understand." She opened the stall gate and held her breath.

The goat did not move, and instead held her head high. Hands trembling, Virta lifted the black feather and brushed it against the goat's forehead. The goat's hide split. Out tumbled a man, bloody and naked—but alive. Sergef.

Virta cried out in joy. She knelt, grabbed a blanket, and wrapped it tight around her love. "I thought I'd lost you."

"Never, my swan," murmured Sergef.

The brothers' treachery, Virta's trap, Sergef's reincarnation—these tales astounded all Nobylisk. The puppet-mistress spun a new shadow-play so that the legend would spread throughout the tsardom.

At summer's end, it came as no surprise that Virta chose Sergef as her husband, with the Tsar's and the people's full blessing.

As for the brothers? Sergef tried making peace with them, and might have achieved it but for Lyonid's shame and Fyobor's pride. The two remained locked for seasons in the same cell, venting fury and blame at each other, even as they continued to grow into their hides. When at last an auburn lion faced a bone-white bear, it was their claws that ended this tale.

The box arrived early afternoon

totally mangled
on my front porch…

Fortunately,
everything inside
was protected by a
thick layer of love, as

you had checked
"fragile", as if there
were plums or
maple syrup
encased

within. When I brought
the box inside to contact
and thank you, I wasn't

quite sure what I would
be thanking you for

as at it appeared to be

empty, its contents
lost in transit…

and so I peered closer,
lifted each flap to
examine beneath
the folds…perhaps
something remained,
had somehow made,
the voyage from
Earth to Mars safely?

And so it had…as there,

wedged in a corner,
partially caught by
a staple, immersed in
glue, was the missing
button to my favorite
sweater that you had
borrowed and promised
to return.

—Terry Leigh Relf

BECOMING OSIRIS

Our stardrive failed us somewhere short of Rigel,
& scattered lifepods like sarcophagi
Against the night's imperishable face:
A vague & transitory constellation
Degrading into novae. Into silence.

The hours of the night are twelve, & endless.
My night-boat drifts dismasted through their currents
Between the jaws of Apep, seeking light.

Orion fills the void beyond my faceplate,
The cloud upon his blade a bleak reminder
Of lives igniting elsewhere…or does ancient
Wisdom hold some hope within its whisper?
Behold Osiris, risen from the West.

The hours of the night are twelve, & fading.
My final breath waits balanced like a feather
Upon these lips to weigh against my heart.

There is no silence simpler than vacuum,
None more complete in innocence. Exhaling,
I seize the agony of wings expanded
Into a spirit slipping from this tomb
Between a hundred gates, a thousand stars.

The hours of the night are twelve, & ended.
Back home in autumn skies, a new Osiris
Rejoins the constellations of the dawn.

—ANN K. SCHWADER

Welcome to our pages, Hank Quesne, with your tale of when days of olde when knights were bold and football was invented. "The Mead Cup" originally appeared in the anthology Travel a Time Historic *(Rage Machine Books, 2005; Nancy Jackson, ed.).*

The Mead Cup

by Hank Quense

"What!" Rowan gaped at King Arthur and Merlin. "Londinium lost eleven to nothing?" Both men sat across from her at a round oak table.

The king nodded.

"But…Londinium has the Rookie-of-the-year in goal and it's the best club in the land after Camelot. How did the Saxon dogs win?" The shocking news overcame her natural reticence in the presence of the king.

"The barbarians are fast and strong." Merlin wore a gray robe and twigs and bits of cheese lay entangled in his chest-length silver beard. "Their goalie is a wizard. And they have two more on the sidelines causing mischief."

"They're serious this time, aren't they?" Rowan said.

"Make no mistake." Arthur pounded a fist on the table. "They mean to capture the Mead Cup."

All three looked to the sideboard where a large drinking horn sat on a three-legged gold stand. Light from candles reflected from the silver and jewel-encrusted bands that encircled it. A gold-hooped barrel caught the liquid oozing from the small end.

"It's very early in the spring to play football." Rowan glanced out the unshuttered window where a cold drizzle fell. "Has the Camelot team even started practice yet?"

"No," Arthur replied. "But I've ordered them to assemble straight away."

"Rowan," Merlin said, "I need your help."

Rowan notched an eyebrow. She wiggled in the chair while awaiting the reason for her unexpected summons.

"Yes," Arthur said. "Merlin will be hard pressed to fight off three wizards. Your healing spells could make the difference between winning or losing. I ask you to join forces with him and use your witchcraft in the defense of the Realm. For seven years, I've held the Cup. Ever since my knights returned from their quests with the Mead Cup and the rules for combat by football." Arthur ground his teeth. "I'll not let the Saxon swine take it from me."

"As you wish, Sire." Rowan bobbed her head up and down. She'd be involved in the game for the most prestigious football trophy in the known world! She'd help defend the honor of Camelot!

The next day, Merlin and Rowan joined Arthur in a meadow outside the castle walls. Colorful pennants marked the corners of the practice field that glistened with new grass.

"We were discussing magical strategies," Merlin told Arthur, "and Rowan wanted a look at the team."

Merlin's description of the brutal Saxon tactics had alarmed Rowan. She would be hard pressed to keep the home team in action unless they were in peak physical condition.

"Any news of the Saxons?" Arthur asked.

"They humiliated Aquae Sulis," Merlin said, "and we just received word of Venta Belgarum's 13-1 defeat. They now march on Camelot."

"This is a practice, Sire?" Rowan pointed to the center of the field where the Knights of the Round Table Football Club drank dippers of mead. "Why don't they run plays or at least kick the ball around?"

"They're working up to it." In his late-thirties, the king had brown eyes and salt-and-pepper hair along with pleasant features and a spreading mid-section.

"Nonsense. Look at the flab on them."

"It's the Mead Cup, you see," Arthur said. "All winter long they've been guzzling its free mead."

"I bet none of them can fit into their armor." Rowan made a mental note to review her healing spells, even the obscure ones. "Your hold on the Mead Cup is in jeopardy."

"And what makes you an authority on football?" Arthur gave her a truculent stare.

"I have ten older brothers and male cousins and they made me play goal on their team."

"I've tried to get them to train harder." Arthur picked at a fingernail. "Unsuccessfully."

"Put me in charge," Rowan said. "I know football and I'll whip this rabble into shape."

"You're a woman!"

"Glad you noticed, Sire."

"Arthur," Merlin said, "desperate measures are required."

"I can train these knights and I can out-coach the Saxons."

Arthur scratched at the dirt with his boot. He looked up and said, "I'll call them together."

"First, I need a club." Rowan pointed to a nearby guard. "That one will do."

Arthur summoned the knights. "This is Rowan. From now on, she's in charge of the team."

"Forsooth, Sire." Sir Agravaine made a face. "I ain't taking orders from a bloody woman. And she's a beldam to boot." The right fullback crossed his arms over his chest and glared at her.

Rowan clobbered him with the cudgel. While he groaned on the ground, she smacked the club into her open palm. "Any other comments?"

The knights took a step backwards and shook their heads.

"We'll start off with wind sprints. Whoever comes in last, cleans out the stables after practice."

"That's work," Gareth said. "Knights don't work."

"Verily. We ain't thralls, you know." Gawaine looked towards the King.

Arthur examined the battlements.

Before long, every knight lay on the ground, gasping for breath. "Mead boy," Lancelot croaked.

"The mead boy is gone." Rowan chuckled. "There's only water."

"Water, you say!" Kay said, with more than a hint of hysteria. "That's for serfs. Knights don't drink water."

"While you're resting, I'll practice with the goalie." She pointed to Galahad, then hiked the hem of her ankle-length black woolen robe.

"Not likely a bare-footed witch will get the bloody ball past me." Galahad sneered at her.

After Rowan kicked ten straight goals, Galahad cried out. "It's a punishment from God for allowing a woman to be in charge of knights."

"Shut yer yap," Agravaine growled. "Every time you screw up, you blame it on God. 'Tis nothing to do with the Almighty."

As the practice continued, Rowan's heart sank from the realization that the prestige of the Realm rested with this group of overweight and out-of-shape men.

On the morning of the game, the sun gleamed on the lush grass and dazzled the eye with light reflected by the dew. The fragrance of spring flowers filled the air.

Rowan had spent a sleepless night worrying about her knights. Despite a week of exhaustive workouts, the men still hadn't reached battle conditioning. She ignored the crowd of noisy fans and approached Arthur, who was biting his fingernails. Merlin stood nearby weaving his fingers through his beard.

"We don't have to worry about the Saxon wizard tending goal," she said, smiling.

"Who is in their goal, then?" Merlin asked.

"A shape-shifting friend of mine. She doesn't know a thing about football, so the only way she'll make a save is if we hit her with the ball."

"Dare I ask about the wizard?" Arthur raised an eyebrow.

"Using a different shape, she lured him into a barn. He's now tied, gagged and naked."

Arthur ran out of fingernails and gnawed on a knuckle while he glared across the field where the barbarians warmed up by drinking large horns of ale and making obscene gestures at the knights.

The knights, looking brave and handsome in their blue and gold tunics, warmed up by griping.

"How come we have to play so early in the morn?" Agravaine said.

"Verily," Gareth said. "What's wrong with after the mid-day meal?"

"And a nap," Kay said.

Rowan interrupted them by sticking two fingers in her mouth and whistling. "A word of caution," she told the knights when they assembled in a huddle. "If you overweight slobs lose the game, you'll have to buy your mead from now on."

"What?" Gawaine cried.

"Aroint thee!" Lancelot looked stunned. "Pay?"

"If you don't believe me, ask him." She pointed to the king.

Arthur, with a bemused expression on his face, nodded.

"Filthy foreigners!" Lancelot shook a fist in the direction of the Saxons. "Invading our land and causing trouble."

"Let's kick their arses, betimes," Agravaine snarled.

In front of the crowd in mid-field, the cheerleaders started a routine. Coached by Queen Guinevere, ten noble maidens, in low-cut, ankle-length kirtles with hennins covering their hair, linked arms and danced a primitive can-can while cheering for the Camelot team—except Galahad. The girls hated him and his holier-than-thou attitude.

As soon as the starting whistle sounded, a burly Saxon rearranged Lancelot's senses with a vicious blind-side punch, and Rowan had to cast a spell to un-addle his wits.

Both sides tested the other with the usual elbows to the mouth, kneecap kicks and groin grabs, but the unprincipled Saxons also resorted to dirty tricks such as concealing iron saps in their fists. Sir Kay broke his knuckles when he kidney-punched an unsporting Saxon who wore armor under his tunic. Kay howled and jumped around in pain until Rowan's healing spell took effect.

On the sidelines, Merlin and the wizards waged their own contest. Lightning bolts, hailstones, and magical itching powders flittered around both sidelines.

Mid-way through the first half, the cheerleaders built a human pyramid. Just as the last girl climbed on top, the structure collapsed in a display of bosoms, thighs, and bottoms as limbs and clothes flew in all directions.

"Eek!" one cried out.

"Jesu Christi!" another wailed.

"Me hennin's gone missin'," said a third.

With the exception of Galahad the Pure, Camelot's goalie, the players froze in mid-mayhem and stared open-mouthed at the pile of undergarment-less maidens. Galahad streaked up field, dribbling the ball towards the Saxon goal where the shape-shifter waved a hand in greeting.

The goal gave Camelot a 1-0 lead and sent the fans into a frenzy.

The cheerleaders, dignity and clothing restored, cheered loudly for Lancelot.

At half-time—with the score tied at two—Galahad complained to Rowan. "The Saxon goals are a punishment from God for letting the cheer-leaders on the field. In the name of the Lord, I demand the sluts be removed at once."

Rowan ignored him. She cast bone-setting and blood-clotting spells as fast as she could mumble them. The knights engulfed her in a miasmic cloud of sweat and blood. Never had she seen two teams with such evenly matched unsportsman-like skills. Every player on the field displayed expertise in knavery.

So too, the wizards. Merlin stayed at a distance to protect the king and players from the shower of fist-sized rocks that bounced off his protective ward.

Rowan looked at her squad while they sat on the ground to conserve their remaining strength. She was exhausted—not physically like her players—but magically. She couldn't fix many more injuries. She squared her shoulders and said, "Anyone know what a hedgehog is?"

Dumb stares gave her the answer.

"Here's how we'll win the game, then."

When play resumed, the Saxons swarmed over the

home team and scored a goal. Galahad blamed the cheerleaders. "Remove the harlots at once."

The maidens ran close to his goal, stuck out their tongues and hiked their kirtles.

The red-faced Galahad turned his back on the girls and didn't see the Saxon shot streak into the goal, increasing the lead to 4-2.

The knights looked to Rowan.

"Keep them moving." Rowan called. "Wear them out."

A few minutes later, Gareth stole the ball close to mid-field and kicked a pass to Palamides, who had been felled by a sap shot behind his ear. Palamides, barely conscious but deep in Saxon territory, tottered after the ball and managed to score before the enraged Saxons descended on him.

The knights tied the score near the end of the game. Both sides now staggered around the field, almost crippled by exhaustion.

Arthur chewed on his sleeve and cast imploring looks at Rowan.

Rowan had trouble swallowing because of her dry throat. A tie game would be a disaster for Camelot because the knights couldn't last through an overtime period. Rowan waited until the knights controlled the ball, then whistled to get her players' attention. "Hedgehog!"

The knights formed a vee-shaped wedge deep in their own territory with Galahad dribbling the ball behind the wall of players. Two Saxons charged into the wall and received bloody heads for their trouble. After the wedge crossed mid-field, a Saxon wizard called out, "Off-side! They're off-side."

"Twit!" Merlin replied. "That rule won't be invented for hundreds of years."

The formation moved up-field a few steps, then halted while the wedge collectively gasped for breath. Rowan kept pace on the sideline. "One more goal and you have free mead."

The wedge lurched forward. The Saxons seized hold of the knights and pulled in the opposite direction. The wedge ground to a stop.

Rowan bit her lip. Exhaustion immobilized her team, and, if the Saxons stole the ball, the knights couldn't defend their end of the field. She grabbed a horn of mead from a spectator, called to her team and spilled it on the grass. The smell of honey wafted up from the liquid.

"I ain't paying for the bloody mead, " Agravaine snarled. "Knock these Saxon miscreants off our lines."

"I never heard of such a thing." Palamides punched one in the face. "Knights paying for mead when it's our due."

"Verily." Kay bent back the fingers on a Saxon's hand and the barbarian released his chokehold on Gawaine. "Next they'll expect us to work for the mead."

"Work!" Perceval exploded. "Forward, my heroes! One more charge and the Cup is ours and so is the mead."

The wedge staggered forward and picked up speed with Lancelot calling cadence. "Left, right. Hut, two. That's the way, lads."

More Saxons threw themselves at the line. The knights hurled them aside.

Merlin conjured an umbrella to protect himself from a shower of pig's feet.

Ten yards from the goal mouth, the wedge split apart to give Galahad a kicking lane. The critical shot smashed into the shape-changer's forehead. She collapsed on the ground while the ball rebounded beyond the wedge.

Rowan sucked in her breath. The ball was loose, and Camelot's goal unattended. She foresaw Camelot's doom.

Gareth, the fastest of the knights, sprang out of the wedge and raced towards the ball. Lancelot followed him. A Saxon dove for the ball just as Gareth heeled it out of the way. He moved to his left for a better shot angle while Lancelot threw himself at a pair of barbarians. All three collapsed in a heap. Gareth lined up the shot and kicked the goal an instant before a berserker smashed him in the head with a forearm.

The referee whistled. "Time, gentlemen. King Arthur's team wins by a score of five goals to four. The King retains the Mead Cup."

None of the players heard the announcement because of the customary and colorful post-game melee.

Rowan hugged Arthur while Merlin disengaged from the losing wizards.

The cheerleaders ran to the spot where Galahad traded punches with a Saxon. The maidens cheered the invader and displayed plenty of skin to distract Galahad.

On the sidelines, a travel-weary messenger rode up and handed Arthur a scroll. The king raised an eyebrow when he saw the seal. He broke it and opened the scroll. His face drained of blood as he read it.

"Bad news, Sire?" Merlin asked.

Arthur looked up. "It's from Theodoric of the Ostrogoths. He says if I don't give him the Mead Cup, he'll come over here, kick my royal arse on the football field and take it."

SF Minnesota

SF MINNESOTA (founded February 1992) is a multicultural, multimedia organization dedicated to improving contacts among groups and individuals interested in speculative fiction, within and outside of the traditional SF community. We have a special commitment to helping make our state's SF community more representative of Minnesota in the third millennium.

Our biggest project is **DIVERSICON**, an August convention exploring diversity in speculative fiction, including diversity of fan groups, diversity in media, and, especially, cultural diversity. Past Guests have included authors Eleanor Arnason, Joan Slonczewski, Maureen F. McHugh, Karen Joy Fowler, Steven Barnes, Tananarive Due, S. P. Somtow, Minister Faust, Andrea Hairston, and Nnedi Okorafor-Mbachu; editor/authors Nalo Hopkinson, Sheree R. Thomas, and Kelly Link; and artists Rodger Gerberding, Christopher Jones, and Melissa S. Kaercher.

Diversicon 17 will be held July 31-August 2, 2009 in the Twin Cities with Guest of Honor **Kay Kenyon** (www.kaykenyon.com).

The **SPECULATIONS READINGS SERIES**, the monthly SF edition of Intermedia Arts' Carol Connolly Readings, has been held monthly (since 1995!) at DreamHaven Books (now at a new location: 2301 E. 38th Street, Minneapolis). Speculations facilitates camaraderie among readers and writers, who hang out after the readings. Upcoming readers:
- **Michael Merriam,** Friday, October 24
- **Jason D. Wittman,** Friday, November 21

Each reading/reception runs from 6:30–7:30 PM, including complimentary refreshments.

The **CLASSIC HORROR FILMS VIDEO PARTY** each fall surveys the history of the classic horror film, including liner notes on the films viewed. This year's entry is Part 17: "Slouching Toward the Millennium, 1996–1998," featuring six films from the period. Saturday, November 8, noon-midnight, Holiday Inn Select, Bloomington MN. Free. Contact Eric at eheideman@dhzone.com for playbill and precise location.

We also host **DIVERSICON PARTIES** at several Midwestern conventions. Other projects to which we make contributions include the **GORDON R. DICKSON FUND** for Clarion West students and *Tales of the Unanticipated*.

The Board of Directors welcomes proposals for additional projects.

SF Minnesota Board of Directors:

Sybil Smith
President
zaan5@aol.com

Scott Lohman
Board Member at Large
scottl2605@aol.com

Bryan Thao Worra
Board Member at Large
thaoworra@aol.com

www.diversicon.org/SFMinnesota.html

DIVERSICON 17

When You Eliminate the Impossible, What's Left Is Diversicon

July 31–August 2, 2009
Twin Cities, MN, location TBA

Guest of Honor: **Kay Kenyon**

Photo by Nomi S. Burstein

Ms. Kenyon, who grew up in Duluth, Minnesota, is the author of numerous novels and short stories. Her work, which features strong female characters and strongly rendered beings of all kinds, often focuses on environmental and genetic doom, humanity's efforts to save itself, and the surprises and consequences that result. Her six stand-alone science fiction novels include *Seeds of Time; Maximum Ice,* a Phillip K. Dick Finalist; and *Braided World,* a John W. Campbell Award Finalist. The second book in a science fiction series with fantasy trappings, *A World Too Near,* just appeared in hardcover; the first book in the series, *Bright of the Sky,* listed by *Publishers Weekly* as one of the best books of 2007 and recently selected as a finalist for the 2008 Endeavour Award, just came out in paperback. Her short fiction has appeared in numerous print anthologies and online venues, most recently in *The Solaris Book of New Science Fiction* (ed. George Mann). She, her husband, and a large orange cat split their time between eastern Washington state and southern California. Visit Kay at **www.kaykenyon.com**.

Posthumous Guests of Honor

Edgar Allan Poe (1809–1849): Author of *The Narrative of Arthur Gordon Pym, Tales of the Grotesque and Arabesque, The Raven and Other Poems,* and *Eureka.*

Sir Arthur Conan Doyle (1859–1930): Author of *The Adventures of Sherlock Holmes, The Hound of the Baskervilles, The Exploits of Brigadier Gerard, Sir Nigel, The Lost World,* and *Tales of Terror & Mystery.*

RATES

NOW: Through the Ides of March (15 March) 2009: Adult $25, Student (ages 5–21) $15, Supporting $5

Through Bastille Day (14 July) 2009: Adult $30, Student $20, Supporting $5, Converting $25

At the Door: Adult $40, Student $30

Mail check or money order to: Diversicon 17, PO Box 8036, Lake Street Station, Minneapolis, MN 55408

For Further Information:
www.diversicon.org
Scott Lohman, Convention Chair: scottl2605@aol.com
General Queries: diversicon@gmail.com

"And I have by me, for my comfort, two strange white flowers—shrivelled now, and brown and flat and brittle—to witness that even when mind and strength had gone, gratitude and a mutual tenderness still lived on in the heart of man." —H.G. Wells, The Time Machine

Heartsblood
by Sue Isle

My summons was to the Railway cop station, still in its original address in the upper section of the central station, though the track itself had never been repaired after the bombings twenty-some years ago. Apathy and lack of money had both been put forward as reasons. Fear, I suppose, might be a third. The attention of the authorities was directed away from the city now, focusing on the underground base in Alice Springs and other possible bases believed but not proven to exist in the desert. The best of the city's skills had drained out, enticed to the Springs under secret contracts. Scientists, engineers, security, medical experts. Who wouldn't go, given a choice?

A market had sprung up among the ruins, hundreds of unofficial stalls, some consisting of a blanket spread upon the ground with goods upon it. People wandered among the crowd reciting the details of what they could provide to you. A walker had to take care, weaving like a snake, murmuring constant flat apologies to guard against offence or retaliation. There was a crowd of kids outside the police station, like unofficial security, aged anywhere from five years old to mid-teens. The police wouldn't take any notice of them unless they did something drastic, but they would act if someone else assaulted the kids. Not so long ago the kids might have been run off or taken to a safe hostel or something, but those places were brim-full. There was no point in noticing. These kids had no parents or family but one another, and they needed and wanted no more.

I slid between them along the narrow space still allowed to get to the doors, running a gauntlet of cries and remarks as to why I might be visiting the police. "For murder," I yelled back. "You want to be next?"

"A confession, how nice," said the cop just inside the door. She had gone through about two minutes earlier, I had seen her from the other side of the walkway. "Can I help you?" she added.

I looked at her just enough to register her appearance; about my height, short brown hair, blue eyes, nice figure. She looked at me a bit longer, adding me to a possible criminal registry in her head. My pants and long-sleeved shirt had no holes or bloodstains or other dirt but they were about two sizes too large and not stylish by any consideration. Beneath the long-sleeved shirt I had on a black T-shirt which must have puzzled her, given the heat, but she only waited for me to answer her.

"I'm from 106 Francis Street," I began.

"The warehouse?"

"About ten years ago, yeah. Somebody died there last night, some of your lot came around, said to come give a statement after sunset. My name's Ash."

"Oh, yes. I do remember now. You live at the top of a long flight of stairs with no phone."

I couldn't help grinning at her resigned tone. "It's a public service to the police, to keep you in shape by visiting me."

"We are so lucky. All right, come through, please. I'm Constable Jamieson."

"Do you have a first name?" I asked, following her past the counter where a very large cop sat as though carved out of granite. He looked as though he would hit as hard as granite too.

"Do you have a last name?" Jamieson countered, waving me through into a small office with an entire wall of bullet-proof glass so that we could be clearly seen by anyone passing by in the narrow corridor.

"Not one I use," I said, unwillingly conceding the point.

"Okay," she said, pulling a laptop towards her on the table. "Have a seat, please. Is it Ash or Ashley?"

"Ashley if you want to be formal."

"If I wanted to be formal, I'd live in another town." She ran quickly through the necessary questions: my age, occupation, family—this took about as long as one needs to shake one's head. Then, "Okay, what happened?"

There was another power failure in the city that night, or perhaps only our area. I had been asleep, since my appointment with Dr. Benson wasn't until eight or so. Akemi woke me up to tell me, a lighted candle clasped in her fist. She was edgy and upset and I'm sorry to say I wasn't exactly sympathetic. "So why wake me up to tell me there isn't any light?"

"Daniel isn't here," she said.

"Well, he'll be back soon, he's got a class to teach." I shut my eyes but immediately opened them as Akemi yelped.

"Don't go back to sleep!"

We both knew that she was afraid of the dark; a bloody inconvenient phobia in our neck of the woods and also for Akemi's line of work. Which was prostitution. No point in being delicate about it even if I was any good at delicate. So I sat up and yawned instead. I'd slept in my clothes, which was usual; not from laziness but because there was little privacy and though my room-mates and I didn't talk about it, I needed privacy more than some people.

Beyond our door there was the usual noise of the building, up a few notches as people became aware of the situation, but it wasn't that unusual so there was no panic. Be it an hour or 24 hours until the power came back, we'd wait. Then there were more shouts on the stairs, and thumps as though someone had fallen or was being dragged. Someone shrieked right outside our fifth-floor door and Akemi eeked. I went to the peephole to see whether it was one of our room-mates. One girl was sprawled headfirst down the stairs and a number of items had rolled loose from her grasp. Food, it looked like, and a laptop computer. Two other girls were busy helping her on her way with their boots. I recognised Charisse, a fairly long-term resident, and her friend from the second floor. Someone further down the stairway growled in shock and pain as the would-be thief slammed into him.

"Shit," I said, jerked open our door against Akemi's protests and made it down the stairs three at a time. I saw the girl on her feet, staggering but definitely not harmless. In her hand gleamed something metal, and Daniel, two steps down, was doubled over and gasping. I jumped at the girl, using all the advantage of my position, ramming my feet into her midsection so that she tumbled, her limbs going everywhere, feet over head, landing broken and silent on the fourth-floor landing.

Not being a trusting individual, I followed her down there, but there was no more to do. She'd jabbed her own knife in between her ribs and that, as Daniel would have said, was all she wrote. Charisse and her friend, of course, had melted away like rats into the walls.

"So you're the person of interest, hm," Jamieson said, when I stopped and looked at her to indicate I was done.

"I just shoved her away from Daniel. She's the one had the bloody knife."

"Sorry. Procedure. Will you agree to a psych-scan to determine your motives?"

I hesitated, really not liking this. Getting noticed wasn't part of my comfort zone. If you got noticed, then Authority was more likely to find some fault with anything else you were doing. Normally nobody cared much if one of us was offed, but this had been in sight of quite a few of 106's residents, even if they had been watching through cracks in their walls.

"The psych will stick to the time and place relevant to the inquiry," Jamieson went on, sounding as though she was reciting from a manual. "Absolutely no invasion of your privacy."

"Come on," I said. "The psych will be digging through my brain. If that's not an invasion, I don't know what is."

"You can have a friend or lawyer present if you want."

"I'll have to check with somebody," I said.

Jamieson sighed. "Okay. You talk to your friend and both of you show up here tomorrow night, first dark. Deal?"

"Deal," I said, vaguely sensing a trap. She seemed to be giving me an out but I didn't feel as though I had one. I got clear of the Broken Line before I slowed down and found somewhere to sit on one of the huge steps of the ampitheatre between the Alexander Library and the station. The Library, unlike the station and the art gallery, had been partly rebuilt and had security in there to protect it. I'd got most of my education reading and talking to people in there since I'd grabbed my life and dashed off with it. Sometimes people even put on plays in the ampitheatre for whoever was about. Several times I had let them drag me into performing in something or other. Ad-libbing Hamlet is an interesting experience, especially when Polonius wasn't too sure of his lines either and tried to fight me off when I stabbed him to death behind the curtain.

Not a good memory right now. I recollected something and delved into a pocket to retrieve my pill bottle, swallowing one dry and coughing a few times before I was sure it was down. After surgery, they would put an internal-release in me, so I would only have to show up at the hospital once a year for minor update surgery. Testosterone would flow in me almost as in a male born—a male born *right*, I corrected wryly. I had always felt male, I just hadn't looked male on the outside. See, my time with Dr Benson had taught me something. I now knew how to quibble. I also couldn't come up with anything better than my first plan, so after a little while watching the lights come on and the people come to life around me, I went home to talk to Daniel.

He was teaching a maths class around the kitchen table. Five students, a big class for him. Even though he knew his stuff, students wouldn't come to people like Daniel unless there was no other option. Fortunately there were enough kids whose parents hadn't had the money or the foresight to book their university places when they were born or who were a shade below the ruthless numbers you had to score. What they would do later, without a legal degree, was another problem, but there were always ways.

"Evening, *Ash*," he greeted me in the pointed way which was intended to remind me I, along with the other room-mates, was supposed to be decently absent during teaching time.

"I'll fetch some water," I said.

"Good boy," Daniel said dryly.

The water transport was a bicycle or more properly a tricycle, a huge thing that took up more space on the road than a motorbike. It was bright yellow, had a rack on the back to which a shopping trolley was now attached, and had once been the property of the Head Injured Society. Anybody riding it certainly looked like a card-carrying member, but it was what we had. When I got it out from under the stairs, I yelled out for other buckets. Charisse, visiting her friend on the second floor, trotted down with two buckets and said, "How long do you think you'll be?"

"As long as it takes me, whatcha think?" I thought about asking her if *she* had been asked to do a psych scan. She should've; she and her girlfriend had been the ones putting the literal boots in.

I was halfway back from the river when the lights went out. Not only the ones around me. I was looking at the buildings up ahead and they went abruptly dark. I got my ponderous contraption off the road at once, knowing someone would be idiot enough to keep driving and rear-end me. There was a crash above and perhaps twenty metres further along. Something small and metallic, probably a defective Eye which nobody had bothered to recharge or repair. A black-on-black shape rumbled past, then a crunch as it ran over the Eye and a yelp as a pedestrian dodged. Without lights, I gave the guy maybe an hour's survival.

I pedalled on the footpath, confident the rattling of the trolley behind the trike was enough warning that something was coming. People cursed me invisibly in the dark but they moved. Someone yelled that it was all over the city, even the cop stations were going to generator power, what the hell was happening? Like ants, people flooded out of the buildings around me until I had to slow down almost to stopping. If I hadn't been fairly close to home, I wouldn't have made it. The fear was rising around me, infecting me. When I got to the building, I heard Charisse calling, "Hurry up," as though I was dawdling, and she helped me get the trike inside. Someone threw a bottle at us, or at the sound of our voices. It broke behind me. I didn't waste breath cursing the guy, I only hustled. In the hall there was light; Charisse had put a candle in a saucer on the bottom step.

"Thanks," I said.

"Is this just our street?" she asked.

"No. I think it's the whole city."

We put the trike back in its spot and she sat to guard the water while I took my first buckets laboriously upstairs. Really didn't want to leave the candlelight, but a few other people were out on the landings with candles, asking what was happening. "Don't go outside," I warned them. "People are wandering around getting worked up."

Akemi opened our door when she heard my voice. "Take this," I told her. "I've got two more to get."

I retrieved our other buckets, then sat watch while Charisse moved hers. Then I made a third journey up the six flights and found refuge. Daniel's students had refused to stay, they'd left five minutes after the lights went out. Akemi got home after that but she had no idea where Kersten and Emily were. Wherever it was, they would do best to stay there until the power came back on.

"Gas is off too," Daniel said, "so we can't boil this water."

"Have we got enough?" Akemi asked.

"For drinking, yeah, about another day. Then we might have to weigh our options."

Shadows jumped from the candlelight as the three of us shifted about, no one wanting to leave the others. There was noise on the stairs, the expected thud of feet but also yells, scared yells. Daniel went to our sole window, opening from the second room, and looked out. "Quite a mob," he said, and we came over, Akemi bearing the candle carefully. We had about five or six candles, I thought. Down in the street about twenty people were yelling to or at each other. Close to them there was a fight going on, a couple of guys beating the shit out of each other next to a car, bashing into it and one of them falling over it. Not far away someone was shrieking in pain. We listened with the guilty relief of people to whom none of the above is happening.

For maybe the first time in my adult life, I desperately wanted night to end.

The lights did not return, but finally the sun came up. There was no sign of Emily or Kersten. Akemi frantically insisted they must have been kidnapped or hurt by a customer and we had to go to the police. "The cops won't know anything," Daniel told her gently. "They were caught up in the dark last night as well."

"I have to go anyway," I remembered, and told Daniel what Jamieson had said. He studied me with an odd expression, as though it wasn't really me he was facing.

"It's been awhile since anything was repaired," he observed. "Maybe that goes for the power stations too."

"Guys," wailed Akemi. "What about Em and Kersten?"

I liked Akemi best of the girls. She never seemed to have to try around me; she simply saw me as a boy and that was it. Kersten and Emily always wanted details of the surgery I was going to have and the effects of the medication, which tended to vary as the pills weren't exactly formal scrip. I was their very own reality TV show.

"Sorry," I said. "What if I report it when I go in? Will you come along as my interview buddy, Dan?"

"Yes, all right," he said resignedly. "It may be our best chance to find out what happened last night."

"Buy a newspaper," Akemi sighed. "God. We could even go listen to a TV or radio, there are enough of them in the building."

Daniel flicked a switch; zilch. "If the power is not back by tonight, it might be more than our health is worth to keep your appointment after dark," he said to me. "It's still early; if we cover up, we could get to the police station quite easily and leave a note for the constable to visit you here. Incidentally, we could also query the day-station officer as to the situation with the power."

"Don't leave me here on my own!" Akemi warned.

"Akemi, you *work* on your own," I retorted.

"It isn't the same."

"Come with us, then."

She eeked some more but eventually agreed. We got our head coverings, drank a mug of water each and headed downstairs to greet the sun. It smacked us over the head in return, just in case all our hiding from daylight had made us forget what was boss.

All the Eyes were dead. They littered the blistering road like big silver marbles, being crunched underfoot by the few vehicles abroad. Akemi shivered and wouldn't talk to anyone, hanging on to Daniel's arm like the fragile flower I knew she wasn't. She'd been more shocked than I had realised. I made brief forays away from them to talk to anybody I saw, known to me or not. Yes, their power and gas was off. The televisions were still working but you only got the test pattern. Radios, only static. Daniel had told me to ask about this but not why, so I asked him just before we got to the police station. "I thought it might have been an EMP," he said. "A high altitude nuclear explosion, perhaps in the desert."

"And it wasn't?"

"Any electronic circuit would have been damaged," he said.

"So why the Eyes?" I kicked one in my path, watched it bounce off the kerb.

"No one cares," Daniel said. "No one left to care."

"That's correct," said Constable Jamieson.

We jumped; she had come up behind us quite silently. Akemi eeked softly. I swore, and Daniel nodded politely to her. All of us true to type.

"We've come to talk to you," he said.

She shrugged helplessly. "Well, I'm the only one you can talk to." She pushed through the doors, a cardboard box in her arms, and we followed. The interior was stuffy but better than outside and without direct sun. "Have some water," Jamieson called as she disappeared with the box. We helped ourselves from the dispenser as directed and I sloshed some over my face. Jamieson didn't come back and after a few minutes Daniel turned to me. "Go look for her."

I found Jamieson in a cramped crib room, just standing beside a benchtop where she had put the box. It held a jar of coffee, biscuits, the general makings you might find in any office. She wasn't crying, to my relief, but she certainly wasn't all right.

"You might as well not worry about the hypnosis," she said. Her tone was indifferent but she gripped her hands into fists. "There isn't anyone up the line to authorise it."

"What's happened—look, will you please tell me your first name?"

"Jenna. What's your last name?"

"Henderson. You now know my big secret…well…" With a sudden jolt of strangeness I thought of what else I hadn't told her. How could I have forgotten *that*? "One of my big secrets," I finished, trying to keep my tone light.

"You're not a minor, are you?"

"No, but my family could still give me trouble if they

wanted."

"They couldn't any more, " she said. Then she did look at me. "They've gone," she said. "All the people who were any use. The last people picked for the Springs base went there last night. We haven't had any government in this state for the past six months."

I tried to put this together with what she had said about being abandoned and what we had seen.

"The city has been abandoned? Is that what you're saying?"

"Yes."

I couldn't get my head around it, which is weird because I've accepted realities which are a lot stranger. The sun has baked the hope out of us over the last two, three decades, over the long years of drought which never really ended. The Government promised new programs and outreaches which would save us and revive us, for wasn't this the best of all possible places to live? But the sun beat down and beat harder, as the ozone hole thinned, and gradually it was accepted, had always been that you lived by night, if you were smart.

I heard myself saying, as though it was somebody else, "But that's crazy. I'm not useless! And you're a cop, how can they say you're not of any use? You're a *good* cop. And Daniel, the guy who came in with me, he's a professor, he teaches maths…"

"At the university?"

"Well, no, they had cutbacks…"

"And what do you do?"

"I act in plays," I said, realising as I spoke how thin it was. "I help out around the building, I fix stuff sometimes." *I spend a lot of time around the Gender Dysphoria Clinic.* "Dr. Benson," I said, interrupting myself.

"Who?" Jenna asked in confusion. Daniel had come to the doorway and I could hear Akemi saying something about checking records. I pushed past Daniel, who tried to grab my shoulder.

"Hang on there."

"I have to see Dr. Benson," I blurted and ran. Daniel yelled something after me but I didn't stop. I pushed the doors open and breathed in fire, as sweat poured down me like an instant river. Vampires don't move around by day, and the Station market had dissolved with the dawn, leaving only a few wrappers and pieces of gaudy plastic strewn on the concrete walkway.

Ten minutes in our ozone-stripped sunlight and you could get killer cancers. I'd already spent more time outside than was safe and bolting along the road to Dr. Benson's was not smart, as Daniel would understate. I felt pretty sick by the time I got to his town-house, one of maybe two hundred in the complex. Some of those places were crack houses or used by squatters or prostitutes or both, but Benson said he needed to be where his clients were. No answer. I tried the door and it was unlocked, so I went in. "Dr. Benson? It's Ash, are you okay?" Stupid. He was probably asleep and had forgotten the door.

He wasn't there. There's a difference between an empty house and one with a sleeping person in it. I went through the place anyway. It was stripped down, a careful, methodical packing away of belongings. Kitchen, bedroom, living room, and finally clients meeting room, bare of most furniture except the desk, perhaps too bulky to shift. On it was a pill bottle holding down a note and I knew it was for me with the same instinct that had told me the house was empty.

"Dear Ash. I know you'll be the one to read this—you're my last client, you know. I stopped seeing anyone else five weeks ago, when I got the final word. A couple of my people qualified for the program but I know now that you won't. I did put your name down but they said no. I hope you can forgive me. Here's all the medication I have for you; it will last another two months. You will have to make your own arrangements to get more, and also make your way to Melbourne in order to stay on the surgical list. Here are the names of some people to see when you get there. Remember, you must do this within two months or risk being dropped from the assignment program."

"Ash? Ash!"

I had no idea how long I had been standing there, but Daniel, Jenna and Akemi were all in the room. Akemi pushed a plastic glass of water at me and I drank it down. I shoved the note out, one of them took it.

"What the fuck…" My voice shook and I had to start again, hating it. "What the fuck is *the final word*? You seem to know what's going on, Jamieson. Why didn't they, whoever they are, pick you?"

In her silence, we read the answer, but she didn't seem to be able to give us a comprehensible reason. "I've got family here," she said finally. "And nobody who was picked meant a damn thing to me. What's a great adventure if you have to do it on your own?"

"You mean, you *were* selected to be part of the Delta Pavonis program?" Daniel asked, patience incarnate.

"I could have been. But I don't know why they didn't pick any of you, so don't push that one."

"They didn't know to ask me," Akemi said. "My friends, you know, the girls I told you about just now? Do you think they were picked—and couldn't tell us?"

Jenna Jamieson made a gesture half shrug, half shaking her head. She walked out of the stripped interview room and we heard water running in the kitchen, then followed it like dumb animals. "We have to drink," she said dully. "Probably we should stay here till dark, not try to walk around any more."

"I never saw a shrink," Daniel said in counterpoint, not really answering her or any of us. "But I know why they wouldn't pick me. What would you say about someone who won't have a phone where he lives or a computer or anything like that—even if we had reliable power?"

"We don't," Akemi began.

"We're broke, that's why," I said.

"The government tracks us by all those devices," he said. "I'm not suggesting voices from God or the Devil, but if you have a phone, people can monitor your phone use, and the same with your computer. They can learn about you, learn whether you are useful to them or should be pruned from the tree."

I couldn't see why he was still obsessing about the government. They'd been gone for six months and we had adjusted, done for ourselves. Those of us close to the street and the wilderness had not even known that they were gone, so how much good could they ever have done us?

Benson was never my father, anyway.

"I'm FTM," I said to Jenna. "That's why all this shit about staying in the program and going to Melbourne. Sex transition program."

"Are you going to go?" she said. Like she was asking whether I planned to cross the road, as though it hardly mattered.

I thought about making some grand gesture, chucking the vial of pills against the wall or something but that was playing their game as well. "I don't know," I said, and put them in my pocket. "Daniel, what do you mean, Delta Pavonis program?"

"That's where the Springs Base people are going," he said. He ran another glass of water, gulped it, filled the glass and passed it to Akemi. "Delta Pavonis is a star, about 18 light years from Earth, which may have habitable planets."

"How do you know that?" Jenna demanded, her tone outraged. "That's last-stage selection material!"

"How does a city constable know *that*?" he riposted.

"We both said no," Jenna said quietly, to me and to Akemi, who splashed water on her hand and ran it over her face to cool her burning skin. "Some things cost too much."

We stayed there until dark, drinking water and sleeping now and then, as we could. Jenna and Daniel talked about running things at the police station. Some of her colleagues hadn't shown up for work last night, she'd said, she could use some help. We couldn't be cops, of course, but we could put something in place, some system to help maintain calm.

When night did fall, Akemi left first, to get something to eat and then go to work. She promised to give Jenna a call at the Station. Daniel and I headed home, also to get dinner, and then he had some students supposed to show up. "I think they will," he said, "but they might be a bit surprised about what I've got to tell them."

I was going to meet some of the players at the Ampitheatre about a new production of *Macbeth* they wanted to put on. We'd decided that last week, so hopefully it wouldn't take too long to convince them it was time to come up with something original ourselves, but then, actors believe they rule the world anyway. Don't believe the quote about poor players heard no more after their hour upon the stage.

It better not take too long. As we stepped out of Dr Benson's deserted house into a city street beginning to stretch and wake into darkness, Jenna tapped my shoulder lightly and I turned to face her. Daniel diplomatically walked on. "I finish around three a.m.," she said. "Would you like to come by—we could go get a drink or something?"

"Absolutely!"

"You could be a bit less of the strong, silent type," she suggested. "I'm sure I'll still like you."

SUNSET ON MARS

The black and white photograph
Of our orange air
Shows a sun as tiny
As a glowing ping-pong ball.
Lack of oxygen shrinks us dry
As dust.
Gray horizon calms us
Even as we recognize
The planet doesn't want us here.
The weather alone knocks us
Back and forth across the net
Never mind the politics of it all.
We're that couple in the picture
Taken outside the suburb
In the foothills of Olympus Mons
Picking through dust for belongings
Our homestead an unintended casualty of the current war.
When asked what we would tell the President
When he arrives in his special shuttle
To survey the damage and offer full support
We said, "We are not the people you want
To talk to about this president."
(That was me; my husband merely shook his head.)
Sometimes a hug isn't enough
To smooth things over
When bodily injury and property damage are involved.
The sun sets on Mars
And we stay here anyway.

—MARTHA A. HOOD

Anticipations

Coming in *Tales of the Unanticipated* #30 (August 2009): There's a prose-poem by Ann Peters and Ellen Kuhfeld, partly inspired by the Babylonian *Enuma Elish*. Barbara Rosen introduces us to a cat with a special talent, while Catherine Lundoff offers an Egyptian cat-sculpture. Stephen Dedman explores the fuss generated by a returning space probe. Terry Faust and Martha A. Hood serve up two very different looks at what happens when a deity drops by for an extended stay. Douglas J. Lane writes about nerd vengeance of the nasty kind. Patricia S. Bowne examines the politics surrounding wood nymphs, while Jason Sanford tells "A Twenty-First Century Fairy Love Story." William Mingin leads us through an epic quest that starts with an unsettled restaurant bill. *TOTU* poetry veteran Cornelius Fortune makes his *TOTU* fiction debut with an account of an orchestra conductor's struggle with a very odd symphony. Newcomer Matthew S. Rotundo studies the legal rights of ghosts, and T.J. Berg makes a chilling *TOTU* debut with the story of a children's book writer who changes her style. Will we do something else that you weren't expecting?